Compiled and Edited
by Xtina Marie

**A HellBound Books LLC
Publication**

Cover and art design by Kevin Enhart

Printed in the United States of America

Contents

Foreword

*I*s *there life after death?*
This question has been the topic of debate for as long as, well, as long as people have found things to debate about. Different time periods, nations, cultures, and religions all have something to say on this matter—some varying wildly—although none have been proven.

'The spirit or soul of a dead person that can appear to the living' is the most basic definition of a ghost. Mention of ghosts date back to the Hebrew Bible.

Throughout history there have been numerous accounts of ghost sightings and hauntings. Folklore passed on from generation to generation. Stories whispered among adolescent girls at slumber parties.

Why is this subject so fascinating? I mean, the percentage of people who claim they have actually *seen* a ghost is relatively small. Yet, in the dark of the night, when we can't easily explain away a sound, our minds automatically jump in that direction.

We all have our personal fears. Ghosts happen to be at the top of my list, and because I am a masochist, I had my hand waving wildly in the air—Hermione Granger-style—at the chance to get to work on this anthology.

18 fantastic horror authors have come together to terrify you with tales of ghosts, spirits and specters. Make sure to keep the light on while you dive in, and absolutely *do*

not decide to investigate on your own when you hear that inexplicable sound from the other room.

Happy Reading!

-Xtina Marie
HellBound Books Publishing LLC

2019

See Mommy Cry
Michael J. Moore

Part One

"Are you off work yet?"

Daniel Porter looks at his phone, thinks about how to respond to the text.

"Yeah. Why?" He presses send. Stuffing it into his pocket, he walks away from PureH20, where he's just spent the last eight hours on an assembly line. His breath turns to fog, expanding like a balloon as it floats away. Burlington, Washington isn't a large town, and the back roads are always dark in the evenings.

In the distance, crickets chirp. Somewhere near the road, something scurries in some bushes. The phone vibrates against his leg and he stops, tenses. It's moments like these that make him wish he had gone to college. No thirty-four year old man should know how much he hates walking alone at night, because he should be able to afford a car. Bringing the phone out, he looks at the screen.

Message From: Kayla.

He selects it.

"I was just seeing if you wanted to come over and have a drink."

His heartbeat picks up as he types, "I don't know where you are," and then resumes walking. The phone vibrates in less than a minute.

"I'm at my house screwball."

"I figured that. I don't know where you live." Before he finishes, it vibrates again.

"Where else would I be at 11?"

Then again.

"lol."

His thumb hovers over the keypad for a moment, as he contemplates a response. He's saved the trouble, though.

"You don't have a car anyway."

"How do you know that?" he finally types, making it to the main road where streetlights illuminate the night, and turning left toward his apartment. It will be at least forty-five minutes from here.

The reply comes fast.

"You told me stupid."

Had he? He reflects on every text and email he's sent in the past week.

"Oh yeah." He presses send.

She was a friend of a friend and he had seen her profile on his wall a few times before she actually sent him a request. It had never been easy to approach, or even talk to women, and having a head of hair that turned prematurely salt and pepper and no real career or vehicle hadn't helped. So accepting it had been as thoughtless as yawning in the morning.

She messaged him right away, asking if they knew each other——they didn't—— then they just kept talking most of that first night. The next day, she sent him her number and they texted all evening. Last night had been their first call, but it had lasted hours.

His cell buzzes again.

Picture Message From: Kayla.

He selects to view it and stops walking when it pops up.

The lighting in the room is poor, but he imagines that's by design. The camera is held somewhere near her point of vision, aimed down her body as she lays on her back. It's like seeing her through her own eyes. She's naked.

He feels himself being backed into a corner. Coming face-to-face with something that for reasons he doesn't fully understand, scare the hell out of him most of the time. His sex drive. All the reasons that he's been talking to Kayla Jennings for the last week, pour out of his subconscious and surface as his manhood begins to press against the inside of his pants. It's been over a year since his most recent breakup, and even longer since he's been intimate with anybody but himself.

He takes in every detail of her body——from the medium sized peeks on her chest, to her toned stomach——and his gaze falls automatically between her legs. Her knees are propped up, her feet flat on a ruffled white sheet. In the background, is a waist-high, rectangular dresser, holding a TV set with chrome picture frames on either side of it. He uses his thumb and index finger to zoom in on her sex. The image comes at him until he's looking into the smiling face of a young girl. It only takes him a second to realize that it's one of the photos on the dresser. He moves it, then stops and goes back.

Kayla's in the picture as well. The girl, who looks like a tiny clone of her, rests on her lap. She looks to be around four or five. Kayla never mentioned having a daughter. He guesses it's none of his business, but she's practically told him her entire life over the past week.

He scrolls across the screen, looking at the other photo. The frame, however, is turned, and all that can be made out are vague colors. Swiping his finger, he looks once again at Kayla's body until his phone buzzes.

"Do you wanna come over or not?"

"I need you to pick me up." He walks.

Then he types again. "If you want to, I mean." Before he can send the message, it vibrates.

Incoming Call From: Kayla.

Taking a deep breath, he accepts, says, "Hello?"

"Where are you?" Her voice is assertive.

"Burlington Boulevard."

"Burlington Boulevard's long, screwball. What part?"

He looks around for a landmark. "You know Dan's Grocery?"

"The mini-mart across from the hotel?"

"Uh, yeah."

"Wait there."

"At Dan's, or the hotel?"

But she'd hung up already.

Walking through the parking lot, he leans against the wall of the convenience store, which is somehow colder than the air around him. His phone tells him it's 11:23. He opens his texts, and looks again at the picture. She has a tattoo on her left ankle that looks like some kind of a cross and chain.

What if she doesn't show?

Killing the screen, he slips the phone into his pocket. Twenty minutes later, Kayla still isn't there. And why would she be? To meet him? To take him home? He experiences a sense of self-loathing that he didn't even know existed as he makes his way toward the road. Not for being him——the man who no woman would ever want a one-night-stand with——but for being wrong. For allowing himself to be fooled.

Then a silver sedan pulls up next to him and even through the dark and the passenger window, he can see her blue eyes gazing up into his. Her golden hair is tied back in a loose ponytail. He just stares until she tilts her head, looking at him curiously. Finally he opens the door, causing the dome light to come on, and sticks his face inside.

"What are you waiting for, fuck-head?" she smiles.

"Uh——excuse me?"

"Are you coming, or not? It's freaking cold out here."

Without another word, he steps in and closes the door.

Part Two

"I'm a little drunk already," she says as she pulls out of the parking lot. Though they're nearly the same age, she looks years younger than him.

"Do you need me to drive?"

Her eyelids hang drowsily, but her smile is wide awake. She watches the road as she speaks. "Don't think so. We'll see how it goes."

Some pop song that he doesn't recognize hums quietly from a speaker on his door. "How far away do you live?" he asks.

"Just over in Mount Vernon." She's wearing pink pajamas and a white hooded sweater with a zipper on the front. "All I have at the house is vodka. That okay?"

"Ah——yeah. Yeah, that's cool." Instead of telling her that he doesn't often drink anyway, he asks her how much she's had already.

She turns her head, looking into his eyes and smiling, not looking away for a long moment. He opens his mouth to suggest she focus on the road, then she uses her thumb and index finger to indicate about an inch. "Just this much," she says, and looks forward again.

Daniel forces a laugh. "Oh. Well that's, ah——not much, I guess."

There's no car seat in the vehicle. Maybe the pictures are old and the little girl's outgrown it. Or maybe she doesn't have the kid anymore. Maybe that's why she doesn't talk about her. She's quiet most of the drive, and it feels like mere minutes before they pull into a driveway in a residential neighborhood and she kills the engine. The music dies and Daniel looks over to see her staring at him.

"Ready to go in?"

"I——ah, yeah." He wills his voice to work properly.

But she doesn't move to get out of the car. "You know, you're everything I expected you to be."

His ears burn. "Ah——thanks."

"Thanks?" She seems to be enjoying herself.

"Yeah. Or I guess I just don't know what that means."

"Exactly what it sounds like, stupid."

"So it's a good thing?"

"If it wasn't, would I have come and picked you up, Daniel?"

He chuckles involuntarily. "Guess not."

"Screwball." She reaches over, covers his face with her hand like a mask. He smells a combination of cigarette smoke and perfume as she shoves him softly. He instinctively closes his eyes. When he reopens them, all he sees is her backside as she climbs out of the car. He steps out, watches as she ascends the few steps leading to her front door.

She looks back over her shoulder. "You coming?"

Realizing that he's staring, he follows her.

"Well," Kayla says as soon as they're inside. "This is it. If you need the bathroom, it's the first door on the left. Don't be sniffing my panties if you find a pair laying around, though."

The house is nice. Though he's only in the living room, it's easy to identify as a three bedroom.

"How do you afford this place?"

"I told you. I rent from my grandma. She gives me the trailer-trash discount." She walks toward what he assumes is the kitchen. "Make yourself at home, 'kay?"

"Trailer-trash discount?" he calls after her.

"Yeah," her voice comes from around the corner. "You know how us white-trash bitches do it. Anything cheap or free."

Daniel sits down on one of two couches around a rectangular coffee table. On the far wall, is an entertainment center with a large flat-screen. Propped next to it, is a picture frame. It's much bigger than the ones on the image in his phone. The little girl smiles at him from a face-shot, where he's able to get a much better look at her. She has curly blonde hair that makes him think of Goldilocks. Her eyes are blue, like her mother's, only wide and alert.

"I hope you're not allergic to cranberry." Kayla walks back into the room, a glass of red liquid in each hand. She sits next to him, so close that her leg rests against his, offers him one of the glasses.

"Thanks." He takes a drink and almost spits it back out.

Kayla laughs, covering her mouth with her free hand.

"Jesus, that's strong."

She sips her own drink, looking into his eyes. In the light, he's able to see just how blue hers are.

Say something, he tells himself, even opens his mouth to form words, but realizes a second too late that he has no idea what they are.

She doesn't seem to notice as he averts his gaze from hers. "So you really walk home every night after work?"

Looking down, he sees ripples in the liquid, wraps his other hand around the glass to stabilize it. "Ah, yeah." He takes another drink. "Every night. I mean five nights a week. Unless I work overtime."

"Does that happen a lot?"

"Overtime?"

She nods.

"Not really. Thankfully," he snickers.

"I just can't get over the fact that you walk. How far away do you live?"

"Um——from here, or from my job?"

"From your job, screwball."

"About forty-five minutes, walking——give or take. There's a shortcut, but I don't use it."

"Really?" She tilts her head. "Well that doesn't make sense."

"Excuse me?"

"Why wouldn't you take a shortcut?"

"It's dangerous, I guess."

"You guess?"

"Well, there are some train tracks that run behind the factory. They cross the bridge into Mount Vernon. I could cut like twenty minutes out of the commute if I used them."

"Haha!" she exclaims. "That's funny!"

"What's that?"

"You called your walk a commute."

"Yeah. The trip, I guess, is a better word."

"Or something. Not commute, though. Screwball. So five nights a week, you walk. In the cold."

He nods.

"And the dark."

"I walk under the streetlights."

She laughs again. "Oh——that's cute. Now I know why you don't take the tracks. Are you afraid of the dark?"

He shakes his head, feeling his face flush.

"Ahaha! Don't lie. You are! I can see it in your lying face! Don't worry, Danny. If the power goes out, just hold onto me. I'll keep the monsters away."

"Daniel." He raises the glass to his lips, killing off half the contents.

"What?"

"Daniel. I, uh——my name's Daniel."

"What? Relax, you big baby. I'm playing. Plus, I think I can help you."

"Yeah? How can you do that?"

"Easy." She takes a sip of her own drink, then licks cranberry juice from her lips. For a second, he's reminded of a movie vampire. "You just have to remember one thing. It's not really the dark you're afraid of."

"No?"

"Nope. It's what's in the dark. And guess what, screwball? Whatever that is, it's in the light too. It's just harder to see at night. So figure out what it is that you're really afraid of, and you'll be able to get over it. Why don't you just buy a car? Then you won't have to worry about the cold at least." She tucks her legs underneath her. "Don't they pay you enough at that water factory?"

"Water bottle factory," he corrects. "And if by 'enough' you mean just enough to survive off of top ramen and water from the assembly line, then yeah. I had a car last year, but I blew a head-gasket, and found out it would cost more to get it fixed than I paid for the whole car."

"You can't catch a bus to work or something?"

"They stop running at nine."

"So you catch it in the morning then?"

"Yeah."

"Then you walk home?"

"Uh, yeah. In the cold. In the dark."

"On a train. In the rain," she says.

"Excuse me?"

"Would you eat me here or there? Would you eat me anywhere?"

Daniel's jaw hangs from his skull until she laughs again.

"Sorry. I used to get in trouble in school for making all the Dr. Seuss poems dirty. You know if you put aside a little money every month, it might take a while, but eventually you'll be able to buy a car. Or why don't you just find a better job?"

He shifts uncomfortably. Even though they've told each other so much over the past week, he has no interest in answering. No interest in explaining that he doesn't know what it is that prevents him from taking steps to better his life.

"You comfortable?" she asks.

He's sitting upright, offering more of his back than anything. "Uh——yeah."

"Oh…kay." She stretches the word out. "Sure?"

"What? Why?"

"You don't wanna go home or anything, do you?"

He shakes his head.

"Tell you what." She sits up, puts her hand under his glass, hoisting it to his mouth. "Lemme help." He washes down the rest of the drink, and the second it's away from his lips, she pushes hers into them, licking cranberry juice as she pulls away. "Why did your ex leave you, anyway?"

That's the last clear memory he has of the night. They talk like they have on the phone. They continued to drink, and soon he's more intoxicated than he's ever been in his life. It all gets mixed up and foggy, from chugging vodka from the bottle, to sitting on the couch together, for what may have been minutes, or possibly hours.

"——when I finish school, I'll be making the big bucks," she says at some point. "Then he'll have to——" And the rest fades out.

"——you should get a——" his own voice slurs. "——a dog, or you could just——"

And they're on her back porch, while she sucks on the end of a cigarette. "Here, this'll help." She pushes it into his mouth.

He coughs and he coughs and she just laughs.

And he's in her bed with no memory of how he got there. She lays next to him. Asleep.

And they're both awake and he's inside of her, her feet near her face and he sees the cross and chain tattoo on her ankle. Then there's screaming. But it isn't Kayla. It's beside his head. It's loud. He looks and sees her daughter standing by the bed, her blonde hair hanging in locks down to her shoulders.

"What the fuck?"

"What?" Kayla moans. "Don't stop." She digs her nails into his back, pulls him further into her. They cut so deep that he grunts.

The little girl screams again. "No, Mommy! No! Please!" Tears pour down her face, soaking baby blue, one piece pyjamas with cartoon ponies plastered all over them. Daniel climbs off of Kayla and rolls over. He pulls the sheet over his naked body and passes out while the girl continues to scream and cry.

Part Three

Every morning a phenomenon occurs in which Daniel Porter finds himself in the dark, yet unafraid. The moment when consciousness replaces the dreams that his unconscious mind has played for him throughout the night and all he sees are the backs of his eyelids. As they open this morning, the darkness is gone, replaced by the bright blue eyes of Kayla's daughter. She's laying on her side, staring at him, smiling. He sits up and the room spins as if it were hurling through space. He immediately lays back down, realizing that it isn't the girl lying next to him, but Kayla. How long has she been watching him sleep?

"I think I'm still drunk," he says.

The sun shines through light blue curtains hanging over her bedroom window, causing his head to ache as if it were full of nails.

"You think?" Her voice is sleepy.

"What time is it?"

"Just past eight. You don't have to work, do you?"

"Not till three," he responds. "You?"

"Day off. You think I'd get that fucked up last night if I had to work?"

"I ah——I don't know. My head's killing me."

She smiles. "Screwball."

Daniel rolls onto his back and looks up into the gold colored light fixture. "Last night was embarrassing. I'm really sorry about that."

"Don't be." She puts a hand on his chest. "I had fun. I even got mine before you decided to roll over and play dead. I'm surprised you even remember."

"I remember," he says.

"Oh yeah? That's too bad, because I thought I was gonna have to remind you."

His stomach flips inside of him. He wants to get up, but the room won't stop spinning. He wants to eat something. To go home. To call in sick and sleep all day. Not to be reminded of last night.

But Kayla throws the blanket off of herself, revealing a pale, nude body, making him aware that he's still naked as well. She climbs on top of him, leaving nothing in between them but the thin sheet. "I don't know why you're so shy." Her smile endures, and he sees for the first time that the only thing about her that isn't beautiful are her teeth. They're slightly crooked and yellow. "It's not like you're a bad fuck or anything. I think that bitch who left you was an idiot." She kisses him and he tastes stale liquor and cigarettes.

"Well, she didn't share your sentiment. I think she did me a favor by leaving anyway."

Kayla just gazes down into his eyes. Hers are still drowsy, but he recognizes sympathy and wishes that she would look away. "Fuck her," she finally says. "Her loss, right?"

"Right," Daniel mimics as convincingly as he can manage. "Fuck her."

Her mouth covers his again, only this time she doesn't pull away. Her body moves slowly, purposefully. Her back arches and her breath grows heavy against his lips. Her pelvis presses into him, rocks back and forth. The movements are subtle, but he finds his headache growing in intensity as blood rushes to his lower region. She moans softly, looking down at what's happening under the sheet. "Maybe you do need a reminder. I don't think I should leave you with just a drunk memory, do you?"

"What about your daughter?" The words spill out of him before he even thinks about them.

Her body grows rigid and her head snaps up, her eyes meeting his. "What?"

"Your kid."

"What are you talking about?"

"If she walks in again—"

She stares at his face as if deciphering a code. "Daniel, I live here alone. I told you that."

"But the girl."

"What girl?"

"Last night. The girl in the room."

Kayla's face moves through a short sequence of expressions, stopping once again on a smile. "You're stupid," she says. "Did she have blonde hair, tits and an ass? By chance were you drilling her?"

"She was wearing blue pyjamas," he says, causing her to sit all the way up. "With ponies on them."

"Daniel, don't play with me."

This isn't fun anymore. If it's some kind of a joke, he wants no part of it. Suddenly, the hangover doesn't matter. It's time to go.

"I think I should leave."

"Damn right you should." Her voice could freeze snow.

He starts to sit up, but she shoves him back down. He looks at her confused.

"What is this, Daniel? Some kind of a sick joke? You creep my page and find out about her or something?"

He tries to sit up again, and again, she shoves him back onto the bed.

"I just wanna get out of here," he groans. "Can I get up, please?"

"After you fucking answer me!" Her palm collides with the side of his face and he sees red. "You think you're cute, Daniel?" She slaps him again.

That's it.

"I DON'T KNOW WHAT YOU'RE TALKING ABOUT!" he explodes. "If you don't get off of me right now, I'm calling the police!"

She stares down at him for a long moment and her eyes become slits before she finally speaks again. "You really don't know, do you?"

"Know what?" He touches the side of his face.

"Daniel, Brittany disappeared a year ago."

Sobriety falls over him like water in a shower. Either she's lying, or insane, and he needs to go. Now. Taking her hips, he shoves her off of him and rolls out of the bed, ignoring the cold which nips at his skin.

"Maybe you just saw her pictures around the house and had a dream. You were pretty fucked up last night, Daniel."

He doesn't respond, just scans the room for his clothes. The floor is littered with her own linen but he spots his pants in the mess.

"Just hold on." She jumps out of the bed. "Let me show you. Please." She bolts through the door, shuts it behind her.

He isn't waiting. He needs to leave, sleep off his hangover, then—after waking up with a clear mind—decide whether or not to block her number. Setting the jeans on her bed, he begins to look for his boxers. When he doesn't find them, he just pulls the pants on.

Shoes, he thinks as the door swings open and Kayla steps in, still completely naked, clutching an aluminum baseball bat.

He throws his hands up, feels his heart jump into his throat.

"Sorry." She climbs onto the bed, swinging the weapon with both hands. He tries to block the blow, but isn't fast enough. It collides with the side of his head and he hears bells as he collapses, landing face-first on the mattress.

"Why?" He hears his own voice as if from a distance.

"I don't know, Daniel." She speaks calmly, almost melodic. "You tell me."

The bat comes down fast and he feels the bones in his left hand snap under its weight. Then it lands on top of his head, sending a surge of pain through his body that makes the hangover seem like nothing but a migraine.

"Please!"

"Fucking screwball," is the last thing he hears as heavy aluminium crashes into his temple and his body falls limp. He sees the cross on Kayla's ankle for a fraction of a second before the world fades to black.

***

Daniel opens his eyes and sees light, smells floor cleaner. His mind begins to process the scene around him and a hallway comes into focus. A woman cries out from behind a door to his right. He's in a hospital, still wearing nothing but his jeans. He looks down at his hand, finding it disfigured and ugly, but there's no pain. A nurse in blue scrubs passes, paying him no mind.

"Hi, Daniel." The voice comes from behind. He turns to see Kayla's daughter standing in her blue pyjamas. She looks up at him bashfully, her hands laced together at her belly.

"Brittany?"

She gives an exaggerated nod.

The woman in the room screams again.

It occurs to him that he should be afraid. Should be panicking. There's no fear, though. Only reality, whatever that means now.

"Brittany, where are we?"

The little girl drops her hands and presses her lips together. She seems to be suppressing a grin. "We're at the hospital, silly."

"I know that. But why?"

She looks down at her feet.

"Why are we here, Brittany?"

"Because," when she looks up, her eyes are wide, hopeful, "I wanted to tell you something." She walks over and stands in front of him.

"Am I dead?"

Brittany smiles from ear to ear, revealing a missing front tooth. "Dead people can't talk, screwball."

He looks around the hallway as the woman cries again. A paper hangs next to the door, announcing, 'Kayla Jennings. In labor.'

"I don't understand—"

"Come on." Brittany takes his hand. "I'll show you."

The world begins to morph until he finds himself inside of the maternity room. A small group stands around the bed as a nurse hands a tightly wrapped pink bundle to Kayla, who lays with her hair matted to her forehead with sweat, smiling down at the baby.

"She's so beautiful," an older woman sings.

The baby stares up, her cheeks drooping, her eyes wide and aware. A tall, muscular man with a military-length, faded haircut reaches out and strokes her cheek.

"That's my dad," Brittany says, watching the whole scene unfold.

"And that's you," Daniel replies.

She nods.

"They can't see us, can they?"

She shakes her head.

"Brittany, why did you want me to see this?"

"You just wait, mister." Reaching up, she grabs his hand again and the room quickly changes. He finds himself in Kayla's living room, only it isn't the way he remembers. The furniture's arranged differently and the picture of Brittany is missing.

Kayla stands in front of the coffee table, holding the baby, whose face is twisted in agony, crying. Daniel hardly hears her though. The sounds are muffled, like listening through water. Brittany's father, whose hair is longer now, stands shirtless in front of her, screaming. Kayla yells back, the words are unintelligible.

Every muscle in the man's face flexes as he raises a hand and strikes Kayla. The sound of the slap resonates clearly and Daniel tenses up. Kayla drops, landing on top of the table, breaking the baby's fall with her own body. Brittany's dad snatches the collar of her shirt, cocks back again as she looks up at him with tears in her eyes.

Daniel doesn't think. He lunges at the taller, more muscular man. But Brittany catches him by the wrist. Then he's in a courtroom, sitting in the pews. Brittany sits next to him.

"What is this?"

"Ssshhh," she whispers, holding a finger to her lips. "Just watch."

Her father stands in front of the judge in an orange jumpsuit. A lawyer in a grey suit stands next to him. The judge's mouth opens and closes as he speaks, but there is no sound. Daniel looks around for Kayla, doesn't spot her anywhere.

"Brittany—"

"Mommy didn't like the way dad kept hurting her," she whispers. "The cops took him away. He doesn't get to come home for a long time now." The look on her face is indifferent. She just stares forward at her dad.

The man shifts his weight from one foot, to the other, his hands together on the wooden podium like he's praying. Daniel just watches. Then Brittany's hand slips into his and he's back in Kayla's living room. Everything is once again arranged the way he remembers it. The photo of Brittany is back on the entertainment center.

Kayla sits on the couch, looking down at a large book which sits on the coffee table. A thin stream of water lines one side of her nose. She sniffs, wipes away the tears with the back of her hand. Next to the book is an empty wine bottle.

Daniel takes a closer look and sees that the book is a photo album. Organized neatly, are pictures of Brittany, of Kayla, of Brittany's dad wearing a military uniform. There are family photos, taken professionally somewhere when Brittany was still an infant. Even copies of the ones he saw in the image on his phone. She's only looking at one though. A picture of her and her daughter's father. They're alone, standing in front of some trees. He's behind her, his arms around her midsection, smiling into the camera. They appear so happy Daniel never would have thought that he beat her.

Then he knows something that he doesn't want to know. All feelings of serenity that he experienced in the hospital hallway flee and he doesn't want to be here anymore. He looks down at Brittany. She doesn't return his gaze, just stares toward the hall with a blank expression. Somehow, he knows what's coming next.

"No," is all he can manage to say as another Brittany comes running down the hall in her blue pyjamas. Her footsteps are small and quick. Within seconds, she emerges into the living room. When she sees her mom, she stops in her tracks, a guilty look on her face.

The Brittany who brought him here watches detached.

Kayla looks up, snaps, "I thought I told you to go to bed!"

"But I'm still hungry," the little girl whines.

Kayla stares at her daughter for a long moment, until Brittany's hands come up and her fingers lock together exactly how they did when Daniel first laid eyes on her in the hospital.

"This is all your fault, isn't it?"

Brittany's eyes grow wide. "I'm sorry, Mommy." She turns and runs back the way she came.

Kayla grips the neck of the wine bottle, stands up. Her own eyes become slits and she bares her teeth, bringing her arm back and launching the bottle at Brittany. It connects with the back of her head and she hits the floor, belly down. Kayla moves on her as she rolls onto her back and screams, tears pouring down her face. Kayla reaches down and takes the bottle, raising it over her head, ready to strike again.

"No, Mommy! No! Please!" Brittany covers her face, curls into a ball.

Daniel tells himself to move. To do something. To stop her. To look away. But his body refuses to obey. Then Kayla's face softens. She sits the empty bottle down on the entertainment center, right next to the picture of Brittany and disappears down the hall.

Brittany struggles to her feet, sniffing and blinking in tears. She touches the back of her head and slowly approaches the table, looking down at the photo album. She doesn't see her mom as she reappears behind her, an orange extension cord in both hands. Kayla's face is tense as she wraps the cord around Brittany's neck and lifts the child up off of her feet.

Brittany's eyes bulge and her hands come up. She tries to dig her fingers between the cable and her skin. Her legs flail. Her mouth opens and Daniel can see her tongue swelling. Amidst choking sounds, a tiny squeal manages to escape. Kayla falls to the floor, bringing her daughter with. The little girl collapses between her legs and begins twitching, staring off into nowhere.

Daniel's mouth hangs open as he watches in horror. He tries to speak, but no words form.

Finally, Brittany breaks the silence from where she still stands next to him, witnessing her own murder. "Come on," she whispers, takes his hand. "There's more."

Part Four

It's dark in Kayla's car.

Funny, Daniel thinks, how the dark is never frightening inside of a car.

They sit in the backseat, Brittany next to him, resting her head on his arm. Kayla's in front of him, driving somewhere in the country.

"She killed you," he says. "She killed you because he started hitting her when you were born. And because you reminded her of him."

Brittany reaches up, hugs his arm close to her face.

"I'm sorry, Brittany. I'm so sorry this happened to you."

The car pulls to the side of the road. Daniel looks out the window, and recognizes where he is. Highway Twenty, headed into the mountains. He's been here many times. The driver's door opens, illuminating the inside of the car. Kayla gets out and closes it behind her. She walks to the back of the vehicle and the trunk opens. When she reappears, she's carrying a small, limp, bundle, wrapped in a white sheet. Setting the body on the ground, she walks to the side of the car. Daniel's door opens and the dome light comes on again.

She leans in, coming face-to-face with him. There's no longer anything beautiful about Kayla Jennings. Her features are stone cold as she brings out a shovel that Daniel hadn't even known lay at his feet. She shuts the door behind her and it's dark again.

Brittany takes him by the hand.

Then they're deep in the woods. There's a flashlight propped up in a tree, and for the first time that he can remember, Daniel wishes it was dark. Kayla shovels dirt into the shallow grave where her daughter lay. Every bit of sex appeal that she possessed when he met her is gone. She's sweaty and dirty and the faces she makes as she works are panicked and hideous. When the hole is filled, she tosses the shovel aside and begins to arrange leaves and sticks over it. Then she falls to her knees.

Finally Brittany speaks. "Are you ready?"

"Ready for what?" Daniel can't look away from Kayla.

"To see Mommy cry."

Kayla's dirty hands touch her face and her body jerks as choking sobs escape her. She tries to suppress them. She pounds both fists into the earth and screams long, loud. When she runs out of breath, she inhales deeply and screams again. Then she cries. She cries and she cries, and something nearby moves in some bushes.

Daniel wonders if she cries because of what she did to her daughter, or because of what the consequences will be if she's caught. It doesn't matter though. A little girl is dead.

"Brittany, can you get us out of here?"

She doesn't look at him, just stares at her mommy and nods. She doesn't take his hand either as daylight appears and he finds himself outside of Kayla's house, standing in her front yard. Brittany stands with him. The early morning sun shines on her hair, and he once again thinks of Goldilocks.

"You're such a beautiful girl."

She looks up at him with shining blue eyes, and smiles.

"This never should have happened to you." He falls to his knees, places his hands on his shoulders. "Brittany, why me?"

She doesn't answer, just holds his gaze until he thinks he might cry. But he doesn't.

Instead, he asks again, "Why did you want to tell me?"

"After Mommy hurt me, I didn't wanna stay home. So I left. I walked and I walked and no one would talk to me. Then I came back. But Mommy didn't talk to me either. I think people can't see me 'cause they don't wanna. When Mommy started talking to boys on her computer, I saw you. I went to your house—or your ap-part-ment? That's where I've been. I like it better there. With you." She reaches out and touches the tip of his nose and he feels a sorrow deeper than he ever imagined existed flood through his body.

"Brittany, I'm gonna make this right, okay?"

Her smile grows wider as she throws her arms around his neck. "I like you, Daniel. You're a good boy."

"Well, you're a good girl." He hugs her back, feeling her tiny, frail body against his. "Thank you for telling me your story."

"Daniel." Her voice is soft in his ear. "It's time for you to go now."

He pulls away and looks at the house. Then back at the girl. "Am I dead in there, Brittany?"

Brittany grins. "I see why Mommy likes you, Daniel. You're funny." She kisses his cheek and the world once again fades to black.

***

He opens his eyes and sees red.

This is it. I'm dead. This is what death looks like.

But the thought quickly flees. He knows better. Death looks like Brittany. Placing both palms on the mattress, he pushes himself up. Pain shoots through his left wrist, causing him to fall back into the puddle of blood he's been laying in.

CLICK-CLICK

He knows the sound. Using his right hand, he lifts up slightly and looks into the barrel of a large revolver.

"Back down." Kayla's voice is calm. She stands off to the side of the bed, still completely nude, clutching the gun in both hands. The bat sits propped against the wall behind her.

"Kayla."

"Down!" she yells. "Now!"

"Okay. Okay." He lets himself fall onto the bed. His brain seems to bounce off of every wall inside of his skull. "Just relax. Don't shoot."

"Why, Daniel?"

"Why what?"

"DON'T PLAY WITH ME! Answer the question! Did you think you would blackmail me or something? Do I look like I have any money to give you?"

He curls into a ball, covering his head as if that will stop a bullet. "I don't know what you're talking about."

"DON'T FUCKING LIE TO ME!" The bed shakes with every word. He knows that she's kicking it. "How did you know? How could you possibly know about her? Nobody! Nobody! Fucking nobody, Daniel. I didn't tell a soul!"

"I don't know anything! I swear to you. I don't know what you're talking about! Just let me sit up, Kayla. My head hurts. My hand's broken."

"Go to hell, Daniel. If you move one inch, I'll put a bullet in the back of your head. Do you understand me?"

"Yes."

"DO YOU?" The bed shakes again.

"YES! Yes I do! Just calm down. Please."

"Nobody," she repeats. "Who else knows?"

"Nobody," he says. "Just me."

"How?"

"I don't know."

"Answer me." Her voice grows low, like she's speaking through gritted teeth.

"She told me." Daniel closes his eyes as tight as he can and tries to gain control of his breathing.

"Who?"

"Brittany. She told me everything, Kayla."

"I hate you, Daniel. I hate you so much. Why would you do this to me? I was nice to you. I even fucked you. I thought maybe you were just guessing at first. You wouldn't be the first to make that assumption. Then you mentioned the pyjamas. There's no way you could have known that. How, Daniel? Tell me."

"I told you," Daniel's voice is desperate. "Brittany told me everything. It's okay, Kayla. I know. I know how he used to beat you. How he hit you with her in your arms. I know. He messed you up. It's not your fault."

"SHUT UP!" she explodes. "SHUT THE FUCK UP! RIGHT NOW!"

"Okay. Okay." He curls up tighter. Though he doesn't look, he can feel the gun trained on him, burning into the top of his head. "I'm sorry. Don't shoot me. Your neighbors will hear, Kayla. There's no way to get away with it. Just let me up please. I'll get dressed and I'll leave."

"Don't move." Her voice is calm again. "I swear to God, Daniel, if you move—"

"I'm not moving. I'm not moving."

"I need to think. Think. One shot. I hear it all the time. Just one. Just one good shot—" She's talking herself into it. He needs to say something before she succeeds. He swallows a shaky breath, opens his mouth to beg, to plea for his life. Then Brittany's voice whispers into his ear.

"Are you ready to see Mommy cry?"

After she speaks there's a noticeable silence that seems to linger for too long, and he knows that Kayla heard it too. It won't be enough to stop her though.

Forget this.

"You won't be able to get me into your trunk," he finally says.

"What?" she snaps.

"I'm too heavy, Kayla. You won't be able to wrap me in a sheet and take me to where you buried her. Didn't you think of that?"

"I'm gonna kill you." Her voice is so low now that it's almost a whisper.

"Move," the tiny voice says into his ear.

Daniel doesn't think. He rolls away as thunder erupts, echoing through the room. The impact of the bullet causes the mattress to vibrate as he rolls off of the bed and scrambles to his feet. The gun goes off again, and his ears ring. He stumbles back against the wall and a heavy slug splinters the wood next to his face.

Kayla jumps up onto the mattress, pointing the weapon between his eyes. Her breasts press between her arms and she bares her teeth, squeezing the trigger again. Daniel can't move. He sees in slow motion as the hammer moves back, then flies forward.

CLICK

She squeezes again. Still nothing. The room once again falls silent except for the sounds of both of their rapid breathing. Then her eyes go wide and her hands drop, the gun still held firmly in one. Her jaw hangs. She takes a step back, staring down at Daniel's side. He looks and sees Brittany standing next to him, tears pouring down her face. She gazes up at her mother and finally breaks the silence with a loud, high pitched scream that stirs Daniel's soul inside of his chest.

"No, Mommy! No! Please!"

Kayla continues to back up until her feet slip and she stumbles off of the bed, into the wall, knocking over the aluminium bat.

"Brittany," her voice shakes. "Brittany-"

Brittany continues to stare at her mom, her face contorted in agony covered in tears.

"Brittany, please." Kayla begins to cry as well. "Please, Baby, don't cry."

Daniel doesn't say a word. Just watches as Brittany and her mom lock eyes and cry together. Then Kayla straightens her body, takes a deep breath. He knows what she's going to do before she raises the revolver and points it under her chin.

"Kayla! No!"

But the gun discharges before he gets the second word out. Her skull muffles the noise slightly, but it's still loud. The top of her head explodes, painting the ceiling dark red as her body collapses into a pile of naked limbs.

When Daniel looks back down, Brittany's gone. He watches the spot, breathing heavily, as if she might reappear, but knowing that she won't. He turns back to where Kayla lay on the floor and stares for a long moment. There's no hate. No relief. There's no longer any sorrow. He figures all of that will come in time, but right now, there's no energy for it.

He lays back, sprawls out on the blood-soaked bed. His head hurts. He knows he needs to call the police—and he will. In a minute. But then he passes out. It's the police at the door who wake him up only minutes later.

Epilogue

The eulogy is a simple one. The pastor speaks of innocence. He speaks of forgiveness. The family sits in the pews and weeps. Not Daniel. He's stone faced in the back of the room.

The funeral isn't for Kayla. It's Brittany's. They held a service months ago, when it was assumed she was dead. But after Daniel led the police to where her mother left her in the dirt, the family insisted on another one. A real one.

It's a closed casket.

Nobody knows who he is, and he prefers it that way. He told the police that Kayla Jennings confessed what she had done to her daughter while she was drunk. Then, the next morning, she attacked him and took her own life. Members of her family tried to meet him, but he refused.

Brittany's father's still in prison.

After the sermon, a sad song plays and people cry harder. That's when Daniel slips out. He watches from a bus stop across the street as Brittany Swanson's tiny casket is carried down the paved walkway and lowered into the earth. A tear builds up in the corner of one of his eyes, threatens to burst out, but he blinks once and it's gone.

Why me? He wonders for the hundredth time. Of all the people in the world, why did she choose him to tell her story to? It doesn't matter though. All that matters is what happened. He's no longer afraid of the dark. He can't explain it, but after the whole ordeal the fear just fled. There are three new scars on his head and he still wears a cast on his left hand.

As he watches the scene across the street, he notices two people standing off to the side of the crowd, which is now gathered around Brittany's new grave. A thin, feminine body with no clothes on holds hands with a little girl in blue pyjamas. They both stand, gazing in Daniel's direction. He looks at Kayla's pale legs, remembering that she was naked when she died.

As if she can read his mind, she smiles. With her free hand, Brittany waves merrily. Even through the distance between them, he can see her missing front tooth. Only then does a single tear finally roll down his cheek. He smiles and waves back.

Brittany turns to leave, but Kayla just stares at Daniel for a long moment like she's looking into his soul. Then a half-smile appears on her face. As he peers into her drowsy blue eyes, a warmth spreads out from somewhere deep in his abdomen. Brittany comes back, takes her hand and she finally turns to leave. Daniel watches as they both move away and slowly fade into nothing.

Brittany has her Mommy back.

The Door

T. Fox Dunham

Still the baby wailed through the door—long since dead but desperate for comfort. Harvey leaned his head on the wood. Night after night after night for three months, he'd climbed the stairs, struggling more with each ascendance, determined to finally go through the door and confront the spirit that taunted his lonely nights. And just as the ritual demanded, he failed.

"Don't cry, honey," he said, comforting—as he would his own child. He gripped the oval knob but couldn't summon the will to open the door. The baby wailed through the clapboard, piercing his spirit—not his child, no longer anyone's child. Its screams shrilled with an ethereal pitch, a sound no human could produce. Calluses marked his palm. His fingers ached from the repeated position, clutching the small oval, but he couldn't face the phantom. "Don't cry little one," he whispered through the door, pawing at the faded and filthy white paint that chipped off the panels. "May is so bright. Summer is coming." He looked out the hallway window, gazing at the rising hills in the nascent fog. The sudden frost melted in the sunlight but the late chill had shocked the magnolia tree, melting its white petals. He'd at least seen another spring, even though the pain worsened, spreading up and down his chest, drilling into his neck. He longed to leave, to go out onto the battlefield and see the hills, but Harvey couldn't let go. He gripped the doorknob until his knuckles whitened, trapped in limbo.

Denise slept downstairs in a chair, not noticing the child's cries. He'd not told his wife about the phantoms. She'd endured enough, watching him decay from toxic chemicals and invisible rays. She suffered as he suffered, and Harvey endured for the promise of a life, the vow of years that he'd made when they married. He refused to fail her, to be a defective husband. He wanted to be whole again, to be more than a shadow of himself, to be her husband once more.

Then it came. The shadow man followed, playing its part in the menagerie. He heard it climbing the stairs, staggering up one by one. The oily silhouette oozed to the floor, bleeding night around it. Harvey shivered, chilled in its presence. He closed his eyes, keeping his back to the shadow. What did they need? Whose child was this?

So many babies died before the modern era of medicine, so the child could have been many. When the turbulence began right after that last oncology appointment, Harvey had looked into the farm's past, expecting to find an ubiquitous ghost story. He'd even researched the property, checked with local folklorists for any clues, yet he uncovered nothing definitive, no key to ending midnight haunting. If he knew the spirit's story then perhaps he could open the door. He knew houses could be haunted, at least heard many stories since they'd moved from Philly to Gettysburg last summer, and he wondered: Could just a door be haunted?

He squeezed the tiny doorknob in frustration, and the baby cried beyond, calling for him, keeping him there. All he had to do was open it but something in his spirit refused him the simple act. So, Harvey waited for it to stop and considered the events of the previous months, remembering how the story started when he found all the doors shut.

All great stories in life begin when a door opens and all great stories end when it closes.

***

Harvey didn't know how to process the doctor's news. He floated, no longer feeling anchored to the earth. He didn't cry. He didn't raise his hands in anger. Harvey just melted onto the seat of the van, trying to be comfortable. The sound of his phone shocked him back, and his stomach tingled, filling with dread.

He read the text from Denise:

What did Doctor Morden say?

He cycled the text and slipped the phone into his pocket. The appointment felt like a faded dream, and he tried not to think of it. What could he really do? He'd just go on as he had and the world would go on and life would go on and time would go on. Medical transport dropped him at the gravel drive to the farmhouse then drove away, but Harvey needed a few minutes before going into the house. He headed over to the barn, stepping through slushy snow with the help of his aluminum cane. The barn had stood since before two armies clashed in the hills of Gettysburg, and during the battle, the Union army tended causalities in the building. He planned to rebuild the barn first then repair the antiquated farmhouse, fulfilling his promise to bring back the dead. The stone foundation held solid and most of the support beams appeared to be strong. He needed to replace the paneling on the barn to recreate its original appearance, since the place had been declared a historic site. People insisted on holding onto the past, and he appreciated the challenge. Harvey finished his survey and scanned the ground for old buckles, bottles, musket balls, any relics of the civil war that might have been dislodged by the early March thaw. He loved living in such an old place, full of memories and history. On the weekends when reenactors recreated the battle, he'd get lost watching them, losing himself in time. So easily here he could forget the present, and Harvey took comfort in that.

Raw wind racked at the land, chilling Harvey, and he walked to the house, leaning on his cane to keep his footing. It surprised him to find the front door open, and he cautiously stepped inside, getting ready to swing his cane at an intruder; of course, the burglar would take one look at his pale skin, emaciated body and the soft short curls growing from his recently bald head and see no contest. He checked the first floor, looking in the closet built into the side of the fireplace in the living room. Something banged the ceiling. "Denise? You home, baby?" The ceiling groaned from footsteps. Maybe she'd come home for lunch. He dragged himself up the spiral staircase, leaning on the wall for support and found the four doors shut. Maybe she shut the doors to prevent drafts. It cost a fortune to heat this place, but it didn't explain why she'd left the front door wide open. He checked their bedroom and found it empty. He hadn't slept in their bed since starting chemo, making a sickbed out of the couch in the living room. Harvey picked up her body spray from the dresser, sprayed it and smelled the sweet lilacs. The aroma reminded him of their time dating—how wonderful she smelled. He'd come back to their bed soon a complete man and once more become her husband. Harvey didn't care what the doctors said. He'd beat this.

After checking the bathroom and linen closet, he moved to the far end of the hall to the last closed door. They'd intended to use the room for some purpose, but he couldn't recall, lost in all their plans when they moved out here from Philly. He thought he heard something—at first, quiet, maybe even a potent memory that had slipped its bounds like a waking dream. Old houses played tricks on the senses, and you could forget yourself, your time. The noise amplified. The muffled sobs of a baby cried through the door, startling Harvey. A tourist family must have wandered off the battlefield and onto their property. He told himself that's all it was, but the weeping came from the house. He gripped the black oval doorknob. His breath quickened. His head spun from low blood pressure. He needed to rest. The child wailed, crying out to be held, comforted. Its sobs shrilled through the thin door, and he wanted to open the door; however, his hand refused the command, subject of some kind of a mental block. His eyes moistened with tears. It needed him but he couldn't twist his wrist. He'd already exercised too much for the day, and fatigue overwhelmed Harvey. He compensated for the weakness, leaning on his cane like another limb, and it slipped, nearly dropping him to the floor. Black silky fluid oozed from under the door, running along his shoes. The door bled. A baby wept. And

Harvey quickly turned and stumbled down the stairs, moving as fast as he could to get away from the door. He could still hear the wailing from the couch, and he slipped two white pills out of a bottle, doubling his afternoon dose. Then, Harvey pulled the blankets up to make himself more comfortable and closed his eyes until he escaped through sleep.

***

Several nights later he and Denise talked while she got ready for her shift at the hospital.

He didn't mention the ghosts to her. Maybe he would if it happened again. "You going to be okay getting in?" Harvey asked.

"They salted the roads," Denise said, preparing his injection. "I just hope I don't get stuck at the hospital. God, I hate when it snows in April."

"Can't you stay home? Claim yeti attack?" He wanted to be with her and no longer felt comfortable being alone in the house. He'd said nothing about the occurrence. Denise would have told him to call Doctor Morden, but what the hell good would that do at this point? The doctor no longer had any power. Harvey had grown weaker, seldom eating, depending more and more on the needle to ease the pain. He'd used the meds to endure any nocturnal haunting but tonight the smoky snow buried him in the house. "I don't want to be alone tonight."

"I can't, babe," she said. "You know. . .patient abandonment. Is there anything I can do to make you more comfortable?" She hadn't looked directly at him since the morning before. Something bothered her.

"Fuck them," he said. "Stay and talk to me like you used to before when your voice was soft. Before the doors all closed to me."

"You're lying to me," she said, finally looking at him. "Doctor Morden asked me if there was anything he could do to make us more comfortable. He can't tell me what you talked about. And he only asks that when—"

She knew that Harvey had failed her, and he sank into the guilt, drowning in the oily well. "Remember all those stories you used to tell me about all the times doctors were wrong?"

"I remember," she said. He waited for her face to light up with hope, to see a glimmer of their future reflected in her eyes. No mirror glowed. No light flickered. A door slammed upstairs, shaking the house. "Bad drafts," she said then grabbed her purse. He panicked, desperate to say something to keep her there.

"You're the one that keeps leaving!" he tried to yell but his lungs resisted. Harvey coughed hard then tasted blood in his mouth. His chest ached.

She clutched the doorknob. "Your sickness. It used to be your, well, I guess your shadow. Now, you're the shadow." Her voice cracked.

"Please look at me," he said. She sighed and fled the house into the blizzard, leaving the door ajar. Harvey wanted to be furious with her but he couldn't. He understood. Denise protected herself, getting herself ready. She mourned. His life would stop. Her life would go on, and she prepared to survive him. His death would just be another door through which she'd have to pass and pass alone. The idea both comforted and enraged Harvey.

No. Doctor Morden is an idiot. I'm going to be fine—and we'll be fine. I'm going to be fine.

Harvey's head twirled from the morphine, and he fled into sleep. Sometime in the night, the door slammed shut upstairs, startling him awake. Harvey stirred on the couch, drenched in sweat. A vice clenched his chest, pressing into his neck, and he fumbled at the pill bottles. He switched on the lamp and found the front door shut. Maybe she'd come home to be with him. "Denise?" Floorboards creaked overhead, responding to his call. Someone staggered down the hall, thumping as it stepped, walking all the way to the south wall.

"This isn't right," he said to the phantasms. "I'm sick." Something struck the front porch, shaking the living room wall. Raccoons had gotten in through the attic before then, escaped down the side of the house, but it sounded too heavy. Something came for him, and he pushed himself off the couch, staggered to the door but fumbled the chain with numb fingers. The screen door wheezed open. Chemotherapy had killed the nerve endings in his fingers, and he couldn't manage the chain. He leaned against the door to bar entry but had little weight left to leverage. The door pushed back.

"Stop doing this to us," he begged. "I'm going to be fine."

The door pushed harder, nearly knocking him over.

"I'm comfortable," Harvey lied, and the house knew it. Finally, his strength drained, and he collapsed to the floor. It opened, revealing the snowy night. Wind whipped the snow, draining the color of the countryside. In the inchoate night, he could make out the barren magnolia tree partially buried by white. Snow piled on the front steps and the front of the porch. The screen door hung open, and Harvey's mind raced, seeking answers and excuses. He watched as the night bled a shadow silhouette, forming the body of a man. At first it lingered, then a dark figure limped forward, coming for the fallen man. He shuddered, guarding himself and focused against the nausea, trying not to vomit. The silhouette stopped at the doorway, leaned down and reached for Harvey. He shivered, embracing himself for its icy presence, yet the phantasm stopped an inch from Harvey's face. For some reason, as if anchored, the ghost couldn't reach him. Harvey couldn't move, paralyzed by the current in the dielectric between them. For minutes, they just hung there until pain gripped his legs. Unable to endure it for long, he finally summoned the courage and pushed the door shut with his cane. Then Harvey huddled on the floor in front of the fireplace, eventually escaping through sleep.

***

Spring seemed to cast out the spirits, and for a few weeks, the house slept. Doctor Morden cut back Harvey's radiation to keep him comfortable. He'd slept easier, even got some work done, debugging the alarm app on the new phone OS. Things felt normal for a time, and he'd forgotten the disturbances, assuming the door had closed on their ghost story. The tourists came back to battlefield, seeking ghosts of a war long ended, and hunters came for deer in the state lands on the park's borders. One morning, the crack of a gunshot echoed across the fields and raked against the house. At first, he nearly called the police, infuriated. What if their kids had been playing outside? However, he decided to check out the situation first. It might have just been a bus backfiring. Harvey put on his jacket and scarf but once outside, he discovered he didn't need the extra garb. The sun warmed his face, and he loosened his scarf, invigorated by the kinder weather. Spring returned to renew the land, moving through the cycle. Dandelions began to bloom, and white buds sprouted from the dark branches of the lone magnolia tree growing in the yard. He didn't see any hunters, but the sound could have traveled far on a sedate Sunday morning. Not hearing another shot, Harvey nearly went back into the house to work more on the app code when he heard a man cry out from his barn. Maybe someone had been hurt. He followed the sound of suffering to the barn, avoiding the stray patches of stubborn crystallized snow still clinging onto the muddy ground beyond their allotted time. A choir of pain sung out from the dry-rotted walls. Men moaned. Some screamed. Their song of suffering played the symphony of the aftermath of battle. Blood stained the pale grass, and Harvey found a pile of stray limbs—mostly severed legs or arms. A group of reenactors must have gotten the wrong address.

"This is my goddamn barn," he yelled. "They do the hospital at the George Spangler Farm."

He looked between the withered planks, and the scene he witnessed couldn't have been staged without Hollywood special effects. Soldiers wearing blue Union uniforms and wrapped in stained bandages rested on mats. Blood pooled, painting the fresh wood a shade of crimson that would eventually fade to brown. Nurses tended the wounded, and in the corner, haggard surgeons treated the wounded. A medic held a can of ether to a young soldier's face while a surgeon sliced into the skin above his knee. He'd heard of such phantom scenes playing out in Gettysburg before, haunting old sites of military significance. Past painful points played out again and again in the area, spinning like a broken record, never letting the world forget. He watched for a moment, commiserating with their pain, remembering the butchery of the surgery that cut the cancer from his lung, and as he watched, the scene dissipated. Before it faded, he locked eyes with a soldier and knew through some intuition or perhaps the look in his eyes that the wounded man would soon die. The causality joined his gaze and regarded Harvey. Each understood the other, sharing coeval fate. The sun rose high behind Harvey, melting away the vision, and he wondered if he had seen the past or if the soldier had seen the future. Who was the ghost?

Harvey went back inside, more perplexed than frightened by the scene. He ruminated on a cautionary tale about a programmer who once held Harvey's job. The guy had coded a critical math error in a digital clock update for their phones, and on a sleepy Tuesday morning, their customers lost an hour. Most never noticed, and for a good part of the day, they functioned as if it was an hour earlier. He'd always wondered if all the digital clocks in the world lost an hour, would anyone notice?

***

As the weeks passed, the wailing child summoned Harvey upstairs, and he still couldn't get through the mental block preventing him from opening the door. He'd leaned against the door until dawn, looking out at his yard. He watched the white blossom sprout from the lone magnolia tree in the yard. It grew stronger, vibrant, and he'd weakened, finding it harder to breathe each day. The pain amplified, and he only found escape in narcotic sleep, knocked out by the morphine at double the usual dose. The walls and furniture of the farmhouse faded, leaking their color, and Denise slipped further and further away as if Harvey had been set adrift down the Cumberland River.

You don't die all at once. Pieces of you fail as you go, and once lost, he'd never recover them.

At night, he summoned the strength to follow the sobs of the inconsolable infant to the door upstairs. He could barely make it up the stairs this time, leaving Denise to sleep downstairs. His broken and burned body could just still support him, and he made it to the door then clutched the doorknob, running out of time to open it. Blood spilled from below the door. He'd stepped in it and smeared it on the floor. It felt so familiar to him as if playing out the event that motivated their flight from Philadelphia to the country. He'd always pushed the memory away, overwhelmed by the diagnosis then the torture of the treatment, but now the cancer had eaten his body away, drained his strength, making him vulnerable to nightmares and memories.

A year ago, he'd come home to their apartment in Rittenhouse Square and found blood smeared on the bedroom floor. Dark patches stained the white carpet of their bedroom, leaving a trail to the bathroom door. The memory played out in his mind, strangling him.

"Denise?" He tried the locked door to the bathroom. "Did you cut yourself?"

"No," she said through the door. "I'm not clumsy. I'm careful. I'm so goddamn careful."

"Let me in?" he said through the door, fighting panic, the urge to yell. The lock clicked, and he found Denise wiping blood off her thighs with wads of toilet paper. The sight kicked him in the stomach. They'd been trying for two years and after much help from physicians, they'd finally created a life— something wonderful made from them both.

"I didn't mean to," Denise said, sobbing. "I hate this city. Smog. Chemicals. All the goddamn noise." Blood stained her hand. "The city killed it."

"We'll get out," he said, mopping up blood from the toilet seat—the wasted potential. "We'll go somewhere peaceful where you'll be more comfortable. Someplace where we can make a nursery. I'll paint it lavender."

"I'm cold," Denise said. "Close the door."

***

Harvey woke crouched at dawn up against the door on the second floor of the Gettysburg farmhouse still gripping the knob. Pain stabbed his chest, overwhelming him, and he labored to breathe. Normally, the night played out and by dawn, the shadow would pass. Still, it waited for him at the top of the stairs, not able to reach him. Something held it back. It beckoned to Harvey, and he wanted to follow it, to understand the story.

He needed it to end.

Outside, the sun had risen, and the trees glowed. He longed to be among the natural world, to join the Summerland and never feel pain or the cold again. As he looked down at the fields, he watched soldiers adorned both gray and blue uniforms march to the trees, heading to distant and foggy hills, and he longed to join them, to be emancipated from their war.

"I can't leave her," he whispered, yet she faded in his mind. His love felt like a movie he'd seen or a book he'd read years ago; he knew he'd read the book but couldn't quite remember what it was about. What was her name? She'd been his wife and had a name, but names no longer felt important.

Other souls joined the final march of the soldiers, fading as they walked, passing the lone magnolia tree. Its nascent blossoms sagged, falling off like drenched white dresses, but it didn't matter. Next year, the tree would blossom again and again as the cycle continued.

He never opened the door and pulled himself up, ripping himself free. Funny, his leg felt fine. Even the pain had eased, and he noticed its absence. Harvey left it all behind at the door he could never open and followed the shadow. Its body had lightened. The black turned to gray and eventually glowed white, wearing a cloak of magnolia flowers. He strolled down the stairs, excited to soon be out in the sun though pausing, missing their home.

In the living room, he tiptoed to the woman, feeling some fleeting connection to her. He didn't wish to wake her and brushed away the hair over her eyes. Life vibrated from her body. She still had so much of it in her, and he knew she'd go on and bring new life to the world. Some part of him had passed to her, and she would pass it on to her offspring if even in spirit. Life would go on. He kissed her on the forehead then opened the door, ending this story. He closed it behind him to begin a story anew.

An Angry Woman
Richard Raven

Sylvia Collier bolted upright in bed, screaming herself awake. Trembling violently as if in the throes of a seizure, her wide and horrified eyes were fixed on the foot of the bed. She was still gasping for breath when a light suddenly came on and she felt the bed dip beside her. She jerked, startled, and was about to scream again when strong and comforting arms wrapped around her. Awareness finally dawning, she realized the light was from the lamp on the bedside stand and the arms were those of her husband, Frank.

"Jesus," she moaned and gratefully buried her face against his broad, hard chest.

"Again?" Frank murmured, one hand stroking her back through her thin nightshirt.

"Yes." Sylvia was still trembling.

"The same dream for the third night in a row?" Frank pulled her closer to him. "And you never dream, or so you've always told me."

"Not exactly the same dream. It was different this time."

"Different how?"

Sylvia pulled from his embrace and pointed. "The alarm woke me up and the figure was standing at the foot of the bed. Only it wasn't an indistinct shape like a shadow this time. There was this eerie glow like a shaft of moonlight and I could see that it was a woman. She had long dark blonde hair." She paused, looked away from the foot of the bed, and added. "I could also tell that she was dead."

"Dead? Are you sure about that?"

Sylvia nodded. "No doubt about it. She was…all bloody and torn up, and her clothes were ripped to shreds. It looked like she had been in some kind of horrible accident. There was blood coming from her mouth and dripping all over the floor. But that wasn't the only thing different about it this time. This time, I talked to her…and she talked to me."

"What was said?"

"I asked who she was, and she said, *'Does it matter?'* in a really hateful kind of way. I told her, yes, it did matter because she was in my bedroom, so I asked again who she was, then I asked what she wanted. She wouldn't tell me her name, but when I asked what she wanted, it made her mad, and she said, *'You'* in this hard, angry voice. Then she laughed—and there was no humor in it—and she said, *'You're my means to an end'.*" Sylvia shrugged. "And that's when I woke up."

"Holy shit," Frank muttered. "What the hell could that mean?"

Sylvia had no idea what it meant. Despite the woman's horrible condition, Sylvia didn't recognize her, so it couldn't be a tragic loss her mind was dredging up. Nor could Sylvia explain why this dream in its two variations had haunted her sleep for three straight nights. It was true that she rarely dreamed—and never as she had since

Saturday night. When she did dream, the few times she could even recall details afterward, they were always a bit...*weird* in a faintly amusing or melancholy way. No different, as far as she could tell, from the dreams of most people she had known who had shared them with her. Certainly not anything as horrific as what she had seen in her sleep this last time—and it was worse than she had let on to Frank. Much worse. The woman had been missing an eye, the empty socket a bloody crater in her face. There were also several other visible wounds to the woman's face and torso. Some of her ribs were exposed, and the jagged stump of the upper bone of her left arm was sticking several inches through the skin.

"Sweetie," Frank said slowly, "maybe we need to get you an appointment to see the doctor. You're due for a checkup, anyway."

Sylvia shook her head emphatically. "That's not necessary. I think it's all the highs and lows these past ten days. It's been a real emotional rollercoaster for us."

Frank nodded. "It's been that, all right. Still, just to be on the safe side—"

"Baby, I've just been stressed out, that's all. The dream is already fading in my mind." Which wasn't entirely the truth. The truth was that the details of a dream never stayed with her for very long, but that wasn't the case with this dream, and even more so this last time. She had been awake long enough that only a few vague and disjointed images of it should remain, but it remained so vivid and lifelike in her mind that it seemed as if it had been no dream at all.

Strange...

"Well, if you're sure," Frank said and there was a clear note of doubt in his voice.

"Yes, I'm sure. I'm also sure this stress will all pass once I've settled into the new job." She was trying hard to believe that herself and to put a positive spin on things. "Besides, I don't want you worrying about me and distracted today." Frank drove a truck for a wholesale food distributor and made deliveries to restaurants and stores all over the city and surrounding counties. He was already dressed and ready to leave for the day, which meant it was a little after four in the morning. "I want you home, safe and sound, so we can celebrate tonight."

Frank grinned, and Sylvia was glad to feel the tension leaving him as she snuggled into his arms. "Oh, we're going to celebrate," he assured her. "Dinner reservations confirmed, and whatever your heart desires after that."

Sylvia smiled. Ten days ago celebrating was the last thing on her mind or Frank's. Ten days ago all she had wanted to do was curl up into a ball and cry like a baby when she learned that her position with an investment brokerage firm, a position she had held for almost six years, had been eliminated. A bit of belt-tightening, they told her, and her position simply disappeared. All the plans she and Frank had made—the car payments and mortgage payments on the house—and all the simple things they wanted to do in the short term...all of it thrown into doubt. They had been married a little over three years, the second time around for both of them, and they were determined to make it work this time. Frank worked like a dog from sunrise to sunset, sometimes six days a week, but it wasn't enough. In those first days after getting the news, Sylvia was consumed with dread by the thought of just what in the hell they were going to do.

"In case I haven't said it enough," Frank said, and he was stroking her cheek now, "I'm damned proud of you, sweetie. First day on the job with Ryan Communications? Damn, lady, talk about a coup. *The* plumb job in this city."

"Thanks, babe, but I think you give me too much credit," Sylvia said, but she was pleased by his sincere words. "All I can say is thank God for Jeannie."

Jeannie Marlow was an old friend from college. They had drifted apart after graduation, and it was the fifth day after losing her job that Sylvia had wandered into a Starbucks, in need of a caffeine fix…and there was Jeannie. She was sitting alone at a table in the back, a latte in front of her, reading a copy of the Wall Street Journal. Jeannie was wearing what looked like a tailored suit with spike heels and dark nylons, an outfit Sylvia could only dream of owning, much less getting to wear. Jeannie had glanced up at her, and their eyes locked. A huge smile had spread across Jeannie's face as she got to her feet.

"My, God, just look at you!" Jeannie had declared and wrapped Sylvia up in a hug. "I didn't know you were even in the city!"

Nor had Sylvia known she was around. Ryan Communications owned the local ABC affiliate TV station in town, but Sylvia had no idea that Jeannie worked for Ryan or that the man maintained one of his two headquarters here in town. This all came out when the two women began talking, catching up. When Jeannie asked about her— *"Husband? Kids? Where are you working?"* —the misery Sylvia had been feeling began pouring out in a torrent. She hadn't meant for this to happen, and even though she had embarrassed herself, Jeannie wasn't quick to shower her old friend with empty pity.

Instead, she offered a solution.

"Mr. Ryan works mostly out of his office on the east coast, and I pretty much run things at this end. But he's about to close the deal on four TV stations in this region and a couple of online ventures, so he's going to be here, off and on, for months. The staff has been short-handed here for almost three weeks now. We lost one of the girls in the office…a rather tragic thing, really." A look of deep sadness had passed over Jeannie's face, but it had disappeared as quickly as it appeared, and she had continued. "We've been trying to replace her, and with this planned expansion, we need to fill the spot. So, what kind of secretarial experience do you have?"

Two days later, Sylvia interviewed with Wesley Ryan and landed the open spot. She gave all the credit to Jeannie, who had spent those days prior to the interview coaching and preparing her. Once Ryan made it official, Jeannie promptly named Sylvia as her executive assistant. She would be making almost three times the money she was before.

"I've got to meet this Jeannie," Frank said. "I'd love to thank her in person."

"You'll meet her one day real soon, I promise. Right now, as much as I love the way you're holding me, you better get going."

"Yeah, I better," Frank agreed. "This is Monday and always a long and crazy day."

After he left, Sylvia remained sitting up in bed, the lamp on. She wasn't due to begin her first day on the new job until nine, and that was hours away. Yet she was certain that there would be no more sleep for her because she still couldn't get the image of the blood-covered woman from her dream out of her head.

"You're my means to an end." Who was the woman and what had she meant by those cryptic words?

Then again, did it matter? It had only been a dream…right? As if to drive that point home, she let her eyes drift toward the foot of the bed.

Okay, satisfied now?

No, in truth, she wasn't satisfied. She couldn't get the notion out of her head that it had seemed too real to have only been a dream. She had seen the dripping of blood, for Christ's sake, and her hands were still trembling! As she looked around the room, a new and unbidden thought occurred to her.

Could this house be haunted?

She had never believed in the possibility of ghostly entities trapped in this realm and unable to move on. Nor had she ever dismissed the possibility. Until a little while ago, she had simply never experienced anything personally to suggest one possibility or the other and had always kept an open mind on the subject. Now she couldn't help but wonder…

It was an old house, built back in the early seventies, but it was well maintained and in excellent condition. The real estate agent who had sold them the house had mentioned nothing about a dark history to Frank and Sylvia. Nor had Sylvia learned from her online research of anything ominous or sinister. No mass killings by a deranged family member or anything out of the ordinary. The couple who had bought the house originally had raised their three kids here and sold it in the mid-nineties soon after the last of their offspring had moved out.

Could the woman I saw have some connection with this place? Maybe a member of the second family who lived here...the Scotts?

Sylvia closed her eyes, drew in a deep breath, and told herself emphatically to knock it the hell off. She and Frank had lived here for almost two years; in all that time there had been nothing remotely like supernatural activity. Nothing she was aware of or could point to with a definitive finger. It was quiet and peaceful here! Yet here she was spooked by what could have been nothing but a nightmare and wondering if she was living in a haunted house!

What next, Sylvia? A monster hiding under the bed or in the closet? A psycho slasher waiting for you in the shower? A rampaging doll some little girl left in the attic that's about to pounce and rip my throat out? Frank, I swear, if you ever bring another damned horror movie into this house and insist on me watching it with you...

Thinking of the closet reminded her that she still hadn't decided what she was going to wear that day. Mr. Ryan had a very strict dress code, something Jeannie had stressed to her. "And there are no casual Fridays, either. He expects his employees, and I mean right down to the maintenance people who are issued uniforms, to look and act like professionals at all times. He can be a difficult man at times, yes, but he can also be a very generous man when it comes to bonuses and perks and so forth. You'll hear stories of his generosity—and all of them are true. So, just take his ways and his rules in stride and roll with it, and you won't have any problems."

With nothing better to do than sit there like a frightened schoolgirl, she climbed out of bed and padded over to the closet. She took her time, going through the choices available to her, and settled on a dark skirt and jacket and a cream-colored blouse. She found her favorite pair of black heels, then went over to the dresser and located what she would need to go with the outfit.

With this chore complete, the outfit laid out and waiting, she went into the bathroom—*so much for the slasher waiting in the shower*—and relieved herself. Then she went back to bed and burrowed under the sheet. She left the lamp on.

Surprisingly, she began to relax, and after a time she was feeling drowsy. She made sure the alarm on her cell was still set for seven and found her spot again under the sheet.

***

Her eyelids fluttered at the sound of the alarm. She moaned sleepily, yawned, and was about to turn over and wait for the alarm to go off again in snooze mode when she stiffened, her eyes suddenly going wide. Something wasn't right. She could feel it, a crawly sensation up and down her spine that there was someone in the room with her, watching her. She raised her head from the pillow, her heart pounding much too hard in her chest, and she looked fearfully toward the foot of the bed. By the light of the lamp and the soft glow of daylight filtering into the room through the windows…

…she saw nothing. The room was empty. She blew out a loud and exasperated breath.

Of course, there isn't anyone standing there, you silly woman! There never was! Her cell was still sounding on the bedside stand.

She threw back the sheet, swung her feet to the floor, and sucked in her breath.

The room was chilly. But, then, it was fall, and the nights were growing cool, the central air finally getting a break. She shivered as she reached for her phone to silence the alarm. At least she had managed a little more than two hours of sleep that had passed without a dream of a dead woman standing at the foot of the bed. Not as far as she could remember…but she really wasn't sure about it because the dream remained. It was still lodged in her head, every detail of it as vivid and horrible as when she had screamed herself awake.

Why is it still hanging on like this? She was still sitting on the side of the bed, staring at her phone in her hand, and letting herself wake up when…

"My name's Samantha Talbot. Remember the name?"

Sylvia gasped and leaped to her feet. She spun around and…frowned, puzzled, her mouth dropping open slightly. She would have sworn the words were whispered to her by someone—a woman, definitely—from the other side of the bed. She had even sensed for just a split second a presence standing there.

But, again, there was no one there, the room empty. The only sound she could hear was the thump of her pulse in her temples.

But the strangest thing about it, as well as the most frightening…was that Sylvia did remember that name. There was, at least, a vague memory taking shape in her mind. She was sure she had heard the name before…but where? She was still trying to pull the memory out of the depths of her mind when…

…her phone went off in her hand. Sylvia screamed and danced away from the bed as she hurled the buzzing phone toward it.

"Damn it!" she yelled between gasping breaths. She realized that she had only silenced the alarm, instead of turning it off, and now the phone was going off in snooze mode. "You're letting this effect you beyond reason!" she told herself sternly.

And it wasn't helping that she was standing there talking to herself. She didn't have time for this. Not today of all days. She grabbed up her phone and turned off the alarm. Then she pulled off her nightclothes, went into the bathroom and started the shower.

The warm spray calmed her down and finished waking her up, and she began to focus on the day ahead of her. Jeannie had said that Mr. Ryan wouldn't be back in the local office until Wednesday. "So, we'll use Monday and Tuesday introducing you to everyone and getting you familiar with the way things work around here. When Mr. Ryan is in town, I always work closely with him and his two assistants. That means you'll be taking over most of my normal duties."

And what Sylvia had seen of those duties wasn't anything she couldn't handle.

So, why the hell am I so nervous and stressed out? That's got to be what the problem is and why I'm freaking out this way. Come on, girl, you've got this. Just stay focused on the day, get through it, then me and Frank can spend a terrific evening together—and we deserve it!

Sylvia climbed out of the shower and shivered. With all the steam she had created, the bathroom should have been like the tropics. Instead, it was chilly, more so than when she had first woke up, her wet and naked body suddenly dotted with gooseflesh. Sylvia grabbed for a pair of towels, wrapped one around herself and was rubbing at her hair with the other as she hurried into the bedroom. There, just beyond the bathroom door, she stopped in her tracks.

Jesus, why is it so cold in here?

Not chilly—*cold*. Only a few steps out of the bathroom —and no longer than she had taken in the shower—and the temperature had seemed to plummet. Hugging herself, she hurried into the hallway, found it was just as cold there as in the bedroom, and checked the thermostat. The tiny display red 44 f.

What?

They always kept the temperature set at 72, and that was what the display had indicated when Sylvia turned the air off before she and Frank went to bed. It was still set for that, and the unit was still off. If anything, with the morning sun streaming through all the windows, the temperature should have risen a degree or two from 72.

Yet even as she stared at the display, the temperature dropped to 43.

There must be something wrong with it. The easy explanation, but one that didn't seem all that plausible even to her. Still, she had to start getting ready for work, so she checked again to be sure the thermostat was set for 72, then turned on the heat and waited for the flow of warmth from the vent in the ceiling above her head. Just to be safe, she or Frank would have to call a technician to come out and check the thermostat and, likely, the entire system.

Back in the bedroom, she dried her hair, put on most of the outfit she had picked out, leaving her heels for last, and was finishing her makeup when the name *Samantha Talbot* drifted through her mind like a cloud passing in front of the sun. She stopped what she was doing and stared at her reflection in her vanity mirror.

There was a decidedly uneasy look in the green eyes staring back at her.

She now remembered where she had heard the name before. The memory had burst into her mind as clear as a cloudless sky. Three weeks ago, give or take a day or so, there had been a horrible hit and run accident out on Highway 79 just west of the city. It had happened just after sunset and both the local papers and every TV station in town aired a piece about the accident. It had remained in the news for days because police were having no luck finding the driver of the death vehicle. A vehicle believed to be a truck since many trucks used the big four-lane into and out of the city. The victim, Sylvia remembered, was identified as Samantha Talbot, aged 26. She was pronounced dead at the scene. There had been a picture of the woman in the news coverage Sylvia had seen…a woman with long dark blonde hair.

And the woman in the dream had looked like something as big as a truck had hit her.

Jesus…

Then Sylvia remembered one additional detail that the news coverage had provided, and she felt a chill that was all apprehension slide down her spine.

Samantha Talbot had reportedly worked for Ryan Communication.

"We lost one of the girls in the office…a rather tragic thing, really." Jeannie had said to Sylvia that day at Starbucks, and Sylvia could recall, quite clearly, the look of sadness that had washed over Jeannie's face.

Was that who Jeannie was talking about? The woman I'm replacing?

Perhaps the latter was the better question. If what she had seen was the ghost of the dead woman—and that was still a big if in Sylvia's mind—why was she haunting her? Because Sylvia was replacing her? If there was a vengeful spirit on the loose, it seemed to Sylvia that the driver of the death vehicle would be the most likely target of a haunting. It didn't make sense, and that wasn't the only thing puzzling Sylvia.

Why is it still so freaking cold in here?

The temperature had come up some, but it was still much colder than it should have been. Sylvia could hear the hum of the central unit and feel the warmth from one of the two vents in the bedroom ceiling.

For the moment, she put the temperature out of her mind and refocused her thoughts on Samantha Talbot. Sylvia was tempted to take a few minutes and go online and see what she could find about the woman, perhaps begin to make a little sense of what was going on. After a quick check of the time, she realized that she didn't have a few minutes to spare. She had a little more than an hour to finish getting ready and to drive into downtown. Maybe there would be a few free minutes at work to speak to Jeannie about Samantha Talbot, provided Jeannie was willing to discuss the subject.

Sylvia quickly finished her makeup, then rose from her vanity. All that was left for her to do was step into her heels and put her phone and a few other items in her purse. She had to turn off the heat, and she was about to go into the hallway and do that when—

—she stopped dead, her toes through her nylons digging into the carpet. Her purse fell from her hands and hit the floor at her feet, and her mouth had dropped open.

Oh…my…God…

The dead woman from her nightmare was standing at the foot of the bed. Sylvia, in those first few seconds, completely forgot how to breathe as she stared at the broken and gore-streaked figure staring back at her with one narrowed blue eye, the other an empty and bloody socket.

This was no nightmare—the woman was ***there***! She looked nothing like the ghostly entities Sylvia had heard about or saw documented on TV. There was nothing transparent or indistinct about the figure facing her. The woman looked as if she had risen from the spot in which she had died and had found her way into the bedroom.

Sylvia, her mouth still gaped open and eyes bulging, felt like screaming and running madly out of the house, but she could do neither. The cold in the room was now the worst it had been—and there was still warm air coming from the vents!

"Glad you remembered me and what happened to me," she woman said. As was the case when Sylvia was asleep, the woman's voice appeared to be the only thing about her unaffected by the horrible accident that killed her. It was a voice that rang with undisguised and barely controlled rage. Thin streams of blood leaked from her misshapen mouth with each word she said. "Unlike many others, including the cops, who forgot about me quick enough."

Sylvia remained rooted silently in place. She tried to speak, but her throat was so dry that she couldn't swallow, much less form words.

"By the way," the woman said, "that you got my job has nothing to do with this. The truth is that I was only a few days away from quitting that shitty job when that truck turned me into roadkill. I'd had my fill of that place and all the two-faced phonies there." She sounded more enraged now, and there was an eerie light glowing in her one remaining eye.

Sylvia cleared her throat, managed to swallow, and got a few words out. "Then why are you here?" Her voice was little more than a raw and hoarse croak.

"You're my means to an end, I told you that. I've been watching you and hubby for days now. He's quite the stud, I must say—but you, of course, already know that. I was here the night after you were hired, watching you two going at it like neither of you would ever have another chance to fuck. It's a wonder you could even walk when he finished with you."

Despite the cold in the room induced by the fear that enveloped her, Sylvia felt a flush of embarrassed heat rising in her cheeks. That she and Frank had been victimized by a dead woman's voyeurism would have made her skin crawl if she hadn't been so terrified.

"The means to what end?" she asked, struggling to keep her voice level.

That was when the dead woman smiled. A smile devoid of mirth and filled with pure evil. "Ah, yes, the purpose and time is wasting, isn't it? But before we get this little party underway, you need to know that you're going to miss your first day on the new job, and whether you still have a job there or not after we're finished really depends on how things go with a certain bitch who, for the time being, will remain nameless. So, now we can begin." And with that, the dead woman darted around the foot of the bed in a jerky, stutter-step motion and rushed at Sylvia.

Sylvia screamed and tried to sidestep the rush. Her intention was to leap upon the bed and scramble from there to the bedroom door. But in her panic-driven haste, her feet tangled together. She stumbled and sprawled across the bed. Then the dead woman was upon her, and Sylvia found herself staring into the bloody face and the one remaining blue eye. There was more evil in the smile on the face than before.

Sylvia opened her mouth to scream, but all that came out was a grunt, then a harsh intake of breath as she suddenly felt like she had fallen into ice-cold water. It was like a paralyzing blow to her senses, the cold sinking into her to what seemed like the marrow of her bones. She couldn't breathe out, her lungs already burning as she thrashed on the bed. Her head began spinning and blackness was clouding her vision. Even as her thrashing grew more desperate, her lungs now on fire from lack of air, the room seemed to be slipping away from her.

Abruptly, the thrashing stopped, her body stiffening as her eyes turned up in their sockets until only the whites shone. Then her body relaxed, and she lay still, her eyes wide open. She lay there like that for almost half a minute...

***

...then her right foot twitches, then the left. She blinks her eyes several times as if to clear her vision. She draws in a deep breath, lets it out slowly, and draws in another. Then she begins the awkward task of climbing off the bed. She sways on her feet for a moment as if the floor has turned to jelly, but she quickly finds a measure of balance. She takes one careful step, then another.

Lucky for me I'm not wearing those heels. I'd end up on the floor for sure.

She reaches the vanity, grabs the edges of it to steady herself, then leans down and stares into the mirror. She smiles at the perfect and matching pair of blue eyes staring back at her.

***

Sylvia saw herself in the mirror, but she wasn't the one smiling, and she was well beyond the point of terrified by the blue eyes in the mirror.

Oh, God...

"A rather nice body you have, Sylvia. You take care of yourself, that's good."

This bitch has **stolen** *my body!*

"That I have, yes, and I'm the one in control now and don't forget it—and don't call me a bitch again. Care to see what happened to the last one who did that only a few days ago?"

Before Sylvia could muster a reply, an image bloomed in her mind's eye as if emerging from out of some strange and alien darkness. The image was of a naked woman, her body streaked with blood, who was hanging from the railing along the second-floor landing of what appeared to be an apartment. Part of the woman's face was covered by her raven black hair, but what Sylvia could see of it was a bluish-purple, her tongue protruding between her swollen lips. The blood was from her neck where the thin rope from which she was hanging had cut deeply into her flesh. Sylvia could see that blood was still dripping from the woman's right foot and pooling on the floor beneath her. The last thing Sylvia saw before the image abruptly winked out was a distraught man standing near the pool of blood, staring up in horror at the hanging woman, and yelling into a phone.

Jesus, that was on the news. The man—the woman's husband—found her like that on Thursday, the day before my interview.

"Her name was Shelly…something or other. It was fun with her and hubby for a few days, but she finally became more trouble than she was worth and I had to hang her. Both of us, really, but with me, of course, it didn't matter. I stayed inside her until the moment she drowned in her own blood. Just so you know, she wasn't the first since me and that truck crossed paths. Remember about two weeks ago the woman that burned to death?"

Sylvia did remember, another incident that made the news. Witnesses said the woman was screaming and on fire when she ran out of her house and collapsed in her front yard. Both of the unfortunate woman's children, ages six and eight, witnessed their mother's death.

"That bitch was nothing but trouble, and it was a pleasure watching her burn."

Jesus Christ, she's going to kill me!

"Not necessarily. It all depends on you and how well you behave and how a certain other bitch reacts to…let's say, my latest acquisition."

"What in the name of God are you doing?" Sylvia screamed. She heard herself, but no sound came from her mouth. It was as if she was screaming into a void.

"Stop that screaming, damn you, I can't even hear myself think. Just shut the hell up and be a good bitch because I have a call to make."

Sylvia, now pushed well beyond the point of terrified, felt herself step unsteadily around the bed, felt herself sit down on the edge of it, and saw her hand reach for her phone on the bedside stand. She was powerless to stop any of it. Her heart pounded and felt like it was going to leap from her chest as she watched Samantha Talbot scroll through the phone's contacts, finally finding the number she was looking for. Sylvia's thumb hit connect.

"Hey, it's me," Samantha said, and she was speaking in Sylvia's voice. That, in and of itself, was frightening on many levels, but the most horrible thing of all about it was the voice that answered the call. Sylvia found it impossible to get her mind wrapped around the sound of that voice or the significance of it. Nor could she grasp just what the hell was going on or why she had been made part of it.

"Thank you so much," Samantha was saying. "Frank left hours ago, and I wasn't sure what I was going to do. I'm ready to go, and I'll be watching for you."

***

For Sylvia, horror piled upon horror in the next twenty minutes or so as Samantha Talbot forced her to pace the bedroom floor in a relentless stalk. Sylvia had easily sensed the woman's anger, but nothing could have prepared her for what she encountered once her mind was joined with that of Samantha. Sylvia had always heard phrases like *malignant* or *black anger*, but only now was she truly gaining a proper understanding of what those words meant. The rage that drove Samantha was even more animalistic in its ferocity than it was when she was alive.

It only added to the madness in which she had spiraled that Sylvia found it harder by the minute to think her own thoughts or recall her memories. Even the memory of Frank holding her when she woke up screaming only a few hours ago was growing dim and hazy in her mind. It was Samantha's thoughts and memories that had taken over and were running rampant through her mind. One second Sylvia was forced to endure vivid flashes of torrid sexual adventures involving men and women, sometimes with multiple partners of both sexes. The next it was the horrible thoughts and images of what Samantha had done to those she believed had wronged her in the past and was quite prepared to do to who she had called—and who should be walking in the door any second now. Back and forth, one memory after another, one thought after another—there was no end to it!

The one constant, and it was a memory and a reoccurring one, was of the sound of an engine and headlights bearing down her; fear that had gripped her in the final moments before the killing impact and a blinding flash of brilliant white before everything went black and silent. This was the one memory that frightened Sylvia the most; every time it played through her mind, she could feel the rage in Samantha amp up and turn darker. The way Samantha kept stomping back and forth across the bedroom floor, growing more impatient by the second, Sylvia believed it only a matter of time before she started trashing the place or simply torching it.

Fire, Sylvia had discovered, was one of Samantha's favorite things.

The malignant entity inside her was almost seething in rage and breathing in shorts gasps through Sylvia's mouth when there a soft knocking on the front door. Sylvia and her captor stopped abruptly near the bedroom door.

"If you expect to live past the next hour, not one fucking word," Samantha hissed. She remained near the bedroom door, waiting and listening. Finally…

"Hello?" called a cheery voice. The voice sent Sylvia even deeper into the tailspin of fear and desperation that held her in its grip. "Sylvia? Are you here?"

"Come on in," Samantha called in Sylvia's voice. "I'm in the bedroom."

Even as Sylvia heard the front door closing, Samantha was moving them toward the bed, where she sat down and forced Sylvia to cross her legs and to assume a relaxed pose.

A few seconds later, a figure appeared in the bedroom doorway. She was a tall woman with dark auburn hair and dressed impeccably in a burgundy dress that hugged every curve. She was smiling brightly.

"Hello, Jeannie," Samantha said, again using Sylvia's voice.

"Hey, yourself." Jeanie came into the room, relaxed and still smiling. "What a morning to have car trouble, huh? Oh, I love that outfit, by the way."

"Thank you."

"So, are we ready to get this day started?"

"In a minute." Sylvia watched her right hand patting the bed beside where she and Samantha were sitting. "First, come here and sit down with me and let's talk a bit."

Sylvia desperately wanted to scream a warning to Jeannie or least try and let her know that something horrible was afoot, but she knew she couldn't wrench that kind of control away from

Samantha. The woman's essence was too strong. Even if she tried it, no telling what the crazy bitch would do. Nor was there any of knowing for sure how Jeannie would react. Based on Samantha's thoughts, Sylvia wasn't entirely sure how Jeannie fit into this whole thing.

Jeannie's smile lost some of its brightness as she glanced at her watch. "We really don't have time at the moment…but what the hell? Today and tomorrow, at least, I'm the boss, so I think we can spare a few minutes." She stepped to the bed, sat down and leaned toward the woman beside her. "So, what's on your mind, Sylvia?"

"For starters," Samantha began in Sylvia's voice, but then changed to her own voice and added, "it's not what's on her mind but mine."

Jeannie's smile evaporated, and Sylvia saw the color drain from her face as she leaned slowly away. Now Sylvia knew what part Jeannie was playing—a forced part similar to her own —but there was still nothing she could do to warn her friend. For a time there was only a heavy and charged silence.

"Samantha," Jeannie breathed barely above a whisper. "God in heaven—*again*? And, this time, it's *Sylvia*?"

"The one person who could get me close to you again."

Jeannie was shaking her head. "I thought after what you did to those other two women—"

"You thought what, Jeannie?" Samantha barked as she and Sylvia stood to face the other woman. Samantha was in such a rage at this point that Sylvia could actually feel the heat of it. Jeannie, surprisingly, remained calm, showing no fear.

There was only a look of deep sadness and resignation that shone like the sun on her face. "You thought you could just wish me away?" Samantha demanded, her voice rising. "That you had seen the last of me?"

"I hoped and prayed for that, yes. I kept telling myself that even *you* would begin to see how pointless this is."

"Pointless," Samantha echoed in a monotone. "That's all I ever was to you, a pointless fling. A chance to find out what it's like with another woman. Then you threw me away."

That they were involved for many weeks were among the memories Sylvia had seen, and she had seen them together several times. It made her feel cheap and sleazy as if she had been spying on them.

"You were beginning to scare me, Samantha. Your anger was one thing, but you were also throwing discretion right out the window. All those times you would slip into my office and lock the door—you were putting both our jobs in jeopardy."

"Spare me the fear for your lofty position crap, Jeannie. The way you bow down and kiss that old bastard's ass is disgusting. Him and his code of conduct—and the dress code he shoves down everyone's throat, especially the women. What cave did he crawl out of anyway?"

"I wouldn't expect you to understand it, Samantha. The worst of it, though, was that I wasn't the only, was I? You told me I was, but it wasn't true. You'd fall into bed with anyone who caught your eye. Even when I found out the truth, you tried to drag me into it with you. That was just too much for me, and I had no choice but to break it off with you."

"And that's why you're to blame for my death!" Samantha yelled.

"No, Samantha, I'm not to blame for that. I felt terrible because you died and I cried for days afterward. But you have no one but yourself to blame. You're the one who wouldn't take no for an answer and went ballistic when I told you it was over. You're the one who jumped out of the car and ran into that highway in a fit of rage…and I had to watch you die. Then you thought I'd fall right into bed with you and those two women whose bodies you possessed. My God, when are you going to stop this…this *insanity* and leave me alone?"

"You refused me—*twice!*" Samantha retorted as if condemning Jeannie for being an idiot. "You left *me* no other choice but to get rid of both of the others. One last chance, Jeannie." She hiked up Sylvia's skirt almost to the waist. "I found us such a great body this time, better than the other two combined. Not as perfect as mine was, of course, but it should serve our purpose nicely. So, what are you waiting for? Come here and show me— *prove* to me—how much you've missed me."

Sylvia wanted to scream and for many reasons, and she would have done it if she had believed she would be heard.

Jeannie had looked away and, Sylvia noticed, she had started to tremble. "That is just so wrong, Samantha. It was wrong both of the other times and even worse now! Sylvia is my friend. She has a husband and, from what I've heard about him, he's a really great guy. I won't do this to either of them. Get it through your head that it's over between us and has been since I broke it off with you." Jeannie paused, wiped at the tears that were now glistening on her face, and said, "Sylvia, if you can hear me…I'm so sorry. I never meant for something like this to happen. All I wanted was to help you, not turn your life into a living nightmare."

Sylvia heard and believed her. Jeannie was as much a victim as anyone else Samantha had involved in this sick and twisted death fantasy game she was playing.

"This has got to stop," Jeannie breathed, slowly getting to her feet, her purse clutched in her left hand. "You're doing this and killing people because of me…I can take no more of it."

"Jeannie! No! For God's sake, don't do it!" Again, only Sylvia could hear her voice. What alarmed her was that she could see Jeannie's right hand easing ever so slowly toward her purse, and Sylvia knew what was in the purse. Jeannie had shown it to her.

"You can stop it," Samantha snapped. "You can stop it all right now. All you have to do is accept the inevitable that we are going to be together— one way or the other. So, what's it going to be?"

"I guess it is inevitable," Jeannie breathed in a resigned, forlorn whisper. She raised her head and locked her eyes with Samantha's blue ones. Sylvia could see the light of determination glowing in Jeannie's eyes.

Jeannie, no, I beg you. There's no help for me, I understand that, so do what she wants and try and save yourself, if you can.

Sylvia saw the light change in Jeannie's eyes, then noticed her friend's right hand was inside her purse. "Sylvia, please forgive me," she murmured, her hand now coming out of her purse. "I do this for both of us, and I hope it works." Then, addressing Samantha, "And I hope *you* at least feel this," she said in a voice of grim resolve as she aimed the can of pepper spray attached to her keyring.

Things happened very quickly after that. The stream of spray hit Sylvia in the face. She screamed at the searing heat that splashed into her eyes and soaked into her skin. The only sound from Samantha was an animal-like growl as she and Sylvia's body rushed Jeannie. Sylvia felt the impact, followed by a quick and eerie sense of falling, then the three of them hit the floor. There was a grunt as breath whooshed out of someone; Sylvia wasn't sure it came from her or Jeannie. Her eyes and face were still on fire and, for the moment, that was all she could think about.

She felt Samantha struggling with Jeannie and heard what sounded like a resounding slap, and the palm of her right hand was suddenly stinging. Then she felt herself push up from the floor and stalk across the room. She heard glass smashing— *the mirror?* —then there was more pain in her right hand, this time much worse. She felt herself again crossing the floor, then a jarring impact as she dropped to her knees. Jeannie, she realized, was again beneath her. There was a bitter and enraged hiss from Samantha a split second before Jeannie screamed in agony. Something hot and sticky splashed on her hands and arms, but Sylvia still couldn't see a thing and could only guess that it was blood.

"Oh, God!" Jeannie wailed, and Sylvia felt more of the hot, sticky splashes.

Sylvia screamed like a lost soul, consumed by fear and pain, her eyes feeling as if they were melting in their sockets.

And it was then that Sylvia began to lose touch with herself, her mind swimming in a growing pool of blackness. She continued to hear the sounds of a fierce struggle and the screams of pain, but it was beginning to seem as if it was no longer her concern. That something, she had no idea what, was pulling her away from the bedroom and the evil insanity going on there. The blackness soon washed over her and she wasn't aware of anything until…

***

…it finally began to recede like a slow-moving tide going out. Her eyes were no longer burning, and it took only moments for her to take in the scene in the bedroom and what was now happening all around her and to glimpse herself in what remained of the smashed mirror on her vanity. All of which sent her scurrying and sobbing out of the house. There was nothing else she could do. She found a bit of refuge from the chaos that had engulfed what had been the epicenter of her world beneath a willow tree in the front yard.

None of those frantically working to save the burning house had seen her escaping it or seemed to notice her huddled form sitting against the trunk of the tree. No one saw her gashed and bloody hands or the blood that covered her face and chest from the gaping wound to her forehead. But it was doubtful that any of them could have seen her even if they had been looking for her, and she knew none of them were. They would only see her…what remained of her… once the fire was out and they found her burned corpse in the charred ruins. They would also find Jeannie, but not as Sylvia had seen her before leaving the burning house. Samantha, the vicious bitch using *her* hands and pieces of the broken mirror, had slashed and hacked Jeannie to pieces. Little remained of Jeannie's once lovely face, and Sylvia had seen the two long and thin slivers of mirror sticking out of Jeannie's eyes.

How Sylvia had gotten the wound to her forehead, the wound that had split open her skull and had obviously killed her, she wasn't sure. She couldn't remember that part of it. The wound looked as if her head had been slammed viciously, repeatedly against something hard and sharp. Perhaps a front corner of her vanity; that was where she had seen her body lying in a huge pool of blood on the floor. Had Samantha killed her or made her, Sylvia, kill herself? Not that it mattered; it amounted to the same thing either way. Perhaps death itself was the reason for the darkness that claimed her. Then, again, perhaps it was because of something else altogether.

Sylvia could only hope that Samantha would leave Frank alone.

There was no sign of either Samantha or Jeannie. Now that Samantha had what she wanted, Sylvia figured she had vanished and taken Jeannie with her. Jeannie had asked for her forgiveness, and Sylvia had already given it. She could blame Jeannie for nothing more than being human. Sylvia's only real concern right now was Frank.

To say he would take all of this hard didn't even begin to come close. Would he be able to move on and start over again? He had already been through a nasty divorce from an unfaithful wife—and now something like *this*? Sylvia decided to wait there at the house for him to return. Just to make sure he was okay and that nothing had so far happened to him. Once she saw that for herself, then she would leave him alone. She didn't want him to catch a glimpse of her, not as she appeared now, or to even sense her presence. She didn't want him to ever feel as if he was being haunted. As she had obviously been since finding Jeannie that day at Starbucks.

On the other hand, she didn't want Samantha, that vicious bitch, to reappear and steal the body of another woman and pursue her lecherous interest in Frank. So, Sylvia decided to stay close, at least for a time, and make sure he wasn't further victimized by a ghostly intruder. If Samantha did return, she had a nasty surprise coming.

For she would find a *very* angry woman waiting for her, and it would be an epic clash.

Tethers
Sarah Cannavo

Sophie's tears started as she and Jason hauled their luggage from Dublin Airport to the rental car awaiting them in the lot, but he didn't notice until he'd swung his suitcase into the Auris's trunk. "Gimme a sec and I'll unlock the d—Soph?" Glimpsing the glittering tracks on her cheeks he let the bag he'd hefted drop, brow furrowing beneath his shaggy brown hair and blue eyes bright in alarm. "Hey, what's the matter, babe? This some sorta jet-lag thing?"

Sophie shook her head, flashing an embarrassed smile as she sniffled and swiped at her eyes. "It's stupid," she said with a watery laugh, pushing back the stray strands of long blonde hair the damp breeze was determined to plaster to her face. "I mean, we're not even in Wicklow yet, and Aileen never stepped foot in the Dublin airport, but just being *here—*" she gestured around them at Ireland itself— "drives it all home. It's finally hitting me that it's all real, that we're doing this." She chuckled again. "Like I said, stupid, right?"

Jason's expression softened. "Aw, Sophie, no, that's not stupid at all." He came around to her and hugged her tightly, rubbing her back and murmuring, "It's all right. It's all right," as she buried her face in the crook of his neck; a few last tears escaped her as she breathed in the comfortingly familiar scent of his leather jacket, the musk of his skin, more grateful than ever he'd agreed to come along.

She'd lost her parents when she was sixteen, in a fire that'd consumed the Kearns house while she was away at camp. She'd been spared foster care by her aunt Lydia, her mother's sister, but didn't particularly enjoy feeling like a familial obligation, as Lydia had constantly reminded her she was, and so Sophie'd struck out on her own the day after graduating high school and had struggled to settle ever since. At first it'd been fun, going where and doing what she wanted, restless, funding herself through her work as a photographer—ten years of that before it started sinking in that the itch she felt to move, to pick up and leave and press on, was actually an emptiness, a need to seek born in some hollow part of her she didn't need a therapist to explain. As the urge to settle grew in her she'd found herself in Yucca Valley, California, a town near Joshua Tree, four years ago, which was where and when she'd met Jason Capaldi, both of them ducking out of a bar fight that'd swelled to involve the whole place. Already in his truck he'd seen her running, flung the passenger door open, and hollered for her to get in; she had, he'd gunned the engine, and they'd sped off into the night just ahead of the sirens and the red-and-blue lights descending like a swarm of pissed-off hornets on the Coyote & Cactus.

Neither of them had ever looked back. They still lived in Yucca Valley, in an apartment above the tattoo shop Jason's brother Jackson owned; Sophie kept up with her own photography but also worked at a photo studio in town—utterly amazed every time she clocked in that it was still open in this day and age—and Jason picked up grunt work at various clubs and music venues in the area, rigging lights and sound systems, hauling cables and equipment, making him what he called "a roadie without the road." It was a good life; she loved her home, loved Jason, and the lost-little-girl feeling that had dogged her since her parents died had faded significantly.

Yet a ghost of it still clung on, apparently, and last year, when she'd seen a commercial for one of those ancestry sites for the millionth time she'd caved and ordered a kit. Sophie knew the Kearns family had its roots in Ireland, but she'd learned those roots were in Leinster—the village of Wicklow, specifically—and that her great-great-grandmother Aileen, before she'd emigrated at twenty-three to America, in 1900, had helped run the family inn—an inn that still stood and still took in guests, albeit under different management. Greene's Inn—where her family had gotten its start, a tangible link to her past.

Sophie had hemmed and hawed about going at first; it'd been Jason, God bless him, sitting amid the towers of maps and tattered books on Irish history Sophie had stockpiled like a lunatic bear lining its den for winter, who'd finally said, "Soph, you know you're going. So go."

"Of course," had been his response when she'd managed a fear-mangled invitation to accompany her, which after everything he'd put up with over the past year cemented his status in her mind as a saint in a black T-shirt and ragged jeans.

So here they were for four days in Wicklow, rooming at Greene's Inn and getting acquainted with the land Aileen had called home before America. Until now, and even during the ten-hour flight from California, the whole thing had had a haze of unreality on it. But stepping out of the terminal, looking around and realizing where they were, it had all come down on Sophie like a hammer blow, Are we really doing this? abruptly metamorphosing into Holy shit, we're doing this! She gave one last sniffle and pulled back, smile steadier as she wiped her cheeks and smoothed her shirt out. "Thanks, Jason."

"You sure you're okay?" he asked, eyeing her carefully.

"I'm good, I swear." She lifted the bag he'd dropped and tucked it into the trunk, nestling it with her camera carefully beside it. "Can't promise it won't happen again, though."

"I'd be more freaked out if it didn't. This is your family, not just another photography gig." Jason stole a quick kiss, then passed her the Auris's key. "I'll get the rest of this crap. How 'bout you check the map again so we don't wind up ass-deep in a bog on our way to Great-Great-Grandma's place?"

Sophie grinned. "Can do." In the passenger seat, half-hearing the droning thunder of airplane engines and Jason's dark invectives against their luggage's lineage as he shoved and rearranged, she retraced the path she'd marked on the map of Wicklow. The directions had come courtesy of Dacey O'Neill, who ran Greene's Inn now with her husband Quintin, the O'Neills having bought it from Aileen before she left with her fiancé, Troy Kearns.

"And nobody's ever changed the name? In all this time?" Sophie had asked with a puzzled grin as she spoke with Dacey three weeks ago, making arrangements for the stay.

Even over the phone the young woman's laugh was clear and cheerful as a brook bubbling in a meadow. "Oh, they've tried. But little places like this don't forget easily; there hasn't been an O'Connell on their land in twenty years, but everyone still calls it the O'Connell farm. So no matter what Quintin's family renamed the inn, it was still called 'Greene's place.' Quintin's grandfather saw it was a losing battle and changed the name back, and it's stayed that way ever since."

Jason slid into the driver's seat, startling Sophie from her reverie. "Ready to go?"

She smiled. "Let's do this."

The infinite greenness of the fields and hills rolling around Wicklow like the swells of a verdant sea stunned Sophie, made it difficult for her to believe half a day ago she'd been watching the California desert roll by, cracked dusty earth baked brittle as bone. Here and there she glimpsed farms, cottages, scattered herds of sheep and cattle like flotsam bobbing on the emerald ocean; with the windows rolled down and a blue sky arcing overhead Sophie half-expected to hear flute music echoing from the hills, glimpse diminutive figures in diaphanous dresses dancing around the craggy gray boulders.

The inn was situated on the road to Wicklow, just outside the village proper, a haven for travellers needing a night's rest before they continued on their journeys. It was a sturdy building of gray stone, the original stables and water pump still in place out back, though Sophie doubted they saw much use these days; cheerful white shutters adorned the windows and banks of bright flowers lined the walkway to the front door. The wooden sign swinging gently in the breeze proclaimed GREENE'S INN in an old-fashioned but uncomplicated script, letters painted an appropriate color. It had two storeys and eight rooms to rent—snug, Sophie's mother's gardening magazines would've called it, cozy.

Since booking the trip, Sophie hadn't known what she'd feel when she actually arrived; getting out of the car with Jason she found the most she could do for a moment was stand there and stare, eyes tracing the texture of the stone, the thick glass of the windows, the bobbing heads of the flowers beckoning her on.

Jason came around and stood beside her, taking her hand and watching her a moment. "It ain't gonna vanish, you know," he said with a small smile, coaxing one back from her.

"I know."

"But hey, you wanna stay out here and look a little while longer, I'm game. By now I figured I'd've already stepped in sheep shit, so since I haven't I'm ahead of the curve."

A window on the upper floor was open, and Sophie's laugh drifted up and danced through it into a room uninhabited, yet not empty.

He was aware of himself as he was everything around him: indistinctly, like a gray haze of the kind that settles over someone between sleep and waking and not inclined to choose one or the other yet. Forms moved beyond his gray existence, and muffled voices rubbed against the cotton batting coating his senses, but none struck with enough force to register for any real remembrance.

Not that he was completely ignorant of his state or surroundings; every so often as he drifted along the glint of sun on a brass bedpost, the clatter and chatter from the dining room below, a closing door would jolt him into a moment of clarity. New pictures on the walls, new voices in the halls, people passing by him with little more than a slight shiver or brief glance around the room. But where was she, *where had she gone? he'd have time to wonder, and then he'd slip back under again, aware only of the fog and a link that throbbed faintly through it, tethering him to the inn. So the cycle had gone, irregularly—for how long? How many days had he been drifting like this? Asleep yet not asleep, awake yet not awake.*

Then he heard the voices.

They came from outside, and he wafted to the window, prickled with a dull curiosity. For a moment he focused, and a moment was all he needed.

Because it was her.

Aileen.

Shock flooded him, followed by solidity—of thought, of memory, of place. At the sight of her, color leeched back into the world; everything gained edges, definition, substance. She was wearing trousers of some kind, and her long blonde hair was hanging unbound instead of in the tight plait she'd always preferred—and mother of God, what was that gleaming hulk she was standing beside?—but her face, her features, that tall, slim body...It was Aileen, older (how much time?) *but unmistakable.*

And there was another man beside her.

Rage replaced shock, a hot bolt of it that shot through him and burned higher and deeper as he watched Aileen and the man talk, laugh—watched Aileen lean in for a kiss before they walked up to the front door of the inn.

No.

Not again.

"Welcome to Greene's Inn," the young woman behind the front desk said as the silver bell above the front door jingled, looking up from the ledger she was marking. "How can I h—" Her warm, red-glossed smile vanished, and though her complexion had been pale to start with, the blood drained further from it as she froze, staring at the couple.

No, Sophie realized, feeling the weight of the girl's blue-gray gaze, *not us. Me.*

Then she shook herself out, flushing and giving a sheepish laugh that nevertheless carried the same tones Sophie had heard over the phone. "Oh, lord, I'm sorry, Miss." Dacey O'Neill's local brogue accented but didn't obscure her words. "But you…you look just like her."

Sophie smiled back as Jason relaxed beside her. "It's all right."

"Not that I ever knew her personally, of course," Dacey went on; her brown hair was half-drawn back from her face, and her loose curls bounced as she shook her head again, hands busying themselves smoothing her sweater—a gray knit, pale as sea mist. "No, she was a *bit* before my time. But—well, you can see why I was so startled."

She stepped aside, heels clicking on the wooden floor, and gestured to an oval-shaped portrait, maybe nine inches tall, hanging on the wall behind the front desk. Coming closer Sophie saw it showed a woman several years younger than herself, seated and wearing a high-necked dark dress with a lace collar, pale braid draped over one shoulder like a pet snake; the hairstyle was severe, the pose—straight-backed, hands in lap—demure, but the faint smile on Aileen Greene's face held a hint of mischief, her eyes a brightness the painter had been skilled enough to capture. And her face: Sophie's, plain and simple.

"Whoa," Sophie breathed. There'd been no photos in the records her search had uncovered; for all she'd known Aileen had been an Irishwoman of the red-hair-and-freckles variety, and the coloring had just been bred out of the Kearns family over the years. But this…*Talk about a link to my past, huh?*

"Jesus, babe," Jason said, gaze swinging from the portrait to her and back. "You sure this isn't one of those you're-inadvertently-your-own-ancestor deals?"

"To the best of my knowledge, no, I didn't *Futurama* myself." Sophie studied it again. "It *is* freaky, though."

"I've seen Aileen up there every day for the last seven years," Dacey said, tossing the portrait a fond smile. "So when you came walking in it was like seeing a ghost strolling through the front door."

"You got any of those here?" Jason grinned. "I always thought it'd be cool to see a ghost."

"If we do, they've kept to themselves," Dacey said. "Quintin and I've never had any complaints, and I don't think anyone in his family did, either." She rested her hands flat on the desk. "But here I am talking your ears off when you've just flown in from the States, luggage piled around your feet and all—I'm sure you're ready to just get into your room and rest already. Here you are, Ms. Kearns, just sign in and I'll see to it you get settled in." Dacey slid the record book across the desk, open and ready.

"Sophie's fine," she assured the woman as she and Jason signed in.

"Then so's Dacey," the innkeeper returned. Sophie liked her already, the warmth and friendliness that seemed more than mere affection. "Capaldi," Dacey said, eyeing Jason's slanted scrawl. "I wouldn't've pegged that—you look like you've got some of the auld sod in you."

"I'm a bit of a mutt, ma'am." Jason scratched at the soft brown hair lining his jaw. "Folks in my family came from all over. But yeah, a few Irishmen snuck their way in there."

Sophie rolled her eyes. "If he gets started with his Murphy Macmanus impression, we really will be here all day."

Jason clutched his chest. "Ya really know how ta wound a man, lass."

Sophie lightly shoved a bag at him. "Stuff it."

"You'll be in room six." Dacey retrieved a pair of room keys on carved wooden tags and passed them to the couple, lips quirking at their banter. "I'll show you to it, if you're ready…?"

Sophie nodded and Dacey slipped out from behind the desk, short dark gray skirt swishing around her long legs. "Dinner's served at six-thirty in the dining room, which is just through there—" she pointed toward a set of double doors across the room, each set with a slim window bright with designs of colored glass and made of the same dark, glossy wood as the panelling and the staircase Dacey led them toward— "but I'm sure we'll be able to scrounge something up for you." She winked.

The upstairs hall was papered the same powder-blue as the lobby, landscape paintings and historical photos hung at even intervals along it; there were four doors to a side, brass numbers and knobs gleaming, and a small end table topped with a bouquet of wildflowers set in vases of milk-white glass at the end. Doors one and three were shut; as Dacey led them to six she said, "We only have a few other guests right now. We keep a small staff, but if you need anything don't be afraid to holler."

"Thanks, Dacey," Sophie said, and as Jason echoed her she felt a draft drift over the back of her neck, icy and quick; she glanced down to the end of the hall and started, wondering how she hadn't noticed before they weren't alone. Just outside room four's open door, a tall, muscled hulk of a man was standing, watching them. He was dressed in dark pants, a white sweater, and heavy boots, a battered scally cap atop his thick black hair; he had a short, wiry black beard, and the eyes beneath his rough brows were piercing, even from a distance. Sophie felt her skin crawl when she realized he, too, was staring at her, far more intensely than Dacey had, his expression stopping just short of a scowl.

What the hell's his problem?

"Soph."

She looked back to Jason. "Huh?"

He gestured into their room "Coming?"

"Oh, yeah. Sorry about that." Looking around she saw Dacey had withdrawn, leaving them to their own devices; the man at the end of the hall was also gone—back into room four, Sophie guessed. One of their fellow guests, maybe, but he'd struck her more as a worker: a handyman, landscaper, one of Greene's Inn's small staff. Shaking off the unsettled feeling his stare had left her with, but unable to wipe the sight completely from her mind, she followed Jason inside.

It was papered in a green-and-cream pattern whose color matched the linens on the inviting double bed. The furnishings were well-kept antiques and the fixtures were reassuringly modern: lamps and outlets, a small attached bathroom with a toilet and claw-footed tub, a bar of lilac-scented soap snug in a dish on the sink. As she and Jason took in their surroundings and unpacked just what they'd need for the night, leaving the rest for after they'd had some sleep that wasn't in coach on a ten-hour flight, Sophie considered mentioning the man's odd behavior to Jason but ultimately didn't—after all, there hadn't been any real behavior to speak of, had there? Just a stare, but Christ, she was a big girl; she could handle a stare. Jason would probably want to find the guy and kick his ass, anyway, and she wasn't keen on starting her journey of self-discovery with a bar fight—although such beginnings had worked out well in the past, she had to admit, glancing with a smile towards the man now sprawled on the bed above the covers.

No, she'd let it go, and if the bearded man kept it up, or did something beyond look in her direction, then she'd mention it. Until then, she was going to enjoy herself.

She was straightening up, toiletries case in hand, when a splash of color caught her eye and she went to the window to check it out. "Hey, Jason, look at this," she said, and he heaved himself out of bed, coming to stand behind her, muscled arms wrapping around her waist.

The sun was setting, staining the sky and low clouds above the distant hills with striated bands of pink, orange, and blue brilliance, like layers within an agate. The colors bled across the horizon and bloomed, mingled, streaked here and there with scarlet like small wounds. Shadows stretched longer across the fields, eager to deepen their hold once dusk surrendered to night, but for now the light lingered, putting on an impressive final display.

"Nice," Jason said. "Want your camera?"

She should've been itching for it; this was the kind of shot she'd wait hours for, ready for the single perfect moment to come along to be captured. But Sophie caught Jason's hand as he started pulling away, drawing him back and leaving her hands over his as she shook her head, smiling.

"I'm all right. I just want to enjoy this."

Once darkness completely swallowed the sky, the couple sat at the foot of their bed, Jason's rough fingers still linked through Sophie's. "So," he said, "how you feelin' so far, now that we're actually here?"

She rested her head on his shoulder and considered a minute. "Is it okay if I don't know yet?"

He kissed the top of her head. "Yeah, I think so."

She smiled. "Thanks." After another minute, she said, "You know, if you ever wanted to dig around your family history, I'd help you out."

He snorted. "Thanks for the offer, babe, but I've got Mom, Jack, and you; that's all I need. I don't want to know which of my ancestors was hanged as a horse thief."

Sophie chuckled and squeezed his hand. "Well, I at least have to be grateful to them for making you possible."

"Whiskey and a broken condom did that, Soph."

She looked at him. "Still."

Jason leaned in and kissed her again, on the lips this time. When he pulled back he had that gleam in his eye Sophie knew and loved, though even as she lay back on the bed, Jason following, positioning himself over her, her lips curled in a teasing smile. "You mean you're not too tired? We had a pretty big day today."

Jason curled his fingers through hers and pinned her hands against the pillows. "I slept on the plane."

Sophie laughed as he leaned down and began kissing her neck. "Sleep on a plane doesn't cou—"

His lips roamed back to hers, and she found she wasn't too tired, either.

"Shit." Sophie dug through her camera bag one more time to make sure—nope, no backup battery pack. *"Shit."*

Jason turned, boots grinding on the gravel of the drive. "What's wrong?"

"My extra battery pack isn't here. I know I brought it, though." She huffed, blowing her hair out of her face as she thought it over. If it wasn't with her Nikon, where'd she seen it? *Suitcase, backpack—backpack!* "It's up in the room. I'll grab it and we'll go, okay?"

Jason nodded, the stiff breeze batting at the map he waved her on with. "I'll be here."

She flashed him a grateful smile and dashed back into the inn, tossing a quick wave to Quintin O'Neill behind the front desk. She and Jason had met him coming down the stairs for breakfast that morning, ravenous after missing dinner; he was a slender, well-dressed man several years Dacey's elder with shoulder-length light brown hair and a slight limp, the result of a recent fall while walking the boreen after a rainstorm. He seemed more reserved than his wife, but not aloof, and he returned Sophie's wave, lips quirking in amusement. "Miss us already, Ms. Kearns?"

"Batteries," she explained, and he nodded sagely and returned to his book, whose Gaelic cover Sophie couldn't read. She and Jason were adventuring today, and Dacey and Quintin had been kind enough to point out spots in Wicklow they should hit during their visit, such as the Wicklow Gaol, the Black Castle ruins, and the Murrough; Dacey had even packed them a lunch in case they didn't wander back in time to have it at the inn. *Nicer in one day than Aunt Lydia was in two years,* Sophie mused as she headed up the stairs.

The man was back.

He was standing outside the closed door of room three, which was odd because that room was occupied by a pair of elderly sisters on holiday from Dublin; Sophie and Jason had met them in the dining room this morning, too. Some problem with the room, Sophie figured, and did her best to ignore the burly bearded man and the recurring chill crawling down her spine. But when she unlocked her door, glanced back, and found he was looking at her with the same intensity as yesterday—maybe even more; he was almost glowering now—anger stiffened her stance, hand tightening on the doorknob.

"Um, can I help you with something?" she asked in as level a voice as she could manage. "I can't help but notice you keep looking at me. Is there something I did—something I can do?"

The man stood there a moment longer, expression never flickering, then turned and walked down the hall and stairs, the wood creaking under his forceful steps.

"Okay, then," Sophie muttered, and went to grab her battery pack.

"That's not a just-connected-emotionally-with-my-roots look," Jason observed as she rejoined him. "Couldn't find your backup?"

She held it up, then zipped it into her camera bag. "That guy was staring at me again, and it's starting to creep me out."

"Wait, what guy? What again?"

Sophie explained and then reached out, snagging Jason's arm as he started striding for the inn, eyes flickering, nostrils flared. "Jay, hey, wait. Don't—where are you going?"

"I want to meet this fucker."

"Jason, calm down. Just leave him alone."

Jason eyed her in stark disbelief. "*What?* Soph, if this sonuvabitch is creeping on you I'm not gonna just stand here and *let* him—"

She tugged his arm gently. "And I admire your intentions, and if he gets worse I'll gladly let you loose on him, but he didn't try anything; he didn't even say anything. I'm pissed and a little creeped out, but I'm not *hurt*. Besides, when I asked him what he wanted he just left. Maybe he doesn't realize how he comes across."

"So I shouldn't go kick the crap outta this guy because he might have Resting Creeper Face?"

Sophie kissed him. "No, you shouldn't do it because I'm telling you I'm all right, and because there are some historic castle ruins with our names on them." She paused. "Well, technically they have the Vikings' names on them, but you know what I mean."

Jason sighed, the fire in him reluctantly subsiding. "Fine. But can you at least promise me if he does it again you'll mention it to Dacey or Quintin?"

"Deal."

He returned her kiss. "All right, then. Let's go break our necks on these ruins."

That bitch.

That striapach.

Not only running around with another man right in front of him, but now with the gall to act like she didn't even know him—him, *Seamus McFaul! Just a stranger in the hall to her, and meanwhile she and that tramp-looking fellow were fucking like beasts in the field. He'd heard them last night from their bathroom, where he'd tucked himself away to fume (since Aileen had awakened him there'd been no relapses into the gray haze, but at times he still hid away, either in the inn or in his quarters out back), grunts and groans and low-throated moans, and even as his rage rose he'd drifted out to watch.*

They hadn't seen him, of course; leaping into that rumpled bed with them would've probably been the only way he could've interrupted their rutting. From his shadowed corner he'd watched his sweetheart, Aileen, offer herself up to her new man like a meal on a silver tray, slim body arching like a dancer's, long lovely legs wrapped around his waist, sweat-sheened breasts bouncing with the cunús's *every thrust; he watched her climb atop him and ride with his hands roaming over every inch of her and her head thrown back, wearing the expression of a lass drawn into one of the Kind*

Folk's circles, unable to stop dancing and not wanting to.

Seamus had watched it all, just as he had Aileen and that God damn Kearns boy, and he felt the same brew of anger and arousal now as then, torn between wishing it was his hands clutching Aileen's taut ass, his lips latched onto her bright pink nipple, his cock seated between her welcoming legs—and the urge to grab the welcoming interloper by the throat, haul him from bed, and make it so. Remind Aileen who she belonged to, and make sure her new man had that lesson driven into his skull right quick. He'd done neither, of course, though it'd taken the strength of Cú Chulainn to resist the pull of both. He had to get to Aileen first, on her own, make her understand that it was him she was meant to be with, not any of these other fools, and then she'd send this one away. After all, what could either offer her that he couldn't? He'd even saved up and bought that ring for her, finer than any innkeeper's daughter could ever expect. Yet here she was giving herself to another man—why? Because he said he loved her, just as Troy Kearns had? They said it, but he proved it, time and again.

Their voices were outside again now, and he moved to the window, saw them arguing, saw Aileen pulling the man's arm, holding him back. Seamus's heart leapt—maybe she was doing it, breaking things off with him. But then their words reached him and he realized they were arguing about him, just not as he wanted them to, and the flame sprung back to life in him, licking and searing every inch of his soul.

The man wanted to challenge him? The fucking interloper, the bastard seating himself so comfortably between Seamus and Aileen, thought he could lay claim to her and Seamus would just give up, roll over with nary a whisper of resistance?

No.

Not last time, and not now, either.

Seamus slammed the window shut so hard cracks appeared along the bottom edge. From his viewpoint they crawled across the interloper's face, and Seamus smiled. It'd do for a start.

Jason kept his end of the deal and didn't go looking for the handyman. But when he was walking around the inn's grounds later that afternoon and the guy showed up—well, what was he supposed to do? Just pretend he didn't see him?

Jason and Sophie had hit some of the sites on their list and returned to the inn around three, planning to space out their wanderings over the last couple days of their visit. She was upstairs in their room now, going through the photos she'd taken on today's trip; she always preferred solitude when she looked over her work, which Jason understood, and so he'd offered to head out for a bit and give her some space. As he ambled around he hoped she was finding whatever she'd come here to find. It seemed she was starting to, anyway; at the harbor today she'd stared out over the ocean, salt breeze skimming her skin, and said, "This is what she saw. Aileen, this—this is where she sailed from. She was younger than me when she did it. And she and Troy Kearns just… left."

"She was brave," Jason had replied. "Brave as hell. Just like you."

Sophie had looked at him with an expression so raw and vulnerable he'd felt helpless before it. "She'd be real proud of you," he'd said anyway.

"Thanks," she'd murmured, and then hesitantly held her camera out to him. "Jay? Could you…Could you take a picture of me here? Please?"

"Yeah, of course," he'd said, and he'd seen her looking at that picture three times on the way home; if she hadn't looked at it at least another three times by now, he'd let Jack tramp-stamp him with 1D 4 LIFE.

A noise nearby jolted Jason from his thoughts, and looking across the inn's yard he saw a man re-stacking a toppled pile of kindling beside a small stone outbuilding. His back was to Jason, but he matched Sophie's description down to his clothes and the cap on his head, and heat surged through Jason; Sophie said she was okay, but it was obvious this asshole's attentions were bothering her, and God damn it, Sophie hadn't come to Wicklow to be glared at by some creeper giant of a handyman.

"Hey!" Jason called, and when the man turned and his gaze fell on Jason, his face darkened, as if he already knew what this was about. *Good.* It would save Jason some time. "Yeah, hi." He stalked closer to the man; it'd rained earlier, and the mud under the slick grass squelched beneath his boots. Drawing up a few feet short of the man he asked, "What's your name?"

It seemed to take great effort for the man to unclench his jaw and speak, as if he was lowering a drawbridge whose gears had long since rusted. "Seamus McFaul," he said, voice deep and rough.

"Hey, Seamus, I'm Jason, and I was wondering why you keep staring at my girlfriend?" He cocked his head, muscles tensed, waiting for whatever the man might do or say.

Seamus stiffened, darkness yawning deep in his eyes. "She ain't yours," he growled, accent clinging to his words like vines on a wall and just as thick. "Whatever ya think you've got with her, ya don't. You're just in my fookin' way."

Jason's eyebrows climbed his forehead. "I'm sorry, *what?*" He shifted his weight on his feet, like an animal preparing to strike, though for the moment disbelief had a slim lead on anger. "We just got here yesterday. Isn't that a little too soon for undying love?"

Seamus stepped toward Jason, heavy hands curling at his sides. "I've been waitin' a helluva lot longer than a day for her, Jason. Only thing is, I'm done waitin'. She's finally goin' ta see I'm the one she belongs with, and then she'll stop hoorin' around with the likes of ya." His grin was a broad, unpleasant thing. "I just gotta show her, is all."

"You fucking—" Jason swung, but somehow the big man moved quick enough to not only evade the blow but return one of his own, fist clipping Jason's jaw hard enough to make scarlet stars dance in his vision. Jason reeled back but kept to his feet and launched himself at Seamus, momentum carrying them both to the ground; mud and grass clung to skin and clothes as they scuffled, grunting as they swung and kicked. Jason had been in more than his fair share of fights over the years, often with men Seamus's size or a group of them, and could hold his own; even so, the handyman's blows were like hammers striking an anvil, and his eyes burned hellishly—it was the look of a man willing to battle tooth and claw for what was his, or what he thought was his, and despite his best efforts Jason felt the upper hand rapidly slipping through his fingers.

Holy shit, he had the chance to think. *This bastard might actually k—*

Then a car door slammed at the front of the inn and Seamus dropped the scarred fist he was cocking and scrambled off, shooting a glance toward Greene's before heading for the old stables. "Yeah, that's right, you better run," Jason said, which even he knew would've sounded more intimidating if it wasn't coughed out as he lay in the mud, dirty and sore and breathless. *Christ, it's your twenty-first birthday all over again,* he thought, then rolled over, groaning as he did, pushed himself up, and went to face Sophie.

"Oh my God, *Jason!"* She shoved her laptop and camera aside and scrambled off the bed, hands hovering near him as though unsure where to touch him without causing more pain. "What the hell happened?" The thought hit, brimming with certainty. "Oh, God. Don't tell me it was…"

"Mr. Fix-It? Yeah, it was." Jason shut the door and limped further into the room. "To be fair, I might've provoked him a bit, but you shoulda heard what this guy was saying. He's cracked, Soph, I'm telling you."

Stomach heavy with storm clouds, Sophie helped the wincing Jason work his dirty leather jacket and shirt off. "Why, what happened?"

"Apparently you're meant to be with him, not me. He was pretty insistent on that. Oh, and he's been waiting for you for a long time, and I'm just what's keeping him from getting to you." Jason lowered his arms, hissing as the movement pulled at the dried blood sealing a small cut on his arm closed.

Sophie's brow furrowed as she crumpled his stained clothes up. "How the hell can he have been waiting for me when we just got here?"

"Trust me, I asked." Jason's boots clunked to the ground as he worked them off his feet. "Oddly enough, he wasn't too clear on the details. And then he said you were whoring around with me, so of course I had to punch the fucker, and there wasn't a lot of room for polite conversation after that."

"Christ." Sophie rocked back on her heels, arms wrapped tight around herself. Her thoughts were swimming, bubbling as her emotions boiled, and it was difficult to fix on one, Seamus McFaul's face filling her mind. *How fucking* dare *he*....She scrubbed hard at her face, trying to clear her head, then said, "All right. Let's…Let's get you cleaned up and taken care of, and then we'll find Dacey and Quintin and tell them what happened, okay?"

Jason kissed her briefly. "Don't worry, I can handle my own wounds. I'll be out in a few minutes. Just make sure you lock that door."

Sophie nodded, and as he disappeared into the bathroom she locked the bedroom door and headed for their bed, lying down with her back to the bathroom. She felt sick, shaky, and she stared at her camera blankly, everything she'd felt before Jason came upstairs utterly wiped away. How could this be happening? What were the odds that of all the places she could've gone, it was here that a guy like Seamus would be, waiting— apparently—for a girl like her to come along and draw all his attention? It explained his scowl today, at least, if he thought she was running around with Jason when she ought to be with him, but how the hell had he come to that conclusion so quickly; had he decided it the second they'd arrived at the inn?

Fuck. She closed her eyes, the pleasant tiredness she'd felt after a day of exploring replaced with a weariness that clung to her bones and dragged her deep into a mental murk awash with questions and possibilities it disturbed her to contemplate. *Fuck, fuck, fuck...*

The floor beside the bed creaked and the mattress depressed behind her as a man's body filled the space behind Sophie; Jason wrapped an arm around her waist, fingertips skimming her belly, and despite the gloom spinning its web around her Sophie smiled, eyes still closed. "Seriously?" she half-laughed, though it was hardly the first time one of them, still stirred up after a fight, had come to the other one looking to burn the lingering adrenaline off. Jason cupped her breast, fingers insistently massaging her nipple, and Sophie felt herself stirring, her body welcoming his touch. "All right," she laughed, pressing her body back against his. "We'll sneak in a round, then head down and talk to Dacey and Quintin."

Jason brushed her hair back baring her throat to him and Sophie let out a soft "Mm" at the light stroke of his fingers over her pulse point. Then he leaned in and kissed the curve of her neck, and she stiffened because accompanying the kiss was the bristle of a beard much thicker and rougher than Jason's facial hair. Her eyes flew open and she jolted upright, all comfort she'd been taking from the man's touch gone, and when she twisted and saw Seamus McFaul in bed with her she scrambled back and screamed.

"Get out, get the fuck out, leave me *alone—!"*

The bathroom door banged open and Jason skidded out. "Soph? What's wrong?"

"Seamus, he—" But in the moment she'd looked away and back, the handyman had vanished, though the feeling of violation that'd flared in her the second she saw his face remained. She wheeled around, frantically scanning the rest of the room, heart pounding. There wasn't anywhere he could've hidden so fast—and how had he gotten in in the first place?—yet he was nowhere to be found.

"Seamus?" Jason came around the bed to her, gaze sweeping the room as he went. "What, was he at the door?"

She shook her head, throat tight, voice thick. "He was in here—he was in *bed* with me."

Anger lit Jason's face but couldn't cover the confusion her words also woke; she saw her own questions burning in his eyes. "Babe, the door's still locked."

"I know. I know." But her skin crawled where Seamus had touched it, her arousal corrupted into disgust. She hadn't imagined it, hadn't dreamt it; he'd been *right fucking there.* "Jay, I know what it sounds like, but that whackjob was *here,* and he was *touching* me, and I thought it was you until he kissed me and I felt his beard, and—I *saw* him, right here in our bed."

Jason rocked on his heels only for a moment, then he snatched his shirt off the chair and yanked it back on. "C'mon. We're ending this shit right now."

They found Dacey in the dining room, giving instructions to Meg, one of the maids. When she saw the couple coming, though, took on Jason's bruised and bandaged appearance and pale, shaken Sophie, she hurriedly dismissed Meg and wove around the empty tables to meet them halfway. "Good Lord, are you all right?"

"Dacey, we need to talk to you about your handyman," Sophie said, and the innkeeper's expression flickered. "There's something seriously wrong with him."

Dacey's brow knit. "I don't understand."

"Maybe he's never given you problems before," Jason said, "but he's been on our asses almost since we got here. Sophie's especially."

Dacey shook her head. "No, I mean we don't have a handyman."

Ice water flooded Sophie head to toe, and she looked at Jason before she forced her voice to resurface. "That's impossible. We've both seen him. Tall guy, brawny, black beard—"

"Hits like a fucking hammer," Jason added, rubbing his jaw. "Old white sweater, black cap, the look of a guy who doesn't get much joy out of life…"

"Oh my God," Dacey breathed, bone-pale, hand flying to her mouth. "That's Seamus McFaul."

"Yeah, that's what he said his name was," Jason said. "But I don't care who the fuck he is;

can't you call the cops and get him the hell outta here?"

Dacey shook her head, for a moment struggling to speak. "No, you don't understand," she finally forced out. "Seamus McFaul is dead. Aileen Greene killed him."

Seamus raged in the empty stable, slamming stall doors while their rusted hinges screamed in protest, overturning crates and a wheelbarrow full of old bridles and tack, the tarnished metal bits and ragged leather spilling out at his feet. He ripped a pitchfork from the wall, hurled buckets and brushes, all the while hurling curse after curse just as forcefully and viciously at Aileen and that man of hers—Jason. His touch she welcomed, yet she bolted from Seamus's like he was Grim Death his own self. And that pup, that upstart, having the nerve to confront him like that, like he was the one interfering in the natural way of things. Oh, he should've snapped Jason's neck when he had the chance, should've driven his head into the dirt again and again until it was no more than mud and pulp, should've dragged him and that shrieking colleen out into the lonely fields and—

He paused his storming, because that idea had brought with it a flash of familiarity, as if he'd considered it before, or even tried it. But he hadn't—had he? He stared down at his hands as though they might provide an answer, but they were empty, and as he fished for memories his head throbbed, a few nagging nudges in his mind that only turned to mist and faded when he tried to catch them. What had he...What had happened...?

But the impression had been strong yet fleeting, and quickly enough Seamus resumed seething, glaring through the stable's doorway back toward the inn and vividly recalling the fear on Aileen's face when she saw who her bedmate was despite the warmth and willingness she'd been responding with a moment before.

The silly little bitch thought she knew what fear was, but she didn't.

Not yet, anyway.

But he'd show her.

"I thought you *knew,*" Dacey said again, having been unable to move past this point since she'd realized, horrified, that they hadn't. "You talked about Aileen and the research you'd been doing and, well, I just figured you'd found out somehow."

Numbly Sophie repeated the shake of the head she'd replied with each time. Her great-great-granny had killed a man—no, *that* certainly hadn't come up in her research. Seated with Jason across the table from Dacey, her head was spinning and her limbs felt heavy—ironic, considering how unmoored she felt, as though Jason's hand on her thigh was the only thing keeping her anchored.

"It's just a piece of local lore at this point," Dacey said, "but like most of that it's managed to live on—this place doesn't forget easily, like I told you." She looked up as the dining room door opened: Quintin returning, closing the door behind himself before, with uneven step, rejoining them and setting down what he'd left to fetch—an old scrapbook bound in green leather and embossed with gold around the edges, a bottle of whiskey, and four glasses.

"I thought you might want some of this," he explained, pouring the drinks, "to make this go down a little easier." He tapped the scrapbook, and Sophie toasted him before downing the whiskey, the burn of it spreading through her and chasing away some of the chill Dacey's news had loosed.

Quintin settled himself beside his wife, across from Sophie. Once Jason and Sophie refilled their glasses, Dacey, face still pale with strain, said, "Neal Greene, Aileen's grandda, opened the inn in 1826. His sons helped run it until his oldest, Colin, left to become a sailor and his second son, Declan, married and became a farmer in Munster, leaving Joseph, his youngest, to take over when Neal died."

Joseph, Aileen's father. Sophie's search had told her that much, at least, and how it'd been just the two of them after Joseph's wife Ciarda had died birthing Aileen. Dacey opened the scrapbook, the first few pages of which held copies of birth, death, and marriage records, as well as the original deed for and an ink drawing of the inn done on paper yellowed with age. She continued, "There was a family who owned some land near Wicklow Town, the McFauls. For whatever reason, they'd come from Connacht and set up here. On the whole, they weren't well-liked; most of the locals regarded them as cruel, shiftless people who'd cheat you or beat you as soon as look at you, and judging by how many times the name McFaul shows up in arrest records of the time for robbery, assault, public disturbances, and the like, they weren't far off.

"But come one season when he found himself short-handed, Joseph Green hired Seamus McFaul to help around the inn—tending the horses and the grounds, repair work, that sort of thing. Seamus, by all accounts, wasn't the friendliest person, and he had a temper quick and vicious as any of his kin's. Joseph, though, saw that he was also a strong lad and a hard worker, and said good men can come from bad stock, so he was willing to give Seamus a chance. Aileen was sixteen that year, Seamus several years older."

Dacey bit her lip, looking at Sophie as though hesitant to continue. Sophie still felt swaddled in disbelief, though a tingling current of dread was beginning to burn beneath it, and the same struggle was playing out plainly on Jason's face. Quintin took over from his wife and went on, "As the story goes, Seamus fell in love with Aileen, though he hid his feelings at first. Even so, he acted as if the girl was already his, often challenging or outright fighting with other Wicklow boys who came to court her. When confronted, he claimed he was concerned about their 'intentions' towards Aileen and was only fighting in defense of her honor, so Joseph kept him on, after encouraging him to not be quite so overzealous.

"Then, when she was eighteen, Aileen met Troy Kearns, who began courting her almost immediately. By all accounts she returned his affection in full, and as both of them were of good standing in town almost everyone regarded it as a well-made match. Seamus, sensing that he now had a serious romantic rival yet not wanting to admit Aileen *wasn't* his after all, finally confessed his feelings to her—even proposing marriage, with a silver ring he'd saved months of wages for, convinced that Aileen would at long last realize her own feelings for him if she only saw the depths of his for her.

"She rebuffed him, however, as gently as she could, for she'd known him for two years and didn't wish to wound him too deeply. Anything other than acceptance was tantamount to a blade in the heart for Seamus, though, and anger quickly replaced fear and hope. According to lore, he kept the ring and declared several times when he was in his cups at local pubs that Aileen would wind up wearing it sooner or later."

Dacey picked up the thread. "Aileen was twenty when Joseph died." His death-notice was in the scrapbook, too, mentioning he was "survived solely by his daughter, Aileen." "She stepped in to run the inn herself, keeping her father's staff on—including Seamus, believing they were past the awkwardness of the situation with him, herself, and Troy. To Seamus, however, it was a sign of lingering affection, a sign that he still had a chance. He bided his time—three more years. Then he proposed again, certain by now she'd be able to admit her love for him. Except this time, instead of just rejecting his offer, she informed him Troy Kearns had proposed and she'd accepted. Seamus didn't take this well, and Aileen finally dismissed him from his job, realizing the situation would be untenable if she kept him on any longer.

"That was the final straw. One night, Troy and Aileen were walking home from town when they were waylaid by Seamus, who'd lain in wait for them in the field they usually cut through. It'd started raining and they were keen to get home quick, so neither of them noticed him until he jumped out and grabbed Troy, roaring that when he got Troy out of the way once and for all he was going to take Aileen away somewhere neither of them were known so they could finally be together."

Jason's hand was still on Sophie's leg; she threaded her fingers through his and squeezed tight, wondering if he felt her taut muscles trembling. The look on his face suggested he was seeing his confrontation with Seamus in an even sharper light, more fully realizing what he'd escaped, and Sophie's heart skipped a few beats as it sank deeper into her, too.

"The men struggled," Dacey said, "Aileen screaming at Seamus to stop. But Troy was on the ground and Seamus was strangling him, damn near killing him. Aileen, though, found a good-sized stone and brought it down on Seamus's head twice. The first blow stunned him; the second killed him."

Sophie could see it, clear as one of her own memories: the driving rain and howling wind, the green fields gone black with night and the storm and the two men wrestling in the mud until Seamus's hands wrapped around Troy's neck, squeezing, his face split by a killer's mad grin and eyes lit with rage and vicious triumph while Troy's widened, whites showing in fear and panic—

—and Aileen, hair and dress soaked and blowing wildly in the storm, stone in her raised hand as she brought it down on the top of Seamus's head with a banshee cry, the crack of the second blow as his skull caved in, face going slack, body slumping to the soggy earth as tendrils of blood crawled from beneath his cap and down his face…

"You can imagine the furor that erupted when Aileen and Troy burst into the inn, muddy and bloody and Troy half-dead where he stood, and once Aileen explained what had happened, the story spread all over town—not that anyone particularly blamed her for doing what she did, or was much surprised by the turn Seamus's obsession had taken, him being a McFaul and everything. There was an inquest, but the decision came back self-defense." Dacey turned another page and slid the book across the table so Sophie and Jason could better see a newspaper clipping dating April 1900 relating the verdict she'd just given—and accompanied by an ink rendering of "the deceased, Seamus Edmund McFaul, thirty years of age," which showed the face that'd been haunting Sophie since she'd arrived in Wicklow, down to his dark brow and thunderous scowl.

Her breath hitched at this confirmation, and she wondered what flashed across her face to evoke such a look of concern and sympathy from Dacey. "Jesus," Jason said roughly, hand drifting unconsciously to his scraped knuckles. "That's— fuck, that's him."

"A few months later," Quintin finished, "Aileen sold the inn to my family. She and Troy had considered heading to America for some time, and in the wake of these events they decided to finally do it. So they went to New York, where they married, and a year later she gave birth to their first child, though I suspect you knew that part already, Ms. Kearns."

She did, but couldn't seem to form a response; her tongue lay in her mouth like a thing long dead, and she couldn't seem to stop shaking no matter how hard she tried. The story—and the implications it raised—swirled in a dizzying torrent in her skull, one word as yet unsaid beating against her the most consistently until finally she cracked her mouth open just enough to say, "So this whole time we were being harassed by a ghost?"

"I thought you didn't have any of those," Jason said.

Looking bewildered, Dacey insisted, "We don't! I mean, we never have—nothing like this has ever happened here, until..." She bit her lip again, gaze falling to the polished tabletop.

"Until I showed up," Sophie finished for her, no blame in her voice. It wasn't anything she hadn't been thinking herself—it was hanging there plain as day. "Looking just like Aileen."

"So you think, what?" Jason's brow creased. "You coming here called him back from beyond?"

"Maybe 'woke him up' is a better description," Quintin said, and everyone looked at him. "The inn and its grounds held great meaning for Seamus McFaul; it's easy to see why his spirit might linger here after his sudden death. But what if he wasn't aware of where he was, or even that he was dead? Perhaps he was lying dormant, so to speak, and then yesterday..."

"I walk in looking like the woman he was obsessed with, with a new guy on my arm to boot," Sophie finished. "So now he's awake, confused, *and* majorly pissed." She looked at Dacey and Quintin. "I'm sorry, guys."

Dacey shook her head and Quintin waved her guilt off. "Even if you'd known this part of your ancestor's past you hardly could've known what your arrival would do," he said. "The question is, what do we do now?"

"If us comin' here is what woke this bastard up, won't he go back to sleep when we leave?" Jason asked.

"Maybe," Sophie said, "but maybe now that he's awake he'll stay that way, and God knows what a ghost like his'll do if he thinks he's lost the love of his life again." She sat up straighter, determination in her voice that was taking its time spreading to the rest of her. "I can't just leave and let this guy terrorize more innocent people. Aileen thought she stopped him before; the least I can do is finally finish it."

"Care to share your plan, babe?" Jason asked.

Her resolution bled away and she sagged again. "Once I think of one? Sure."

He wrapped an arm around her shoulders, his warmth and solidity reassuring even though the bruise blossoming on his left cheek, staining the skin beneath his eye, carved a deep pit open in the core of her. "It's all right, Soph. We'll figure something out."

"I just wanted to see where my family came from." She laughed hollowly. "Now the ghost of a psycho handyman thinks I'm my ancestor and wants to put a ring on it by any means necessary."

The ring. Sophie jolted, the thought echoing like the chime of a struck bell. "Dacey, Quintin, whatever happened to the ring Seamus bought Aileen?"

Dacey shrugged. "No idea," she said as her husband echoed her movement. "It was never mentioned in any reports, and the inn's interior's been redone a few times since it was sold— nobody ever mentioned finding a silver ring tucked away somewhere."

Quintin eyed her shrewdly. "What are you thinking, Ms. Kearns?"

"I'm no expert, but don't ghosts sometimes get attached to objects, not just places? That ring sure as hell held meaning for him, and if it was still here—if not in the inn itself, then at least on the property somewhere—maybe it helps tie Seamus to earth." She caught a glimpse of herself reflected in the whiskey bottle, saw a shine in her eyes and color returned to her face. "And if we can get rid of it, we can get rid of him."

It was thin. It was very fucking thin. A hundred and nineteen years had passed; the ring could've been lost, stolen, pawned, or flung into the harbor by Aileen herself after Seamus's death. And even if it was still hidden away on the ground of Greene's, she had no proof it was the link binding Seamus to the living plane—love and anger, hatred and pain, were capable of creating lasting ties all on their own; spilled blood and shared hearts were potent, powerful things.

Yet Sophie couldn't shake the notion that'd lodged in her mind, that the ring was the key and finding it would give them the leverage they needed over the jealous spirit.

Now if we could just find the damn thing...

But they didn't, despite the thorough search of the inn they made; Greene's only other remaining guests, the holidaying sisters, even searched their room after Dacey explained a previous guest might've lost a "family heirloom" in it. Darkness found Sophie empty-handed and staring morosely out the window of her and Jason's new room across the hall from their first—not that they thought a change of sleeping space would keep them safe from Seamus if he chose to show up, but Sophie couldn't look at, much less get into, the other bed without feeling sick, which Jason understood. He just wished he knew what to do now, instead of just standing there helpless, watching her, knowing she was coming undone inside no matter how blank her expression was as she looked out over the night-soaked fields, a far cry from the hopeful woman awed by the sunset yesterday.

"Soph?" he tried, when she didn't respond walking over and resting a hand on her shoulder, trying to ignore the sparks of pain shooting from his battered knuckles. She stirred then, shifting in her seat but staying silent, and he kissed the top of her head. "Say somethin' or I start singing 'Danny Boy.'"

She chuckled, at least. "The way you'd do it, I think it'd be considered a war crime."

He laughed back. "Guess I'll stick to the offstage stuff." He kissed the top of her head again, murmured, "Comin' to bed?"

"Might as well." Sophie stood, looking resigned. "Not sure I'll actually get any sleep, though."

Neither of them did, lying side by side fully dressed in bed. Every creak, every rattle and gasp in the air vent was Seamus returning, every moment they spent with eyes closed a vulnerability. One of them would drift off for a bit, then snap back to wakefulness when the other was startled by a shadow dashing across the wall or the cry of a fox in the fields. Jason's adrenaline flowed through the night like something molten in his veins and he hated it, hated the sharp-edged ready-for-a-fight state when there was nobody around to fight, and when there *was* it was a murderous ghost. What was he supposed to do, wrap his knuckles in rosary beads and see if that helped next time?

Near dawn he drifted off, mind a jumble of moments from the last few days: Sophie snapping photos on the Morrough, the rolling sea and ships bobbing in the harbor, the first glance he'd gotten of Seamus stocking wood near the outbuilding…

For fuck's sake. "Sophie!" She'd finally dozed off, too, but his idea overrode any regret he might've felt at waking her. As she blinked awake, lifting her head from his chest, he said, "There are other buildings here. The stables, that shed or whatever it is—it's a long shot, but what if Seamus hid the ring in one of them?"

Sophie stared at him, then put her hands on his cheeks and gifted him with a hard, deep kiss he would've enjoyed more without the bone-deep pang her touch woke in his sore jaw. "Baby, you're a fucking genius," she said, pulling back, eyes bright.

He snorted. "Tell that to my teachers." He scrambled after her as she bolted off the bed. "Hey, wait up."

Their third day in Ireland came in gray and damp, the low wind tinged with salt. Jason, Sophie, Dacey, and Quintin crossed the yard under a sky like slate, having decided to check the stables first, but stopped dead just inside when they saw the wreck someone had made of it.

Three guesses who, Jason thought as Quintin said, "This is impossible. I don't think we've been here in two years."

"Again, not an expert, but I don't think ghosts need a key," Sophie said, hefting an overturned wheelbarrow upright. "You think he overheard us, came here to get the ring first?"

"Maybe, but you want an honest opinion?" Jason surveyed the chaos. "Dude was just throwing a temper tantrum." He grinned crookedly. "Take it from a guy who's thrown a few in his time."

Whatever Seamus's reasons for wrecking the place, the ring wasn't in the stables, either. The other structure, Dacey told Sophie and Jason, was where they kept gardening tools and the like; it'd been standing as long as the inn had, and was the last building on the grounds Seamus would've had access to.

But at first it seemed as big a bust as the inn and stables; Jason and Sophie spent over an hour combing the outbuilding's cramped, sod-scented interior, Dacey and Quintin unable to fit alongside them, and their only accomplishment was avoiding tetanus from the scrape of a rusty rake. "I think we have to call it, babe," Jason said, dust furring his lungs, muscles burning as he swung a sack of fertilizer out of the way, and Sophie slumped back against the wall on her haunches, groaning. "It was a good idea, though," he tried to console her, but from the look she wore, it wasn't taking.

"It would've been a better one if it'd worked." She braced her hands against the wall to lever herself up. "Dacey mentioned something about calling the parish priest; maybe that'll—" She paused halfway up, looking back at the stone wall.

"Soph?" Jason came closer. "What's up?"

"One of these stones feels loose." Sophie turned fully, fingers skating over the stones until she found the one that shifted at her touch and worked it free like a tooth from its socket, its edges scraping at the crumbling mortar that'd held it in place.

At first the palm-sized gap seemed empty, and the disappointment that sank leaden in Jason's gut flickered across Sophie's face. Then she reached in, sweeping her hand around, and brightened. "Holy shit, there's something in here!"

It was a little parcel of stained burlap, bound up with string Sophie snapped and cast away. The burlap fluttered as she unwrapped it—her hand was shaking. And when the sacking fell away there in her palm sat a silver claddagh ring, slightly tarnished but its delicate craftsmanship still evident.

Sophie looked up at Jason, beaming in disbelief. "We fucking *found* it."

"I guess they aren't kidding when they say Ireland's full of magic." Triumph surging in him, Jason leaned in for a closer look.

And was grabbed from behind and hurled outside.

He'd let them stew in their fear and uncertainty overnight; anticipation of an attack could sometimes be more unnerving than the attack itself. But when Seamus flung their door open he found the room empty, bitter dismay curdling within him as he prowled the inn, hunting them. Maybe they'd fled, and then it was his turn to fear because if they had they were out of his reach; he'd discovered that for some reason he couldn't leave Greene's grounds. Every time he tried he felt like a hound straining against a chain, unable to go beyond its length.

He was down in the wine cellar when he felt a sharp tug on the chain, a pull that passed with a white-hot sharpness through him. Confused and alarmed by its strength he went back upstairs and found he could follow it, feeling the tether shorten as he followed it to its source: the stone shack out back, where Aileen and Jason were examining something glittering dully in Aileen's palm.

The ring.

His ring, which the interloper was grinning at—planning to steal it? But like Aileen, it wasn't his, wasn't his, WASN'T HIS—

Seamus swept down to remind him.

"Jason!" Sophie screamed, scrambling to her feet as he came down hard a few feet away, rolling briefly before he came to a groaning stop. She started after him, heart hammering, but Seamus appeared between them and smacked her aside before advancing on Jason, grabbing him by the

collar of his shirt and, though Jason was no small man himself, lifting him easily as a rag doll, his boots dangling several inches above the ground, legs kicking weakly.

"Fucker…You wanna fight, put me down an' I'll give you one," Jason muttered, dazed yet defiant.

Seamus's grin was dark and cold, blackly amused. "I doubt that, boy."

"Seamus McFaul, you put him down right now."

He didn't, but he turned and looked at her, grin vanishing. Even now she was amazed at how solid he seemed, how indistinguishable from a living man. She was also scared shitless, but she drew herself upright and spoke like she wasn't, a technique that'd served her well in the past. Against jackasses in bars and on the street, admittedly, but a bully was a bully no matter the country or century. Tightening her grip on the ring Sophie said, "Leave us both alone."

Seamus's eyes narrowed; his heavy hand crept to Jason's throat, tightening slightly. "I'm not lettin' another man come between us, Aileen."

"I'm not Aileen!"

Seamus's grip relaxed, and Jason gasped thinly for breath. Not seeing a way to ease into it Sophie pressed on, "Aileen is dead. She died decades ago. So did Troy Kearns, and so did you. You're dead, Seamus. You have no place here anymore."

Seamus's expression flared. "You're lying!" he roared, and Jason scrabbled at the hand strangling him again, face flushing as he choked.

Sophie risked a step forward. "No, I'm not. My name is Sophie Kearns, and that—" she pointed at

Jason— "is my boyfriend. We came here tracing my family history. I'm Aileen's great-great-granddaughter." When Seamus stayed silent, dark eyes darting between her and the struggling Jason, she moved another step closer. "You're lost. You're confused. I'll explain everything if you let Jason go. *Please.*"

Dead.
Dead?
But he was here.
Wasn't he?
Because as Aileen—Sophie?—spoke, there were two sets of images overlapping in Seamus's mind, surging through his skull at full flood: a rainy night, thunder grumbling over the horizon as he crouched in the knee-high grass, currents of fire pumping through his blood...the blonde woman and Jason heading up the walk towards the inn...

Aileen...

The smell of rain and mud thick in his nostrils, vision swimming scarlet, a woman screaming as a man—Troy? Jason?—choked in his grip...

Dead?
No.
But...

Seamus shook his head like a man trying to dislodge something unpleasant clinging to him. "No," he muttered. "No..."

"Seamus," Sophie urged, eyes locked on Jason. "Let him go."

He did, and Jason gasped as he hit the ground again, sucking down grateful breaths as he scrambled away.

Sophie rushed to help him up. "You all right?" she asked.

"Maybe," he said hoarsely. "You know what you're doing?"

"Maybe." She looked at Seamus and found confusion had softened his expression, and her heart skipped a beat. Could it really be so easy? If she explained the situation, would that be enough to get the ghost to move on, wherever he might have to go?

"Sophie?"

Dacey. She and Quintin, summoned by the commotion, were coming out the back door of Greene's, eyes widening when they saw the ghost for the first time. They started toward the couple but Sophie waved them back as she would from a wild animal, then looked back to Seamus as he said, grinding each word in his throat, "Sophie...Kearns? Aileen's great-great-granddaughter?"

She nodded, a smile daring to flicker across her face. "That's right."

She had one more moment to hope, then Seamus's expression contorted into one of pure hatred, his eyes embers set alight with Hell's own flames. "I'll have to settle for killin' you, then," he snarled, lunging for her.

She had a moment to think telling him she was descended from the woman he'd been obsessed with and the man he'd hated probably wasn't the smartest of moves, and then he was on her.

He remembered everything.

The rejection. The dismissal. The black rainy night.

And the bolt of pain as that bitch brought the stone down on his skull, and again, and then darkness.

The gray haze.

Drifting.

And if what this woman said was true, if Aileen and Troy were as dead as him now and she was a result of their treacherous union, the least he could do to pay back some of his pain was keep their line from continuing.

It would all end here.

Sophie felt her breath fly from her as she plowed into the ground, just barely managing to keep hold of the ring. Her ears were roaring; she was dimly aware of Jason, Dacey, and Quintin rushing toward her, but her immediate focus was on the weight of Seamus as he followed her down, teeth bared, dark eyes burning brighter. He was no featherweight Casper, but she managed to get a fist up before he pinned her, snapping his head back as she connected. A moment later Jason was yanking on Seamus, and the ghost twisted with inhuman speed to deal with him. Sophie managed to squirm free and finally set the ring down, poising herself above it on hands and knees, slipping from her jacket pocket the chunk of stone she'd pulled from the wall.

"Seamus!" she shouted, and when he wheeled around and saw her a wordless cry of horror escaped him, rising as he dove for her again.

But before he reached her, she raised the stone.

And brought it down on the ring.

Fire exploded through him, ripping him apart as it went. Memories sliced through his mind, each one razor-edged, and as stone struck silver again Seamus screamed.

The tether was gone. In its place a rift was opening, one only he seemed to see, and he didn't like what was waiting on the other side of it; suddenly the brief darkness of death, even the numb gray haze of in-between, seemed far more preferable. But there was a new pull on him now, one that wouldn't be defied, and it dragged him inexorably into that yawning maw, closer, closer...

Seamus flickered, like a print captured on bad film. The solidity was leeching from him as he writhed, rooted in place; gray wisps were rising like steam from his dissolving form, but as the wind carried them to Sophie they were freezing cold and carried the reek of decay.

She kept hammering at the broken ring, beating it into even more twisted shards of silver, and as the screaming ghost appeared to fold in on himself she struck one last blow, powering it with a cry of her own rage and pain. The vibrations of it travelled up her arm, but the strike had deeper ripples than that, and Seamus McFaul disappeared in a rush of sulfur-scented air, his shrieks and curses abruptly cut off.

For a moment Sophie stared, unable to believe it, and then adrenaline drained away and she sagged against Jason as he wrapped his arms around her, the weight of the day crashing down on her. The stone slipped from her fingers and a few tears slipped down her cheeks; she nodded as

Jason asked urgently, "Soph, are you all right?", and relief swam through his expression.

"Oh, thank God," Dacey said as she and Quintin clustered around the couple.

"So it worked, then," Quintin said, looking down at the broken ring. "Mr. McFaul's finally left our world."

Sophie nodded again. "I think so."

"Good riddance," Jason muttered, still holding her protectively.

Sophie looked at Quintin. "You wouldn't happen to have any of that whiskey left, would you?"

He smiled. "For you, Ms. Kearns, I'll open a bottle from my private stock."

Sophie gathered the pieces of silver from the ground, metal cold in her bare hand. As the group headed back to the inn, the rain started to fall.

The rest of Sophie and Jason's stay was pleasant and uneventful. The morning of their last day in Ireland they visited Wicklow Head Lighthouse, where the sea took the remnants of Seamus's ring; Jason stood behind Sophie on the shore, wrapping his arms around her waist as she leaned back against him, their jackets speckled with salt spray and the occasional raindrop.

Sophie had been quieter since ridding Greene's of Seamus—not distant, Jason thought, just…thoughtful, trying to process everything that'd happened. God knew how long it would take her—take them both, he amended, mind going to the necklace of bruises he was heading home with and the experiences heaped behind them. But he'd be there with her as she did it. It was her journey, but she didn't have to make it alone.

"So." He nuzzled her hair. "You find what you were looking for?"

Sophie smiled. "I think I get now why people say to be careful what doors you knock on. But hey, all of it's my history, so I guess I can't complain. I went looking, after all."

"Jack's gonna shit himself when we tell him."

She laughed. "Maybe I'll start a side gig as a ghostbuster when we get back to the States. I've got prior experience now." She shifted. "What time does the flight leave, again? I want to make sure we get to say goodbye to Dacey and Quintin before we have to go."

The innkeepers, though grateful to Sophie for ridding them of a potential spectral menace, had needed some convincing that neither she nor Jason held them accountable for their trip's unexpected detour through the Twilight Zone, or would refuse to step foot in the inn again because of it. Their relief on discovering this wasn't the case was endearing, and Jason knew he'd come back when Sophie did. "Don't worry, we got time." He threaded his fingers through hers and kissed her knuckles. "But, uh, I changed our flight. We're not heading straight home from here."

Sophie twisted to look at him. "What? Why not?"

"Because I did a little research of my own." Jason kissed her lips. "Trip's not over yet, sweetheart."

The cemetery in upstate New York was a small place full of graves mostly from the turn of the century, shaded by trees whose dark branches still dripped with runoff from the earlier rainstorm. Aside from the dead, Sophie and Jason were the only ones around; by the look of things Sophie guessed these graves didn't get many visitors.

"Kane, Keane…It should be somewhere around here," Jason said, pausing to brush moss from a cracked headstone.

Sophie's breath caught. "Jason. Here."

He came to stand beside her, in front of a rectangular gray stone bearing the names Aileen Fiona Kearns, 1877-1946, and Troy Egan Kearns, 1877-1951. There was a claddagh here, too, the hands clasping a crowned heart carved atop the names and dates, but these hands were cradling, supporting, not grimly grasping, clinging to something that was never theirs.

Sophie's throat grew thick, eyes blurring hotly. "Thank you," she said to Jason, not for the first time since he'd told her their destination.

"You did all this to connect with your roots," he said. "I figured you should get a chance to see where the ones who planted them ended up. " He started to step away. "I can give you some time by yourself if you want."

She caught his hand, tugged him back. "No, don't. I mean, could you stay with me? Please?"

He squeezed her hand back. "Yeah, of course."

Slowly she knelt, reaching out and running her fingers over the cold stone. Aileen, who'd killed to save the man she loved and then crossed an ocean to start a life with him—a life that had led, generations later, to Sophie's own. Aileen, who'd thought she'd rid the world of Seamus's cruelty once and for all. *Don't worry,* Sophie told her silently, wondering if wherever she was she already knew, *I finished what you started.*

Just as when she'd landed in Ireland, approaching the grave she didn't know what she'd feel when she reached her destination. *Overwhelmed* came to mind as she knelt there now, but there was also a rush of fondness and respect for this woman she'd never known, which helped ease how shaken she still was by her ghostly encounter. But above all there was a warmth of the sort she hadn't felt since her parents died, the sense of a hole being filled—not a feeling that she knew or understood everything, but that it was all right if she didn't. Maybe she'd always be finding her way, but she could still be happy with where she was, and as Jason knelt with her and held her tight, letting her cry, she was.

Eventually Sophie took a rubbing of the gravestone, giving it a final pat before she and Jason stood. "Ready to head home?" Jason asked as she carefully slipped the rubbing into the cardboard tube he'd brought for her.

Home. Sophie smiled. "Yeah. I am."

Amongst the Gorse
DJ Tyrer

"This must be the place," she said as the fifth, or possibly sixth, farm track we had followed that day appeared to be the one we wanted. There was frustration in her voice.

"Well, you did insist on remoteness," I reminded her. Cordelia had wanted a break from her busy schedule and had decided to rent rooms in a cottage for a week. She worked as an investment banker, a high-pressure role where the adage that a woman had to work twice as hard to be thought half as good remained true. She had been well on her way to a breakdown.

She snorted in reply, concentrating on negotiating our way up the rutted track to the lemon-yellow cottage.

"Oh, I hope this is it," she commented as we halted in front of it, "it's lovely! Roses around the door, just like I imagined!" They were yellow to match the colour of the house.

"Ever so romantic," I told her, leaning over to kiss her cheek.

We got out and went to the door, which was already opening. A woman about ten years older than us stepped out to greet us.

"Hello, you must be Cordelia; I'm Sylvia, we spoke on the phone; and, this must be Louis. I am pleased to meet you."

From what Cordelia had gleaned from her, it seemed that Sylvia had only just begun renting out rooms. I wasn't certain if she was just being ingratiating or if she genuinely was glad to see us. Even if it was the former, at least she seemed keen for us to enjoy our stay.

"And, we you," Cordelia replied, adopting that unfortunate tone she had when being polite to those she considered her inferiors. "This place is even more lovely than I expected."

"Why, thank you. Well, do come in. Here, let me help you with those bags."

Cordelia, of course, would never dream of carrying heavy bags when I was around to do it for her; feminism ended at the close of the working day for her. She took in one small bag, leaving it to Sylvia and me to bring in the bulk.

"I'm quite alright," I told her.

"Oh, it's no problem. A little hard work never hurt anyone."

"Thanks." Was that a dig at Cordelia?

"So, what is it that you do?" she asked as we went inside.

"I paint. I'm an artist," I expanded in case she mistook me for a painter and decorator and asked me to redecorate her lounge.

"Really? Successful?"

"Not really. I've sold a few paintings, but fame and fortune have evaded me so far."

She laughed, then paused to direct Cordelia through to our room, before telling me that her late husband had been an amateur artist. "He was even placed in a couple of local competitions."

"Is that one of his?" There was a semi-abstract, painted largely in different shades of yellow, of what appeared to be the cottage, at the head of the stairs.

She shook her head as she deposited the bags at the foot of our bed. "No. He bought it at an art auction. He thought it looked like this place. It was by...Steve Scott, I think."

"Really? It might be worth something. He was quite successful. Worth making sure it is sufficiently insured." Cordelia didn't seem to have heard, for which I was grateful; Scott was a touchy subject with her.

"Oh. Um, well, this is your room. I hope you like it. My room is just across the landing."

Was it my imagination or had she given me a pointed look as she said that? She certainly wasn't unattractive. Cordelia didn't seem to have noticed anything; she was busy admiring the view.

"It's really nice," Cordelia commented. "Just right."

"Good. Well, supper is at seven, so I will see you then."

We thanked her, then began to unpack. I found an old book of poetry on the bedside cabinet on the side I slept. It was bound in yellow and looked like it was of the decadent school. I couldn't really imagine Sylvia reading it and wondered if her husband had collected poetry in addition to the art.

"We should go for a walk," Cordelia decided when we had finished. "That's what you do in the country. Must you bring that?" she asked, nose wrinkling, as I picked up my portable easel.

"I might want to paint something."

"Whatever. Just don't expect me to hang around."

"You are supposed to be relaxing."

She sighed. "Sorry. I can't quite get into the sedentary frame of mind. Oh, well, let's go for this walk."

There was a footpath at the rear of the cottage that led across the fields to the gorse-clad moors beyond with their glorious display of yellow. Out on the moors themselves, the path was not quite so clearly marked, as if long untended.

"It would be easy to get lost out here," I commented, "although it is lovely. I think it would make a beautiful painting—if I've got enough yellow!"

"It *is* soothing...Louis, what's this?" she was pointing at a stone protruding from the profuse growth of heather and gorse. "It looks like a gravestone!"

"I think it is." It certainly looked like one. I went over to it and knelt down to scrape it clean of moss. "Yes, there's a name...Edward Atheling."

"Isn't Sylvia's surname Atheling?" She framed it as a question, but I knew she knew the answer. Cordelia had an amazing memory. "Is it her husband?"

"Yes and no; at least, not unless he died about a century ago. I guess it's his great-grandfather. The family must have been in this area for ages, maybe even at that cottage. We should remember to ask her when we get back."

"I don't like it, it's creepy..."

Cordelia had balked at buying a flat beside a graveyard. She was a hard-headed woman in so many ways, but death just creeped her out. Her parents had both died when she was quite young and she hated to be reminded of mortality.

"It's not as if it's near the cottage, darling. Look, see, there's the roof of the cottage. I doubt you could see this area. Let's move on. Look, sheep."

That, at least, distracted her. I would have preferred to look at the grave a little longer, maybe paint it, but didn't want our break to be ruined before it had really begun. I wondered why the mysterious Edward Atheling had been buried out on the moor. It was strange. There didn't seem to be any others, but I did wonder if any more of the family was buried about here amongst the gorse.

We wandered freely and returned in time for supper, a lovely meal of roast lamb and traditional vegetables. It was only after that I realised we had forgotten to ask about the grave. Probably, Cordelia preferred to ignore it altogether. I took the opportunity to read a little of the poetry collection I found earlier.

"Any good?" Cordelia asked, looking up from a Harlequin Romance. Her preference in poetry was for Shakespeare out of a sense of intellectual snobbery.

"It's okay, although this Wantage fellow had a rather jaundiced view of humanity. I prefer something a little more upbeat. Well, 'the Phantom of the Past would go no further,'" I quoted, "and neither shall I! Goodnight."

"Goodnight." We both switched bedside lamps off and lay down to sleep.

***

I awoke to see someone standing in our bedroom doorway, a silhouette that barely stood out against the darkness of the landing. For a moment, I thought it was Cordelia, but I felt her move beside me. It had to be our host.

"Sylvia," I whispered, "is that you?"

For a moment, I thought maybe my luck was in. But, she didn't reply and gave no gesture. I began to wonder if it was actually her. Could it be a burglar, way out here? What should I do? All I could think to do was lie there and stare at the vague outline of whoever it was

Then, the figure moved. They seemed to turn and step out from the doorway. I jumped out of bed and headed for the door, still lacking any clear idea as to what I would do if it was an intruder—or Sylvia, for that matter. I had covered about two-thirds of the distance when there was a sudden loud crash from outside the room, as if someone had just fallen straight down the stairs. Shocked, I ran out onto the landing and snapped the light on.

Although the bottom of the stairs was shadowed, it was pretty clear there was nobody at their base. It didn't seem too likely that they might have fallen any distance away or been able to crawl away—and the crash I had heard had not sounded the sort of fall you just walked away from without pause—but, I headed gingerly downstairs to investigate. Although the odds seemed to be against discovering an active burglar downstairs, I was worried that I would discover a mangled corpse.

I switched on every light on the ground floor and checked every room, just to make certain, but there was nobody about, no blood, no signs of forced entry, nor any indication that anything had actually happened. I felt a chill despite the warmth of the night and a sense of confusion. I was certain that I had been awake, not sleepwalking, and I certainly hadn't been dreaming in bed. Had I imagined the sound of the fall? It didn't seem credible. Wearily, I walked back upstairs having returned the downstairs to darkness. Neither Cordelia nor Sylvia had come out to investigate; maybe it wasn't so incredible to imagine it had all been in my mind.

As I climbed back into bed, Cordelia stirred awake and asked, voice heavy with sleep, what I was doing.

"I thought I heard someone downstairs." I didn't want to tell her what I thought I'd heard; I was already beginning to feel foolish.

"What?" She was awake now. It had probably been a silly move saying that much. Cordelia lived in mortal fear of intruders, despite never having been burgled.

"It's alright; I went and had a look around. I must have been dreaming; there was nobody there."

Was I trying to convince her or myself that all was well?

***

I felt shattered in the morning. I had had trouble getting back to sleep and spent too long tossing and turning. What a start to our break! Perhaps it reflected some underlying worry niggling me. Maybe my mind just hadn't been ready to switch off.

I decided to go for a walk alone—Cordelia pouted that we were supposed to be on holiday together, but I needed to get my head straight. They say that green is supposed to calm the mind, but I found the yellow of the gorse soothing as I ranged across it, working the nervous energy out of my system.

I found myself back at the grave of Edward Atheling. I hadn't brought my easel, but I did have my sketchbook, so I sat down nearby and began to doodle my impressions of the site. There was something forlorn about it.

"It's lovely up here, isn't it?"

I jumped at the vocal intrusion, a line marring the landscape I was drawing.

"Oh, I'm sorry, I've made you spoil it."

I turned to find Sylvia standing nearby. "It's okay. It was just a rough sketch in case I want to paint the scene later. Here, you can have it." She accepted it with a smile. "Did you know this grave was here? It's a bit of an odd place to be buried, don't you think?"

She shrugged. I had the impression she wasn't too keen to discuss the grave. "He wasn't much loved, so was buried here, out of the way, to be forgotten." She paused, then added, in a whisper, "Unfortunately, the dead don't sleep easy on the moor."

"Pardon?"

"Oh, sorry, nothing..." She smiled, suddenly, and said: "I've been alone a long time, Louis. Even when my husband was alive, I was alone, emotionally, physically. I yearn for human company...if you understand me..."

I did. I laid aside my sketchbook, stood and crossed to her, took her in my arms, kissed her. There was something wonderful about giving ourselves up to passion amongst the gorse—she had brought a blanket for us to lie on—and Sylvia was like a woman possessed, unrelenting in her desire. When we parted, she was aglow with vitality, whilst I was shattered and exhausted. I had to sit there, watching her walk back towards the cottage, to recover my breath. Cordelia had never drained me like this. It was only at that thought that I realised the risk I had taken—what if Cordelia had come looking for me? Was it worth throwing our love away for some moment of passion, no matter how torrid?

The glow of delight quickly evaporated, leaving me feeling guilty and a little stupid as I trudged back. I was also a little freaked out at having made love beside—no, I think, atop—a grave. I might not share Cordelia's hang-ups on the subject, but this did seem wrong. It made me wonder about Sylvia Atheling. I had taken her for a sort of Mrs Robinson in my mind, but, now, I was beginning to think, perhaps, that she was a bit weird; predatory, even. Maybe that was just my guilt and embarrassment projecting negative qualities onto her, but I no longer found her quite as alluring.

She was having a cup of tea with Cordelia when I entered the cottage and her genial greeting was so convincingly genuine that I almost doubted that our encounter had occurred outside my imagination. I would have imagined she had been here all along had I not been able to feel where she had bitten my shoulder at the height of our passion. How I was to conceal that from Cordelia, I had no idea; I was an idiot!

I joined them, feeling very nervous. Sylvia was completely unfazed and I had to wonder at how she managed: I began to suspect she was no stranger to illicit affairs, no matter what she claimed.

The rest of the day passed in something of a blur, my mind being preoccupied with replaying what had happened out on the moor and Sylvia's calmness and my own confused feelings. Her cool demeanour was a little bit disturbing, certainly unnerving, and made me feel all the more awkward.

My only relief was that, when I came to wash before bed and checked my shoulder, the bite mark had faded away to almost nothing, a slight redness and bruise that were nearly invisible and would mean nothing if detected. That was something to be thankful for.

Cordelia was in an amorous mood when I climbed into bed, but I had to decline, my encounter with Sylvia still having left me drained. She went to sleep in a huff and I soon joined her.

***

I awoke with a start to an unpleasant sensation of menace. For a moment, I thought it was the sensation you can get when you awaken from a nightmare and your confused mind is not quite caught up with you being awake. But, as I opened my eyes, I saw that there was a shadowy figure at the foot of the bed. It wasn't Sylvia; it was the bulky figure of a man. I was certain that was what I saw, that it was no dream. There was a man at the foot of our bed and I could feel malevolence in the stare of his unseen eyes. I couldn't help but let out a little cry of shock.

At that sound, the figure turned and strode out of the room and, as I sat there, upright in the bed, shocked, once more I heard the sound of an almighty crash as if he had thrown himself down the stairs.

"Y'alrigh', darlin'?" slurred Cordelia, stirring sleepily.

"Yes," I lied. She didn't seem to have heard the crash and I didn't know what else to do or say. The man had been real, I would have sworn to it, even if I hadn't clearly seen him. Yet, what had just happened?

I knew what I would see when, finally, I dared to rise and look: nothing. It made no sense at all. The only explanations I could conjure up, marvellous and mundane, were the equally ridiculous and unpleasant notions of phantoms and vivid hallucinations that I couldn't bring myself to believe; didn't want to believe. None of it made any sense. Was I going mad?

***

It was not a lie when I told Cordelia, the next morning, that I needed a lie-in.

"I had such trouble drifting off," I explained. "Then, I slept so badly. I might as well not have slept at all."

"I slept like the dead," she replied, her tone seeming to imply that she suspected me of some act of deliberate holiday sabotage. "I hope you aren't getting ill."

"I don't think so. I think I can't quite have wound down. Give me this morning and I'll be right as rain."

She tossed her head, telling me that she was going to go for a walk. Cordelia had been talking about going to an equestrian centre, but obviously didn't want to go alone.

Within minutes of Cordelia leaving, Sylvia was in our room and showing scant regard for my weakened state. Her unwanted attentions meant I was feeling no better by the time Cordelia returned.

"You *are* looking rather sickly, you know, Louis," she opined as we sat down for a traditional roast dinner.

"He just needs to build his strength up," Sylvia told me, doling out additional portions onto my plate. To me, it seemed as if she were blatantly smirking, yet Cordelia appeared oblivious and just concerned for my health.

As it was, I could barely bring myself to eat anything, let alone all that had been heaped upon my plate. I felt utterly awful. Having an attractive older woman throwing herself at me should have been the stuff of dreams, but was proving more of a nightmare.

I was excused from helping clear the plates away, so went through into the cosy front room and sat down in a deep and comfortable chair. Pieces of gorse, heaving with their wonderful yellow blooms, had been laid upon the mantel, brightening the room.

Cordelia and Sylvia entered together, but the latter seemed surprised, and not pleasantly so, to see the gorse.

"What is that doing there?" she asked.

"Oh, I gathered some; I thought it would help cheer Louis up. It looks so lovely, don't you think?"

"You shouldn't have brought it in," Sylvia told her.

"Oh, honestly!"

"It's very bad luck to bring gorse indoors. Carry gorse in and you carry death in with it..."

"Oh, poo! That's just superstition!" She was using her condescending tone again, but I could detect an undercurrent of unhappiness.

Sylvia gathered up the gorse and carried it out.

Cordelia turned to me and asked, "You don't think there's any truth in that, do you, Louis?"

"No, of course no, it's just an old wives' tale..."

"It's just that I gathered it up by that grave. That's where it grows best."

Well, that explained her sudden nerves. I was a little surprised that she had even gone back up there. I doubted she would be sleeping too well that night. Having had the notion that gorse was connected to death planted in her mind, it would doubtless play upon her subconscious that this cottage was located amongst the gorse, surrounded by so much of it. The yellow flowers had seemed so beautiful, but, now, suddenly, had a morbid, oppressive element to them that made them unpleasant to us. It was strange how an impression could swing about so suddenly.

"Oh, I wouldn't worry about it. I mean, all sorts of plants grow on graves, and nobody says you'll die if you bring any of the others home."

"I suppose so." I could tell she wasn't convinced.

The rest of the day was tense and we retired to bed in no good mood, snuggling together in a vain search for comfort.

***

That night, when I awoke, it was with a scream. Cordelia had rolled away from my embrace and into a foetal position on one side of the bed. I, in turn, had stretched out, almost spread-eagle on my back. Thus, when I opened my eyes, it was to look directly up into the face of a man fifteen or twenty years older than me, shadowed but still clearly staring down at me with a look of rage. Something landed on my face as he jerked his head back and headed for the door.

Cordelia awoke with a startled shriek of her own as the crash from down the stairs occurred as before. Fumbling for the lamp switch, she demanded to know what was happening, if I was alright. Suddenly, the room was drenched in light as she found the switch. I blinked and could almost imagine that I'd been dreaming now that the menacing darkness was banished.

My doubts were swept away as Cordelia turned to look at me and asked, "What is all that over you?"

"What?"

"On your face and hair," I reached up to brush myself as she went on, "it looks like dirt and leaves."

Cordelia was right; it was soil and bits of gorse. I remembered stuff falling onto my face as the man had moved. The soil and gorse had to have fallen from him. It had been no dream. Then, my sleepy brain got into gear and asked why soil and gorse would fall from a man's head. Involuntarily, my mind thought back to what Cordelia had said about the gorse she had brought into the house. It seemed too fantastical to be true, yet it seemed so obvious that I felt sick to my stomach.

"Louis, what's wrong?"

"It fell from a man. He was standing there, by the bed, looming over me. It fell from him. Do you understand me?"

She was confused. "I don't–" she started to say, then an expression of horror swept over her face as she reached the same conclusion that I had. "You don't mean...?"

I nodded. "It seems too incredible to be true, but..."

"I don't want to stay here, Louis, I want to go home!"

I shook my head. "Not now. I don't want to go into the darkness. Besides, he only comes once a night."

"Once? What the hell are you talking about?"

"I've seen him the last two nights—once in the doorway; last night at the foot of the bed. Each time, there was a loud crash."

"I thought I heard something..."

"I wonder if, maybe, he died falling down the stairs. I'll ask Sylvia in the morning."

"I'm scared."

"Don't worry, we're safe now and we'll leave tomorrow." I hugged her close and stroked her hair, repeating my words like a mantra until she fell asleep in my arms.

***

Cordelia woke first when the sun rose and, this time, it was her scream that woke me.

"What is it?" I exclaimed, shocked and confused.

"Look!" Cordelia didn't mean anything specific—she meant everything: the house looked utterly different to the house we had grown to know. Last night, it had been homely. This morning, it was ruinous. We were lying on bare floorboards in a damp and mouldy room utterly lacking any pleasant touches. I couldn't believe what I was seeing.

"You are seeing this, too, aren't you?" she asked me.

I nodded. "Yes. Yes. Is this real? It can't be real..."

"Can it?"

I shrugged. I didn't know what to believe.

We staggered to our feet and found our suitcases in the corner of the room. I left Cordelia getting dressed and went out onto the landing. The rest of the house was in the same dilapidated state as our room.

"Sylvia?" I called out, walking to her bedroom door. The Scott painting was long faded into nothing, just sun-yellowed and mould-mottled canvas. "Sylvia, are you there?"

No answer. I hadn't really expected one, even as I opened the door in order to make certain she wasn't there.

A few minutes later, we were out at the car. Cordelia was all for leaving immediately, but there was something I needed to check. I headed around the house towards the moor.

"Don't go!" Cordelia called after me. "Don't leave me alone!"

"I won't be long. Then, we'll leave."

"Hurry up, Louis!" I heard her shout after me. "Hurry up!"

I walked out amongst the gorse, the path no longer visible, to where I thought we had found the grave. It was there and, beside it, there was a second grave. Unwillingly, I reached out to scrape the moss off the gravestone and read the name carven upon it: *Sylvia Camilla Atheling*. She had died a few years after her husband.

I shivered at that, but was all the more disturbed as I noticed something flapping atop the grave. It was a piece of paper twitching in the breeze, held in place by a stone. I reached down and plucked it out from under the stone. I recognised the sketch, of this area; it was the one I had given to Sylvia.

Crumpling it, I tossed it away, allowing the breeze to snatch it up and send it tumbling away across the gorse. I turned away, not wanting to know more.

The Kiss of a Phantom
Kev Harrison

"And here is your key, Mr Jackson," said the sleepy-eyed receptionist, handing over an antiquated room key with an even older-looking fob the size of Daniel's forearm. Daniel glanced around reception. He was totally alone. In hindsight, this hotel might not have been the best choice to cheer him up after the break-up.

He dragged his small suitcase across the polished floor to the elevators and pressed the 'call' button. He glanced up at the art deco display, bulbs illuminating each floor's stained-glass label in turn as the lift slowly descended. The doors slid open as it reached zero and he stepped inside.

Daniel shrugged his shoulders. The lift whirred as it climbed towards the sixth floor. He stepped out and turned right, as the receptionist had instructed, moving into the east wing. 632 was the last room on the right.

Motes danced in the afternoon light as he opened the door. The windows were ajar, allowing a light breeze in, disturbing the accumulated dust on the tired furnishings. Daniel placed the suitcase onto the luggage rack and perched on the edge of the second bed, near the window.

He glanced around the room, a smirk creeping onto his face when he noticed the old tube TV, locked into a wall-mounted stand high up in one corner. "Shithole," he said softly. He dug into the pocket of his hoodie and pulled out his phone, checking for messages. There were none. No texts, no missed calls. He wasn't missed, then. He touched the power button, the face of the phone turning black. Then a reflection in the screen caught his eye.

Female.

Voluptuous.

His eyes darted away, doing the maths to figure out where the reflection had come from. He looked out of the window across to the west wing of the hotel and there, in the room opposite was a maid.

Standing on a chair, she was leaning out of the open window, cleaning the pane with a cloth. Her maid's outfit was no match for her breasts which shimmied from side to side as she wiped. Daniel felt fire in his cheeks.

He instinctively ducked below the window ledge, his brain sending mixed messages to stop looking and to do anything but, all at once. His curiosity won out and he knelt by the window, his fingertips over the edge, eyes wide, fixed on the scene before him.

The room phone burst to life with a loud 'brrring.'

Daniel spun around, jarring his arm and landing on his arse. He found his feet and hurried to the handset between the beds. "Hello?" he said. He carried the phone over to the window. The maid looked at him. Smiled. She stepped down from the chair and flattened down her uniform, then disappeared from view.

"Mr. Jackson," the languid voice of the receptionist. "Housekeeping informed me that your room was unoccupied last night."

"Okay," said Daniel, then paused.

"There are no towels in the bathroom, so I'm sending someone up with them right away."

"Okay," Daniel said again. The phone at the other side disconnected.

Daniel lowered himself into one of the room's two upholstered armchairs and clicked the power button on the cumbersome TV remote. The screen slowly fizzled to life, a snowstorm of interference masking the picture. He tapped the channel up button, found only five terrestrial channels, then pressed power off, feeling defeated.

A loud knock at the door made his heart thump in his chest. He ambled over and turned the release, easing it open. A young man, in the old-fashioned uniform of the hotel, pressed two folded bath towels into Daniel's chest.

"Taahls," he said in an accent so rough it could cut glass. Daniel looked at the towels, then up at the man.

"Thank you," he said. Then he noticed the maid. *The* maid. The one who had been cleaning the windows. She beamed at him, her lips candy apple red, contrasting with her milky skin. She winked. Took a step away from the housekeeping trolley, revealing shapely, stockinged legs. Daniel went to repeat his thanks, but couldn't spit the words out, gibbering meaninglessly.

"Nuffink else for yah?" The young man began dragging the trolley towards the elevators before Daniel could respond. Daniel watched the sway of the maid's hips until they were out of sight, then closed the door.

He laid the towels on his bed, beside the window, then sat back on the armchair. He paused for a moment, eyes closed. On the dark canvass of his eyelids, his mind painted the curves of the maid, her figure filling the bust of her pinafore dress to bursting and the skirt hitched up to reveal stocking tops which delicately pinched at the flesh of her thighs. He opened his eyes and tried to slow his shallow breath.

He found himself staring at the door without realising. Then, after a swift glance around the room, he stood up and bolted out of the room. He waited by the elevator, nervously humming a tune to himself. The heavy doors parted and he stepped inside, pressing 'G' for ground level.

Walking out into the reception, the place remained deserted. The same tired-looking man who had checked him in earlier stood at the desk, reading a thick, leather-bound book. Daniel decided to check the restaurant first.

He swung open the saloon-style doors and heard them thwack back and forth while closing behind him. There were thirty-something tables, immaculately set for dinner, though Daniel had yet to see another guest in the place. The lamps on each table were panelled glass, the cutlery bone-handled. He shuffled down the aisle between the tables, then stopped at the end to peer through the porthole window into the kitchen.

The place was dead. A host of polished, silvery instruments hung in various locations. Nothing moved. He turned back and paced his way to the reception area once more.

"Can I help you?" the sleepy voice of the receptionist asked.

Daniel stammered for a moment. "Erm…no…I don't *think* so."

"If you're looking for the games room, it's on the other side. Billiards, skittles and cards." He gestured with a limp arm, towards an arched doorway on the opposite side of reception.

"Oh," said Daniel. "Yes, that's right. Thank you." He put his head down and hurried over. He turned the brass doorknob and pushed. The rich red of the walls absorbed much of the light, low lamps over the games tables creating yellow halos, punctuating the gloom. Daniel's eyes began to adjust, picking out a silhouette beside the corner bar.

He moved closer, eyes fixed on the shadowy shape. The sound of the closing door mechanism startled him. He spun around, cheeks flushing as he realised the source of his fear. He cursed under his breath, then stopped as a laugh bubbled up from behind him. The sound surrounded him, bombarding him from one side and then another. Ice wound its way down Daniel's back. He took a breath and turned to face the bar.

She stood there, the maid, her eyes fixed on him, one hand on her hip, the other arm extended toward him, a single finger beckoning. Daniel glanced over his shoulder, but there was no-one else. The gesture was intended for him. He walked towards her, eyes locked onto her features. Light danced in her eyes, while her lips parted slightly, revealing just a glimpse of her teeth. "He...hello," said Daniel, his voice wavering.

The laugh came again, her lips turning upward into a smile, the sound reflecting from the panelled walls. As he got closer, she opened her hand, inviting him to place his in hers. He reached out and let their fingers intertwine, hardly noticing the cold touch of her skin. She pulled him closer, taking his other hand and placing it at the curve of her hip. He moved it downward, feeling the roundness of her behind and then her lips were on him. Soft and full, they brushed against his.

Daniel closed his eyes and allowed her to guide him. She pulled him closer, their bodies now pressed tightly together, his chest firm against her full breasts. He unhooked his fingers from hers, teasing her hair back from her face and stroked her cheek.

Her skin was so soft. So *cold*.

He opened his eyes wide. Dead eyes looked back at him. Dark, sunken, with none of the fire that had made them so wickedly irresistible. Her plump lips were blue, veins tracing meandering paths from them across her cheeks.

"Kiss me," said a voice, though her lips remained perfectly still. Daniel pushed her away and she stumbled into the bar. Her uniform was dishevelled now, the blacks of her skirt and pinafore a tired grey, her stockings laddered in multiple places.

She licked her lips with a black tongue, leaving a translucent snail-trail of saliva around her mouth. She darted forward, hands reaching for him. He jerked away and sprinted for the door, her shoes beating an uneven rhythm behind him. His palms slammed into the door, and he frantically twisted the doorknob.

Locked.

A cold hand grasped at his shoulder, twisted him around. She was thinner now, the illusion of life slipping away before his eyes, replaced with corruption, wastage and decay. She lurched forward, tendons and veins boldly visible in her neck, lips puckered. Daniel ducked, wriggled free of her grasp and made a dash for the window, weaving between the high billiard table and the lower one, set for cards.

Again came the thrumming of heavy feet behind, her lumbering gait arrhythmic. Daniel reached the window. Clawed at the catches. Levered the window upward, cool air rushing in. An arm jerked forward above him, little more than bone now and slammed the window down. Daniel glanced up. Papery skin covered the skull whose eyes bored down into his. "Kiss me," the words came once more, from nowhere and everywhere. He dove for the ground, cold tiles rising up, thudding into his jaw. He scrambled forward, tasting blood from his bitten lip, and squeezed through the space to the bar.

Without thinking he grabbed two bottles, whisky and rum. He turned and threw them as hard as he could at the advancing maid. Fragments of glass exploded in all directions as the bottles atomised on impact with the advancing skeletal figure.

Still she stalked closer.

He turned back, finding vodka and brandy. He let fly, two direct hits, shards of glass, like deadly hail, filling the air. She staggered backward, then marched on, outstretched fingers like twigs of bone.

Daniel pressed himself to the wall, reached up, finding something. He tugged at it. It was stuck to the wall. He heaved and managed to pull it down. Turned it in his hands. A mirror. He flipped it around, held it out towards her. The maid froze, jawbone hanging open. A scream emanated from the empty maw, high-pitched, rasping. Then she was gone.

Daniel slid down the wall, his chest heaving. His eyes scoured the room for signs of her, but all they found were shards of glass, refracting the dim light. He hauled himself to his feet and stumbled to the door. He tried the knob. The door opened without resistance.

The weary-looking receptionist placed his book on the counter in front of him. "Are you okay, sir? I heard a commotion."

Daniel approached the counter. "I… I broke some bottles. I'm sorry."

The man's eyes widened. He fished a pair of glasses from his jacket pocket and positioned them on his nose. "It was her, wasn't it?" he said.

Daniel stammered. "H-her? What?"

"The mirror, sir." The receptionist gestured towards Daniel's right hand.

He hadn't intended to bring the mirror with him. He held it up and looked at his face. Bright, red lipstick stained his lips.

"I'll take care of it, sir. You be on your way now."

Mark Is Still Missing

David F. Gray

"Yeah, but I'm starting to get a little nervous."

I dreamed that on New Year's Eve, but it doesn't matter. It happened. I know, because the second time it wasn't a dream.

I'm making a mess of this, but that doesn't matter either. Last week, just as the knife slid in, I caught a glimpse of the blue house. For the first time in months, I actually have a chance…if I can get past *him*. I'm loading this document into my computer because if—*when*—the barrier cracks, I'm going to push through it. If I don't make it back, I want someone to know what I've done and why.

You see, something took my son, and I'm going to take him back.

No parent should ever have to suffer the loss of a child, but it happens. Sickness, accidents, human monsters who prey on the young; sometimes, it just happens.

It happened to me.

God, it hurts to type that.

Mark, my twelve year old son and only child, disappeared six months ago, between one and three-fifteen on New Year's morning. The images that fill my mind are merciless and brutal. I see him caged like an animal for the amusement of some insane pedophile. Worse, I see him buried in a shallow grave, planted where no one will ever find him.

And those are the good days.

On the bad days, I think that something else has him, or almost has him. It's something so wrong that it cannot be conceived by the waking mind. It's all I can do to hang on to my sanity.

Jenny is not so lucky. I visit my wife three times a week, but she no longer knows me. She doesn't know anyone. She just lies in her bed, staring at something only she can see. The doctors try to offer some hope, but I can see the truth in their eyes. Jenny's mind is gone, buried deep in whatever world she's created for herself.

Even after all these months, I still remember every detail of the dream.

It's New Years Eve. I have to work, but I'm going to meet Mark at a party at around two in the morning. In typical dream logic, some of my long lost friends from high school will be there along with Mark's friends. I've made it a point to get each of them a gift certificate from a local restaurant.

I leave work and drive to the party. I'm a little concerned because it's in a bad neighborhood...drugs, gangs, and a crime rate that would make the south side of Chicago blush. It's also my neighborhood. God knows I've tried, but I've never been able to afford better.

I find the house and pull into the driveway. It's a tiny wooden number resting on concrete blocks. The white paint is faded and the entire structure tilts to the left. I go inside and find Mark sitting on a worn red couch watching television.

"How's the party?" I ask.

"Dull," he replies. "They're all asleep." I glance around and see that he's right. Everyone is sacked out on the floor, blankets pulled over their heads.

"Then let's go home," I say. Mark nods and we walk out of the house. My Mustang is still there in the driveway, but for some reason we decide to walk. It's a warm Florida night, so we go to the nearest intersection and take a left. Our house is maybe two miles away, but it's two miles through a bad neighborhood on the biggest party night of the year. We walk in silence, but suddenly I realize that I've forgotten to give my friends their gifts.

"Hang on a second," I tell Mark. "I'll be right back." I turn and trot back toward the old wooden house. Just like that, I abandon my son. But it's all right. It's just my dream, you see. Sometimes, we do things in our dreams that we would never do in waking life. At least, that's what I keep telling myself.

I get back to the house. This being a dream, I don't realize that it is now much larger, painted bright blue and two stories high. It is also on the other side of a street that had become a part of a much nicer neighborhood. I go inside, but everyone is still asleep. I leave the envelopes with the gift certificates on a table where my friends will find them and leave. Once outside, I see my Mustang sitting right where I left it. I suddenly realize I have left Mark alone. Pulling my phone out of my pocket, I hit the speed dial.

"It's me," I say when Mark answers. "Are you all right?"

"Yeah," he says, "But I'm starting to get a little nervous."

"Okay, hang on. I'm on my way back now." I get into my car and pull out of the driveway. When I get to the intersection, I see that the two lane street has now become a busy four lane highway. I pull out, make a left and hit the gas. I keep an eye peeled for Mark, but everything is different. Long, never ending strip malls line both sides of the highway. Their glaring neon lights make me squint so hard that I can't see the pavement. I stop the car and get out. I'm starting to get scared.

I must have made a wrong turn, I think. I leave my car sitting in the middle of the highway and start running back toward the house. The neon lights disappear and I am left in darkness. I keep running.

Then, out of the darkness four figures appear. It's Jenny, along with her parents. The fact that my in-laws are both dead makes no difference. To my immense relief, Mark is with them.

"I've been looking for you," I say. Then I do a double take. The boy is not Mark. At least, he's not my Mark. He looks like Mark...sort of...but he's a good five years younger. "Where's Mark?" I ask, but Jenny ignores me. The four of them walk past me and disappear into the darkness. Suddenly I am terrified. Not only have I abandoned my son, but now I can't find my way back to him.

I make it back to the intersection and for an instant I see the tidy blue house. *I'll start from there,* I think, *and retrace my steps.* I turn the corner, but without any hint of transition, the house disappears. In typical dream logic, I can still see it, but even so, it's gone. Something has come between me and it...some kind of barrier. Far worse, there's something lurking within that barrier. I take a step forward, but the thing stirs. It sees me, and it *knows* me. I can't take it anymore. I flee.

I don't mean that I run. I flee.

I think that, at that moment, my waking mind decided that enough was enough. It took that dark dreamscape, crushed it into a tiny ball and hurled it deep into the recesses of my mind. I jerked awake and found myself lying in my own bed next to Jenny.

I glanced at my alarm clock and saw that it was three fifteen a.m. As in my dream, I had worked until well past midnight. Unlike my dream, there had been no party. Both Jenny and Mark had stayed home and watched the New Year come in on television. I lay there, heart pounding. After several minutes I couldn't stand it any longer. I slid out of bed, padded down the hall and peeked into Mark's room. His bed was empty. I stared at the tousled sheets.

He's in the bathroom, I thought, *or probably getting a drink of water in the kitchen.* But he was gone. The window in his bedroom was locked, and there was no sign of a struggle. He simply disappeared.

I don't remember much about that night. I ran about our tiny house like a madman for several minutes, convinced that Mark was somehow staying one step ahead of me. Finally I woke Jenny. I told myself that she had let him stay overnight at a friend's house and had forgotten to tell me. The fact that I had looked in on him when I got home did not matter. My mind was grasping for any possible explanation. Jenny thought it was some kind of horrible joke, but gradually she realized that something was very wrong.

We called the police, of course. They searched the neighborhood but came up empty. Mark did not magically appear the next day, or the next week, or the next month. The police continued their investigation while Jenny and I slid deeper and deeper into our own private hell.

We didn't think things could get any worse, but after a month, we discovered that we were now suspects in Mark's disappearance. The local news ran the entire story and suddenly we found ourselves huddling in the business end of a hurricane. Our friends deserted us and people at my job shunned me. That was it for Jenny. I came home one afternoon and found her lying on the floor, curled up with a pillow between her legs, staring into the distance. She's still staring.

After that, I moved through my day to day life like a dead man. Three months after Mark's disappearance, late one evening, I was again brought in for questioning. Bill Davis, the detective in charge, was on a mission. He was convinced of my guilt and nothing was going to sway him.

"Tell me exactly what you did when you discovered Mark's disappearance, Mr. Grant," he began. An hour later, he flat out accused me of murdering my son. "We've seen it a hundred times, Steve." He liked calling me Steve, even though I told him I preferred Steven. "A kid defies his father and the father lashes out in rage." He leaned across the interrogation table. His breath smelled of coffee and stale cigarettes. "You need help, Steve," he said. "I can get you that help. We can end this once and for all. Just tell me the truth and let me help you."

"I've told you the truth," I said, closing my eyes. "You just don't want to hear it." He growled, stood up and started the whole thing all over again. Five hours later, he stormed out of the room. I was released with a stern warning to not leave town.

A few days later, I was fired. Until last week, I spent my days staring at the walls of my house. The bills were coming due. We had always lived paycheck to paycheck, so I had maybe a month before the power and water got turned off. I didn't care. I wanted to die.

Then, eight days ago, my cell phone rang. It was around five in the afternoon and I had no intention of answering it, but the ring itself managed to penetrate the fog that had wrapped itself around my mind.

It was Crazy Train, by Ozzy Osborne, and it was Mark's ring. I pulled the phone out of my pocket and stared. Glowing in the twilight, Mark's picture stared back at me. In an instant, the mind numbing terror and despair that had been my constant companions for six months vanished into nothingness. My heart soared. *He got away,* I cried silently. *Oh thank you God, he got away.* I hit the 'accept' button.

"Mark? MARK! Please let that be you!"

"Yeah, but I'm starting to get a little nervous." It was Mark's voice, and for a moment, that was all that mattered. Tears suddenly soaked my cheeks.

"Where are you? Just tell me where you are and I'll come and get you." For a moment, there was nothing. Then…

"I'm starting to get a little nervous." Now I actually listened. Mark's voice was dull...*pale*. It seemed to be coming from a long way away.

"Where are you?" I screamed. "For God's sake, just tell me where you are!" A loud clash of static made me wince, but I kept the phone to my ear. I heard Mark's voice again, but the static made it impossible to understand him.

"MARK! ANSWER ME!" The static grew worse, but finally I was able to make out four words.

"It's…dark…he's close." And the line went dead. I hit the redial button but the call did not go through. After several tries, I gave up and called Detective Davis. I could feel his disbelief as he listened.

"I think that your mind is trying to tell you to come here and confess," he said in that dull, flat professional tone that I had come to hate.

"You self righteous bastard," I growled. "My son is out there. Now you get your fat, lazy ass in gear and find him, or so help me I'll…"

"You'll do nothing," snapped Davis. "You'll stay right where you are while I check this out." He hung up, and called back a few hours later.

"No calls have been made to your cell phone, Steve," he practically crowed. "And your son's phone has not been used since his disappearance.

Now, why don't you drop the act, come in and talk to me."

"Screw you," I snarled and hung up. I thumbed the 'menu' button on my phone but there was no record of Mark's call. My heart sank. *It's finally happening,* I thought. *Move over, Jenny. I'll be checking in soon.*

At that moment, my phone went off in my hand. It was Crazy Train, and the display clearly showed Mark's picture and name. At that instant, I wanted to slam it into the wall so hard that it would never ring again. I actually raised my hand to do just that, but of course, I couldn't. Instead I thumbed the 'accept' tab and raised it to my ear.

"Mark?" My voice was a harsh whisper. I heard the sound of heavy breathing that seemed to go on forever. It sounded like someone running. "Mark," I pleaded. "Please son, talk to me. Where are you?" The panting stopped and was replaced by something much worse; weeping. It was Mark's voice. I was sure of it.

"Mark," I tried to say, but the name stuck in my throat. Suddenly I was sobbing, matching Mark breath for breath.

"Why…did….leave…me?" His voice was fading.

"I'm sorry," I said. It was almost impossible to breathe. "Oh dear God I am so sorry!"

"…I…can't…hear..." Those were Mark's last words to me. The line went dead and when I checked the menu, there was no record of his call. I threw it at the couch and fell to the floor, sobbing. I don't know how much time passed, but after a while I stopped crying. I lay there, eyes closed, hearing Marks voice in my mind. *Why did you leave me?* It was a brutal accusation, but after a while I suddenly realized something. My eyes snapped open.

"Wait a minute," I croaked out loud. "I never left you." It was true, of course. When I came home from work on that terrible night, Mark was already in bed. I only abandoned him…

"In my dream," I whispered. It made no sense, and yet, it did. I sat up, thinking hard. I could feel my mind circling a truth…not a fact, but a truth. I think that it's something buried deep in all of us, something that we refuse to acknowledge. It has to do with that border…*barrier*… between asleep and awake. I think that that if we did manage to acknowledge it, it might drive us mad. It's an old truth…an ancient truth.

No, I won't write any more about that. Even here, at its fringe, I can feel the madness pushing at me, trying to get in. For Mark's sake, I can't allow that.

I had to do something, so I got in my car and headed deeper into the neighborhood. I had a rough idea of where the party house might be…the white one, not the blue one. I had never seen it of course, except in my dream, but I knew, or more accurately *felt*, where it might be. It was the illogical logic of dreams, but I was determined to search every street.

At first, it didn't work. There were a lot of decaying white houses, but none of them matched the party house. Night fell and darkness grew thick over the neighborhood. I pulled onto one of the narrow side streets and got out of my car. I reasoned that I had been on foot when I abandoned Mark, so maybe I needed to search on foot. It was a foolhardy thing to do, but I was exhausted and not thinking straight.

I don't think I realized it until I came to the next intersection. I paused at the stop sign and scanned the area. After a few seconds, I discovered a wonderful fact. I was excited. Against all odds, I was getting close. I could feel it. I took another long look at the surrounding houses, and suddenly the dark landscape in my dream began to match up with reality.

Oh my God, it's working, I thought. *I just have to find the way to go deeper in.* I didn't begin to understand what I was thinking and could have cared less. I knew that if I could find the house, either the white one or the blue one, I could find Mark.

"You don't belong here," said a harsh voice. I whirled and came face to face with six dark figures. *I'm a dead man,* I thought. They were young, in their late teens. All of them were bigger than me, and all of them were armed. Four of them had wicked looking knives. The one in front held a sawed off shotgun, while the final gang member held a massive pistol that was pointed straight at my head. "The way is closed," said the young man with the shotgun. "What's ours is ours, and what's his is his. This is ours." He spoke dull, flat English with no trace of an accent or any kind of 'street lingo.'

"Wait," I cried out, holding my hands up. "I just want…"

They rushed me. I turned and ran, but they caught me. What followed was brutal. They took turns. The ones with knives used them with surgical precision, inflicting dozens of shallow, painful cuts on my face, arms, legs and torso. The other two used their fists and feet. In minutes I was a bleeding, broken mess. I sank to the pavement, but 'shotgun boy' grabbed me by the scruff of the neck, yanked me to my feet and held me close. His breath reeked of dead things.

"What's his is his," he said again, "But sometimes he lets us have our fun." He grinned and I think I screamed. For just an instant, I saw something reflected in his eyes. I don't remember what it was. I don't *want* to remember.

I caught a sudden movement off to my left. An instant later, I felt a searing hot pain in my right side as a knife slid between my ribs. Shotgun Boy let me go and I fell forward. Darkness pushed in on me and I started coughing up blood. *I'm sorry Mark,* I thought as the lights went out. Then, just before I lost consciousness, I saw it…the blue house. It was there, just a few lots away. I could see it, but more importantly, I could *sense* the white house hiding behind it. *I'm there,* I thought. *I found it.*

I saw something else as well; tentacles. There were dozens…hundreds…of them, and they were everywhere. Even in my barely conscious state, or perhaps because of it, I could see that they were infesting the neighborhood, straddling the street and winding through each and every house. Some were mere threads. Others were like gigantic pythons, throbbing with some kind of unimaginable power.

Six of them, each the width of a good sized rattlesnake, were running straight to the gang members. I managed to raise my head. The tentacles ended at the base of each gang member's neck. Like their larger kin, they pulsed with some kind of dark obscene power.

My mind grew even darker, and as it did, the blue house shimmered and faded while the white house grew sharper. Behind the white house I sensed the portal. It was closed, but as I watched, it slowly opened. I tried to scream again, but only coughed up more blood. Standing in the opening to that gray land that existed between asleep and awake was a figure that...

No. I won't go there. That barrier between consciousness and unconsciousness exists for a reason, but there is something that lurks beyond that barrier that does not belong there. It is real. It is vile. It is beyond ancient.

I stared into the portal, past that...invader...that had no right to exist in our world of light, and beyond it I could sense the countless screams of terror of children who had been dragged into the darkness.

And one of those screams belonged to my son.

I reached out a hand, as if somehow I could reach into the portal and drag Mark back into my world, but that obscene creature blocked my feeble effort.

MINE. That single word blew past my fading senses, shattered my will and drove deep into my soul.

MINE. I could feel my last spark of life being crushed out of existence. The voice behind that word spoke of a power that existed before our universe was born.

MINE. The third time it spoke to me, I was given a vision. It was not given out of kindness or compassion. That lurker in the portal knew nothing about such concepts. It was given as a warning.

A timeless war fought over billions of eons. Countless universes born, only to be shattered into oblivion by this war. Another and another, the cycle of unimaginable destruction repeated over and over, until at last a victor emerged. The vanquished scattered, hiding from their conquerors within a brand new universe, nursing their strength. They needed sustenance, and one of them discovered our children. It found that it could reach through their dreams and drag them into a place where it could feast off of their life energy.

I saw a web of portals that stretched throughout time and space, linking not only our dreams but the dreams of billions of other races on billions of other worlds. I understood that the thing at the portal was at the center of it all, a bloated spider, feeding, growing stronger and stronger.

MINE. For the final time it spoke, this rapist of dreams. I could feel my very essence being compressed into a tiny, fading spark, soon to be extinguished. Then the vision faded. The portal disappeared, along with the white house. I was back on the street, surrounded by the gang. Sanding above me, Shotgun boy grinned again.

"What's his is his, and what's ours is ours." I thought of the tentacle burrowing into the back of his neck and understood just how wrong he was.

"You're…all…his," I managed to croak. Then a booted foot smashed against my face. My last thought was a rerun. *I am a dead man.*

As it turned out, I was wrong. Someone called the police. They were on scene in two minutes. The paramedics arrived almost at the same time.

The gang fled, melting into the neighborhood. I was rushed to the nearest hospital. After six hours of emergency surgery, I stabilized. The knife thrust had not been fatal, and while the cuts were plentiful, they were not life threatening. I spent a day and a night in intensive care, another day in recovery and the next five days in a semi-private room, thanks to the fact that my insurance was still in effect. Yesterday I was discharged. The doctors all say that I'm lucky to be alive. I can't argue the point, but it's irrelevant

I know where Mark is, and I'm going to get him.

There's so much I don't understand, like godlike beings fighting an ancient war or one lone soldier feeding off our dreams. There is one thing I do understand; one single, devastating fact. I don't know why, but the creature that took Mark did not come through my son's dream, it came through *mine*. Which means it's my fault. If I had not abandoned him in the dream, he would be with me today. Insane? Maybe, but it's the truth.

Here's another truth. Mark is still out there. Maybe he's managed to somehow stay free. I don't know that...my phone has been silent...but I have to hope. It's all I've got.

It's late now, well past midnight. It's still agony to move. I'm not even close to full strength, but I don't care. I'm going out again.

A moment ago, I peeked through my bedroom window. The street was quiet and the houses were dark. The single streetlight painted everything in harsh, amber tones. All seemed normal, but then I let my eyes defocus and wander. The neighbor's hedge rustled in a certain way, and the oak tree in my yard creaked and bent. In my mind, I saw tentacles. I shuddered at the idea that they may very well be infesting my home.

What's his is his. I don't know why *he* chose this God-forsaken neighborhood, but I am certain that he's watching me, waiting for me to make another try for Mark.

I'm not going to disappoint him. That vision, I'm certain, came from him...his way of telling me that getting my son back was futile. I don't care. Tonight I'm heading deep into the neighborhood. I'm going to keep prodding and poking. That barrier is old. Maybe the portal isn't the only way in. Maybe there is a crack somewhere that I can squeeze through.

Also, whatever it is that took Mark is old beyond old, and more often than not, the old are also frail, even senile. A fool's hope? Maybe, but it's all I have. If I can find a way in, then maybe I'll have a chance. If not, well, at least I'll know that I tried. I won't abandon Mark...never again.

I can't think of anything else. I'm going to e-mail this document to Detective Davis. I have no doubt that he'll have a bed ready for me next to Jenny as soon as he reads it. It doesn't matter. If I can bring Mark out, all will be forgiven. If not, then I won't be coming back.

Something rustles outside my window. Maybe it's a stray cat, but I don't think so. I'm out of time.

I love you Jenny. I always have, and I always will.

Hang on Mark. I'm coming.

* * *

Memo: To Captain Rachel Ferguson
From: Det. William Davis
RE: Case MP-TPA-1104, Grant, Mark
Boss:

Here's a copy of Steven Grant's e-mail. According to the time stamp, it was sent just hours before his disappearance yesterday. Forensics has confirmed that it was sent from his computer. As you can see, he is deeply disturbed.

I am now certain that Grant was responsible for the disappearance of his son, Mark. We've distributed his picture to every local and federal agency, so I doubt he'll be able to elude us for long. As for his son, well, I've got a bad feeling that if we ever do find him, it will be in a shallow grave in an abandoned lot somewhere in his neighborhood.

On a personal note, I take full responsibility for Steve Grant's disappearance. I didn't think he had the guts to run. If you let me keep the case, I won't rest until I find this bastard. You've got my word on that.

Bill.

Collector of Ghosts
Jon O'Bergh

In an overlooked corner of the antique shop sat the oblong box, gathering dust. Swirling geometric designs of inlaid wood and mother-of-pearl decorated the lid. Its size suggested the overbearing parent of a jewelry box, with precious heirlooms hidden within. Yumiko spotted the box first, and her voice dropped to a reverent hush. "Bethany. Look at this."

Bethany ambled over and gasped as she lifted the lid. The compartments contained a game board, two sets of cards, a pair of hexagonal dice, and six game pieces in the shape of skulls. She unfolded the game to reveal the checkerboard floor plan of a grand Victorian house. Bold, old-fashioned letters with hooks and swirls spelled out *The Mansion*. "From the style of the drawings, I'd guess this is over a hundred years old," she said. "Possibly from the late eighteen-hundreds." She picked up one of the game pieces, then another, studying their detail. Each skull looked hand-crafted from different materials: silver, cinnabar, ivory, gold, obsidian, and bronze. "We've got to buy this."

Yumiko nodded. "How much is it?"

Bethany turned the box around and located a white sticker scrawled with the price. "Thirty-five dollars. Oh my God! That's a steal. I wonder why it's so cheap."

"Don't ask, or the owner will probably say he marked the wrong price." Yumiko looked through the two sets of cards, admiring the florid patterns that framed the edges. Those marked with the word *token* on the back depicted items representing each room. The other set, with the label *draw*, contained a variety of instructions. "It's still in remarkable condition, as if it didn't get played much."

"Arjun will appreciate this since he's studying game theory. I think Josh would get a kick out of it, too. He might even want to turn it into a game app." Her voice grew excited and breathy. "We can invite them over to play the game with us this weekend. What do you think?"

Yumiko nodded, though not because she agreed. She felt ambivalent about Josh, with his pushy braggadocio. The first time they met, freshman year of college, his way of speaking instantly grated on her. Especially how he sprinkled sentences with "bro," even when addressing Yumiko or Bethany. But she kept her impression to herself for the sake of harmony with her roommate.

The shop owner rang up the purchase, oblivious to any discrepancy between the item's real value and the number on the white sticker. The two women pooled their cash and handed it to him, holding their breath lest he decide to change his mind about the price.

Friday night, the four friends gathered at the apartment of Yumiko and Bethany. When Yumiko opened the door, Josh strutted past her and blurted out, "Let's see this game you're so excited about."

"We'll get to that in a bit," said Bethany. "But first, what would everyone like to drink?"

As she attended to the requests, Josh sprawled on the sofa, his arms spread across the sofa's back like a raptor in flight. "Man, what a rough week. I bombed the Lit quiz." He laughed off the failure.

Yumiko kneeled on the other side of the coffee table, facing him. "You need to take your classes more seriously."

"I take them seriously," he squawked.

"I mean besides the gaming classes."

Arjun remained standing. Yumiko could tell he was deliberating where to sit without impinging on Josh's appropriation of the entire sofa. Finally, he sat in the chair to her left. His long legs chevroned against the table while his thin arms dangled over the armrests. He reminded Yumiko of a daddy-long-legs, that awkward but beneficent insect that would sometimes get stuck flying around her bedroom, and how she would always have to help it find its way outside.

"You didn't come to our study group session." She tried not to sound judgmental, but could not look Josh in the eye.

He waved away her observation. "Yeah, I know. I was busy, bro."

Right—busy playing Warcraft, she thought. She glanced at Arjun, but his face betrayed no hint to validate her suspicion. She laid out the game board on the coffee table.

Arjun leaned forward to examine the board. "Wow! This is really impressive. I like how the walls of each room are drawn to give a three-dimensional perspective, like you're actually looking down from above."

"I thought you'd appreciate it," said Bethany as she brought over the beverages.

Josh grabbed the box and read aloud the rules painted on the underside of the lid. The object of the game was to acquire a Token card from each room by landing on a Token square, then be the first player to exit the mansion through the front entry or back porch. While doing so, the players needed to avoid ghosts that manifested via the Draw squares. The ghosts could help or hinder the player, depending on the Draw card's directions.

Arjun picked up one of the dice. "These are unique." He turned it around, looking at the numbers inscribed on each facet. "Traditionally, dice have been designed using Platonic principles that describe the ideal number of sides of a three-dimensional object. So that would be four, six, eight, or twelve sides. But these have fourteen. Very unusual. Each number one through seven appears twice."

"Seven is a lucky number in Japan," Yumiko said, trying to be optimistic.

Arjun nodded. "Yeah, it's lucky in many cultures. But the seventh month in China is also known as the ghost month. And fourteen is considered unlucky because the Chinese word for *four* sounds similar to the word for *death*."

Josh laughed, tossing aside the box. "So that's why there's no fourth or fourteenth floor in my building. And no thirteenth floor. Just more stupid superstitions, bro."

"Stupid? You think so?" Yumiko did not consider herself to be superstitious, but thought about her mother's obsession with propitious signs. Growing up in a household where certain actions were considered auspicious or inauspicious meant that a current of unease ran through her whenever she ignored her mother's admonitions. "You're telling me you wouldn't be even slightly reluctant to live on the thirteenth floor?"

"Nah. It's just a number. Besides, you can call the thirteenth floor whatever you like, but it doesn't change the fact that it's still the thirteenth level. Same goes for four and fourteen. Skipping the number doesn't really accomplish anything."

"I don't think it's a matter of the number as an abstract concept in a sequence," Yumiko said, remembering how the Japanese word *shi* meant both *four* and *death*, similar to Chinese. "It's more a certain quality of the number, its associations—what we think about when we say the word." She turned toward Arjun. "What do you think?"

"Numbers have many interesting properties, but luck isn't one of them."

"Perfectly logical answers," said Bethany. "Exactly what I'd expect from Mr. Game App and Mr. Game Theory."

Arjun clasped his hands together across his belly. "And what's wrong with logic?"

The question fired Yumiko's passion, and she jumped in before Bethany could answer. "Nothing.

But it can lead to rather unsavory outcomes if not tempered with heart."

He pursed his lips, pondering the statement, then smiled. "Okay, I'll accept the logic of that premise." He raised the die close to his eyes. "Looks like it might be carved from bone."

"Ooh, spooky," said Josh with exaggerated sarcasm while his hands quivered in the air. "I hope it's not—*human* bone."

Yumiko looked away, trying to hide her impatience with his irritating humor. The laughter of the others sounded to her more a polite response than genuine amusement. She wondered why Bethany seemed to tolerate Josh so much better than she did. She watched Bethany sitting beside him on the sofa, leaning slightly in his direction. With his legs and arms splayed, he exuded a relaxed confidence that evidently some women found attractive. But to Yumiko it just looked sloppy. Not like Arjun, folded up uncomfortably in his chair, which she thought endearing.

Bethany had never admitted as such, but perhaps she was attracted to Josh. That could explain why she seemed to overlook his many faults. Bethany normally came off as less tolerant than Yumiko, a fiery spirit who could change her judgment about someone in an instant if she felt slighted.

The friends selected their pieces and placed them in the Vestibule according to the instructions. Josh rolled the highest number, giving him the first turn, and pumped his fist in the air with a triumphant "Yes!" After rolling again, he moved the obsidian skull forward and announced that he was heading to the Kitchen.

Bethany shook her head in mock displeasure. "Typical. Always looking for something to eat."

Yumiko rolled next, and advanced her cinnabar skull into the Music Room. She shouted in delight when she landed on a Token square. "Okay, first player to capture a token."

Bethany chanted, "Go Yumiko, go Yumiko."

Arjun rolled fourteen. "All right, high number." His silver skull landed on a Draw square, so he picked the top card from the pile. "*Advance directly into the Vault and take a Vault token.* Cool."

Josh peered at the Vault's perimeter of solid black lines and snickered. "Yeah, but the only other way in or out of the Vault is to roll doubles like snake eyes. Through here." He pointed to a secret passageway leading from the Ballroom. "Looks like you might be stuck in there a long time, bro."

"Maybe. But you'll all have to come in sooner or later to get a token."

Bethany's gold skull followed Yumiko's trail through the Music Room and into the Dining Room. Josh rolled an eight, moving forward seven spaces into the Kitchen before reversing direction to land on a Token square. Yumiko groaned and accused him of cheating.

"There's nothing in the instructions that say you can't reverse direction during a move," he argued.

Yumiko continued to protest, but Arjun jumped in to support Josh's reasoning. She shrugged. "Okay, then, if we can be flexible with our interpretations, don't complain if I try something outside the box later." The dice rattled in her fist. "This sound reminds me of the xylophone part when I played first violin in *Danse Macabre*. Did you know that Saint-Saëns used the xylophone to suggest the sound of skeletons dancing?"

Josh crossed his arms. "Roll the dice already."

Yumiko shot him an angry look as she threw the dice. They clattered across the board, coming to rest to display a seven and a six. The number thirteen. Yumiko felt the same tingling unease that came when she approached a ladder on a sidewalk or woke up on Friday the thirteenth. The light in the room started to dim.

"What's happening?" said Bethany.

Arjun slumped back on the sofa. "I feel strange."

Yumiko rushed to the light switch, but flipping it repeatedly had no effect. The light continued to drain away. There should have been street light spilling in through the window, but Yumiko found herself engulfed in blackness. "Are you guys still there?" She heard Bethany's voice nearby. Then, from somewhere distant, came Josh's reply. She called out for Arjun. Silence.

The sudden flaring of light startled her. But the unfamiliar surroundings, lit by the gas flames of a chandelier hanging above a dining table, startled her even more.

Bethany stood on the other side of the table, mirroring Yumiko's panic. She grabbed the back of a chair. "Where the hell are we?"

"I think we're—" Yumiko halted, stunned to consider the possibility. "I think we're in the mansion."

"How can that be?"

Yumiko opened her mouth as if to answer, but could only shake her head. She looked down, somehow feeling responsible for their predicament. She realized it was an irrational reaction, yet she was the one who had rolled the number. She was the one who had discovered the box in the antique store. "I'm so sorry. If I hadn't rolled a thirteen..."

"It's not your fault. One of us would have rolled a thirteen sooner or later. It must be like a portal to another dimension."

Josh entered the room, drawn by their voices. "I was in the Kitchen, just like in the game."

"I can't believe this is happening," said Yumiko. "Where is Arjun?"

Josh scratched the back of his neck and frowned. "He must be stuck in the Vault."

Yumiko let out a cry as she spotted a skeleton in the corner. Clothed in the dusty remnants of a dark plum-colored Victorian dress, it slouched with its back against the wall, legs outstretched across the floor. Bony hands emerged from lace sleeves. Tufts of hair had come loose from the once stylish pompadour, lending the skull a deranged look. Yumiko ran over to clutch Bethany's arm as Josh approached the skeleton and kicked at its hips.

"Don't!" shouted Bethany.

"Why not? She's obviously been dead a long time." The skeleton collapsed sideways onto the floor.

Yumiko turned away, still clutching Bethany's arm.

Josh nodded toward the bricked-up windows. "No exit through there. I bet we'll find the front and back doors bricked up the same way." He thought for a moment. "We need tokens."

"What?" asked Bethany.

"Tokens. Like in the game. That must be the only way we can get out of here."

Yumiko let go of Bethany's arm and picked up a plate.

"Get something easier to carry," said Bethany, reaching for the silverware. "Like this spoon."

Yumiko set the plate down and chose a teaspoon. "So what happens when we've collected something from every room?"

Josh and Bethany glanced at one another, their fearful looks conveying a simultaneous realization. Josh spoke first, pointing to the skeleton. "Only one of us gets to leave. Whoever collects all of the tokens first."

Yumiko shook her head. "No, there must be another way."

"It's in the rules, bro." He grabbed a knife and clutched it in his fist like a weapon.

"So what are you going to do?" asked Yumiko. "Race off by yourself to each of the rooms?"

Josh gazed at the knife in his hand, unable to look either woman in the eye. "I don't see any other way."

"What about Arjun?" asked Bethany.

"You'll waste time trying to find a way into the Vault. Who knows if it's even possible." He took a deep breath that lifted his chest. "Okay, then, I'm going on to the other rooms."

Yumiko slammed her hands on the table, making the dishes and silverware rattle. "I can't believe you would be so callous. There must be a way to work together to get out of here."

Josh sneered. "Sorry, but there can only be one winner in a game."

Yumiko's mind raced. An image came to her, and she saw herself playing in the orchestra, each instrument weaving its part to create a unified tapestry of sound. "What if...What if we held hands once we collected all the tokens, as if we were a single organism?"

Josh pocketed his knife. "And if it doesn't work?"

"Then we can draw straws, or...or something."

Josh headed toward the door. "Go ahead, if you want. I'm going to do it my way."

"Bastard," Bethany spit out, glaring at him as he left. She turned back to Yumiko. "Now what?"

"Let's try to find Arjun. If the layout here is the same as the game, there should be a hidden passageway that connects the Vault to the Ballroom."

They passed through the Main Hall, pausing to grab a small silver tray sitting atop a credenza. Yumiko slipped the teaspoon in her pocket, but anxiety made her grip the tray so tightly her fingers began to ache. She had seen such a tray once in a movie—a period drama. A butler had held it out to collect a visitor's calling card. She could not imagine anyone coming to call here. Who could have built this monstrosity, and for what purpose? The horror of their predicament made her fearful, and she could not dispel the guilt that somehow she was responsible. She still seethed, too, at Josh's decision to strike out on his own. Then again, his selfishness shouldn't have surprised her. He had always been something of a jerk. It would be hard to forgive him. *If we get out of here alive*, she thought as she spied another skeletal body slumped in the far corner, clutching a bowl filled with tokens.

Unlike the well-furnished Dining Room, the Ballroom sat largely empty, just a few chairs scattered along the perimeter and a flock of music stands in the corner, clustered like flamingoes. The women's voices echoed as they called Arjun's name and felt their way along the wall, pressing on the wood. Yumiko was certain a secret passage lay on the other side, if only they could figure out how to access it. She scrutinized the edges of the wood panels for evidence of a thin gap that might signify a hidden door. She listened for changes in the sound of their knocks that would indicate a hollow space. All the while, she was aware that they were losing time. Josh would be collecting more tokens. Soon he would have all he needed. The thought made her pulse quicken.

At last, Bethany pushed on one coffered panel that clicked open to reveal a cubbyhole. She reached in and pulled a large white knob, which swung open a portion of the wall beside her. Only a bit of light from the Ballroom's flickering gas sconces penetrated the dark corridor.

"One of us should stay out here just in case," said Bethany. "I'll go in to find Arjun." She entered the narrow passage and disappeared into the gloom, calling his name.

Yumiko felt something brush against her thigh and jumped to the side. Looking around, however, she saw nothing. Then it touched her face. She brushed the air to clear away what felt like a cobweb, too distracted to notice the teaspoon edging out of her pocket until it struck the floor with a clatter. As she stooped to pick it up, it slid several feet away from her. She took a few steps toward it, and it slid toward the door. She tried a third time, watching with frustration as it reached the threshold. Determined not to abandon her post to chase it further, she rested her fists on her hips, one hand still gripping the little tray. "Whoever or whatever you are, I know what you're trying to do. Don't think you can play me."

A chair catapulted across the room, making her flinch as it crashed into the wall beside her. She spun around and saw the heavy brocade draperies rustle. A bone-white, emaciated hand emerged from behind one drape and grasped the fabric. Yumiko gasped and clutched the tray to her breast. She trembled, imaging what horrible face might match the hand and appear next. But the sound of Bethany and Arjun emerging from the passageway caused the hand to withdraw.

Bethany held up some coins. "Look, tokens from the Vault. I told Arjun about our plan."

"Good." Yumiko noticed that her teaspoon had vanished from the doorway. "I hope you still have your spoon, though, because a poltergeist seems to have stolen mine."

Bethany felt her pocket. "Yeah, still there."

"Whatever spirits are in this room are getting upset. One of them threw a chair at me. Another one's hiding behind that curtain. So we should grab a token and get out of here as fast as possible."

Arjun gestured toward the music stands. "We can take some of that sheet music before we move on." He approached the stands, but as he reached for one sheet, all of the music scattered, tossed into the air by an invisible hand. Arjun tried to grab a couple of pages as they floated toward the floor, but something snatched them out of his reach. Bethany ran up behind him and put her foot on a sheet that had settled on the floor, then bent down to retrieve it before it could be snatched away. In one swift motion, synchronized like a herd fleeing a predator, the three friends ran out of the Ballroom.

In the neighboring Parlor, they found more skeletons. Someone had tried to break through the wall, but solid stone blocked the other side of the hole. Chinks dotted the stone, evidently from the fireplace poker that lay abandoned a few steps away. Whoever had attempted to escape had made little progress, the effort ending in futility. The building was entombed.

A moan rose from behind the sofa. Yumiko froze, still spooked by what had happened in the Ballroom, but the two others moved forward to investigate. Arjun reached the teenager first and helped him sit up. "How long have you been here?"

The boy's eyes fluttered open. "I don't know." His voice was weak, almost a whisper.

Bethany kneeled beside him. "What's your name?"

"David."

They helped David stand. He wore an Alice Cooper T-shirt and cut-off jeans that ended just above his knees. Bethany asked how he had become trapped in the mansion.

"I was playing a haunted house game with my friends, just like this place. We were transported here when I rolled a thirteen."

Yumiko nodded. "Just like what happened to us. Where are the others?"

"Evan made it out. But he left Tim and me behind." David hung his head and wiped a tear with the heel of his hand. "Tim's dead."

Bethany put her arm around his shoulders. "We'll help you get out."

He looked up at her. "How?"

"We're collecting tokens together. We have a plan. Do you feel strong enough to walk with us from room to room?" David nodded. "Good. Then let's get our token from here and move on."

The group found more bodies in the Library in various stages of decomposition. One couple huddled in the corner, holding each other, their faces mummified with the mouths open in a silent scream. A woman in a skinny, beaded flapper dress and pearls had expired sitting in an armchair, looking as if she were still waiting for the party to begin. The room presented a gruesome history of twentieth century fashion. Arjun grabbed a bookmark and they hurried out.

When they reached the Music Room, they encountered Josh with a tureen under one arm. He offered a half-hearted smile. "Oh. I see you found Arjun."

Bethany glared. "Yeah, we got him out of the Vault, no thanks to you." David emerged from behind the three others. Seeing Josh's surprise, Bethany explained, "This is David. He ended up trapped here while playing the game, like us."

Josh placed a dollhouse-sized piano into the tureen. "He'll just slow you down. Look how weak he is."

"Maybe." Bethany held up one of the coins. "But you still have to find your way into the Vault by yourself, where there's no light, to get one of these. Good luck with that."

Josh looked from one friend to another, taking in their displeasure. "Well, then, I guess I should get on it." A tight smile flitted over his face, vanishing before it had time to set. "Only four rooms to go."

"I ought to slug you," said Arjun. "But it's not worth the effort."

Rather than attempt to pass through the impromptu blockade, Josh exited via the side door through the Dining Room. Yumiko heard his footsteps quicken on the hardwood floor as he left the Dining Room and scurried down the hall.

Bethany frowned. "We should try to stop him. What if he collects all the tokens first?"

"He won't," said David. "Trust me."

Arjun organized the team, dividing up the remaining rooms. "Yumiko and David, Kitchen complex. Bethany, can you handle the two rooms by the back porch? Good. I'll go to the Conservatory. Meet back in the Main Hall as quickly as possible."

They dispersed for their missions. Yumiko sent David into the Pantry while she collected an item from the Kitchen. One room to go. She opened the door of the Storage Room. Unlike the other rooms, this one offered no illumination, which unsettled her. She instinctively groped for a light switch before realizing the house lacked electricity, and laughed to herself at such a reflexive habit. But the silent laugh did little to conquer her dread. Something stirred in the corner, crouching amidst the supplies. The head craned upward to look at her. In the dim light, she could just make out wrinkled skin stretched taut across the skull, and a nose eaten away to bone. Two coal-like embers smoldered in the eye sockets. Disheveled hair fell alongside what remained of the face. The ghoul began rapidly clicking its teeth.

Yumiko hesitated, uncertain how to get past the creature. Yet there was no other option. She took a tentative step forward. The creature stood, raising its hands to reveal fingernails sharpened to points. Yumiko took another step, and the ghoul rushed toward her. She screamed and ducked to the floor, forcing her shoulder into the ghoul's shins, which sent it tumbling over her. As she jumped back up, she noticed beside her a mop standing in a bucket. The ghoul clambered back to its feet and now stood blocking the doorway.

Yumiko wielded the two cleaning items like a sword and shield as she advanced. She thrust the mop into the ghoul's chest, pushing the creature into the Kitchen. It grabbed hold of the handle and tried to swing her around. But she let go and charged with the bucket. David ran into the room, drawn by her scream, and picked up a rolling pin. Together they attacked the ghoul's head until the skull snapped off and flew across the room. The body collapsed with a brittle xylophone flourish as the bones hit the tile floor. Without pausing to catch their breath, Yumiko and David scampered out of the room.

Back in the Main Hall, Arjun gestured to follow him to the Vestibule, but Yumiko grabbed his arm. "Wait. We should get Josh, if he hasn't already left."

Bethany grumbled. "The one who was so quick to abandon us?"

"Look, I never really cared for him, but I won't let myself fall prey to the same lack of compassion that makes me dislike him."

Arjun considered the logic of Yumiko's remark. "No, Yumiko's right. He may have made a pretty selfish decision, but he's still our friend. He'll probably have made it into the Vault by now."

Arjun led them to the Ballroom. The secret door remained ajar. "Josh," he called out, "you in there?"

A faint reply seeped out from deep within the dark space. "Yeah, I'm here. I'm trying to find some coins."

David stepped up to the cubbyhole. Reaching inside, he pushed the knob, and the door swung shut.

"What are you doing?" cried Yumiko.

David's arm dropped back to his side. "It was 1972 when my friends and I found the game and started to play."

"Wait, what? If you were a teenager in 1972, then..." Yumiko's sentence died as she understood his meaning.

David shut the small panel of the cubbyhole. "If someone is to win, then someone has to lose. Someone always has to stay behind. Those are the rules."

"This is madness," said Bethany.

David handed over his Pantry token. "I was going to steal your tokens, but you were kind to me. Hurry, though. You don't have much time to escape before the other ghosts try to keep you here. We're always looking for more company."

The three friends hastened to the Vestibule, with David trailing behind, then joined hands as Yumiko placed her free hand on the front doorknob. "I hope this works." The floor trembled slightly, releasing a fine rain of dust from the ceiling. Yumiko looked one last time at the boy, a wistful expression on his face as he stood beneath the archway that led into the hall. "Goodbye, David. And thank you."

The gas flames went out, followed by absolute silence. Moments later, the light began to return. Yumiko heard the chirping of a bird and the hum of a refrigerator grow louder. She relaxed, realizing her plan had worked. They found themselves back in the apartment. But the box and the game had vanished.

"I'd like to burn that box so no one else ever has to experience the horror," said Bethany. "That game is demonic."

Yumiko looked down at the floor. "I feel terrible leaving Josh behind. Even after what he did." The thought of him trapped in the dark Vault, slowly starving to death, made her shudder.

"There's a reason we made it out and he didn't," said Arjun. But Yumiko could see how unsatisfied he felt with that logic.

Bethany just shrugged. "He revealed his true nature. I don't feel bad about it one bit."

***

The following day, the friends visited the antique shop to find out if the owner knew anything about the strange game.

"Do you remember where you got it, or who brought it in?" asked Yumiko. "Anything at all?"

The proprietor shook his head. "I can't even remember how long I had it. I buy and sell so many things."

Yumiko looked defeated. Bethany asked for a pen and scribbled out her phone number. "Listen, if you recall any clue, no matter how insignificant it seems, please give me a call. It's really important."

Once the friends had left, the shopkeeper reached below the counter and withdrew an oblong box, hand-decorated with geometric designs in bone, shell, walnut, cherry, and ash. In a few days he intended to place it back on the floor among the other antiques, tucked away in a secluded corner to await discovery by someone new. He caressed the lid and, with a grin, said, "That makes one more ghost for the collection."

The Dancing Dead
Dustin Chisam

It was a perfectly lovely church. As was the cemetery it overlooked. The wrought iron fence enclosing the property was a uniform black, not a bit of its sheen giving way to rust. The grass was perfectly cut, the trees trimmed and fallen branches quickly cleared away. It was pristine *and* serene.

Cemeteries were monuments. Consolation, reassurance that departed loved ones are never too far. So knowing this, it's easy to see the serene expanses of grass and stones as beauty. Some might even go so far as to say that to think of them as frightening is to misunderstand. That to imagine them as they are in gothic horror movies—tilted markers overgrown with gnarling yellow weeds, with a fog rolling in through a rusty gate hanging off a hinge—is missing the point. As fun as it may be to creep one's self out, cemeteries are a place of comfort. Amy certainly thought that one should respect this solemn perspective out of respect for fellow mourners. Too bad her three companions patronized the boneyard for more ghoulish reasons.

"They say this is one of seven gateways to hell here on Earth," Freddy intoned. He was a human ham hock, burly and deliberate in his movements. "And that on Halloween night, Satan himself visits the grave of a child he had with a witch who's also buried here."

Andy shuddered, his baggy shirt rippling over his tiny frame as he did so. "Why'd you have to tell me that now?" But while he was the most skittish of the group, the glee on his face was still obvious.

Kelley was like another Freddy—round and solid, but half a head taller and a ruddy ginger as opposed to Freddy's dark hair. "So you haven't heard about the werewolf in the trees, I take it?"

Amy rolled her eyes. They were Freddy's friends, and when she and Freddy had split for a few months, she hadn't kept up with them, either. Now she stood at the gate of Spring Grove Cemetery on the night of All Hallows', one of her favorite holidays. As much as she would enjoy this any other night, now she was kicking herself for letting Freddy talk her into this. There were parties to go to, attractions to patron. But all this beautiful graveyard could make her think was that she wished her aunts Elsa and Millie could have been buried in half as nice a place. At least if it looked a little more Tim Burton-esque she might be feeling it a little more.

Freddy had exchanged favor after favor to get a set of keys to a cemetery that had more urban legends about it than the last 3 US presidencies. All in the name of being able to go legend-tripping on Halloween night and having it all to himself.

"Oh, did you see that, Fred? Amy rolled her eyes. What's the matter, are you not a believer? Are we gonna have to fight?"

Amy chose her words a little carefully; she was sure she didn't imagine that particular joke of Kelley's seemed a little sincerer this time: "Sure I believe. It's just that these stories are so crazy that I'm willing to bet it's *all* made up."

"Oh, so you'd be more on board if there was just, like, one murder in its whole entire history?" Kelley chortled.

"Maybe if they'd just put in a bunch of security cameras they'd have proved all the legends a long time ago," Freddy shrugged. "Anyway, their loss. We're the ones who'll be famous after tonight, not them." That wasn't the first time he had shown that strange certainty about how this expedition was going to unfold.

A single click of the hefty padlock, and a barely audible squeak of hinges, and they were in. Freddy closed it behind them, locking it, killing the promise of any cooler plans for the night of Samhain.

"So anyone who wants to pay their respects to any family here are S.O.L.?" Amy asked, amused.

"Yup," Freddy replied as he rattled the chain, waiting for the clatter to subside. "Too many looky-loos who didn't want to go through official channels. All they needed to do is slip the weird ass caretaker a hundred spot after plying him with a few drinks."

Ghost hunting had long been one of their favorite hobbies. Freddy had a keen sense of sussing out what was needed for every location—be it a public place, a private property, he knew what to do. He knew when to ask permission, negotiate the details with the owners, or just skip to trespassing. But getting the keys and being allowed to enter unsupervised—he had outdone himself this time.

Spring Grove was almost perfectly designed, if you were of the ghost hunting mindset. A winding road that led up to a small two story church at the top of the hill, surrounded by neatly polished, gleaming headstones. Amy was surprised at the number of statues and sculptures that she had only seen in more fanciful depictions of cemeteries—most of those completely fictional. She said as much.

"Yeah, there used to be a bunch of rich people, who were usually from Chicago, who were buried here up to the 20s," Freddy explained. "The stock market crash brought that to a halt. But… services continued up there another 15 years." And Freddy nodded up at the church.

It was an old stone building. Amy was raised Catholic, and was used to attending mass in more cavernous houses of worship. The first time she had ever attended a service in a tinier Protestant church, it had come as something of a shock. But looking at Spring Grove's tiny, ancient church, the antiquity seemed to add a sense of majesty to it equal to any of the giant Catholic churches she had attended. It seemed to almost be a natural formation of the earth with the barest of modifications to make it a symbol of holy ground. All in a building barely bigger than the smallest of two bedroom houses.

"Should I do it?" Andy cut into her thoughts, pulling an empty beer bottle from his backpack, and assuming a throwing stance.

"Yeah! Just don't shit your pants when it doesn't break, or I am *planting* your ass in the trunk for the ride home!" Kelley urged.

While Andy seemed to be trying to work up the courage to throw it against the wall of the church, Freddy leaned over to Amy:

"Supposedly a glass bottle won't break no matter how hard you throw it against the wall," he explained. Finally, after a few more seconds of shifting his weight from foot to foot, Andy threw the bottle. He was no major leaguer, or even a Little League rookie, and after spinning a dozen times, it *clanked* against the ancient stone, and landed in the grass, whole and unmarred. Andy looked at the others with an expression that was a strange mélange of terror and glee.

"Movies used unfired or sugar glass when they break stuff," Kelley shrugged. "It is *really* fucking hard to break a bottle compared to in the movies."

"Well, I can try again later," Andy shrugged.

"No, you can't," Freddy said. Despite his jovial tone, there was the hint of warning in it. If Andy caught it, he maintained a casual air.

The keys jangled, sounding melodic as they sang a plea for entry. The largest key, one that looked fit to lock a dungeon beneath an ancient keep, was slowly inserted into the lock that seemed just as antiquated. Whereas everything else about the cemetery seemed shiny and new, everything about the old church seemed to shout to the heavens its contrast. And true enough, the well-oiled gate was far more well cared for than the enormous wooden double doors of the church as they didn't so much as creak as they *roared.*

"That is the mother of all creaking doors. We should record it and sell it to a movie studio. We could make it the new stock 'creaking door' sound effect."

And it still had more of that cacophonous groaning to do before one of those heavy double doors was open wide enough to admit them. Her senses told Amy immediately that the interior of the old church was not nearly as well cared for as the cemetery. A dull potpourri of offending odors wafted about—mold, decay, stuffiness, dust—all tickled her nose, one of her least favorite parts of this hobby.

The caretakers had evidently given up on the inside—there was graffiti on the floors and walls, and trash on the floor. Amy noticed that the trash was faded—beer and soda cans, food wrappers—a lot of them had packaging designs she knew were several years old. Most of the graffiti was pop culture occultism—pentagrams, more than a few 666s, and beseeches to the Dark Lord himself. But it was just the stuff moody teenagers who mistook angst for pathos wrote.

"Okay, a nice, tranquil, well cared for cemetery isn't good for the narrative. *Now's* the time to start taking pictures," Freddy announced, pulling his digital camera out of the backpack. Amy still thought of what they did as "legend-tripping," not "ghost hunting." The few pieces of equipment they had only payed lip service to the idea. All in all, this would simply have been an afternoon out that would end up shared in a new album on Freddy's Facebook, nothing more.

Andy pulled out his own "EVP recorder"—or rather, his ordinary tape recorder endorsed by the most popular ghost hunting reality star of the moment and embossed with his name.

"What is your name? How did you die? Do you have a message for us?" The usual list of EVP clichés.

Kelley actually owned a camera with a thermal setting. He almost looked like a serious researcher as he scanned the inside of the church, as he didn't break the silence with a litany of stupid questions.

But it was Freddy whose actions were a hard right from their usual ghost hunting routine. He had pulled an ancient 3 ring binder from his book bag—the yellowed plastic creaked and squeaked as he slowly opened it.

Amy, curious, approached the altar. Freddy was standing on the other side of the pulpit from her, facing the ruin that once seated a small but devout congregation. And in Amy's eyes, what he did next was a defacement of that legacy. He pulled out a single piece of dark chalk. Or what looked like chalk, because he seemed to be able to write as easily on the wax surface of the candle as he did the marble altar.

On he drew, covering the cross with arcane and occultish symbols, and when he reached the base, on he drew. The strange, unidentifiable symbols seemed to lead to and up the sides of the cross like circuits. One single candle holder was the only other thing on the altar, and Freddy placed a single small wax candle from his bag into it. The last symbols he drew seemed to twist around the candle holder on the cold marble. Double checking the symbols, he closed the binder and stuffed it back into his bag, saving the lighting of the candle for last.

"Okay. Time to go. We have until the candle burns out," Freddy said, leading the march to the back of the church. Andy and Kelley quickly fell in behind him. Amy knew when he was withholding for dramatic effect and knew it would be useless to ask for answers. So she followed, if not as eagerly as the two minions.

The back door, which was in a room that the years had stripped of all of its former context and purpose, was just as heavy as the front. Amy looked at the spiral stairs to their left and longed to climb to the bell tower, as crowded as it would be. But that wasn't what Freddy was interested in. They took a sharp right after descending a tiny, rickety porch, and came across a cellar that looked like so many one would expect to find in Tornado Alley

"Okay, the cellar, just like the maintenance guy said." Amy saw the alarmed looks that Andy and Kelley weren't clever enough to completely conceal. It was only when Freddy popped the hatch and went in first that the other two seemed to remember they were his de facto henchmen and followed. Amy sighed, and did the same.

She couldn't see anything except the steps—they seemed to be carved out of the earth, and a stone wall was all that they could see on all sides.

Wham! And instantly, they fell into darkness as the heavy doors slammed shut

"Okay, nobody use any lights. Don't turn around—it's already too late. The only way is forward, now. We're going to link hands and I'll guide us out. Got it?" Freddy seemed to know what to do. And in the silence that followed, Amy knew that Andy and Kelley were hesitating at their dear leader's orders for the first time in their lives.

"Why? W-why c-can't we use any lights?" Andy stammered.

"And who shut the door?" Kelley demanded. "It's *way* too heavy for—"

"What, you think I'd bring you here if I wasn't hoping to see something?" Freddy asked, with that familiar edge in his voice that had led to their breakup. "Link hands! We've got until that candle burns out."

"How big can a cellar be that we have to do this?" Amy said, reluctantly taking hold of Kelley's paw in the blackness.

"*This* cellar? Ehhh…pretty big." Freddy's casualness was—well, at this point Amy was tired of analyzing and sussing out every hidden meaning of her now *ex* (again, though she wasn't going to share that until she got home)-boyfriend's ever more cryptic statements.

They turned seven times. Left, left, right, left, right, right, and left. This had to be a cellar as large as a school auditorium given the length of time between turns. Amy had been to a haunted house once as a child where she and her friend had been wandering around a section that was a pitch black maze for over ten minutes. Some trick that she couldn't recall was used to allow others to escape without those behind them seeing, but they couldn't find it. It got to where a performer from the part just outside had to come in and break character and explain they were in a room no bigger than a large living room before he guided them out. But given the sheer amount of time she rubbed her free hand against the wall between turns, she knew there was some serious distance between turns.

The idea of an enormous basement under a small church wasn't that unsettling until Amy reminded herself that this was a cemetery. Would she rub her free hand against bone jutting from the walls?

But on that last left, she heard climbing footsteps. Again, sneakers on stone. And after listening to the twenty-six steps, she heard another set of cellar doors swing open. But when she followed Freddy, Andy, and Kelley out and looked around, she realized it had been the same steps, the same cellar door…in theory.

If they had succeeded in their little adventure, Amy had imagined a situation where they all saw a single figure floating among the gravestones that they would mistake for another legendtripper, only for this newcomer to slowly fade away—hopefully on film. But what was revealed when they stepped out into the open was so instant and undeniable that it destroyed any of Amy's notions of what was in the other side, and how close it truly was to the world of the living. Freddy slowly led the three back into the church. There were no questions as they walked to the front door—and looked out into the cemetery, as Freddy pointed at them to crouch and keep their heads down when they looked out.

The cemetery had changed. It was every menacing graveyard depicted in films and then some. It was as though a sincere memorial had been slowly corrupted by those buried beneath, their moldering bodies releasing a poison that altered earth and plant. The trees seemed more pointed, jagged, and sharp. The statues less naturalistic in the low light and more exaggerated, and the gravestones larger and also more angular. The corruption and festering of the dead became the corruption and the festering of the earth, plants and markers above. As far as Amy could see, there was only blackness beyond the cemetery gates. And above it all loomed a night sky that glowed a dull red, a featureless shimmering orb in place of the moon.

This is what the post Apocalypse looks like, Amy thought numbly. *A dead world—not destroyed, but a world* for *the dead to trample around like they were* alive again.

"You did it," Kelley said in a quiet, wheezy voice Amy never imagined he could muster.

"W-we...I think we should—" Andy could barely get the words out, he was shaking so bad.

"You know we can't just turn back around," Freddy said quietly. "Get to the windows, and keep your heads and your voices low." They all went to what had been large stained glass windows in the world that they belonged in. Now, only black tracing the formerly ornate patterns and artwork remained, offering an unencumbered view. The men took the right one; seeing this, Amy decided she'd have the left one all to herself.

"You don't want any lights from your cameras alerting anyone," Freddy explained as Andy and Kelley started to point their cameras down at the cemetery below. Sheepishly, they pocketed both of their devices.

Amy's heart was pounding with anticipation. Ghost hunting had been their shared interest, and she was willing to forgive every lie, every shitty thing Freddy had ever done simply for making this moment possible. But she knew this was too easy, knew there was a catch. There would be hundreds of videos like this on YouTube if it was this easy to get proof like this.

"I'm going to trust you all not to scream," Freddy said. "Farmer's Almanac says the sun should have just gone down in the real world." *The real world*...this went well beyond a mere surprise for a night out. This was the kind of thing that merely destroyed the worldview of the unprepared if they were lucky, and their sanity if they weren't.

They ascended—many clawing their way out of their graves, but a few rose, as if they were lighter than air and the dirt was nothing. The earth easily parted for them as the water parted for a dolphin leaping from the oceanic depths.

Decay brought about a conformity to the masses, erasing the line between young and old, the thin and the fat, the rich and the poor. In death, they were almost as one. From this distance, they were as large as the distance between the tips of the thumb and index finger of an outstretched hand held at arm's length. Amy imagined that she saw a few details that differentiated them from the church, but realized their anonymity was key.

Amy's imagination had run wild through it all, and she, who imagined innumerable worlds for herself that she would rather walk in than the one she called home, readily took this all in. In the red glow of this new cemetery.

The large mausoleum in the center of the graveyard was opening, and one more of the dead emerged, filing out in different directions, already knowing their assigned spots.

The last to emerge was taller than the rest, and moved with a languid grace that somehow marked it as whatever passed for a leader here. But instead of a crown, it wore a ragged top hat. But despite this obvious mark of masculine dress, Amy couldn't bring herself to think of the leader as a *him*. *It* was all this wight could ever be to her.

It was a phonograph, the horn seeming to be larger in comparison to the machine than most she had seen pictures of. With a jerk, four legs popped out and embedded themselves in the earth, leaving the phonograph four feet off the ground. And Top Hat did its work, and cranked. It seemed to turn the handle for several minutes before finally stepping away. All at once, the dead cast off the flowing burial shrouds that trailed behind them as an eerie music emanated from the horn.

It was not wholly unpleasant, but there was a promise, a hidden meaning beneath it that was not meant for the living. It might make one's fillings tingle. It would cause birth defects when played to the unborn. It would tell an ill person on the edge that he *should* take his AR-15 to work on Monday morning. It was *wrong*, because Amy and her companions did not belong here.\

Their shuffling gaits gave way to a more fluid (movement), as they finally cast off the seeming facade of rigor mortis, for it was more than blood and muscle that animated them. That unfamiliar tune put a jaunt in their step and dance in their dead hearts.

"You remember reading Goethe in college, Amy?" Freddy whispered as loud as he dared to her. "This is just like one of his poems. *Totentanz*, or 'The Dance of Death.' Maybe Mr. Goethe learned a few of the same tricks I did and survived to write about it."

It was beautiful. Their motions were not perfectly in sync, but their style was. Over the next ten minutes, their movements could be described as ballet, swing, Celtic, and styles whose names and cultures she couldn't begin to guess at. Every change in style was instant and shared among the entire group. And whatever they had been in life, in death their grace and skill kept their heads pointed to the sky only some of the time, so effortless were their flips.

"You know, with all of the different calendars and feasts, how is it that we chose October 31st as the day this sort of thing could happen and be 100% right?" Kelley asked, mercifully remembering to whisper.

"Humans gave the day this significance just because they believed," Freddy whispered. She really wanted to ask him how he knew all this, but knew there wasn't going to be any time, not now and not later.

One shroud blew in the wind. It was obvious that they all would wrap themselves up again before returning to the grave. In this wind, that could actually be the breath of gods or spirits as in the myths of old, it would never go beyond the reach of its owner. Slowly it tumbled and danced toward the church

It was so perfect. The angle was perfect. So entranced were her fellow churchgoers that she easily shot her arm out the window and grabbed it and they never even realized what had just happened. Stuffing the shroud into her jacket pocket, she was feeling immensely proud of herself in that instant.

"We need to get out of here," Amy whispered to the others. The music was still as strange as it ever was, the dead as graceful and energetic as they ever were. The three men were so still as they peered out that Amy wondered if they had been hypnotized. It was only after a few seconds that Andy was able to divert an infinitesimal amount of his attention to her. "While they're distracted," she added.

"Be quiet," he hissed. The chattering teeth of their merry band was entranced just like his buddies.

"No, we have to get out of here right now. We can sneak back down into that magic cellar. I thought you said we had a timetable, with that candle—"

"A timetable and a condition," Freddy whispered. "The living just can't walk in the other side and walk back out like nothin'." The other two tensed at this and looked at each other, as if this was a signal they had been waiting for—and all three crawled under the window and stood when they were past it. Freddy slowly advanced on Amy, pulling a large Rambo knife from his pocket. She knew it was a Rambo knife because he had saved up his allowance for months when he was ten to buy it from an ad in the back of Soldier of Fortune magazine. He hadn't been allowed to actually hold it until he was much older, but it was one of his most treasured possessions. Amy knew this was it, and let him advance.

"I've probably told you how much I don't like being dumped. Kind of an understatement. And I sure as hell hate being dumped by the same bitch twice—yeah, I know what you were thinking. Caretaker told me the story about this place. He believed it, too—that's why I had to get him drunk. Says someone has to stay behind so the others can come back to the real world. Guess who that's going to be?"

They were louder now—like they knew they were protected if they were heard. And Freddy was less than six inches away, looking for some fear in Amy's eyes to give him a little satisfaction. But he could see none, and before he could say something, the other two jumped in.

"You always called me a chickenshit," Andy snapped. "I think going along with this little plan was pretty damn brave, don't you think? I certainly do."

"And you know what? This is what you get for bashing on H.P. Lovecraft all those times." Freddy and Andy gave him a brief look of incredulity. "What? I don't need that big a reason to go along. It was *your* idea."

"So do me a favor, babe. I just wanna see if you're gonna cry. Since you always brag about never ever crying."

"You know what's great about living in a small town?" Amy whispered. Freddy seemed taken aback by the question, and the total lack of fear. "Everyone you meet is probably a mutual friend. Like the cemetery groundskeeper who babysat me when I was little and warned me after you got the secret of this cemetery from him when you lifted his keys. When you said 'I know just the person' to him and thought he'd sleep it off and forget."

Instantly, he was dancing as the stun gun she had slipped out of her pocket was pressed into his ample gut, and his beloved Rambo knife clattered to the church floor. Instantly, he stumbled, down on one knee. Kelley and Andy stood behind him, their mouths agape. They hadn't expected this turn, and they hadn't expected her to run for the back door.

Freddy's trembling fingers grazed the back of her boots as he weakly tried to grab her ankle; Andy was the fastest, but he took a split second to assess the situation; and there was no way Kelley could catch her on even her worst day—so with all of this she had a full second after she closed the door to the back room, slamming it shut on the shroud as she left it with each half in each room. No way they'd be pulling it out.

The deadbolt was there. It was there because she needed it to be. She was making the better offer to the dead; they didn't even know the trespassers were there, but they knew Amy would make this deal. So the Other Side favored her, knowing she would give three where Freddy, Andy, and Kelley would only give one. It saw fit to help her, because of her generosity.

"They want the shroud, you guys," Amy informed them through the door.

She quickly climbed up the bell tower steps, and risked one last look at the Dance Macabre below. But it was no longer a dance. As unified as all of their movements were in their rise, gathering, and dance, so too were they unified in their march up the hill. But one was different—all had their shrouds back on, save one. And there was an animal aggression in his gait none of the dead had shown so far.

Top Hat, however, stopped halfway up. It alone looked up at the bell tower, at Amy. She saw a silver glint flashing from its empty sockets. She had a moment where she thought she had made a horrible mistake in hesitating, in needing to *see*—

It offered her a single bow, done with the same flourish of all of the revenant's movements. And it joined the others, back into the march.

Amy took her time going back down the stairs. No sense in panicking and tearing ass out—three for one was a fantastic deal. She didn't savor their pleas on the other side of the door as they furiously tried to break it down. Three pairs of fists hammered away, until there came the same loud creaking—the doors of this parallel church were just as uncared for as those in their world's. The soft, rustling voice that called out could only be Top Hat's.

"Dance with us." But there came another. And Amy had a pretty good guess who it was.

"I want my shroud!" And he seemed to cover the distance from the entrance to the church to the back door by midsentence, so that *shroud* came from right outside the door. The screams began, and the bangs, and the tearing, and the trickle of blood that welled under the door. The shroud was pulled as if it were a tablecloth yanked without disturbing the tableware on top of it.

And the screams faded just as fast as the shroud's owner had crossed the church.

Amy took one last look at the blood seeping under that door before heading out. Down that same porch, a left turn again, and down the cellar steps she went. This time, she closed the doors herself. Down those twenty-six steps. Left, right, right, left, right, left, and left one last time before coming to twenty-six more steps and out the cellar. Back into a night with a pockmarked moon, innumerable stars in the sky and a faint blue tinge. Back into a cemetery that was a place of comfort and remembrance, into a night alive with the sounds of the living alone, in all its forms—insects, owls, and no haunting, otherworldly compositions. Back into the church for one last bit of unfinished business. The candle was almost burnt out now. As she passed, she blew it out, and ran her hand over the symbols Freddy had drawn, smearing them. Now there was no cellar and no cellar door, Amy knew.

She exited through those double doors with their deafening creak, and she took the care to lock behind her before marching out back to the cemetery. At the gate was her old friend, the caretaker, looking at her in disbelief.

"You did it." Amy nodded in reply. She pulled out the keys she had snatched from Freddy's jacket pocket in the split second before he had fallen from the stun gun shock.

"Think you might want these. I know you have your spares, but I'm sure you don't want to leave this hanging so your bosses would find out they got lifted when you were passed out at the bar."

The groundskeeper looked at Amy in disbelief, catching the keys as she tossed them back to her old friend.

"We'll tell them me and Freddy got in a fight and I ran into you here, so you gave me a ride home." The caretaker nodded as they went through the gate. Amy took one last look at the church, and thought she heard a few faint, familiar notes before she continued to the garage across the street where the caretaker parked his truck and where Freddy had parked his car.

"I can't believe you actually went," he said. "I mean, after I warned you—" Amy held up her hand to placate him.

"You know someone else'd be their sacrificial lamb if I didn't step up. And you know the only one who's more eager to see ghosts than Freddy is me. I'd say this is about the best Halloween ever."

The Long Woman
Bill Davidson

Johanna Robbins first heard about the long woman at the breakfast table. Jason had finished his half hour in the pool and was now on a longer haul; persuading Izzie to eat and hoping to get her to nursery in time to avoid being late himself.

Izzie spooned in the tiniest of morsels and wiggled violently side to side on her seat, as though listening to a song nobody else could hear. Without looking up, she said, "The long woman's come in here."

Her head was still down so all Johanna could see was the froth of her white-blonde hair, lighter by several shades than her mother's, but otherwise pretty much the same. The daughter of tall parents, she would hopefully one day sprout up, but for now she was tiny and skinny as a rake, even for a three-year-old. Getting her to eat, anything at all sometimes, was a constant and worrying struggle.

Jason leaned in but, surprisingly, didn't say, "Will you stop wriggling and finish your breakfast."

Instead, he winked over her head and said, "Your Mummy's a long woman."

Izzie rolled her eyes, a habit she'd picked up lately, imitating, Johanna knew, her father. A picture-perfect copy.

"Mummy's not long. She's *tall*."

"So, who is she then, this long woman?"

Izzie was matter of fact. "I do see her in the night. She does come above my bed."

Johanna and Jason exchanged quizzical glances, a frown in there as Izzie added, "She sees me."

It seemed that was all she had to say on the subject, so Johanna tapped the back of her hand to get her attention. "What's she like?"

Izzie was still wiggling but now she stopped to give this some thought. "Long and blue."

Then she crammed the remains of her cereal into her mouth, barely leaving enough room to be able to say, "We're doing sunflowers."

Johanna watched her slide off the chair and head towards the hall at a run, more up and down motion than strictly necessary, clearly the only thing inside her head now a morning of planting sunflowers with her nursery friends. Jason shrugged, kissed his wife and followed in her wake.

Later, when it was much too late, Johanna would replay that first morning in her head, recalling how neither of them took their daughter, and her story of a long blue woman above her bed, seriously.

Now, left alone, Johanna took coffee into her study and got on the phone, checking emails while she spoke. Robbins Wealth Management had been doing good business and these days she seldom had to attend the office herself. She made three appointments for the day, one with the potential to pay her mortgage for three whole months, if it came off, and that would be a huge relief.

Because, it didn't matter how much you made, and she made a lot, a house in Kent with its own internal pool was more than could be easily afforded.

***

Johanna got back to the house feeling bushed and a bit flat—none of her visits had turned into solid business—kicked off her heels and threw her keys on the table, already calling for Jason and Izzie. His car was out front, so she knew they were home.

The idea of the long woman, long not tall, had kept coming back to her all day—that line, 'She does come above my bed' snagging unsettling little hooks in her mind.

Still calling, she walked around the modern villa she couldn't quite think of as home. All squeaky oak floors and hard angles, there was nothing homey about it. No answer, so eventually she had to check the pool room, feeling anxious and vaguely irritated about having to go in there.

The pool was the reason they'd bought this place, and she had known they were going to buy it as soon as Jason put the estate agent's particulars in front of her, the excitement in his voice.

"Check it out, Jo. This place has its own pool!"

Jason, the one-time county swim champ. Johanna the woman with a paralyzing fear of water any deeper than a cup. She didn't even like walking into the damn room, seeing the water in there all slippery and shimmering. The echoey sound of the place, the smell. It made her throat tighten and ticked her heart rate up just thinking about it.

Jason had convinced himself, for no good reason, that she'd somehow get over her phobia just having a pool so close at hand. They had spent a few stressful mornings in their swim suits while he tried to get her to lie back and relax as he held her. Even tried giving her swimming lessons, but no dice. Now, she took a steadying breath before opening the door into the overheated, chlorine smelling space and froze in place, not believing what she was looking at. Not wanting to believe. Her husband and daughter floated in silence, face-down in the water. Stretched out and flat, Izzie's hair formed a near-white halo around her head.

Terrified of water or not, she came at a run, slithering to a stop at the edge of the pool as they burst upwards, both at once, snorting and laughing. Catching sight of her, Izzie cried out, "Mummy! We did do eleventy elephants!"

Jason smiled up at her. "You don't fancy putting your swimsuit on, hon? Just sit at the side with us? You don't even have to come in, if you don't want to."

Izzie nodded furiously, grinning wide with her hands clasped before her like she was begging, tugging hard at Johanna's heart strings even as she backed away. How she hated disappointing that girl.

"I'll start dinner. You two have fun."

Jason smiled, but she caught his disappointment too. He just couldn't hide it, even though Johanna had told him the story; how she had come this close to drowning when she was a kid not much older that Izzie. She had found herself out of her depth in the river near her childhood home, panicked and thrashed and struggled, and then just gave up. She could remember it now, watching her own bubbles escape as she sank into the green water, not really minding as darkness closed in. Not minding it at all. Then, her father's hand had grabbed her, and she was hoisted into sunlight and air and couldn't believe how easily she had given up her ghost.

Jason had squeezed her hand. "That was then, this is now. You couldn't drown in that pool if you tried."

***

Nighttime. Johanna fluttered between sleep and waking, sliding in and out of a dream where weeds tangled and dragged at her, deep underwater. She gasped and came awake, with a sudden burning need to see Izzie.

She slid out of bed, leaving Jason snoring lightly, wanting to check on her daughter straight away, just make sure everything was okay. The house was dead quiet as she padded across the hall, the only light a dim bar at the bottom of Izzie's bedroom, coming from her little nightlight.

Johanna turned the handle carefully, not wanting to wake her.

It was chilly in there, surprisingly so, and in the instant that she opened the door, she thought she caught blue motes of dust, sparkling in a plane across the middle of the room like the afterimage of her dream. In the corner, the gaudy unicorn mobile swung lazily on its string.

Izzie blinked her eyes open and turned her head as Johanna stepped to her side, kneeling to smooth those ridiculous white curls and press her lips to the powdery skin of her forehead. Just breathing her in.

As usual, Izzie put her arms around her neck and squeezed tight.

"Mummy?"

Johanna kept her voice to a whisper. "Shh, honey. Go to sleep. Aren't you cold?"

Despite the coolness of the room, Izzie's hair was slightly sweaty. She was already falling back asleep. She shook her head.

"Not cold."

Then she mumbled something, just as her eyes closed and her breathing evened out. Something that might have been, "The long woman's cold."

Johanna stayed there for a while, her hand on her daughter's chest. Not yet willing to leave her on her own.

***

There was no talk of long women at breakfast and, in the light of day, Johanna felt ridiculous because she had let it spook her. Still she listened close to her daughter's chat, alert for any mention. Izzie said, "Josh says I'm slow-coach."

Jason frowned, "You can run fast!"

She shook her head. "I'm slow-coach."

Johanna watched her go off with her husband minutes later, her hand over her heart. Her tiny, skinny daughter who wouldn't eat. Of course she was a slow coach.

It wasn't until much later, when Johanna was reading her favorite bedtime story, Cowboy Baby, that the long woman finally got another mention. Lying back in bed, Izzie rubbed her upper arms and did one of her dramatic wiggles.

"The long woman is brrrr! Cold."

Johanna took a moment to answer. This was, after all, the girl who managed to convince her nursery teacher that she had a pet pig, called Simon, that had its own bed in her room. The story had unraveled when she claimed that Simon was also blue.

She kept her voice even. "What does she do?"

Izzie immediately stretched up and out, arms out to the side as she opened her eyes as wide as they would go. She tilted her head side to side, the movement slow as she waved her arms in sinuous motion.

Then, not noticing her mother's expression, she said, "Night, night Mummy."

***

There was no dream of drowning that night, but Johanna surfaced from sleep as though she had been slapped and was out of bed and on her way to Izzie's room before her limbs had any kind of chance to wake up. Again, she was careful opening the door.

Izzie, looking heart-achingly small, lay on her back, arms stiff at her sides and staring straight upwards at…Johanna's breath caught in her throat and she shook her head hard, thinking if this was a dream, she wanted to wake up right now, wanted this image as far gone as anything could go.

A woman, bluish-white and longer than Izzie's bed, floated, only inches above her. This might have been a corpse in its coffin, but it was face-down, so that its nose almost touched Izzie's. Its arms were flung wide and *moving*, just as Izzie had shown them.

Everything about this thing, this ghost, because surely that's what it was, was blurred and ill-defined and nothing stayed still. Even the air around it rippled and shifted, electric blue motes drawn into a shimmering plain.

The woman's eyes were wide open, staring down, and so was her mouth, but her features were indistinct and in constant, wavering motion.

It took Johanna less than a second to take all this in before she threw herself across the room, screaming as her hands came up, claw like. Izzie had time for one brief yelp before she was dragged bodily from under the figure.

Johanna's forehead grazed the woman's trailing finger, a burst of white-cold pain across her skin. Shrieking at the long woman, cursing, she backed up to her room and threw the door closed. Jason was on his feet, not all the way awake but already in a fighter's stance. He looked around, searching for the threat.

"What's happening?"

Johanna spread herself against the door as Izzie hurried to her father, telling him, "The long woman's come in here, Daddy."

For a moment, they stayed like that; Johanna wide-eyed and taking huge, shuddering breaths, flat against the door. Jason staring in confusion whilst cradling their daughter.

He asked, again, "What's happening?"

"There's something in her room, Jase."

"What sort of thing?"

Johanna didn't want to use the word 'ghost', not in front of Johanna. She didn't want to say *the long woman* either. She just shook her head. Then, feeling the throb of pain there, put her hand up to her brow.

Something else she managed to avoid saying, "I thought ghosts couldn't hurt you."

Jason was a big guy, wide in the shoulder from all that swimming, but Johanna could see how tentative he was, crossing the hall; scared. She stayed in the other bedroom, holding Izzie tight and watching as he pushed the door all the way open. He leaned slowly across to peek inside.

Taking a steadying breath, he stepped through the door, his movements quick and almost bird like. After a moment, his shoulders sunk to a more normal level and he turned back to where she stood, shaking his head. Still, his voice was no more than a whisper.

"Nothing. I can't see anything."

The room, when she finally stepped into it, was normal. Everything familiar and ordinary. The unicorn mobile was perfectly still.

***

Izzie curled between them that night, sleeping happily as the adults lay awake, staring at each other. At one point, Jason whispered, "Come into the lounge, so we can talk about this."

She shook her head. "I'm not leaving her, Jase."

Johanna got through the following day on autopilot, not quite landing the deal of the year, the one that would pay the mortgage for months, but it still looked promising.

By silent agreement, they put Izzie to bed in their bedroom that night, undoing six months of determined parenting. Johanna left the door open as she came back through, so that she could check on her. She intended to do a lot of checking.

When she returned from an extended reading session, and multiple time-wasting kisses, Jason greeted her with a glass of red wine and a long hug.

"What was that, last night?"

She searched his eyes. "Do you believe me? Believe it was real?"

Jason touched the mark on her forehead, but gingerly. It was a raised weal, nasty, like a burn.

"I believe something happened. I've got to be honest, I'm struggling to get to what."

"I saw her, the long woman. I saw her as clear as I see you now."

He must have seen something in her face, because he asked, "What?"

"That's not right. She wasn't clear, she was…it was like everything about her was blurred, kind of rippling. Like water or something."

"Could it have been a dream?"

She shook her head. "No way. Izzie saw it too."

"So…"

"I think it's some kind of ghost. I can't believe I'm saying that out loud." She shook her head. "It was right there, hanging above her, Jase!"

"I can't think what to do. Call Father Brennan?"

She had been thinking the very same thing. She put her hand on his, squeezing.

"Let's just wait and see. Maybe I scared it away."

He sipped his wine. "What I'm wondering, why now?"

"What?"

"We've lived here for over a year. Why is this happening now?"

"I don't know. But what I do know, if it comes back…" Johanna's face contorted, her lips pulling away from her teeth. "… it's going to have to fight me."

***

Johanna struggled to get to sleep, even though she'd only had a few hours the night before. It was harder with three of them in the bed, and Izzie, though tiny, took up more space than either of the adults and was just such a wiggle.

Still, eventually Johanna sunk into a dream about moths and dark water, coming awake when Izzie tugged her arm and said her name, a long drawn out, "Mummy."

Like it was two words.

She was lying flat on her back and when her eyes flickered open the long woman's face was right there, immediately above hers. It floated, blue and rippling but still somehow intense and intent, mere inches away. If Johanna moved, their noses might touch.

She felt her eyes widen as she tried to pull back through the pillow, breath stuttering in her throat but going no further, in or out, like her lungs had been stunned. Her hair rose in terror and cold, and her heart raced, booming hard and painful in her ears. Being careful not to raise up even a millimeter, she creaked her neck around to look at Izzie, who stared back with big blue eyes as she was pressing into her shoulder. On the other side Jason slept on, a normal, mundane sight.

Izzie whispered, "The long woman sees you now, Mummy."

Johanna didn't want to turn back but had to. The woman floated, face to face and toe to toe. Its jaw hung loose. Everything about it was in gentle motion as it hovered, its surface flowing, like river water. It wore a long dark coat, spread wide to cover the bed like the wings of a gigantic bat. The air around it shifted and glistened like oil.

She wanted to creep a hand out, shake Jason, but just couldn't do it. The woman's face was hard to focus on, but not so she couldn't make out its mouth when it started slowly opening. Keening now, not loud but high in her throat, Johanna tried again to shrink away into the bed.

The mouth kept opening till it was frighteningly, impossibly wide, and a horrible gurgling bubbled from its throat. Not words, just a horrifying, throttled noise. She could *see* it, like oily blue bubbles, streaming through the air.

Jason was suddenly on his feet and shouting, trying to drag his wife and daughter away as the long woman broke up and dissipated, neon blue lines chasing each other into nothing.

In the sudden glare of the overhead lamp, Johanna turned to see her husband huddled by the door, wide eyed and terrified holding her daughter.

"What the fuck? What was that?"

Johanna still couldn't get her stunned lungs to work properly, so it was Izzie who answered. "The long woman. She does see Mummy."

***

They were in the living room, drinking brandy. It burned Johanna's throat, but she welcomed it, for now.

Jason's hand shook as he took a sip. His voice shook too, when he said, "You were really yelling in there."

She shook her head. "I didn't yell."

"Sorry, honey, but you did. You shouted, 'Don't do it'."

She frowned and widened her eyes and sipped her brandy, trying to get her own trembling under control. "Did I? Jeez."

She tried the words out in her mouth, "Don't do it."

It didn't feel right, she was sure she had shouted no such thing. Izzie was on the couch beside her, head in her lap, and had, amazingly, fallen asleep.

"What do we do, Jason?"

"We call Father Brennan. That was a..." He looked at his sleeping daughter, then shrugged and dropped his voice to a whisper. "That was a ghost.

An actual, all the way real ghost. Or a demon. Whatever the hell it was, we need help."

***

Father Brennan did his priestly thing; praying around the house, blessing it, using a silver aspergillum to sprinkle holy water. Johanna made a bed for Izzie on the couch and the adults, including the priest, spent the night awake, hour after hour waiting through the darkness for a long woman who didn't come.

The next day, Jason went to work, even though he'd had little sleep, taking Izzie to nursery. Wanting some normality, he said. Not letting it destroy us, he said. Johanna watched her daughter bounce off towards the car, holding Jason's hand as she skipped.

Johanna herself was so tired that she couldn't imagine doing anything like skipping, ever again. She lay down on the couch and closed her eyes.

This time, Izzie wasn't there to wake her. She came awake all by herself, alone in the house, the ghost's face above hers, inches away. She tried to hold onto herself, hold herself tight, even though her heart felt like it might burst or stop, it pumped so hard and crazily against her ribs. She blew out a few shuddering, panicky breaths, breathing right into the woman's face, and tried to slide away, slithering off the couch onto the floor. The long woman kept pace with her, its features rippling and changing, but staying just above her own.

Its face was as ill-defined as before, but there was a desperation in the eyes that bored so hard into hers. As Johanna watched, its mouth opened, and kept opening. Again, a sound that she could see but not hear streamed from the ghost's mouth. Johanna put her hand over her face, and screamed.

When Jason came home, Johanna was curled into a ball against the couch. He hugged her and rocked her, and said, "We're not sleeping here tonight. I'll book us into a hotel."

It was a few minutes before she could even find it in herself to nod. Over Jason's shoulder, she could see Izzie, looking on with concern for just a moment, before skipping away.

***

At Johanna's request, the hotel they booked into wasn't in town, or anywhere near it. It was sixty miles away. Izzie was excited, filling the back of the car with soft toys. Johanna couldn't stop trembling, couldn't keep her voice even. The long woman's face kept coming back at her again and again. The expression was…what was it? Insane?

She spoke out loud, but quietly, so only she herself could hear. "Desperate. She's desperate."

They spent what might have been a pleasant evening in the hotel restaurant—there was a play area for kids—then they went to bed early, turning in just after eight because they were just too tired to keep going.

At around two in the morning, Johanna's eyes popped open to find the long woman, screaming silently above her and screamed right back.

***

A month later, and Robbins Wealth Management was in trouble. Johanna could avoid going into the office most days, but she was still the director, the beating heart of the enterprise, and she was missing. By the end of the month, she was about as missing as a person could be.

Nothing worked, and nothing helped. Father Brennan brought a specialist exorcist who didn't impress the long woman one bit. The long woman who, as Izzie said, saw *her* now. Saw her every single time she allowed herself to drift into sleep, as though she was just around the corner, lying in wait for her. She no longer seemed to see Izzie, thank God.

Johanna had stopped going to bed, and refused the sleeping pills the doctor had prescribed. Instead, never much of a drinker, she drank, first brandy and then, when she started buying her own, vodka. And so she would fall into an alcoholic doze, just about the only sleep she got.

Jason would often come hurrying from the bedroom to take her in his arms, hold her till she stopped shaking, or at least shook a little less.

He would sometimes tell her he had heard her again, yelling, "Don't do it".

She could never recall shouting and it didn't feel right.

The early hours of the morning became the worst for Johanne. She took to wandering the dead and empty streets, feeling more and more like a ghost herself, sitting on playpark swings or walking around strangers' gardens. It felt, with every time she encountered the horror of the long woman, like she was slipping further away from herself, the person she thought she was.

Sometimes, often, she would step silently into the bedroom, just to stand over Izzie and watch her sleep, curled tight into Jason's side. She could watch for a long time.

Once, she leaned in to whisper, "I see you, but I'm a tall woman. Not a long one."

***

Mid-morning on a rainy day in September, Johanna came back drenched from another long, exhausted walk, barely able to move her feet. She picked up a bottle of vodka and drank from it as she wandered the empty rooms, not even bothering to take her sodden raincoat off. Swallowing vodka like it was water, she ended up in Izzie's room. She lay down on the bed but wasn't going to let herself sleep. Sleeping was done with, so far as Johanna Robbins was concerned. Something that belonged to life before the long woman.

She hadn't taken the sleeping pills, not wanting to deal with the long woman whilst she was drugged, but started swallowing them now. One after another, emptying the blister pack, all washed down with vodka. When they were gone, she lurched to her feet again, feeling the slowness already in her limbs. Time to sleep, at last. Time to rest.

She caught sight of her haunted, exhausted reflection, a crazy woman in a soaking coat, and told it, "Everybody needs to rest."

She looked around her daughter's room, and picked up a stone that Izzie had found on the beach, one beautiful day in June. Just one of those breathless days of high sky and sun that she once took for granted. Wincing with the pain from fingers, blistered from scratching them through the long woman's face, she stared at the stone as though it held some deep mystery, then dropped it into the pocket of her coat. She wandered the house, picking things up, random weighty items that could fit into her pockets. After a while, her coat was so heavy it sunk her at the knee.

She was so damned tired, but the smell of the pool hit her like a slap as soon as she stepped through the door, clean and sharp and full of chlorine. She finished the bottle and threw it, right out into the water. It splashed, and bobbed, merrily.

Johanna slow-walked along the poolside, barely pausing before stepping off into three feet of water, steadying herself before wading towards the deep end. She got to where the water bubbled at her mouth, making her cough, and kept going. She hadn't had her head underwater since she was a kid, had forgotten the fuzzy underworld, the sound of bubbles running against her ears.

She kept her eyes wide and stared into the blue, hair floating around her, then opened her mouth, screaming her daughter's name in a sudden furious burst of air. All her air. She screamed again, but this time with water.

It wasn't so bad, she decided. Just like in the river where she had felt that it was very nearly okay to let go and disappear. Everything was already wavering and slipping away as she felt herself sink, finding her proper level to float, one well below the surface. Staring now at the tiled floor, she even smiled.

Then, a vision of Izzie came into her mind, so strong and clear it caused her to gasp. Her daughter with sweaty, blonde curls as she lay, sleeping, in bed. Johanna watched her beautiful girl, content in that moment simply to look.

Izzie blinked, surprising her by opening her eyes so they were staring at each other. A nice image to slide away to nothingness, until a noise made her look sideways. It took a moment to recognize her own self standing there, terrified. As she watched, this Johanna turned from scared rabbit to ferocious, screaming madwoman, diving in to snatch Izzie away.

The darkness she had been seeking closed in, but everything had turned on that moment and she didn't, she absolutely did *not* want to die. She wanted to live, to be with Izzie and see her grow. The version of herself who took Izzie was gone and she went on a desperate search, needing above all things to warn her. She had to find her, get to her and warn her.

In a drowning moment, she discovered a sleeping Johanna, lying with Izzie curled beside her. As she watched, the woman opened her eyes, so she screamed out her warning. A second later another Johanna lying on a couch, yet another closing her eyes in a hotel room. She found her and found her and screamed out her warning, *don't do it.* Over and over, like a tape loop, or the pages of a fast-flicked book.

Until, finally, the last page turned, and Johanna Robbins was gone.

Good Dog

Nathan Helton

*C*lick-clack. Click-clack.
The nails on her paws made a tapping noise clearly indicating a limp as the dirty, black dog kept a steady but slow pace down the side of the dark highway. The floppy ears listened acutely for something, anything. They twitched.

Her body stiffened for a pause, and then swiftly slung itself into the cover of the ditch line just before the headlights came around.

The vehicle pulled a gust of wind behind it, a tender caress in the summer heat of the night. Everything quickly returned to black. The dark head rose up, waited. There could be another interruption just ahead, and darting on and off the road in such an expedient manner was hard on her old bones. She wouldn't risk coming out into the open so soon. Not now. Not when she was this close.

***

The old man loved to sing. She would lay beneath the kitchen table, her belly welcoming the cool of the hardwood floor, and he'd belt out whatever sounded good to him at the moment—Van Morrison, The Eagles, Nat King Cole, The Bee Gees—it was all the same to her.

Every day the sun comes up around her
She can make the birds sing harmony
Every drop of rain is glad it found her
Heaven must have made her just for me
When she smiles so warm and tender
A sight for sore eyes to see

Her dark brown eyes, an obvious relayer of her wisdom and calm demeanor (though not as keen and observant as they used to be, evidenced by the many fat squirrels that hung around), would drift closed in the lull of a verse with her head still hanging, only to snap back open when he would emphatically groan out his favorite parts of the chorus. He'd eventually trail back off, the volume descending and the words morphing into a soft hum, and she would lower her head to rest on her paws, resolve to eventually roll on her side, and finally off into a nap. Such sleeping used to happen a lot around the house.

As far back as she could remember, it was just the two of them; in fact, some of her dreams still returned her to their hikes in the forest when she was much younger. His light laughter followed her off-trail as she would take off, a coal-colored blur betwixt thick patches of overgrowth and fallen trees, to try to catch the gray rabbit always a body length ahead.

Such trips ended after he went away in the ambulance the first time. A long night to never be forgotten. Lonely. The first one she could remember being alone on, in fact. The house was different when he was gone during the dark, and so urgently. Sounds announced themselves as if promising danger; the *creaks* of the boards were more foreign, more intrusive. The streetlight would paint the rooms in a dingy amber, a poor substitute for the warmth of the bright sun that hopefully followed him to where he was at the moment. He needed its care more than she did—maybe it was making things better—that was the hope, anyway.

***

She heard and smelled the rain far before it reached her. The cool drops, first hesitant, soon transitioned into a steady stream on the worrisome walk. The sun would rise soon, but the weather appeared to be locked in for the time being. Her wet fur helped to cool her core, and the panting slowed just slightly. The aching joints had long since stopping being intermittent; every moment brought a stabbing pain stout enough to halt a breath or elicit a whimper, should there be anyone worthy to hear the noise. There was no stopping, however, unless it was for water. With the sky falling at the current rate, surely there would be a puddle ahead in the next little while.

***

Once the old man returned home, he was only able to break away from her a single time. On that occasion, she must have fallen into a deeper sleep than intended, for she woke up to an empty bed one morning. Her heart thumped wildly. She called upon her nose to find him, and it led her reliably into the kitchen, where he met her with a knowing chuckle. She sighed in relief.

His essence seemed diminished; his vitality decreased by the day. She could smell it, too...more and more as days passed. It was a stench she cared nothing for, as she knew it was the cause of the pain, loss of appetite, and the extra long hugs. Bright smiles gave way to half-grins, and days spent mulching the small tomato garden in front of the porch led to elongated naps with the television on.

As pathetic as it had become, the singing and the humming never stopped.

On one of the days, she remembers him telling her something, his love and warmth coming through the gravelly, worn voice. It was in a tone she hadn't heard before. When he was done talking, he nodded in a confirmatory manner. She stared, his form filling her view, waiting for something after the talking. A hand reached out and caressed the right side of her face, which reflexively drew a smile out of her.

After that, the horrible smell started to dissipate. The man found new strength, made walking laps around the house, ate more fruit (a piece or two handed down to the dog bowl, of course).

The son would visit from time to time. He used to arrive with a lady and two kids, which she adored, but they hadn't been around for a long while, now having reached the point to where their scents registered no longer. His default aroma was expensive cologne masking cheap cigarette smoke.

She could only gaze upon the son with solemn attentiveness. He would confidently flop her ears about as he strolled past, which she detested, as it was never a show of affection; merely a gesture of dominance and pity at worst, and an ignorant, passive action at best. His dropping by would ensure that the next few moments would cloud the home with a tension that left both her and the old man exhausted at day's end. Though the two looked similar, there was little else that bound them.

One particular visit, the second-to-last one, in fact, ended with the son bringing out a stack of papers. The old man, now bespeckled, read attentively over the pages. The son leaned over, elbows on knees. She chastises herself now for not paying greater attention, but the fight was definitely over the content of what the son had presented. The old man did not make it all of the way through the stack before, in an exasperated manner, closing it all back up as he had first seen it. His glasses, slowly removed, reflected the light of the bulb above him as the conversation continued. Her master spoke unsurely, but slowly and calmly. He tapped nervously with his foot. The son smiled, his wolfish grin baring stained, yellow teeth.

Then, with a jubilant *yip*, he strutted out of the home, his car engine momentarily ripping away the serenity of the neighborhood as he sped deep into the night.

***

While the daylight removed a great deal of her ability to evade notice, progress was not, and could not, be hindered. The road had carved itself through patches of heavy forest for as far as she could see. She would have to maneuver through some yards eventually, which posed danger of exposure, but there was no other way to where she needed to go.

The town was just ahead.

***

The old man rested back into the sofa once the son had made his hasty departure. He stared off into the distance—probably nowhere in particular. She didn't like this mood. She jumped up on the couch, and, despite how it made her hips feel, laid down beside him, her shoulder pressed against his right hip. Her head, facing forward, tried to tilt up to see him, but she couldn't locate his face. Her inquisitive gesture caused him to wrap his right arm over her side, petting her softly, and then she rested with him, hoping her presence could diminish the heat of his strife.

***

The forest now behind her, she was moving along sidewalks and trotting quickly across the sleepy neighborhood streets. She had been sighted a couple of times by morning commuters, the necks of those within the car twisting about, observant of the dirty black stain in their suburban idyll. One particular vehicle passed and slowed abruptly, and the familiar noise of an engine decelerating reached her ears. She knew to pick up her pace. She perceived without looking that she was about to be followed. Her route must be broken up, just for this moment. The intent of the driver, however noble, must be disregarded: Until she was done, there was no rest. No friends.

There were many more houses in this neighborhood than in her old one. Plenty of places to hide.

She darted down the street to her right, despite objections from the cracked pads of her paws, dealing jolts of heavy discomfort only amplified by the increase to her top speed, which is to be considered a slow gallop. She looked ahead. A patch of woods lay up and to the left; to her right, a painted, wooden fence with an opening.

The car was approaching quickly. Almost in eyesight.

Her preference was the left, but the risk was simply too great. She would certainly be seen. Would they wait her out while she stayed in there? Maybe call someone to forcibly take her? Breaking line of sight and keeping away was the objective. Frustrated at the choice, she curled around the open gate of the wooden fence and whipped out of the view of the street.

The vehicle rolled to a stop on the other side of the fence. She could hear a commotion within. A woman's voice—children, too. Minutes passed, the voices eventually stopped, and the four wheels began to roll again.

Again the vehicle's wheels slowed to a standstill, just past the fence opening. A door opened and shut. She looked around the yard. She needed to hide somewhere else. She trotted deeper into the property, around the house in front of her and away from the fence opening, the vehicle, and the street. She was all of the way on the other side of the house when she finally heard the vehicle door again slam, followed by the sound of it driving carefully, but away.

***

One time long ago, the old man sat on the porch, a cheeseburger on a plate to his side. She drooled excessively, casually walking up to the plate, but was stopped with a stern command. Her eyes fixed themselves to the food while he thought. Once the idea hit him, he reached over, broke a piece of cheese off of his dinner, and held it high.

Sit.

She jumped for the cheese. He beckoned her back and pushed her rear to the ground.

Sit.

She went for the plate. He swung his hips to the right, boxing her puppy body out, and lifted the plate away. He swiftly pointed to her nose. She was experienced enough already to know that she should pay close attention. Defying him whilst the pointed finger was out was not a good idea. The plate was returned to its former spot, and he tried yet again. He gingerly pushed her rear down until it was as he had preferred.

They repeated the process, with him speaking every time they did it. This continued on until she was about to go mad with hunger.

Sit.

She smiled, panting wildly, her eyes almost bouncing around in her head. Her head wobbled left to right. She whined for just a moment, and then she did it.

She sat. The old man smiled. He gave her the cheese.

They did it again. There was some meat with the cheese this time. Sitting wasn't all that hard, turns out. Some bread was with the next bite.

The old man repeated the command-and-reward process until he was pacified. It had apparently gone on better than he had imagined. He picked up the plate to eat the rest of the burger. One piece left now. As he was about to toss it in his mouth, he caught something out of the corner of his eye. He looked down.

She was sitting.

***

As the imminent threat pulled away, the hum of its engine was soon hardly discernible amidst the background noise of the neighborhood. Her guard lowered slightly. She caught wind of something else. Her nose drew in air; it processed instantaneously and her mouth began to fill with saliva.

Cheese.

She turned her head, following the scent, her hunger dictating her actions; she warred inside her mind, knowing she could not delay, but the need was too swift, too formidable. The chase of the aroma allowed her to recognize her surroundings behind the house—a small backyard covered in soft grass and edged by a continuation of the same wooden fencing from where she first entered. But that wasn't all. Sitting at a small table, facing away, sat a small girl.

The sight of food prompted the dog's stomach to remind her well of how long it had been since she had last eaten, but the consequences—the prospect of failure—must be considered. It was time to go. She turned to leave, and she must've rustled with less care than she imagined, for a friendly, high-pitched voice rang out across the yard.

"Hey, doggie!"

She turned her head to regard the child, who had already stood up from her table and was waving slowly. "Hi!" The greeting was accompanied by a beaming smile.

The black dog slowly resumed her walk away and off of the property. She had trotted and made it almost to the front yard again before she heard the clumsy *thumps* of a child's running feet behind her.

"Where you going?" The girl asked pleadingly.

The smell. It was stronger now. It piped itself up her nose, demanded to be noticed. They were both stopped.

"Are you hungry?" She paused for a moment, knowing not to rush the dog and scare it away. "Well...are ya?"

Turning her head completely, she saw that the girl was only a few steps away. She had a cheeseburger extended forward, held tightly in hand. The hunger pangs exploded, now near an unbearable level. The long snout pushed out breaths in fast rhythm, regulating and trying to persuade. She needed to go. It was not much longer now. She was almost done with what she needed to do.

The little hands put the burger on the ground. "Here," she spoke calmly. "I don't wanna scare you. I'm not gonna hurt you. I promise. Take it." She backed up and continued to do so until the dog could hardly see her form around the bend of the house.

The temptation was insurmountable. She trotted forward and took the cheeseburger, swallowing it with only a few chews, which drew a giggle from across the yard. "Wow! You were hungry." She appeared to think for a second. "Hold on," she commanded. "I'll be back. *Don't move.*"

With that, the little girl scampered out of sight. The dog, again by herself, looked in all directions. She wasn't wary of a trap, but she'd been wrong before. She walked cautiously back to where the girl had gone. The table was unoccupied, but the door to the home was wide open. The absence didn't last but a moment, though; the girl returned with a bag, running as fast as she could and only stopped when she was nearly a body length away; the point at which the dog tensed up. The child knew she had committed a most suspicious act, so she hurriedly stuffed her hand within the bag and pulled out a cookie. "More food, see?" She placed it on the ground, as she had with the burger.

The cookie was gone in a flash. More giggling.

This time, the cookie stayed in her hand. The brown eyes met hers, two emeralds beneath a head of long blonde hair. It all began to seem safe.

Gently, the dog took it from her hand in a drool-filled transaction. The resultant, excitable jubilation the girl had been giving was stifled by the realization that her hand was now covered in dog spit. She nervously smiled and wiped it all off on her yellow sundress. "Okay. Want a few more?" She reached back into the bag.

A *click* and a *thud* emitted from the front yard, and the dog again stiffened. She ignored the pleas of the girl as she trotted to where she had entered the property in the first place. The opening was closed, and beside it stood a man, who looked just as surprised to see her.

"Uh...hey, dog?"

The little girl came barreling around the yard, yelling at the top of her lungs. "I found a dog! We've been having lunch!" She stopped and caught her breath. "He's nice," she informed cheerily.

The father was careful, doing nothing to give the dog sense to believe she was in the way of harm. "Lunch, eh?" He finally looked at his daughter. "I'm half afraid to ask what you were eating."

"Burgers!" She yelled. "Also, cookies." She raised the bag proudly.

"You fed the dog...burgers and cookies?"

She shrugged. "We don't have any dog food."

The father raised his eyebrows, acquiescing to her logic before lowering himself to a squat.

"Well," he said while staring at the dog, "I see that you have a collar. Let's see who you belong to."

He slowly lurched forward for a second, but stopped when the dog took a few steps back. "I'm not going to do anything to you. I just want to read your collar."

He tried again to the same effect.

The little girl stepped in. "Give him a cookie!"

"Well, hold on just a minute, missy. How do you know it's a boy?"

She thought for a second. "I don't know, I guess." She looked at the dog and craned her head until she had almost flipped herself over. "A girl?"

The father looked from where he was, squinting his eyes. "Yeah, I think so, too."

"You think she has puppies somewhere?"

"Nah, I wouldn't say that. She looks like she's up there in her years. See her fur? Lots of white spots. It's possible, but I doubt it."

"Can we keep---"

The father had seen the question coming. "Whoa! Hold your horses. I don't know if this is an agreeable arrangement for all involved. How do you know this dog wants *you*?"

"Because I will love her and bathe her and feed her. And we can play and watch TV when it's too cold to go outside."

"Okay, that's...not an answer, but that's really nice of you." He thought about making another step forward, but decided against it. "Where's your mom?"

"Inside."

"Does she know about this?"

"No," the girl replied sheepishly.

"Hmm." The father stroked his chin. "I'll tell you what," he said looking back at the dog, "first we need to see who she belongs to. There's no need in getting too attached if she belongs to someone else."

The girl's devastated expression said all that needed to be said. He needed to appeal to reason. "Look at it this way...there might be some little girl out there that's missing this dog real bad. What if you had a dog for a very long time and it went missing? Wouldn't you want whoever found it to call you?"

The young face displayed a change of mood. Her cheek muscles loosened and her frown dissipated. "I guess so," she hesitantly replied.

The dog, amongst all of the talk, remained still. She felt she knew what was coming next. She had to stay open to all avenues of escape.

"I need to get the information off of her collar, but she's not going to let me close." He stood up again. "Hand me a cookie."

The daughter excitedly walked over and placed one on his palm. Without looking, he abruptly shoved it into his mouth, looking over to her with a mischievous grin. She laughed with a hint of outrage. "What! That's for the doggie, not you!"

"Are you kidding? I'm hungry, too! Who do you think bought these? You've fed everyone in this yard but me so far!" He let her laugh subside before continuing. "Okay, for real now." He reached out to her. "Cookie, please."

She reluctantly slapped the treat into his hand. "Don't eat it, dad. It's for the *starving dog*."

He turned to the dog, who swallowed hard in the presence of the food. There was a hint of a wag in the tail, but the father wasn't sure as to what it signified. "I'm not going to harm a hair on you, little doggie," he cooed. "I just want to see what's on your collar. After that, you can run around the yard for a bit."

The cookie drew toward her mouth, only fingertips skirting the edge of the treat to prevent any nipping of the skin or nails. The dog kept a keen eye on the other hand. She feared that from there would be the danger of capture.

The little girl tried to assuage the fear. "Don't worry. It's all going to be okay."

The father followed her statement up by speaking to no one in particular. "I really need this to work. I don't want to spend all day feeding a dirty dog handfuls of cookies."

The treat was very close now. Inches away. The dog slightly opened its mouth, but its legs tensed up, ready to jump, to strafe away if needed. Then she saw it— the other hand started to move. It was a trap.

"Good doggie!" The little girl yelled as she made a tiny jump.

The dog's eyes glanced to the girl's movement, and the father had found the moment to act. He lunged his free hand forward and grabbed the collar. Immediately, the dog jerked away, writhing and bowing back, flopping the best she could, like a fish on a hot dock. In a second, she was free again, but the collar remained in the man's hand. There was a sigh of relief as the father raised and inspected the tags. "I guess that'll have to do." He rubbed the dirt off of the dingy, metal ovals to uncover what appeared to be a phone number, a name, and an address. "No dog name on the tag," he informed, "but I have a last name—*Peters*—and the address is...Alleghany?" He looked at the dog, which had backed its rear against the fence. In all of the commotion, the girl had somehow rushed to her side and was softly petting her back. "Alleghany," he repeated.

"What's that?" The daughter asked.

"It's a town, one about, oh, two hundred-ish miles from here." His puzzled expression was not lost on the girl.

"So that's bad?"

"It's a heck of a long way to be from home, is what it is. I wouldn't know if it's necessarily *bad*, my dear, but I guess there's only one way to find out." He rubbed the tag just a bit more. "Guess I'd better give this phone number a call." He looked one more time at the dog. He saw desperation, sadness. Exhaustion. "She's in a bad way though, sweetie. Now that I think on it...maybe it's best if we just take her to the vet and let them work it out."

The hands formerly petting suddenly wrapped around the dog affectionately. "Sick, maybe?"

"Who knows." The father thought. "How about this: You stay out here and watch her. Take care of her. I'm going back inside to see about the vet and her owner. We'll figure out what we need to do from there. All right?"

"All right." Her response was forlorn, but he figured it could have been worse. He made his way into the house. "Good, good," he said to himself. "I'm glad this happened. It's not like I had a thousand things to do today already…" He trailed off as the door shut behind him.

The dog immediately trotted to the gate at the fence, breaking away from the arms of the girl. "Wait!" She begged. "We're taking you home, little doggie. You'll be with your family soon, don't worry."

Whines blew forth from the black dog. Jumps, scratches at the gate. A muffled bark at first, and then a loud one.

"I can't let you out. You'll just run away!"

Frantic scratching now. More reverberant *thuds* as her paws banged up against the gate and rattled the latch. She swung her head from side to side.

"You're acting all weird. What's wrong?"

The spastic movements continued on but for a moment, and then the dog, running up to the girl nose-to-nose, gave a big lick to her face. She then backed up several steps, gave out a hefty, bellowed bark, and pushed her paws against the gate, scratching down it as she came back to all fours.

The girl thought. She looked back to the house. She could see no movement. No parents. She returned her gaze to the brown eyes. They were pleading, encumbered with a wisdom she was ill-prepared to fully comprehend, but old enough herself to acknowledge for its mere presence. The stare broke some sort of barrier; she suddenly understood what needed to be done. The small hands reached up and flicked up the latch. The gate slowly swung open.

The dog looked upon her for a few blinks, then passed through the opening and back into the street.

***

The son and the old man at first had a screen door between them as they spoke. There were tones of hostility, followed by apology and regret, then a cycling back around to hostility once more. She hadn't sat down since the son's car roared into earshot. Neither had the old man. She watched them both strictly, her eyes volleying back and forth to each speaking face. The son's brawny arms flexed as they spread out and grabbed the door frame. He bowed his head and listened, as if the old man's words were trying to blow him straight off of the porch.

The bowed head lifted once the old man was done talking, an expression of acceptance failing to overshadow a clenched jaw signifying unparalleled rage. With the speed of a snake, he pushed off of the pane, his hands out and up, as if trying to discourage a physical attack upon him.

There was something she didn't like about his eyes. Despite the color, they were dark. Predatory. She nonetheless held silent and watched.

The old man's anxiety was all but a visible aura to her, easily sensed without the need to observe his misty eyes or snarl of a frown. She hated that frown, and hated the son for fostering a situation in which such an expression was warranted. The old man had spoken his peace, nodding in a confirmatory manner, and, before turning away from his son, he made some parting remarks, each as sharp as a spike, before walking back toward the kitchen. As the old man passed her, they exchanged a look. He paused, unblinking. The frown, and with it the anger, melted away without incident. He smiled and began to hum. She wagged her tail, swishing it back and forth across the floor.

Behind the old man, the screen door lightly smacked back to its closed position.

***

Somewhat re-energized by her meal, she spent the rest of the afternoon stealthily moving past what felt like an innumerable collection of homes. She re-routed herself repeatedly, opting out of a path that would have taken her straight through a park full of people; one particular detour lost precious time when she again was sure that someone was pursuing her.

For all of the shade that she passed under, no amount of respite seemed to alleviate the disregard and brutality of this late-afternoon sun. Her eyes began to blur as she broke into a long stretch of street without any tree cover. She blinked hard. The brightness, the reflections off of glass—it made her feel all the more vulnerable, as her sight felt dulled enough to miss a looming danger. Her chest heaved, breathing hard to keep her body temperature down.

She passed around a street corner, timidly looking before trotting along again. At the end of the block, she came to a four-way stop. A man, just ahead, calmly walked his own dog, a small, white terrier, along a yard, the property line established by a tall chain-link fence. In a rush, four dogs, each black as night and as large as wolves, stormed to the end of their territory with a grand ferocity. Booming barks echoed out of unison; the fence sang out in distinctive *clinks* as massive paws pushed and pressed their weight, not expecting freedom from the containment but ready to capitalize should the event occur. The man reacted in accordance with his leashed pet, picking up the pace and working to break beyond the dogs' sensory reaches, the man muttering to himself in curses in the midst of his quickening. She elected to remain still for a moment, letting him walk comfortably past her next turn, which she could see just ahead. There was no telling how he'd react at this point to a dog off of its leash after that ordeal. No sensible reason to press the matter and find herself in another crisis.

The man and his dog had disappeared from sight for a few breaths when she pushed off with her good hip and chose to continue on. She wearily pressed alongside the chain-link fence, her head facing forward and turning only to observe the surroundings just ahead.

The dogs made no noise as she went by, nor did they move.

Once she put another short length of street behind her, a familiar smell found her snout. She was able to follow her nose singularly now should she have felt the need, forsaking her other senses. Passing homeowners preoccupied with mowing lawns and the carrying in of grocery bags, she zeroed in on a small home at the termination of a dead-end street. A large, white truck obscured the front door, but talking and yelling could be heard around the property. Uniformed men began to intermittently carry boxes up a ramp and temporarily disappearing into the back of the vehicle, working fast and stopping only to move out of the way of colleagues. She hopped over the curb, entering the yard, and hugged the edge of the property to the right while trying her best to remain invisible. As she rounded the truck from afar, she caught a glimpse of a familiar man standing in the flurry of movement. She tensed up, stiff as granite. The smell was intense now.

Expensive cologne. Cheap cigarettes.

**

The son grabbed a pillow from the couch, one that she herself had rested upon many times during naps in afternoon serenity, and thrust the old man to the floor with a hand upon his throat. She only first thought to bark, hoping the mere threat would break them apart.

The son positioned the pillow over the elderly face, swatting away arms that moved too slow to make any difference.

She next lunged forward, mouth agape, and sunk her teeth into the son's right forearm. She thought to wrench her teeth into the meat, to work her jaw with all of her strength, but her bite was only meant to be a warning, not a full-on attack. She released the arm. The pillow raised immediately; she heard a gasp of air. The old man's hands began to extend, to help him crawl away from the danger.

In a blink, her head seemed to be facing another direction. A throbbing pressure hugged the left side of her face, and a massive arm seized the back of her neck. The pain was incredible. She yelped as loudly as she could, trying to break free.

She knew she was being dragged to the bedroom. In the midst of her cries for pain, the idea dawned upon her that maybe all of the danger had shifted to her now. Maybe he was safe from harm; in fact, he might be escaping this very moment.

They reached the bedroom, and the hand of the son slung her with all of his might. She landed on her left hip, and a searing stab of pain coursed through her; despite the injury, she brought herself to all fours and started to make her way back to the kitchen, and to the old man.

As she made her way forward, the son grimaced at his wound before turning and slamming the door behind him.

Her paws scraped frantically against the wooden barrier, and she could feel her weight cause a slight bend in the door, but nothing more. Her barks were chained tightly together, repeating in a manner of stout determination. Desperation sat in as the house became eerily quiet; the old man's yelling was a muted but brief affair. The barking stopped as the situation necessitated that she change her tactic—she looked around fruitlessly to see if there was another way out, a moment marked by soft whimpers and emotional anguish. The room glowed orange for a period, and then not at all. The pain in her hip crawled back into existence, a cramping uncomfortability that made it difficult to stand any longer. Maybe the sun went with him, like last time.

The night was without noise. She would know; she was listening the entire time.

The morning brought stomping upon steps. A voice, not the old man but, yes, somewhere in the house, was distinct.

She barked as loud as she could and waited for the door to open.

Footsteps called closer to the door. A shadow revealing two legs peeked from underneath. The knob turned, the opening of the doorway widened, and she leaned her head right to see her liberator. The kind smile and face looked down upon her.

It was a neighbor.

Her fur bounced lightly as she ignored her hip and exited the room. She looked around, smelling, searching. It didn't take her long. He lay on the kitchen floor, motionless, which is right where she had last seen him. His mouth was frozen in throes of a primal scream.

She sniffed him and put her wet, cold nose upon his cheek. It had easily driven him out of sleep in times past. Every time but this one.

***

After a while, the son watched as the men began to exit the home with either small items or nothing at all. He nodded in approval, waving the men goodbye before walking back into the house. The doors of the trucks were soon slammed shut and they all drove away from sight, leaving choking clouds of exhaust that fought to dissipate. The front door remained open, allowing the evening breeze to slip in unabated.

A dirty, old black dog crept in as well.

The house was mostly bare, save for some boxes and trash bags. Just inside the living room, she could hear him to the right and down the hall. Her timing was perfect. Just as it had the last time she had seen him, the sun spilled autumn tones about her. She faced the hallway head-on, her attention and desire unwavering, and she waited.

***

The same neighbor that had freed her from the bedroom had volunteered to adopt her. The house, despite the welcome and understanding she received, felt hollowed out. Her hunger abandoned her. Food would come frequently and aplenty (in her familiar bowl, one of the few things brought from the old man's house), but it would remain, touched only by the passing flies. The guilt and the grief consumed and enveloped. Sleep would come on occasion, but it was accompanied by the grim re-living of it all. The days took on an ethereal component; the absence of the old man pushed her into a limbo. Just in case she had been mistaken this whole time, she kept close to the door, watching for her friend.

***

Sporadic pops and shuffling noises poured out of the lit room down the hallway. Without preview, the sound of increasingly loud footsteps echoed in the hollow home and out casually walked the one she hated most. He jumped in a startle and stopped, dead in his tracks, his face smacked with disbelief. He was only silent for a pause. "You," he managed to say. An unsure sneer drew up the side of his face. "You're a long way from home, dog."

She remained as still as a statue.

"You're not mad at me about what happened, are you? You here to even the score?" He leaned his head to the right, trying to get as full of a look around the room as he could, just in case anyone else was around. "I guess that'd be the only reason you'd show up, eh? From the looks of you, I'd say it's a given that you walked." He continued to study her appearance.

She still did nothing. His words brought out no reaction from her. The sun ducked behind the nearby mountains, and the house went all but dark.

"Listen," he said with a laugh, "I'm almost outta this place. I'm about to go far, far away where even *you* can't find me—and don't get me wrong—I'm really impressed you made it here." He took a cautious step forward and looked upon her with pity. "You're the only other thing that was there that night. Trust me. He was suffering. I did us both a favor. I know so much that you never will. Now go find someone else to hang out with."

A street light flickered on. It caused slices of light to dive through a window covered in half-opened blinds where the son stood. He gave her a moment to register his words, then exhaled deeply. "Go on! Get outta here. Piss off!" He waved his hands outward.

She held firm, but began to slowly growl. One borne from the deepest parts of her pain.

"All right," he said as he started to walk toward her with his arms at the ready. "Have it your way."

***

On one particular night, one not too long before, she awoke abruptly experiencing what, at first, was a faint feeling of familiarity. She raised her head up and studied the silent room. The air felt at once heavy, and colder. Her hair seemed to suddenly stand on end, a sensation beckoning her attention to a dark corner. Something was there.

It made a noise.

***

To compound the effect of her growl, her upper lip raised to produce her most fearsome snarl. She kept as-is while the son was now a step away. He paused one last time to ascertain the angle at which to grab her, and started to make his move before he heard a commotion behind him.

He stopped and angled his ear back toward the dark of the hallway. The light from the room he had come from had been turned off. The streetlight remained the sole illuminator.

He knew someone was in the house. He brought himself upright, turned away from the dog, who was no longer growling, and leaned his head forward. "So you brought the dog, huh? I'm calling the cops!"

No answer.

"I'm going to beat this dog down and then I'm coming back there to do the same to you if you don't come out of that damned room. You don't know me. You don't know what I'm capable of."

The response from the darkness was not a set of words, but a hum. A soft humming. It was exiting the room.

"Is this supposed to scare me? Try again."

The humming continued, growing slightly in volume and clarity as the noise entered the hallway.

"Is this really how you want to spend your evening, pal? Come here and I'll give you something to hum about."

The humming stopped.

"Now what?"

The ashen face leaned into the light through the blinds. The eyes were piercing, cold daggers into the soul; the mouth was fixed open, frozen from the pain of death.

Two old hands grabbed the sides of the son's head, squeezing and pressing nails through the skin and into the skull. Now fixed to him, the arms pulled back, dragging him down the hall and into the room. The door slammed behind them. The screams began at a high-pitch, and ended as a subdued gurgle.

***

She left the hallway, walking out of the front door and into the night. Chirps and whirs of nearby insects sang a sweet tune she associated with days long ago, back when she was much younger. Her body ached, but she now felt better than she had in quite some time. She made her way down the street, brave and unafraid. She wanted some water. Definitely a nap. Something to eat, eventually.

Maybe a friend in a yellow sundress.

***

No one ever answered the number on the dog's collar, so taking her in felt like a natural move, much to the little girl's delight. They named her Cookie.

"And if a man shall meet the Black Dog once it shall be for joy; and if twice, it shall be for sorrow; and the third time he shall die." — *W.H.C. Pynchon*

Never Say Never
Brian James Lewis

The older boys laughed as the little kids' feet scampered across the leaf covered field and disappeared down the path into the woods. Tyler slid a joint out of his battered box of Marlboros, sparked it up and passed it around. Benny took a deep hit and passed it on. Then he slid four cans of beer out of the deep pockets in his hunting coat. Popping his open with a practiced thumb, he handed the others into the waiting hands of his friends. Tops popped, Benny belched loudly and eagerly sucked on the joint as it came around again. The other guys chuckled nervously at the sudden blast of sound. While the chances of them getting caught by a parent or tattle-tale kid were pretty low, it wasn't wise to advertise. Still, if they had to wait for the little kids to get a head start on the infamous "Snipe Hunt," they might as well enjoy it. So they chilled and smoked quietly until Eric cursed, flicking the tiny speck of a roach into the fire.

"Burn your fingers, bro?" Tyler grinned at him.

"Yeah…Always fucking happens!" Eric scowled into the fire, as if it were to blame for his lack of skills.

"Well, you know what they say, practice makes perfect!" Tyler nodded while reaching into his jacket for the Marbs again. "Why don't we try that again, gentlemen?" Tyler's voice was already raspy and smoke burned at 18. His old man was okay with that, long as he didn't set the barn on fire and work got done. But Jake Yoakum probably wouldn't be very happy about the tiny patch of weed Tyler grew behind his toolshed.

"Hell yeah!' said Benny. His hand reached out greedily for the lit joint, and he sucked down another major hit. Sip and smoke, smoke and sip. They'd done that often enough in this location that it would seem weird not to. Benny had become kind of a weed hog, but nobody said anything. It wouldn't be long before they'd all be off doing different stuff and nobody'd be smoking up here. Benny saw Adam watching him and asked, "You bring them sacks?"

Adam nodded and pulled the rolled-up feed sacks out of his pockets. Each of them had to contribute something to the Snipe Hunt and the sacks were Adam's. His Mom was big on using them for cute crafty stuff, but tonight the boys would be using them for a scarier purpose. Nothing like a quick tumble in a dark feed sack accompanied by some scary noises to dampen a few pairs of overalls! Then just before the little guys got too freaked out, the older boys would come to their "rescue." After that, a quick walk would take them to Yoakum's Barn for a Halloween party of hot crullers, apple cider, and a bunch of lame party games put on by the grandparents.

The Snipe Hunt was an annual tradition that had been around for ages in the farming community of Blaine Forks, Pennsylvania. Years ago, the four boys sitting around the fire had been wide-eyed little kids. Just like tonight's group of ten, they'd also gone out hunting for the Snipe with fishing nets and pillowcases. Now as a sign of their impending manhood, they were the ones in charge of the little kids tonight. After carting everyone up to the campfire in his Dad's old red pickup, Tyler told the kids a few scary ghost stories and a couple jokes. Then it was time to send them out into the woods to capture that elusive Snipe! Adam smiled when he saw one kid wearing a pith helmet and carrying a butterfly net. If anybody was going to get the Snipe, it would be him.

The fire crackled merrily, and tonight was a good one to be straddling that line between still being a boy and becoming a serious working man. So the guys were full of jokes and ready to have fun.

"Who the hell wants to go bobbing for apples?" Tyler chuckled. "I'd rather have Theresa Schaefer bob on my knob, if you know what I mean!" He winked at Adam as he passed the joint over to Benny, who was sitting next to Eric. Even though he dutifully chuckled along, Adam knew that his skinny, runty size would probably make him the last of their bunch to bed a babe.

The other two laughed like loons, their faces looking like evil jack-o-lanterns in the firelight. It was as if the night was changing Eric and Benny for the worse. Adam felt his old pal, anxiety fluttering in his chest, so he focused on the weed and beer, hoping they would loosen him up enough to enjoy the evening. The guys talked and laughed about whatever came up as they sat around the fire for the mandated half hour. That was the right amount of time for the little shits to get themselves all in a frenzy trying to find a snipe that could attack at any moment or, according to one dissenting voice, not exist at all.

"Never has been, never will be!" cackled Eric. He was a cruel young man who enjoyed killing cats and cutting open live squirrels. Another favorite activity was picking the legs off insects and lizards one by one, laughing as the animals writhed in pain. The squirrels actually shrieked, which made Eric excited to the point of erection. He was itching to use the sticks that he'd lovingly cut and cured so they weren't too supple, nor hard enough to leave much of a mark on the little rug monkeys. Tyler and Adam were not nearly as excited about them as he was. Benny didn't give a crap either way. All he cared about was getting toasted.

As the guys laughed and got their buzz on, Adam heard dry leaves crunching underfoot. The sound seemed to be coming from behind him. He glanced back to see if any of the sharper kids were trying to circle around and catch them at their own game. But nobody was there. His eyes tracked a fast movement, but no face. Probably just a deer or something…He leaned back into the warm orange glow of the fire and happy sound of laughter.

"Whatever! Take Theresa if you can get her. I'd rather have Julie Sbarra! Now that's a rack!" Benny argued with Tyler who continued to ramble on about the wonders of Theresa. All of which was pointless since Theresa and Julie were at the Halloween Dance with their dates while they were busy chaperoning the Snipe hunters. Oh well, a guy could dream, right?

The Keystone Ice and multiple joints worked their magic, making the half hour fly by. Soon it was time to creep quietly down the hill after the kiddies. Tyler stood up, belched and farted. As he was stretching his back, something caught his attention. Adam watched as his gaze flicked behind them.

"See something?"

"Naw…guess not. Thought I did for a minute."

"I did too, earlier. But it sounded like it was right behind me."

"Yeah?"

All four of them looked around wide-eyed for a few seconds. Then Eric burst out laughing and poked Adam in the ribs with one of the sticks.

"Haw-haw! You guys are FUN-NEE! Ain't nothing out there! Now shut up and grab a stick!" Adam shrugged at Tyler, who still looked wary, but they each grabbed a stick and gritty feed sack. Then they joined Eric and Benny who were busy hamming it up.

"Oh dear, Benny! I think the snipe is going to get US!"

"Goodness! Whatever shall we do?"

"Well...I've got a nice sturdy stick! So I'll just whack him like this!" Eric shouted as he sliced down a large bunch of ferns.

"Ooh! My hero!" Benny swooned, laughing so hard that he nearly fell down.

"Shut up, you fuckheads! You're ruining everything!" Tyler hissed as he grabbed their collars and shook them. "We don't tell the kids that there never was a snipe! We don't mess with tradition! Am I clear on that?" His announcement was followed by an uncomfortable silence. Tyler took it to mean that even though the boys were pissed off, they were going to do right and resume their quiet creep into the woods. Then they'd round up the runts, scare them a bit, and take them back to the barn. After which, they'd party a little more.

Unfortunately, he couldn't see their faces like Adam could and that was too bad. Maybe Tyler was right, but that didn't make it any easier for Eric and Benny to swallow. Adam could barely recognize the two guys that he'd grown up with. Both their faces were rigid with anger and nearly purple with rage. He wanted to warn Tyler and tell him to back off before it was too late, but fear wired his mouth shut.

Before he could get anything out, Eric and Benny turned on Tyler and began beating him with their sticks. Then they crammed their feed sacks down over his head and arms, cutting off any chance of retaliation. Tyler tried to run, but Benny knocked him to the ground. Then both guys kicked him in the balls repeatedly and finished with a couple boots to the head for good measure.

Eric was breathing quite heavily and it wasn't just from the exertion. Somebody gasped nearby. He turned his head to see that Adam was staring at him and Benny with a horrified look on his face. It was an "I'm gonna tell" look, if he ever saw one. Eric snatched up his stick and bellowed

"We've got one more customer, Benny! Let's get him!" Then he went tearing off towards Adam, feeling more excited with every leap, until he was moaning. He couldn't wait to get his hands on him!

Adam was certainly no strongman. In fact, he weighed in at barely a hundred pounds. But the one thing his sleek body was made for was running. There really wasn't any choice. Either he'd end up like Tyler, all trussed up like a country ham with his privates aching, or he could take his chances on the brand-new Nikes he was wearing and roll. He ran for it with all he had, flinging away his stupid feed sack. What was so great about frightening kids, anyway? The best way to enjoy fall in the forest was during the daylight hours. He ran here often and knew many of the paths well. In the afternoon, the towering trees were majestically beautiful. The explosions of color from their leaves was like a silent fireworks show that made Adam wish he'd paid more attention in art class.

But in the night, all the magic disappeared and the paths became dark tunnels where anything could be hidden. Hell, you could hide a school bus out there in the dark and nobody would ever know! Slivers of moonlight illuminated the path just enough for him to follow it, but the beauty was gone. Adam shook his head and headed for the hills.

Eric stopped for the dropped feed sack, since his was still wrapped around Tyler. His blood was at a murderously erotic boil. They would catch that wimpy little fuck! Then they would whip him. Oh yes! Whip him HARD. Whip Adam until he bled. He couldn't wait to use his stick over and over! The thing that lived inside Eric rose up, nearly blinding him with its power…

"C'mon, Eric! He's getting away!" shouted Benny. He turned back to see what was slowing his partner in crime down, only to be sorry that he had. "Dude, really? What are you doing? Stop that!"

Eric looked down to see that his hands were busy with other things besides the feed sack. His cheeks burned and he struggled to make his feet move. But his legs felt weak…Whoa…His whole body was woozy and wobbly… Suddenly, he face planted as everything let go and relaxed.

Benny was a strong weightlifter, but he was built square and stocky. He also tended to keep a good amount of fat around his middle. The kids at Hunterdon High didn't usually make fun of his gut more than once, because it earned them a quick black eye or bloody lip. Well, if they were within arm's reach. Otherwise he was stuck yelling wheezy, out of breath threats at them instead. That was so fucking annoying! There were a few skinny little pricks at school who could always outrun him. However, Benny was going to make sure that Adam wasn't one of them. If Adam got away and shot off his mouth to Tyler's old man, Big Jake, things were going to be very uncomfortable for a long time.

Adam risked a quick look over his shoulder and saw that Benny was chugging along behind him. But he was whistling like a steam engine.

"You just wait right there!" Benny huffed. "I'm going to beat your ass!"

As fun as that sounded, Adam had no intentions of following that order. The moon rose out of the trees, which helped him see the path better. He could also see that Benny still held a feed sack in one hand and a stick in the other. His big steel toed work boots slammed the earth fiercely with every stride, crushing sticks and kicking rocks. But Benny's big body needed more air. Damn weed! He shouldn't have hogged it so much! Smoking was bad for the pipes. Still, Adam was surprised at how close Benny was to him. He expected to have a much greater lead…

"Crack!" Adam whipped his head around to the left, expecting to see Eric leaping at him from the darkness. But Eric wasn't there. He was too busy lying flat on the ground in a state of ecstatic paralysis. His body would be gloriously immobile for at least another ten or fifteen minutes. Thanks to the rush of feel good chemicals released by his body in response to its first orgasm, all he could do was pulse in ecstasy.

Even though Adam saw nothing, he felt a strange pocket of warmth engulf him for a minute. Not only that, but the air smelled…meaty, like fried baloney or the breath of a giant carnivore. What? Now where the hell did that thought come from? Maybe he should just be happy Eric wasn't whipping him. Except this wasn't really a great time for him to relax. Benny was still chugging along behind him and if Eric wasn't on his left…

Then he must be on his right! Adam whipped his head around. Nope, nothing except trees and scrubby bushes. It probably wasn't the best time to think about them, but Adam wondered where the hell all the little kids were. So far, all the commotion hadn't scared up a one which seemed a little weird. He forgot about them the next minute when Benny began shouting at him again. "Hey! Hey…you!" Then he fell silent.

Thud! went Benny's body as he collapsed in a wheezy, gasping heap. His brain was so oxygen starved, he could see a face peering at him from the deeper woods. It looked kind of like a long fox with luminous green eyes and freaky tongue. Was that Adam? Man, if this was what Tyler's shitty home-grown weed did to you, he was just going to stick with beer from now on! First he couldn't run worth a shit and now he was seeing things. Great! What he really needed was to take a little rest. At this point, he didn't even care what Adam did. He could tell the fucking President, for all he cared. How had things gotten to this state? Benny tried to remember, but everything faded to black.

Adam watched Benny fall and felt relieved. That would give him the opportunity to rest and also to go check on Tyler. Hopefully he'd gotten himself unstuck by now. But if not, Adam would be able to pull the sacks off. Then they could try to put things back on track. He started walking towards Benny, but heard stealthy footsteps coming towards him from the deeper woods and stopped. Of course! It was all just a trap! Benny was just pretending to be crapped out and when

Adam came back to check on him, BANG! Eric would beat the hell out of him. Then they'd double bag him like they had Tyler, laughing their heads off as they left him behind. Nope! He wasn't falling for that shit! Adam began running away again, going deeper into the woods on paths he'd never gone down before.

The thing in the woods watched Adam leave. Once he disappeared from sight, it moved onto the path and approached Benny. It's long, serpentine tongue whickering out ahead of its face. The smell was good, and the quantity plentiful. A little sweaty, yes, but that just added flavor. The thing was hungry, so very hungry. Its elongated fox face opened slowly, revealing rows of razor sharp teeth that glistened with saliva as the tongue measured things. When it figured out how big Benny was, the creature's head expanded like a balloon so it could take him in the least amount of bites. The tongue danced excitedly and a drop of saliva hit Benny's face.

"Hey! Mom? It's Saturday...I don't have to get up early." Benny mumbled, wiping the moisture off of his face with one hand. His eyes opened slowly to large green luminous ones staring at him from a huge tiger striped fox head. Then the tongue wrapped around his waist and pulled him into the cavernous mouth. His screams were abruptly cut off as the mouth crushed him like a vice and the tongue darted out to catch any escaping blood. The Snipe ate quickly. With every gelatinous sounding crunch, the head slowly shrank back to its usual size. To curl up and nap would have been wonderful. But there was so much to do before the sun came up and it was forced to hibernate for at least another year.

Since the oversensitive boy had run even farther away from the others, the Snipe ignored him for now and went back down the trail towards the two bigger victims. With a slither of its forked tongue, the creature that had been released by Eric's loud and stupid assertion that it had never existed, set off down the trail in the boys' direction. Sometimes people needed a little proof that spirit creatures do exist. Unfortunately, the boys wouldn't be able to share their knowledge. The little one was a believer, so it wasn't necessary to chase him down. But if the boy kept going North there was a chance, they'd cross paths near the snipe's lair. What a pleasant thought...

Tyler's cell phone rang, lighting up the screen. It was 8:45pm, but there was no answer and the phone went to voice mail. Jake Yoakum frowned at his own phone and put it back into his pocket. Where the hell were the damn kids? They should have been back by now! Some of the mothers were beginning to fret, along with the grandparents and it was dragging down the festive mood of the Halloween party. If Jake just zoomed out of there, he'd risk getting them all riled up. Not to mention he'd be stuck using Pop's ancient station wagon. Tyler had taken everyone up to the field in his truck because that creepy Eric's was a god damned germ freak and wouldn't let any of the kids ride in his car. Not that many people would've fit in the tiny Fiat, but shit, that wasn't neighborly! He'd be having some words with the boy once everybody showed up.

Speaking of creepy Eric, it turned out that he had himself a visitor. He'd finally woken up from his post-orgasmic snooze and was still foggily wondering where everyone was. Boy! He couldn't wait to go scare the shit out of those kids they'd sent on a "snipe hunt." Ha-ha! Everyone knew that was the corniest old trick in the book. Snipes didn't even exist! It was just a way to get little kids to burn off some of their Halloween candy energy and give the big kids a little fun at their expense. Snipes! That was hilarious. Eric laughed until he switched to screaming as the foxy head of the snipe came slithering into view.

"What the fuck is *that*?" Eric shrieked. It looked like the result of a boa constrictor mating with a fox. The nightmare creature kept getting closer. "Holy shit! Guys? Hey, guys?" Eric's voice was climbing as the Snipe grinned, showing off blood smeared teeth. Its long serpentine tongue flickered out. Well, well…Mister "Never-Never" came with some special sauce. How nice! The eyes glowed green in appreciation of this bonus. As the scratchy tongue moved across his face, Eric realized that this thing was for real. It wasn't a joke and the guys weren't going to help him get out of dodge. It was up to him whether or not he was going to live long enough to tell his grandkids, or anybody, about this thing. His fingers clutched the ground and found the hickory stick he'd made. Then, in one quick movement, he struck the Snipe's tongue with it. With an angry hiss, the beast recoiled.

"Ha-ha! How do you like my stick?" Eric crowed. The snipe growled at him, then went into convulsions, making him cheer. "I knew that would work! Especially when you're just dealing with a dumb animal! Ha-ha!" He started backing away with his stick held high, but his victory was cut short when the Snipe's head whipped forward and spat a shiny metal thing into his face so hard that it broke his front teeth.

Eric plucked the metal thing out of his mouth and looked at it. "What the hell?" Did this weird ass creature shoot bullets? He wiped the blood off the oval shape and found himself looking at Benny's WWF belt buckle. "Oh no..." Eric moaned through bloody lips as he stared at it. "What happened to Benny?" he asked the grinning, ballooning head of the Snipe. It didn't answer, but he didn't have much longer to worry about his friend's fate, anyway. Instead of extending its tongue for another stick slap, the snipe's head turned vertically and the open mouth slammed down over Eric's body. Then it closed, crushing him with so much force that the sounds of his bones breaking echoed through the trees. It chewed, pausing a moment to eject the three-foot-long piece of hickory wood, then swallowed Eric with a happy moan of its own.

Tyler lay nearby in his feed sack covered state. His balls ached from all the kicking and he was groggy from the unexpected attack. He wanted to get up, but he couldn't because the two hard cloth sacks were fitted so tightly over his upper body that he could barely move his arms. "Goddamn bastards!" He roared, but it was barely audible through the two layers of fabric. He'd always known that Eric was a creep. The guy got his jollies doing, "experiments" on obviously suffering creatures and posting them on YouTube under the handle, Professor Pain. But Benny? Now that surprised him. Sure he was more brawn than brain, but still…Well it just showed that you didn't always know a guy! Tyler rolled himself back and forth on the ground hoping to loosen the bags. It was slow going, but he thought he could feel movement…

Jake Yoakum was trying not to pace around the brightly lit barn and ruin the festive mood, but damn it, he was getting nervous. Either something had gone wrong or the boys thought they were being funny. Well this Dad wasn't laughing. The agreed upon plan was to let the little ones do some Snipe hunting for an hour max. After that everybody was supposed to head for the Halloween party in the barn. He'd called Tyler's phone multiple times after things went past the hour mark and finally left him a curt voicemail. Still, no call back, nobody arrived, just nothing. He was just about to ask Pop for his keys, when the barn door squeaked open making one of the mothers scream.

"Here they come!" yelled Yvonne Mooney, when her littlest, Ralph, squeezed through and ran into her arms. He was followed by another boy until all ten little kids were in the barn. But nobody seemed ready to party. In fact the youngest, Carl Hutchins, sat down and immediately fell asleep. They were all filthy and quiet. While the mothers fussed over the kids, Jake looked out the door. Nobody else was out there.

"What the hell?" Tyler yelled from inside his feed sack prison. Something heavy hit the ground near him and suddenly he felt kind of warm. There was also a stink like rotten meat that came with whatever it was. "Guys? Come on! I think you've done enough damage for the night!" Nobody replied, but something sharp poked through the feed sack and sliced it open. "Finally!" Tyler shouted. "I'm glad you bozos are finished! I can take a joke, but…Damnnn!" His relief turned to terror as he pushed open the sacks to reveal a pair of luminous green eyes and a grinning mouth full of razor sharp teeth.

The Snipe was feeling pretty good after two large meals, but still needed more food to prepare for its next hibernation period. Once it entered the cave, it wouldn't be able to leave the bewitched entrance after the sun rose. Then it had to wait for the next nonbeliever to make their opinion. Usually every Halloween, but sometimes longer. Not enough food meant dying and the Snipe hadn't survived for well over a century by not taking care of itself. The little ones would have been so sweet and delicious! But the ruckus caused by the bigger boys ruined all of that! There went all those lovely meals…

Then the Snipe stumbled over just what it needed, another large meal of human flesh. It was even gift wrapped! Well, well things were looking up! So handy and quick, but where was the fun in that? It was a creature who enjoyed the chase, screaming, and the delicious smell of fear. Having something unaware of its fate was no good! So the Snipe gave Tyler a chance by pulling the feed sacks off of him. The effect was priceless.

"AAAAAUUUGGGGHHHH!" Tyler screamed as the serpent with the tiger striped fox head moved closer and opened its mouth. Looking like a cartoon character, he tried to run as fast as he could away from whatever the hell was after him. Benny must've put a roofie in his beer or something. There was no way this thing could be real! But instinctively, he knew it was. Deep down he'd always feared that Snipes were actually real and now he knew. Sadly, he wasn't going to be able to share his knowledge with humanity because this one was getting to work fast. Even though Tyler's feet were moving, they were just flailing in the air as he was lassoed by the Snipe's long tongue. Then he was flying high, free as a bird! Until the monster's jaws slammed shut around him like a bear trap and everything went black.

The mothers and grandparents had finally gotten the children into party mode by giving them espresso spiked hot chocolate. They also played some fun kiddie music to bring the energy up. While that was nice for the little ones, Tyler's Dad just couldn't keep a smile pasted on his face. Something was wrong and much more of this hokey Halloween happiness was going to make him scream. Finally, after pleading an upset stomach, Jake was able to get outside the barn for some "fresh air." But as he walked briskly towards the other vehicles, Jake discovered that Pop had already driven off in the old Chevy wagon. Shit!

He stood at the end of the drive for a minute while weighing his options and decided against frightening the children any more than they had already been. Instead, he began walking up the road to the hayfield. He had a set of keys to his truck and intended to drive it home with his son in it. If Tyler was lucky, the walk would work out some of his anger, but Jake sincerely doubted that it would.

As the party sounds faded behind Jake's footsteps, the Snipe was heading back to its lair. It had hoped to score that last young, tasty meal before going into hibernation, but it could deal. This wouldn't be the first time and it sure wouldn't be the last. Plus, the Snipe was starting get pretty tired and it didn't want to risk not being able to enter the den upon its return.

The trails converged and became narrower until Adam found himself stumbling down a single path that was overgrown but smooth, like it had been in use for a very long time. He hoped that it would take him into town or at least, closer to home. However, things got increasingly more rocky and craggy until Adam found himself at a dead end up against Christy Mountain. "Balls!" Adam shouted at the solid rock wall in front of him.

"This is some bullshit!" he sobbed. After walking and running what felt like miles, this was his reward? To turn around and go all the way back to where you started from? Well, fuck a duck and nuts to that! Adam kicked the rock wall with his shoe, only to watch in disbelief as his foot disappeared inside of it. As he looked closer at the wall, he saw there was an old tunnel hidden in plain sight. It was an optical illusion caused by the colors of the rock. Even though it looked dark in the tunnel, it seemed like a better choice than going back the way he came. For all he knew, Eric and Benny were close behind and ready to torture him in some new way that Eric had wet-dreamed about. Fucking creepos! Besides, there must be a shorter way to reach the farm and Adam figured this might be it. He took a deep breath and stepped inside.

As Adam was stepping into the dark tunnel in hopes of being rewarded for all his efforts at staying alive, Jake had finished his walk up to the hay field turn-in. He could see his old red pickup parked near the tree line. It was deathly quiet there, which threw the idea of extended partying out the window. Maybe when he opened the door he'd find Tyler fast asleep. Instead, all Jake found was his son's cellphone on the dash. It was full of messages from him. He shouted for the boys but there was no answer.

The tunnel was beginning to smell bad and Adam was losing hope that this was really an escape route. He didn't want to turn around though because maybe he was close to something and didn't know it. About all that he knew for sure was that his Nikes were definitely not new anymore! No dazzling whiteness was left for him to follow as he kept trudging forward. Adam was trying to remember who'd made that speech about it being the darkest just before dawn, when he walked face first into a rock wall. The tunnel had petered out to nothing. Shit! He was going to have to turn around.

As the Snipe travelled the boulder strewn path that led to its lair, it smelled something. Just a trace, but it was a good smell. A lively smell of sweat and fear. The Snipe started feeling excited. Maybe it hadn't missed that last meal, after all…

Jake looked for the boys. He found the embers of their fire, a crushed pack of Marlboros, and some beer bottles. Nothing very odd. He kept on to where the paths went into the woods and slipped in something gooey. There was a hickory stick in the middle of whatever it was and it smelled disgusting. That damn Eric and his animal experiments. He couldn't even do a simple Snipe Hunt right! Jake wiped his hands on the bandanna he kept in his back pocket and walked on.

Adam fought his way back towards the open end of the cave. Man, he was exhausted and just wanted to lay down…It was taking so long to get back. He hoped that by now he'd see the light of dawn from the mouth of the tunnel. Instead there was a flaring up of two green headlights that seemed to be moving closer. Maybe Tyler's Dad had come to look for them! Adam ran towards the lights, yelling "Mr. Yoakum! Mr. Yoakum! It's me, Adam McCoy! Over here!" The headlights moved towards him. Yahoo! He was finally getting out of this nightmare! Then he smelled that meaty odor and the air became hot. He hadn't noticed a warm spring when he'd entered the cave but now something was dripping on him…

The Snipe got happier the farther he travelled into his den. The last teenager had trapped himself inside the cave, a possibility the Snipe had only dreamed about. Now that it was really happening, the creature chuckled and grinned at his good fortune. There was no way out. Having this last good meal before dropping into his year-long slumber would be so much better. As his glowing eyes searched the cave, the little twit came right to him.

"Help!" cried Adam. The quick movement, the meaty smell, the warm air, all reminded him of the fire and when Benny was chasing him. He heard the screams and knew something had happened back there but he didn't feel the need to go back and check. In his opinion Eric and Benny deserved whatever they got. There was a slithery sound and something grabbed him around the waist, pulling him into what felt like a room full of razorblades.

The Snipe chewed and swallowed his meal. It was so full and tired that it nearly forgot to roll the boulder in front of the entrance. Moving slowly now, it heaved the massive hunk of stone in place then made its way to the rear of the cave. The snipe yawned, turned itself three times, wrapped itself into a ball, and drifted into pleasant dreams of next Halloween's feast. He couldn't wait until the next snipe hunt and foolish nonbeliever.

Back at the barn everything was quiet and cleaned up until next year. All the children had been carried home to bed. Most of them slept soundly with the exception of little Ralph Mooney who kept waking his exhausted parents with his terrified tale of the Snipe. His father cursed the teens for taking things too far. It was one thing to inject a little excitement into Halloween, but sometimes these kids got a little over the top. He and his wife finally got little Ralph to sleep with some warm milk laced with honey and just a bit of Dimetapp. Art Mooney shook his head. "He has big green eyes and looks like a tiger snake!" Ralph had whispered to them. He would have a talk with Jake Yoakum in the morning about *that!*

It turned out that Jake was beginning to feel kind of like little Ralph Mooney. He was facing a situation that couldn't be possible, yet it was. He looked and looked, but all he found were a few feed sacks. A couple of them were shredded up pretty bad, but Jake couldn't make any connection.

It was like a stage that had suddenly been deserted by the actors. Any moment, he expected to see them come striding down the hill with laughter in their eyes. But they didn't. Just a few hickory sticks strewn about and that was it. Jake called for them, hoping there was a chance they were nearby. "Tyler? Boys! Eric? Let's go guys! Benny and Adam? Where are you guys? Fellas!" The only answer he received was the cawing of a crow that seemed to be mocking him. Four boys gone for no earthly reason. Jake Yoakum slowly walked back to his truck. Then he sat down inside of it and cried.

Wandering Grove
Trevor Newton

"It's almost six," Carolyn said. "I should get home before Kenneth comes in from work." She reached across Richard's chest, opened the dresser drawer and retrieved her wedding ring.

"I don't understand why you bring that in just to take it off," Richard said. "You could just leave it in the car."

"Really? That's it?" She looked back at him. "You don't want me to toss it in the lake, file divorce papers and move in with you?"

"Come on, that's not how I meant it."

"The further away it is, the more permanent this seems." She sighed, sitting up. "I'm not a twenty-eight year old bachelor, like you. I'm almost forty. I have children to think about."

Carolyn stood and Richard grabbed her wrist. "I want to see you as soon as I'm back from this job."

"We'll see, Dick."

"I'll leave a phonebook in your driveway again."

Carolyn retraced her steps from the bedroom to the front door, gathering her clothes off the floor. She returned to the bedroom fully dressed and sat on the edge of the bed. As much as Richard detested the remarks of throwing the wedding ring away and filing divorce papers; he had to admit it was true. He wanted nothing more than to come home to her every day, eat dinner with her and fall asleep in each other's arms. But she was right, she didn't just have a husband to think of, she had kids, too.

"What's this new case about?" Carolyn asked, smiling. Richard knew it was an attempt to steer away from what weighed heavily on both their minds.

"I honestly don't know how to answer that," Richard said.

"Well, you said you *find* things for people. What does this person want you to find?"

"This guy sent me a letter instead of an email, so I know he's nuts," Richard said, picking the envelope up off the dresser.

"How do you figure that?"

"People who still send snail mail typically all do it for the same reason: they think someone's watching them. Besides, his letter seems like something written by a drunk. It starts off sounding like he needs help finding his daughter, which is above my pay grade, then delves into finding some sort of town called Wandering

Grove. I'm supposed to meet him at Cafe Tipping Point tomorrow morning at seven."

Carolyn's disinterest was obvious. She leaned over, placed a hand on his cheek and kissed him. "See you again sometime."

Richard counted her footsteps and, when the front door clicked shut, pictured himself running after her and kissing her, like the happy ending to a romance movie. Instead, he fell asleep with knots tightening in his stomach.

It wasn't hard to distinguish his client from the regulars of Cafe Tipping Point. The man was old, at least in his seventies, and a few months past needing a haircut and shave. "You must be Mr. Miller," the man said, extending a frail, bony hand. "I'm Dr. Allen Young. I wasn't sure if you'd show." His English accent was thick, like an actor in some obscure, dated film.

Doctor. Wow.

"I try to respond to all my clients, though I have to admit, your letter isn't very clear. I'm not sure what you're looking for."

"My daughter," Allen said, sitting down in the booth. "Did you want a coffee?"

"No, I'm fine." Richard took a deep breath. "Listen, missing persons is *not* what I do. I find missing *items*. Possessions. I'm afraid you've wasted your time. You'll need to contact a detective."

"A detective won't help me. He'll just snicker at my expense, call me crazy, maybe even have me admitted now that I'm old."

"I don't understand."

"My daughter passed away in nineteen sixty-eight."

Richard stared at the man, studying him. He almost expected him to laugh, to laugh at wasting his time or maybe maniacally like some sort of escaped lunatic on the fringe of reality. But he didn't. He just stared back, with tears on the verge of cascading. Richard stood up and slid out of the booth. Allen grabbed his arm, looking up at him. "She's in Wandering Grove."

Richard jerked his arm from the old man's grasp. "Wandering Grove isn't even real. I googled it this morning. Nothing."

The old man laughed, showing many discolored and half rotten teeth. "You won't find it on *any* map, young man."

"You should go to a psychiatrist," Richard said, walking to the door.

"She's there because I killed her!"

Patrons darted their eyes around wildly before landing on the old man. Low whispers resounded throughout. Richard hung his head low, flushed from embarrassment and walked outside. He expected the old man to follow him after the hysterical reveal, but he stayed seated, tracing Richard's path with his dark eyes, staring with such intensity that veins protruded from his forehead.

***

Kenneth sat in a rocking chair on the front porch of his home, smoking a cigar and reading a newspaper. Richard had watched him for two hours, waiting for him to either leave or go inside. He looked happy. Richard wondered how the expression on his face would change if he marched up the porch and told him he had been sleeping with his wife for a year. His grip around the phonebook tightened.

Just go inside, you motherfucker.

Carolyn, smiling, opened the door and called him inside. Richard looked at his watch: noon. Lunchtime.

Richard cranked his Honda, drove parallel with their driveway and tossed the phonebook out the window. He sped down the road, ignoring all the stop signs between their home and his apartment.

He wandered around the apartment aimlessly, watching television, checking emails, attempting to cook a meal. The old man's final message echoed through his mind.

She's there because I killed her!

What could that mean? The man was a doctor. How could a man of such intellect *be* so crazy? But, what proof did Richard have that he *was* a doctor? He *said* he was, but he could just as easily be lying through his teeth hoping it would further the validity of his tall tale.

The doorbell rang. Richard quickly squirmed off the couch. Carolyn was rarely able to sneak away on the weekends, but maybe Kenneth took the kids out somewhere and she claimed to have a headache. He opened the door with a smile and the hollow barrel of a .357 grinned back at him.

"I'm coming in," Allen said.

Richard slowly backed away from the door, bumping into the kitchen table. "Doctor, let's not do anything crazy here, huh?"

"We're going to Wandering Grove, get what you need."

"You should think about what it is you're doing. You could go to jail for this."

"I'm done thinking!" he shouted

"All right, all right."

"No one has believed me for decades, Mr. Miller. The thought of doing this has been in the back of my mind since nineteen seventy-five, when two detectives laughed in my face. *Laughed*—at a man who lost his child. I'm seventy-three years old now, Mr. Miller, and this thought is no longer idly lingering in the back of my thoughts. I want to see my daughter. I *will* see my daughter. It's my dying wish."

"Dying?"

"Lung cancer. I've six weeks at best."

"It doesn't make any sense."

"And it never will, Mr. Miller. Life will *never* be fully comprehensible. Now, let's go to your car. We've a long drive ahead of us."

The old man wasn't lying—they drove for well over five hours while he gave directions, Allen never taking his aim off Richard. He turned down a dirt path amidst a dense forest as instructed.

"Park. We'll have to walk the rest of the way."

Fall leaves crunched underneath their feet. Allen stood behind Richard, walking with a slight limp, a gun in one hand and a cane in the other. "We're almost there," Allen said.

"You expect me to believe that there's an entire town somewhere in these woods?"

"Something like that."

Richard squinted ahead. Through the now darkening forest, a bright yellow light swirled between two tall, wicked trees. Its size grew as they walked closer, extending well over twenty feet into the sky once they were upon it. It churned audibly like a wooden pole running through a tub of lard, vibrating the surrounding air and providing a candle-like heat. Richard's mouth hung open, his eyes wide with surprise, confusion. He looked at his hands, his arms. The color of his skin and clothes no longer clutched uniqueness, but succumbed to thick radiating yellow. Allen tucked the gun in his waistband. "I suspect that won't be necessary anymore. Will it, Mr. Miller?"

"What is this?"

"It's a portal I opened in nineteen seventy-one. After my Suzie passed away, I spent all my time at the library reading up on witches, dark magic and the occult. With what little money my wife graciously allowed me to keep after our divorce, I traveled the world to gather all the ingredients to open it. It took me seventeen months, but I did it."

"What's on the other side?"

"Wandering Grove, you fool. I thought you would at least be able to make that connection."

"What *is* Wandering Grove? And if you know how to get there, why do you need my help?"

"Because my daughter is in there. Somewhere." Allen tapped a cigarette from a soft pack, lighting it. He coughed violently from the first inhale. "I don't know exactly what sort of place it is. It's something like purgatory, but not precisely. It's a middle-area, where people go after the exact moment of death. It's a place of journey and self-exploration—until they reach Heaven or Hell."

The duo slowly walked through the portal, and the leaves and forest turned into a roadway. It was two lanes, but wide enough to easily accommodate six. Allen looked around, squinting, then pointed at a road sign. "Birch Lane," he said. "It's important we remember that. You never arrive in the same place twice, but in order to leave you must do so from your last point of entry." Allen jotted the name down on a notepad.

"It's dark, but—"

"Not a normal dark, yes," Allen finished. "It's always like that here, a timid grayish blue."

They walked further in, passing a rusty sign that announced they were a mile away from the city limits. A gas station, looking long abandoned, showed up as they finished walking up a steep incline. An elderly man in a wheelchair was banging his fists on a vending machine, screaming at it. Richard started to walk toward him, but Allen annoyingly grabbed his arm again. "Wait."

Allen picked up a rock and weakly tossed it toward the wheelchair bound man. The man reacted, looking around. "He's a Wandering Soul, not an apparition."

"What does that mean?"

"It means he can hear us, see us, interact with us. But we shouldn't. We're outsiders and fiddling about with his journey to his final resting place isn't wise."

The man's screams grew louder, molding into desperate cries. Richard shook his head and walked across the road into the gas station parking lot. Allen sighed behind him. A note was taped to the back of the man's wheelchair. Richard took it off, reading it. *KID FUCKER COCHRAN,* it read.

The man wheeled around, eyeing Richard, then the note. He snatched it from Richard's hand. "Them no good fuckers are always pulling this shit on me!" he shouted. "I ain't never touched no kids! Not never! Them townspeople was liars, every one of 'em! Billy Cochran ain't never touched no kids!" He turned his attention back to the vending machine, pounding his fists against it. It was vacant of snacks, except for one dead rat in the top right corner. The man raised his fist over his head, shouted, and slammed it against the machine with all his might. The rat finally came loose, falling into the bucket. He reached in, grabbed it and tore at its dried flesh with his gums. Richard walked back to Allen, his late-afternoon lunch bubbling in his stomach, daring to expose itself.

Richard couldn't shake the *feeling* of Wandering Grove. The smell reminded him of spending winter break at his grandmother's cabin in Vermont. Mothballs, lotion, the charred bits of a dying fire with grease mixed in from roasting weenies the night prior. The air felt thick, like a cloak clinging around his body. Shuffling could be heard around them; in the woods. If Richard reacted quick enough, he'd catch a glimpse of the monstrosities dwelling in the woods. Claws, snouts, sharp teeth. They appeared lathered in some sort of liquid, shimmering off the light from the moon.

"They're what happens to a Wandering Soul when they never find their resting place," Allen said. "It's rare, and it can take centuries, but it does happen."

"Jesus."

"They wish."

Allen's limp was getting worse. He groaned with each step and, once they were a couple hundred feet into the desolate city, he collapsed against a set of stairs that lead up to a modest home. Richard attempted to help him up. "No," Allen said. "I'm sorry, I need to rest."

"Take all the time you need," Richard said, taking a seat next to him.

Across the street stood an apartment complex. Many of the lights were turned on, illuminating the occupants tending to seemingly everyday chores and activities. Watching television, cooking, Yoga. Richard counted the story's: twenty-five.

"People live here?" Richard asked.

"Some souls find their way to Heaven or Hell fast. Others, not so much. It's why I have faith that we'll find my little girl."

"Would she still be...*little*?"

The old man's eyes wandered from his feet to the city that lay before him. He took a deep breath. "No," he managed. "I guess she wouldn't be. Not if she's still looking."

Two small boys, no older than ten, started walking toward them. Allen laid a hand on Richard's arm, looked him in the eye and shook his head. "Look at their *beings*," he said. Richard wasn't sure what he meant. He squinted, studying them; their features. They were both white-skinned and blonde haired, dressed in overalls and vintage looking caps. Neither wore shoes.

Then he noticed it. Ever so slightly, you could *see* through them.

"It's a past soul's apparition," Allen said.

"I don't understand," Richard said, standing up.

"When a soul finds his or her final resting place, an apparitional image is left behind. Think of it like a scene in a movie. It'll show you the defining moment that lead them to either Heaven or Hell."

The boys passed by, not paying any notion to Allen and Richard's presence. Richard followed them.

"You shouldn't do that! You may see something you wished you hadn't!"

He didn't listen. This was all too fascinating. One of the boys held an old glass Pepsi bottle filled with a transparent, yellowish liquid.

"You bring the kitchen matches?" one of them asked.

"Darn tootin'," the other replied. "Stole 'em from momma this mornin'."

"This is gonna be wild, Bucky."

After a few moments, they stopped and looked down into a hole. The one with the bottle began pouring it inside, drizzling it. Richard looked inside and his heart lurched in his chest. At the bottom, several small cats and a couple of rabbits were inside, crammed together, trying to shake the liquid off their coats.

"Hey, HEY!" Richard shouted. He knelt down to grab the boy with the matches and his hands went right through him. The boy lit the match, and the two of them shared a sinister smile with one another. Richard got down on his stomach and tried to pull the animals out but it was no use, his hands went through them as well. The match was dropped into the pit. Flames roared from its opening, but Richard felt no heat. Only sadness, as crying mews were drowned out by the crackling of the fire. He stumbled away from the scene, back to where Allen was still sitting, and vomited on the sidewalk.

"You should listen to me," Allen said, smoking another cigarette.

Thunder roared in the distance and wicked streaks of lightning struck the earth. Allen planted his cane and pulled himself up. He walked up the steps and opened the door to the abandoned home.

"What are you doing?"

"It's almost night," Allen replied. "We must stay indoors until morning. Those damned souls you saw in the woods earlier—they come out at night."

The interior of the home smelled of dry musk and rot. The floorboards creaked with each hesitant step and dared to give way. Allen closed the door behind them, locking it, then tugged on an old dinner table to prop against it.

"You're thinking they'll try to come in?" Richard asked.

"I brought a man with me once, some twenty or thirty years ago now. We were pen pals for a while. I spilled my discovery to him one night when I'd had too much to drink and dropped the letter in the postal box. Two months later he flew from Scotland to the states, hellbent on going with me. I told him it was too dangerous but he was the exact opposite of everyone else. He begged me to take him. We holed up inside of a store that night. The windows were huge—you could see straight in. That was our mistake. When they came out, they could smell the *real world* on our bodies. It drove them mad. They aren't able to register that we're human, or any sort of living being, for that matter. They just smell that smell, and try to climb through your body as if it's a portal back home. The last image of that Scotsman is burned into my mind. The thing had shoved its head and arms down his throat, shredding him on the inside. Several of them chased me back to our entry point. I barely had enough time to throw my hex bag on the ground and return."

"Jesus."

"It's important that no matter what we hear tonight, we don't open the door."

The storm grew more vicious; the wind howling and whistling through the cracks of the decayed walls. They shared a sleeve of stale saltines Allen had brought along. They were moist from sitting in his overcoat. They talked like normal people for once, discussing politics, sports teams and childhood memories—the warped world outside the walls seeming far and irrelevant. Soon they found themselves sharing a cigarette and drifting into a somber doze.

The thunder roared once more and lightning struck against a tree nearby, jerking them both awake. But that wasn't the only noise. A moaning, a small desperate cry was coming closer. Allen put his finger over his lips, signaling for Richard to be quiet. He shuffled into a squatting position, delicately lifting himself up to look out the window. A woman, no older than thirty, wearing a halter top and leopard leggings was walking around in the street disoriented. She would have been beautiful, but awful pulsing tumours leaking thick cream-colored liquids cursed her otherwise fascinating appearance.

She caught his glance from the window.

Richard ducked. "Shit."

Her tumultuous wailing rose and soon she was running to the door of the house, beating on it and begging to be let in. *"Please, oh please, let me in. He's going to kill me. He's cut out my baby."*

Allen shook his head at him.

"You have to let me in! I'll die out here—oh God—I'll die out here. He says he'll feed it to me once he's got me."

Richard stood up. "She needs help," he said, walking to the door.

The old man stood, breathing heavily, and took the revolver from his waistband. "I haven't been wrong once!" he shouted. Richard looked at him, then to the door and back again. "I'm telling you, if you open that door, it will be detrimental!" The whites of his eyes beamed through the hollow darkness.

"She's not like what I saw in the woods!" Richard shouted back.

"Yet!" Allen replied.

Her pleas turned to laughter. Richard stepped back from the door, his heart thudding in his chest.

"I know all about your little affair," she said between snickers.

"Don't listen to her," Allen said.

"Oh, but do. You think she only spreads her legs for you? Kenneth and Carolyn have had an open marriage since they took their vows. When she's not pumping your cock, she's pumping your neighbor, and the neighbor next to him...and so on. She's even thinking of marking you off her list. You're hanging by a thread, Dick. Soon you'll be all alone with only your pathetic make-believe detective job to hold onto."

The door shook within its frame, jarring back and forth, echoing through the house. Richard covered his ears—her voice sounded strangely like his mother's.

"I don't miss you, Dick," she said. It *was* his mother. *"Dying from that brain tumour was the best thing that ever happened to me."*

"Whoever you think she sounds like, it's not them. I promise you," Allen said, limping to the door. He fired his revolver at the door twice, and outside the thing thudded against the pavement. He turned back, looking into Richard's eyes, which were now tearing up. "We should get some rest. Tomorrow we strategize."

Sleep came in increments, never longer than half an hour before disturbed by either thunder or animalistic sounds in the night. After losing count of interruptions, Richard finally propped himself against the wall and waited for Allen to wake up. The storm was dying down. The wind no longer stirred, and the rain tapered off into a drizzle.

Allen awoke to find Richard staring off into nothingness, amidst an obvious deep thought. "You're awake," he said, jarring him back to reality.

"Yes."

"What were you thinking about?" Allen asked, sitting up and rubbing his eyes.

"Yesterday, when I followed those kids. Their *defining moment* was setting a hole full of animals on fire."

Allen grunted.

"I couldn't interact with them. I tried touching them, but my hands went through them. Same with the animals. But the hole…the hole was there. I stuck my hand into it. It was real."

"I fail to understand your connection."

"It's like…it's like this place generated something for their apparitional image to be accurate." He turned his head, looking deep into Allen's eyes. "Where did your daughter die?"

He deeply exhaled through his nose. "At our home."

"You know the streets here well, I take it?"

"Most of them."

"Are any of them the same name as the street you lived on when your daughter passed?"

Allen's eyes widened, wildly tracing around the room. "Y-yes."

Richard nodded. "That's where we go, then. But, you realize, if I'm right about this—"

"Then she's passed on. I won't be able to interact with her. Yes, I know."

Richard nodded again, standing up. He helped Allen get to his feet as well.

The woman from the previous night had melted into a liquid silver, mixed with the cream-colored secretions from her tumours. Her clothes floated in the substance. Allen lead the way, his limp now more stiff than ever, and Richard followed close by. Wandering Soul's stared at them, sizing them up, and Allen periodically looked back at Richard. He was done following and interacting with these beings, as outlandish and fascinating as they might be. His apartment seemed like a lost paradise right about now.

He thought of what the woman had said, wondering if it was true. Was Carolyn really having multiple affairs? It didn't matter, he decided. What he was doing was immoral and ultimately a waste of time. It would never lead to anything serious or permanent. Once he got back to the real world, he would cut off the relationship and pursue something more ordinary. A relationship that wasn't just spending time in bed, but going out to dinners and parties together, publicly enjoying each other's company without worrying about gossip or being caught. Normality; luxurious.

"Do you want to hear the weirdest thing someone hired me to find before this?" Richard asked, breaking the silence.

"Sure."

"I had just flown back into America from Nepal. I spent months there helping a group of explorers locate some sort of statue. I get back home and the first guy that hires me needs help finding a quarter. He says he earned that quarter helping his father herd sheep and transport them to an auction house. It was the first piece of money he'd ever earned and on his way to spend it in town, some bullies took it from him. He begged them to give him back the quarter, and you know what they did?"

"Hmm?"

"They threw it in a lake and said if you really want that quarter, go find it. But he couldn't swim, and the quarter sat at the bottom of the lake for forty-seven years. He tells me this whole story in an email and says money isn't an object for him, he'll pay whatever it takes. I dig a little deeper into the guy's name, turns out he worked for Wal-mart way back in the day when they gave their employees a shitton of shares. He sold them sometime in the late nineties, and put the money into fucking Amazon on a whim. Guy's worth millions upon millions.

"I hired an entire scuba team to assist on the dive and paid out of pocket. We had no contract or anything, he could've pulled out at any minute and I would've been fucked. But he didn't. He wanted that quarter and, three months and seventeen thousand dollars later, we found it.

"He paid in cash, too. I'll never forget that day. I handed him twenty-five cents in exchange for twenty thousand dollars. There's some sort of lesson to be learned there, but I'll be damned if I know what it is."

"That's quite a story, Mr. Miller," Allen said.

"I thought so, too. Then you brought me to this place."

Allen chuckled and stiffly turned left in the middle of an intersection. It was the first time Richard saw Allen in a normal sort of state. Even through their discussions before the woman's arrival the previous night, his stiltedness, his hesitation to be vulnerable in the slightest, was still present. But not for that split second of morbid laughter.

It fell into a blank expression as Allen looked up at the road sign: Hartford Dr.

"This is it?" Richard asked.

"Yes."

They walked down the road. It was a suburban area; Floridian style houses planted firmly on concrete slabs, white picket fences, slanted driveways, well manicured lawns. Dusty Mercedes, Lincolns and Cadillacs lined the driveways. A few Wandering Souls were about in the yards, looking into the windows of the homes, touching and surveying the cars. Perhaps longing for their old lives, reminiscing before finally succumbing to inevitability. Some looked their way as they passed. They weren't like the others. They smiled and waved, then awkwardly put down their hands as Allen and Richard paid them no attention.

Allen stopped dead in his tracks, dropping his cane, falling into a deep bout of tears. He fell to his knees, clutching his heart. Richard looked ahead at a house on the left side of the road. A little girl with blonde pigtails, wearing a red dress, was playing with her dolls in the driveway.

"She's gone!" Allen shouted.

Richard knelt down and forcefully lifted the old man back to his feet. Tears cascaded down his cheeks, filling the cracks of his withered, wrinkled skin. "You can still say goodbye."

"You don't know what happens next," Allen said, turning around.

The car in the driveway started reversing. The girl screamed to no avail, and the bumper connected with her head, knocking her unconscious and thudding against the pavement. The tire rolled over her face, reflecting the most egregious popping sound Richard had ever heard.

She's there because I killed her!

"Her defining moment," Richard muttered under his breath.

"Yes." Allen looked up and back where they had come, his lips still curled and trembling. "She didn't live long enough to be defined by anything heinous or heroic." His eyes closed. "Her death *was* her defining moment."

Richard nodded. The apparitional image began to repeat in the distance, and Richard attempted to urge Allen away.

"No," he said, jerking away from Richard. He dug into his overcoat and retrieved a small hex bag and a wad of money. "Go back the way we came. When you get there, throw the hex bag against the ground at the exact point of entry."

"What about you?"

"I won't be returning with you," he said. The popping noise repeated behind them. Richard winced, gritting his teeth. "The money is for your time."

"Won't you become one of those…*things*?"

"Perhaps," Allen said, nodding. "This is my mistake to deal with. My punishment to accept."

Richard slowly nodded. "You're sure?"

"Yes, go on. Before nightfall."

The two boys were heading back to their hole of doomed animals, on their way to cement their fate, now a little more transparent. Fading away.

Billy Cochran never made it into the city. When Richard passed by, his intestines were tied to a light pole and his body slowly swung back and forth like a pendulum. His eyes were glazed in a smoky black, his final facial expression portraying fear and confusion, frozen now in death.

Outside Richard's apartment building, a mustached police officer was ticketing an old Pontiac for being illegally parked. He had no doubts of who it belonged to.

The phonebook was on the kitchen table. A heart-shaped note of legal paper laid on top, saying: *I came by, but you weren't here. I hope the job is going well. I'll try again tonight if I don't hear from you. You shouldn't leave your door unlocked.*

Richard tossed the phonebook and written note in the trash. When a knock came from the front door later that night, he didn't answer.

The Children in the Courtyard Garden

R.C. Mulhare

For my mother, Ida

"You sure you don't need me to do anything else?" Diane asked, a pucker of unnecessary concern folding her smooth, young brow.

Marcelline rested her age-creased hands on the edge of the kitchen counter in her new apartment, glancing away from her daughter. "I'm fine, you've done enough." She gazed out the window overlooking the courtyard garden in the middle of the apartment complex in a more thickly settled part of Manuxet, a trio of Victorian houses broken up into apartments. She thought she saw movement among the bushes and small plots dotting the garden, but the wind could have shaken the bushes.

"You sure? I'm going to the store anyway."

"You've done enough with the unpacking. I need to do things for myself, you know. I'm old but I'm still spry." Marcelline smiled with what she hoped looked like reassurance. "I'd like to see Connor and Madison more often, though."

"They're only a phone call away, too, Mom. Just ask and I'll bring them along."

"Every time I ask, you say they're busy with sports or Scouts or schoolwork or something." She didn't remember Diane and her younger sister Cecily having so many extracurricular activities, but they grew up in a different era. When did kids these days get to be kids? "I'll walk out with you, if you like. I need some fresh air after all this work."

"Okay, but if you need anything, just call." Diane held her arm out. Marcelline slipped her shoulder under it, hugging her.

They stepped apart. Marcelline and Diane walked out into the hallway and down the three flights of stairs to the stoop. When Diane had driven away, Marcelline buzzed herself back into the apartment house, fetching her jacket.

She went to the mailbox in the entryway, unlocking it and collecting the mail. She let herself out the rear door leading to the courtyard.

The fresh air blowing through the doorway smelled of recent rain and damp leaves. The bench she saw from her window had dried off, though puddles glinting with spring sunlight still filled in the lower parts of the gravel walk. She sat down to open her mail.

Footsteps crunched in the gravel, pausing before her. "Are you a grandmother?" She looked up from her letter. A red-headed, freckle-faced boy about five or six, clad in a green long sleeved jersey over denim pants, stood before her.

"Yes, though I don't get to see my grand-kids as often as I'd like," she said. "Do you live here?"

"Yes, up there." He pointed to the window below the one in her kitchen.

A girl about nine or ten, with darker red hair than his and clad in a violet jersey under overalls, approached. "I'm Justin, what's your name?" he asked Marcelline, paying no attention to the girl.

"I'm Marcelline." The boy asked many questions, but kids liked to know as much as they could about the world around them.

"Justin, are you bothering this lady?" the girl asked.

"No, he isn't," Marcelline said. "I'm new here and probably strange to him. I don't mind him wanting to get to know me."

"It's not strange, it's home," Justin said.

Marcelline tried not to chuckle at Justin's gaffe. "And you are?"

"I'm Melanie," the girl said, careful, as if circumstance had made her guarded around adults. One couldn't blame her, with all the strange people who wouldn't think twice about harming a pair of friendly children.

A dog barked nearby. From around the corner of the hedges a pug ran, trailing a leash. The dog's owner, a short, dark woman, puffed after it.

"Go away, doggie. Go home!" Marcelline shooed the dog with her hand. The dog snuffled up to her, putting its paws on her shin. The dog's owner grabbed the dog's harness, pulling him away, apologizing profusely in English and Spanish before carrying away her pet.

Marcelline glanced about. The children had gone, doubtlessly startled by the dog. She couldn't blame them. The dog had startled her, too.

Too busy out here, she thought. Gathering her mail, she went inside to read her letters over a cup of tea in the privacy of her kitchen.

* * *

The next morning, she took the bus downtown to buy stamps at the post office and lined tablets of paper at the dollar store. She would only have had a short walk there if she had stayed in the house where she and Francis had lived on the other side of Manuxet. But cleaning so big a space had sapped her energy. After Francis had passed, Cecily had done her best to help even with her health problems, but it had all proven too much and she had passed. Marcelline had sensed, almost from the day she gave birth to her younger, frailer daughter, that the girl would not live long. With too many memories haunting her, she had agreed when Diane and her husband Bruce offered to help her downsize the contents preparatory to her moving out and putting it up for sale. With their own house, they didn't need one.

Spotting a turquoise playground ball among the seasonal items, she added that to her cart, thinking the two children might like it.

By the time she returned to the apartment, the sun had come out. She deposited her bags in the kitchen. Taking the ball with her, she went to the courtyard. Sitting on the bench, she tossed the ball up toward the milky blue sky and the undersides of the budding branches on the few shade trees.

"What are you doing with that ball?" Justin asked, close to her head.

She tossed the ball up to the sky again. "I'm playing catch with God." The ball fell back, into her waiting hands. "He always tosses it back."

"Can I play, too?" Melanie's voice asked. The two children approached from behind the bench. Marcelline stood, tossing the ball into the air. Justin ran to catch it, fumbled it, then pushed it with his foot to his sister. Melanie grabbed it and tossed it to Marcelline. She caught it and tossed it back to Melanie. The girl tossed it into the air. It came down almost into Justin's hands, falling from them. No surprise, he was so little.

Melanie, running to grab the ball, brushed against her. Cold from the girl passed through her clothes. "Are you kids chilly out here? Do you want me to find you a jacket?" She could loan them two of her sweaters for now. Perhaps Diane had saved something from the old clothes not yet sent to the thrift shop.

They played for some time, till the sun turned behind one of the houses, casting the courtyard in shadow. "Would you be able to come up to my apartment? Would your parents mind?"

Melanie tossed the ball to Marcelline. "We'd rather play in the garden,"

Marcelline caught it. "That's probably good. It gets you out in the fresh air. If it's all right with your parents, and if you want to come up for a visit, my door is usually open. I should go make my lunch. I could make you some sandwiches if you like."

"We should go too," Melanie said, tossing the ball to Marcelline and taking Justin's hand.

"May I walk up with you?"

"I'd like that," Justin said. The pair followed Marcelline as she buzzed them into the house and up the first flight of stairs.

On the second floor stairs, she turned back to speak to them. They'd vanished. If they'd run past her, she would have noticed. Perhaps they'd turned back and gone up the fire escape. Perhaps they had reason not to let her see where they lived.

In the hallway outside her apartment door, she met Joffrey, the building superintendent, on a ladder, changing a bulb in the hallway ceiling light.

"The boy and girl who play in the yard, what apartment do they live in?" she asked.

Joffrey looked at her, adjusting his safety goggles. "I can't give out that information."

"Can't or won't?" she asked, smiling.

"Can't. The property manager doesn't want to take chances with security."

"I suppose you can't be too careful these days. But that information would be safe with a gentle older lady," she said, trying not to wheedle.

"Unfortunately, no, not even an older woman." He hefted his tool kit, coming down from the ladder and folding it before shouldering it. "My brother-in-law in the FBI helped trail and capture a guy working for a baby broker who turned out to be a harmless, grandmotherly-looking woman."

Marcelline shuddered. "Ugh, it's always the least likely looking people who do the most terrible things. Well, thanks for being honest."

Later that afternoon, she went downstairs, looking for the two children. She heard a dog barking behind the door of the apartment below hers, its owner scolding and shushing it in what sounded like Chinese. It didn't seem likely that they lived there, as the dog in the yard had scared them off, unless they didn't like strange dogs. Marcelline went back upstairs, deciding she had spent enough time hunting around. She had letters to write.

* * *

"Have you thought about getting a cat?" Doctor Langstrom said, examining Marcelline during her semi-annual physical a week later.

"I've never really cared much for cats. And I'd hate to look like the stereotyped older woman living alone with her cat."

"What about a dog?" she asked.

"I'm not sure if my building allows us to have dogs." Though the apartment below and someone in the building across the courtyard had them. And a dog might scare off the two children she had befriended.

"So you're alone in your apartment?" she asked, looking Marcelline in the face.

"Yes, but I'm far from lonely. I have penfriends I write to as often as I hear from them. One lady in England calls me on the telephone once in a while, and I'm making friends with the other people in the building as best as I can. It's hard to be lonely with so many neighbors."

"I suppose that helps. Now, I'll call in a refill on your heart medication and the blood pressure medication. They should be ready later today. Other than that and the results from the blood work I'll order, you're doing all right, though I'd work on finding some people to talk with more often."

"Thank you, doctor."

* * *

She nearly had a heart attack when the pharmacist told her the copay for her medications. "Are you serious?"

The pharmacist tapped several keys on his terminal. "I wish I made the prices. There's coupons available online. That takes time to set up, and you need the rebate now."

"I'm barely able to afford to eat at that price." Marcelline dug in her wallet for her bank card. This would dent that month's Social Security payment, and she'd have to food shop at the dollar store, which meant less food in smaller packages. *It's like the business people want to kill off a bunch of paying customers from starvation or not treating our illnesses,* she thought.

She stopped at the dollar store next, passing by the Market Basket, wondering if the cashiers who knew her would worry something had happened to her. Something had to give and improve these straightened circumstances. She bought a few boxes of pasta salad, crackers, canned vegetables and canned fruit and jarred spices to perk up her meal.

Down near the cleaning products, she spotted the lady from the apartment below her, shopping by herself, no sign of any children. Maybe she'd asked another neighbor or a family member to watch them while she shopped, though most people would bring the kiddies along for a short trip like this.

Something moved in the corner of her eye and she nearly jumped. "Marcie, how have you been? I've barely seen you since Francis died," Selma, the nearest neighbor at her old home, said, approaching her.

"Oh, I've been busy moving into an apartment over in Manuxet," Marcie replied. "I only just got settled the other day."

"Oh? Where did you move to?"

"I'm in Jaquith Estates, up on Smithen Street."

Selma reared back as if from a spider, blinking. "You moved in there? Didn't anyone tell you about that place? Several people have been murdered there over the years."

"You have to be kidding. It seems like such a nice, quiet place. There's a lady with a little dog there, and a pair of children, a boy and a girl, who play in the courtyard garden almost every day."

"I hope those children have a family that keeps a close eye on them, so nothing happens," Selma said, looking around as if to make sure no one eavesdropped on their conversation. A pair of young male clerks in blue jackets walked by, one pulling and the other pushing on a wheeled platform piled with boxes to stock the shelves. She waited till they had passed before she continued.

"You make sure you keep your doors and windows locked, especially at night. You don't want to wake up some morning with your throat slashed open."

A female clerk who had paused nearby as she replaced some cans of nuts on a shelf darted a worried frown at Selma before she walked away more quickly than she had approached.

"You could be exaggerating. You scared that poor girl away," Marcie said.

"I'm warning you because I don't want to lose my best friend," Selma said. "But I'll come by to see you some afternoon."

"I'll keep some tea on hand for you," Marcie said, as Selma moved on, pushing her carriage toward the checkout.

Returning to the complex, she looked up to the facade of her building, to the windows below hers. Nothing moved within their frames.

Once Marcie had entered her apartment, someone knocked at her door, setting her heart thumping. She tiptoed to the door, peering through the peephole. Diane stood at the door, looking around. Marcie unlocked the door, letting her in.

"Mom, I was in the neighborhood and wanted to see if you needed any groceries?"

"Oh, I just came from the store. I'm good, but...thank you for coming," Marcie led her inside, into the kitchen. They chattered while unpacking the bags, sharing anodyne thoughts and information. Then Marcie looked Diane in the face from the corner of her eye. "Diane...could you run a search of some kind on...crimes that might have happened in this apartment complex?"

"Of course I could," Diane said, reaching into her purse for her phone. With a quirk of concern in her throat, she asked, "Are you having second thoughts about moving in here?"

She told Diane about Selma's comments. Diane tapped at her phone, studying the screen intently.

"Well, it wouldn't be the first time Selma exaggerated a news item she'd heard or colored the facts of something. Remember the time she kept insisting that a bear was knocking over her garbage cans?" Diane said,

Marcie took the box of tea from one of the bags, rummaging in the cupboards over the counter for a place to store it. "Yes, and it turned out to be a Newfoundland dog that got loose from a yard up the street and around the corner on Wayside Road. But the size and shape of that dog would make you think they were keeping a bear in their yard.

"Rats, I forgot to get animal crackers."

"What, to share with those kids you've talked about? I could get some."

"Thanks, but don't go to any great lengths to fetch them. Speaking of those kids, when we're finished here, would you like to come with me to the courtyard?"

"Sure thing."

They put away the last of the groceries, stowing the fresh vegetables in the refrigerator. Diane fetched her jacket from where she'd hung it on a chair in the living area, and the two went down to the courtyard.

The sun had gone behind a cloud by the time they got outside. Marcelline found the ball under the bench and tossed it to Diane. Her daughter tossed the ball back to her, but it flew wide. She got up and walked after it, so different from the girl who ran after it with her sister. Marcelline hurried after it, keeping an eye on the path for any movement.

Something moved in the corner of her eye. She jumped, looking to Diane, who sat down on the bench, tossing the ball right to her.

"Did I startle you?" Diane asked.

"A little. I wasn't expecting that. I was watching for those two little kids." The woman with the pug entered at the far end of the courtyard, letting her pet do his business under the hedges.

"Maybe they're busy with their homework or some after school activity?" Diane asked, tossing the ball up and catching it.

"I don't think it would be an after school activity. They seem to come out here about this time of the day. Let's give them a few more minutes?"

"Does the lady with the pug dog come out here often?"

"Usually. She lives in the building on the right, with her husband who works nights. I don't see him much."

Diane tossed the ball to Marcelline. "So they're always out here when you are?"

Marcelline caught the ball, tossing it up in the air once before tossing it back to Diane. "More or less."

"Have you seen anyone else talking to them or playing with them? Do they have family around here that you know of?"

"I haven't met their family, but there's plenty of them around here. They must belong somewhere nearby." She looked behind Diane, still seeing no sign of her little friends. The thought crept into a far corner of her mind: perhaps she had imagined the two children. Perhaps her lonely imagination had invented them as a way to feel less lonely in this new place? She pushed it aside. If she would imagine something of that nature, wouldn't it make more sense if she imagined Cecily or someone else close to her?

Diane's phone pinged. She tossed the ball back to Marcelline, taking the phone from her pocket with her other hand. "Text message from home. Madison wants some help with her homework and Bruce wants a second pair of eyes on a spreadsheet."

Marcelline placed the ball in her lap. "I'd better let you go then."

"I'll call you later, once I sort out everything at home," Diane said, turning back toward the unit.

Marcelline rose, the ball under her arm, looking around one last time, seeing no sign of the two children. "Let me walk you to the door, okay?"

Diane smiled. "Of course."

As they walked to Marcelline's building, she thought she heard small footsteps crunching along the gravel walk.

* * *

The next morning, Marcelline had just collected her mail and headed upstairs, when she met her downstairs neighbor coming up from the basement with her laundry.

"Mrs. Lee?" she called. Her neighbor looked up, wrinkling her brow slightly. "Hello, how are you?"

Mrs. Lee shook her head, rolling her eyes. "Fine, fine. Too much laundry to wash."

"I hear you. I had to pay too much for my medicines," Marcelline said. "I saw you in the store yesterday and I wanted to talk to you. Could I give a few little presents to your children?"

Mrs. Lee blinked, shaking her head. "What? No. No children here. They're grown and live in California."

"They do? I met two children in the garden who said they live here."

Mrs. Lee shook her head again, looking past Marcelline into the hallway. "No young children here. I'm sorry. Maybe they live in another building near?"

"Maybe. I'll ask the superintendent if he knows. I'm sorry to bother you."

"No, no trouble. You get lonely, you come down here. I'll make tea and dumplings for you," Mrs. Lee said.

"Thank you. Maybe tomorrow? I've had a long day already today."

"That works. Now you go rest," Mrs. Lee said, patting Marcelline's hand before shooing her away gently.

* * *

"It's taking longer to sell the house than we thought," Diane said, over the phone the next day. *"Bruce wanted to pull the listing and try again*

with another realtor, but we're sticking with Borstead for a little while longer."

"What if you lowered the price?" Marcelline asked. "Like your dad used to say, I'm not made of money, and it looks like what I have is going to run out quicker than I think. We had so many bills after he died and after we lost Cecily. You sure it wouldn't be all right if I moved in with you? I can help around the house."

"That's a good thought, Mom, but we're a bit crowded as it is, after Bruce's sister moved her family in with us."

"You could sling me over a clothes hanger in the screen porch closet. I won't mind," Marcelline suggested, laughing.

Diane laughed, the line rustling, but Marcelline heard a tiny sob in her reaction. *"No, no, I wouldn't do that to you. Besides, there's a lot of noise here lately and you'd never have any peace to write your letters."*

"I do have plenty of that, almost too much."

"What?" Someone yelped in the background and something clattered. The connection crackled rhythmically, as if someone chuckled.

Marcelline raised her voice to be heard over the racket. "I said it's almost too quiet here."

"Ah, I suppose that's not a bad thing. Oh, before I forget it again: I looked up some police reports on your complex..." A pause, the line rustled. Marcelline thought she heard voices, but interference from some other line might have broken through. *"You still there?"*

"Yes, the line sounded a little weird."

"I hope you're sitting down, because I have some not good news."

Marcelline sat down on the kitchen stool. "Do I want to know what you mean by 'not good news'?"

"For once, Selma wasn't exaggerating. There's been some unsettling cases linked to the complex."

"Cases? You're serious?"

"Yes, I'm afraid so. A young man disappeared from one of the apartments, number 402B. He let himself in and never came out. He vanished without a trace, except the police found traces of blood in the bathtub drain. Then a pair of children vanished from a hallway. No one saw them leave with anyone. The police did a door-to door search, but turned up nothing. They even dredged the canal nearby."

"A boy and a girl?" The words popped out of Marcelline's mouth before she could stop them. What felt like ice water ran down her spine. *I'm as bad as Selma,* she thought. *Plenty of children could have lived there and come and gone for different reasons.*

"Mom? You okay?" Diane called.

"I'm fine, I felt a little queasy for a moment."

"I hope I didn't just scare you with that information."

"No, no, it's okay. I'm okay now."

"If you're not comfortable in that place, we can work something out so you can stay with us."

"I signed a lease. I'm not sure I could break it till I've lived here six months."

"We could get a lawyer to work that out."

"I appreciate that, but it would cost us all money, and that's not something we can risk. I'll just be more careful about locking my doors."

"Would you rathe—Hold on, I'm getting a ping on the other line."

"I won't keep you from work. I should get some fresh air anyway. Call me when you get a minute."

"I will, Mom. Love you." The call disconnected.

Marcelline sighed, hanging up the phone. Turning back to her kitchen counter, she carefully split her tablets, first in half and then in half again, halving the doses prescribed. This should stretch the medicine longer, making it less effective, but she couldn't keep paying that much money so often. *Maybe when I'm done here I could bake some cookies from that mix in the cupboard*, she thought. *I could bring some to Justin and Melanie when I find where they live.* She put that thought aside. So many parents these days fretted over what their kids ate. She wouldn't want their family angry with her. Their parents might order them not to see her again afterwards. It might look strange, too. An odd, old woman giving out treats, like some urban version of the witch in *Hansel and Gretel*.

Once she took her medicine and had breakfast, she put on her jacket and taking the ball, went to the garden. She sat down on her usual bench and tossed the ball up into the air, catching it.

A shadow moved across her line of sight. "Playing catch with yourself?" Joffrey the superintendent asked, his voice muffled. She looked up at him. He'd paused before her, a garden sprayer in hand and an industrial dust mask over his face.

"Playing catch with God, we called it when my kids were little," Marcelline said.

He pulled the mask down around his throat. "I suppose that's one way to describe it."

"I was keeping busy while Justin and Melanie show up."

Joffrey shook his head, avoiding her gaze. "Excuse me?"

"The brother and sister who come around-"

"There's no children here by those names."

A cold hand closed on her heart. "I've seen them in the garden. Justin said they live in one of the apartments here. Maybe they live nearby?"

Wariness flickered in his eyes then flitted away. "They probably lived here, but they moved to another neighborhood. They likely come here to play because it's familiar."

She nodded. "They probably feel at home here. But don't let a foolish old woman like me keep you from your work."

"I wouldn't call you foolish, just lonely, like most people." With that, he lowered the mask and moved on, spraying more weedkiller under the bushes as he headed to the screened ball court at the far end.

The children didn't show up that day. Marcelline wandered the garden, as pointless as it seemed, looking for them, watching for movement. The sun moved behind the further house. She went inside to make her lunch, then decided to take a walk in the neighborhood.

Coming home, she buzzed herself in and returned to the garden. A few older men played bocce in the screened court, laughing and chattering and joshing each other in Italian. One waved to her, grinning. She returned the wave, fey and dispirited that she had not seen her little friends.

Maybe she should get a pet animal, a canary or even a goldfish. She called Diane, but the call went to the answering machine. She contemplated calling Bruce, but his office wouldn't want her making a mere social call. She checked the date on her library books. Those could wait till tomorrow, as the last bus wouldn't leave her time to browse much before it made its return trip.

She ate some crackers and an apple, along with some tea, calling it a night. No point watching the evening news: it rarely showed anything good. Channel surfing only wasted time she wanted to fill up, and it smacked of keeping the TV on at all hours of the day, something she had scolded the girls for doing.

She curled up in bed with her Bible, until her eyes grew too heavy to read. As she switched out the light, a soft sound like a child's sigh rose from below, likely a product of her lonely imagination.

* * *

She'd made the right decision, going to the library the next morning. She found several new books she hadn't read before. A listing by the checkout desk, for a book club caught her eye, and the young librarian at the desk spoke glowingly about it, encouraging Marcelline to join. She agreed to it. This would get her out of the apartment and she could make some friends. Cecily would have loved it. It could have shone some light into the darkness that crept into her life.

The thought crossed her mind, she could down the entire ration of medication and go to her frail Cecily, crushed by the world. Had her mind created the two little visitors to fill the gap that Cecily's passing had left in her life?

But if she took that step, she might risk her chance to find Cecily in the world beyond this world. Cecily had fallen from a lifetime of pain eroding her grip, but her choosing this course of action didn't come from that weariness.

* * *

The next day, despite how tired it left her, she walked several blocks to St. Patrick's Church nearby for morning Mass. Afterwards, she visited the cemetery down the road, walking through the aisles to the family plot, with her Francis's fancier marker and next to it, the newer marker for Cecily, with its carved willow branch. The flag on Francis's grave had tipped, and the last of the flowers had faded on Cecily's grave. *I should have brought more*, Marcelline thought, removing the faded flowers. She straightened Francis's flag, hoping an animal brushing past it in the night had tipped it.

The wan sun slid behind the clouds rolling in. Always so much rain at this time of the year, as if something sprinkled the earth with water to awaken it, she thought, walking faster on her way back to the complex

As she entered her hallway, Joffrey emerged from her apartment, toolbox in hand, likely after letting himself in.

"Were you working there on a Sunday?" she asked.

"There were electrical surges in the building today. I had to make sure nothing happened in every apartment." He didn't look at her as he passed along the hallway. "Can't risk fires starting from a shorted appliance."

"No, not at all. Thanks for stopping by. It's very thoughtful and careful of you," she called after him.

"All in a day's work." He didn't look over his shoulder as he descended the stairs.

Once she'd taken off her coat, she went straight for the kitchen, making herself a cup of tea.

In that day's slot in the pill organizer, she found a tablet she hadn't quartered. Likely she'd overlooked it when she'd divided them. Perhaps the Sunday rest included resting from scrimping on her medications. No telling what a lower dose could do to her heart and health if it went on long enough.

Something burned her throat. Her breath caught in her lungs. Her stomach roiled inside her. She pawed at her throat as she tried drawing a full breath. She stumbled against the refrigerator. The back of her head hit the freezer door handle. Everything slid sideways before going black.

...She stood in the kitchen, looking around in the half-light glimmering in the windows. *How long have I been out?* She wondered.

Justin and Melanie stood before her, as if awaiting her arrival.

"Have you seen a girl named Cecily?" she asked.

Melanie shook her head. "No. Not yet, but sometimes there are other people here. We see things that the people out there can't see or won't see."

"Is this heaven?" Marcelline asked.

"It is now that you're here." Justin said, and took her right hand.

Melanie took her left. "Now you can always be with us."

Hallowed Treason
Nikki D. Freeman

*T*he circumstances couldn't be more perfect, Jake thought, taking in the scenery around him. Months of unproductive worry melted off his shoulders like hot wax. The full moon illuminated the dew settling on the untended grounds making the premises sparkle like a diamond mine, casting the carefully placed rocks into shards of silvery monuments. A solemn sight spotlighted by the moon; this land was a treasure chest of research for Jake Hagstrom. *And if all goes as expected, a guaranteed spot behind the cameras as the dollars roll in, making me rich and famous.*

"The night we've been waiting for and she's late," he mumbled sourly. Laying a camera case on the floor of the ninety-six faded blue van he referred to as the Scooby-Don't Mobile, he swallowed his pride and proceeded with the work ahead.

"Just like a woman, hey Boss?" Bobby Carlisle teased, nudging Jake's shoulder as he passed by. "Wouldn't you agree, Blackburn?"

Erica rolled her eyes. That cocky son-of-a-bitch got on her last nerve. "You would know," she called back, kicking herself for playing into his obnoxious-ass game. "Keep in mind, Kara's pulling two jobs on top of spending her a.m. hours trampling through godforsaken territories with us. Give her a break."

"Two jobs? Then how come she's always whining about how broke she is? Besides," Carlisle said, wrapping a beefy arm around her waist, "she's going to miss the Hound from Hell."

"No big deal," Erica said, untangling herself from his embrace. "She'll see you tomorrow."

"Enough guys," Jake called, tired of their constant sardonic arguing. "Let's set up. We're wasting time."

Jake had offered to pick Kara up after her shift last night at Louie's Bar & Grill so they could all ride up here together, but she'd hastily declined. *Why? Because of the stupid fight two weeks ago?* God, that woman could hold a grudge. It had been *Suzanna What's-Her-Name*, the curvy blonde, who had nestled next to *him* at the bar as he downed a shot while waiting on Kara to finish her shift. It'd been *Suzanna What's-Her-Name*, the lilac-fragranced woman who kept touching the back of his hand each time she'd laughed at his stories. And it had been *Suzanna What's-Her-Name*, the persistent siren with blood-red nails, who had followed him home that night without him knowing. *She'd* rang the doorbell after he'd dropped Kara off at her apartment. *She'd* invited herself inside for a nightcap. And, by God, *she'd* taken it upon herself to answer his cellphone while he was in the bathroom taking a piss. Nothing fucking happened between them. Sure, it could've, but Jake wasn't that kind of man. Although the question remained: *Would* something have happen had Kara's call not ruined the mood?

Kara hadn't spoken to him but twice since that evening; once to accuse him of infidelity, and the other was to state that she would drive her *"own damn self"* to the investigation site. *Suzanna* had shown up at his home again when he failed to make an appearance at Louie's for several nights in a row. With Kara's ongoing silent treatment, what the hell was he to think? Certainly not that they were still together.

Or are we?

It's been two fucking weeks now!

Kara knew of Jake's dreams when she'd entered this relationship. She knew his passion for investigating the paranormal. She had developed an obsession of her own after a few late nights in abandoned houses. She said it was... *what was the word she'd used?* "Intriguing." And when she'd learned of his desire to catch Madeleine in action, she had insisted on coming along. "I wouldn't miss it for the world." *Those were her exact words.*

Jake sneered. "For the world, huh? Right. Just over a stupid misunderstanding."

Bobby checked the flash on the Canon Sureshot 85.

"How 'bout the camcorder? Is it set up?" Jake asked.

"Sure thing, Boss. Aimed right at Maddie's grave. Want the night vision scope on as well?"

"With this moon, I don't think we'll need it. But grab the PT100. I have a feeling there's going to be some freezes all around the site. I don't care if the temperature drops one degree, give Erica the signal so she'll start recording." Anticipation tickled his gut. Placing the tape recorder on Madeleine's feeble headstone, Jake plugged in the external microphone to ensure quality reception. Tonight, two and a half centuries after her death, he was ready to mingle with her spirit.

Four strategically placed rows of unmarked stones protruded from the pine needle carpet except for the chunk of stone standing alone in the upper left corner of the clearing. It set distanced from the rest. In the antebellum period, the laborers had buried their own under the watchful eyes of the white men so that there would be no privacy to plan attacks against their masters' families in order to escape. If this was truly Maddie's grave, it could be gathered that Madeleine's fellow slave-hands had been aware of her carnal sin, shunning her even in death.

Sightings of Madeleine's ghost had traveled hundreds of miles to thousands of ears from a handful of local folks visiting the cemetery during the twilight hours... usually teenagers searching for a secluded country hideout to pet and probe without the threat of interruption from the local police. However, serenity was not what they'd received during Virginia's hot summer nights.

Throughout his years of investigating, Jake had never wasted his time in a cemetery due to one main belief: Why would spirits haunt their own graves? No sense lay in such a concept. In fact, graveyards were the least of all places that would be haunted. He'd always scoffed at the Ghost Hunter Wanna-Be's for even considering it. It was mid twentieth-century mental asylums, salvaged plantations, and Civil War battlefields that were ripe pickings to gather proof that life goes on after death. Hell, even junkyards filled with the mangled cars of drunk drivers were more ideal for catching a hint of afterlife existence than a graveyard.

Yet here we are.

The legend of Madeleine had captured his interest with the speed and skill of a trap-door spider. The mystical tale crouched beneath the rumors of the local town, awaiting an unsuspecting Jake to pass through. He'd held no interest in this redneck town except for a quick bite to eat and a refill on gas six months earlier. The arachnid leapt out to grab him in the guise of a gossipy waitress named Martha, hauling him down into the burrow of suspense, stimulating his curiosity with its poisonous bite.

"It's no secret 'round these parts," Martha carried on, leaning her bulk against the side of Bobby Carlisle's booth seat. She eyed Jake as if he was already a celebrity. "Evil roams that land. You can ask anyone 'round an' they'll tell ya it's cursed, and no Braveheart nor fool would set foot on that ground after dark." Her baby blues shone below unevenly arched eyebrows that had obviously been drawn on with a black sharpie. "God, I've never met a real-life ghost hunter before!"

Bobby, who had scooted closer to the window, distancing himself from the straining threads of her navy smock, threw up his hands and mumbled, "Am I chopped liver?"

Martha paid him no mind as she paused long enough to inhale before rattling on. "July seventh makes two-hunerd an fifty years ago since that slave girl was kilt crossing Hallow Road, running directly in front of her master's horse and cart. She was buried with the other Negros who'd passed on before at the far corner of his plantation. Rumor has it he'd ne'er even questioned why she was runnin' away. Ain't that a shame?" Martha clicked her tongue in rhythm to her shaking head. "Poor dear." Quick inhale. "The house I grew up in was haunted. Oh, brother, let me tell you, I ain't ne'r been so skeered in my life. The closet door in my bedroom would open and shut all by itself." Inhale. "This one night when I was babysittin' my lil brother…"

"Excuse me," Jake said, sliding out of his seat, "your wonderful tea has hit bottom." He obliged her with a pat on the arm and a hearty laugh before hurrying to the restroom to allow his ears a moment to reattach themselves after her yakking. Locking the door, he sighed. *Let Bobby and the gals be her audience awhile. Kara will ride me for it later but I'm out!* He snickered at the at the thought of her bruising his bicep later with a sharp-knuckled frogging, but oh well! Truth be told, he hadn't *actually* lied to make his escape. His bladder *was* full. However, Martha's tea had been syrupy-sweet and lemony enough to make even his dick pucker as he pissed it out.

Jake shook the last drop off Little Jake, zipped his jeans and approached the sink. *All I need is one monumental capture to get the network's attention. This could be it!* He studied his reflection, realizing the scruffy beard would have to go when he finally got his show. No one takes a country-bumpkin seriously. He'd been working on his speech for years now, slowly eliminating the southern drawl from his vocabulary. He was a man that would be taken seriously, no matter what changes he had to make for himself. His no-nonsense stare came naturally, thank God. That was one thing he didn't need to practice. His chocolate eyes could captivate a woman immediately... any woman, so he had no doubt they would be able to do the same to a whole audience. He was Jake, after all. Confident and ready to grab the world by the balls.

Balls... warm hands firmly squeezing...

Jake jumped backwards. "What the hell?" he breathed, gawking at his crotch. He swore he'd just felt someone touching his boys. *And how long has it been since Kara and I have bumped uglies? At least a day or two. I'm overdue.* He laughed, chalking it up to his vivid nymphomaniacal imagination.

Are you imagining these fingertips running through your hair? Jake's hands froze beneath the scouring stream of the faucet. *Have it be!* He closed his eyes, rolling his head into the massaging digits as they traced every inch of his scalp. He pictured Kara, leaning into him and lacing her hot tongue along his earlobe. His hardening cock pressed against his zipper. He leaned against the porcelain sink, adding more pressure... more pleasure. The fervent breath encircling his ear grew chilly as if Fantasy-Kara breath was sucking on a peppermint. *"Maaassster."*

Eyes snapping open, he stared into the russet eyes of young black woman standing behind him in the mirror's reflection. He jerked around. Nothing but a piss-stained toilet. His heartbeat pounded in his ears. Hesitantly, he turned to face the mirror once more, his eyes begging him to spare them from looking. Only his own pale reflection stared back. He left without bothering to turn off the sink, thankful that when he'd reached the booth, Kara was paying the check and Martha had moved on to another table occupied by new victims with fresh ears.

Pressing record on his phone, Jake began documenting the story that had led him and his team *(minus Kara, of course)* out here in the middle of nowhere. "It is July seventh, twenty-nineteen. We're setting up in a servants' cemetery near Hallow Road, hoping to capture a sighting of Madeleine Copperstone, a young slave girl…"

Stories of a baby crying in the distance were reported. Many had claimed that a young Negro girl dressed in a flowing white gown had circled their vehicle, peering into the windows as if searching for something she'd lost. Dissatisfied, she would turn away and disappear into the forest separating the burial ground from Hallow Road, a narrow unkempt road that had originally led to the plantation centuries earlier. Occasionally, curious boys tried to follow her despite their date's protests. There's nothing more thrilling than the opportunity to play Macho-Man in the presence of a maiden. No matter how macho the testosterone-ridden teens appeared, they rarely traveled the forest all the way to Hallow Road for fear of seeing the Hellhound. The road still served as a shortcut to James River from town, although most people took the long way around.

"Remember what I always tell you," Jake said, turning to his scanty crew. "Don't be ashamed to say a prayer before we start. I don't know if it really helps, but it sure as hell don't hurt."

Carlisle bowed his head. "Lord above, please hear my prayer. Let me streak not my underwear."

"You're such a jackass, Carlisle," Erica groaned, turning her back to conceal her rolling eyes. "Come on, Kara, don't leave me stranded out here with Jake and this prick." Grabbing a digital camera, she paced the area, snapping pictures at random, careful to stay within a hundred feet of the men. Kara was supposed to bring the walkie talkies. Without them, and with such a small crew, it was too dangerous to wander off alone. Anything could happen, from snapping an ankle in a concaved grave to startling a bum resting behind a headstone. The latter had happened twice during the past seven years of their studies when they'd ran into squatters in abandoned houses. Erica shivered. Those bums had been scarier than any apparition they'd ever seen.

After Martha's ramblings at the diner, Jake had made reservations for a private tour at the Rosenburg Plantation on the anniversary of Madeleine's death. They'd arrived early that morning, following a long gravel driveway up to the three-story Georgian mansion built in seventeen twenty-five. The ten-foot double French doors faced the James River which, in the colonial times, had served as a roadway for shipments and supplies. Each brick of the house had been fired right here on this property. The manicured lawn boasted of magnolias, crepe myrtle, black locusts and tulip poplars, as well as dozens of assortments of flowers and bushes. Jake felt as if he'd stepped back in time as he exited the Scooby-Don't Mobile.

Donning a Civil War issued muslin shirt and brown canvas pants held up by cracked leather suspenders, Sorio Mason matched the era of the people who had lived on the plantation during the late eighteen-hundreds. However, his bald head made Jake think of a genie in a bottle ready to grant three wishes. Sorio skipped down the porch steps to greet them. He had agreed to give Jake and his crew a personal tour of the Rosenburg Plantation before opening hours. Sorio grabbed Jake's hand, shaking it vigorously. "Glad you could make it, Mr. Hagstrom." Likewise, he shook Erica and Bobby's hands. His jolly blue eyes, framed by laugh lines, lingered a little too long on Jake. *Despite the dress-code, his sassy demeanor would fit in better in the banana-forest bars of Los Angeles than here where petticoats and tobacco were necessities,* Jake thought, matching Sorio's smile with a half grin.

His heart lay heavy in the prison of his chest. He checked his phone, sighing. *God, Kara, I wish you'd just call me.* He'd spent months by her side anticipating this day, going over the details together, and learning all they could on the history of this place. There should be four of them following the tour guide into the foyer right now. He'd tried putting himself in her shoes, but the task proved nearly impossible since he personally knew the whole story. Her accusations came from mere assumptions. And *what* she didn't know couldn't possibly hurt her, except that she was damn sure in her own head that she *did* know. All the nonsense helped Jake to stave down the guilt of what she really couldn't possibly know about Suzanna What's-Her-Name's second appearance at his home.

"Notice that the ceilings are twelve feet high," Sorio said, extending his right hand in a grand arched gesture above his head. "This is because one of the main purposes in this design was to keep the home as cool as possible since the Antebellum era had no luxuries such as fans and air conditioning as we do. Heat rises; therefore, the ceilings are high to keep it cooler down here at our level. Many plantation homes had an elaborate spiral staircase such as this one here in the main hallway. This is so the master and his wife could make a grand entrance during parties. Follow me into the parlor…"

Jake checked his phone again. *Fuck!* He found it hard to concentrate on Sorio's memorized speech as he led them through the home. Jake didn't care about the cabriole legs on the tables and chairs, nor the hand-carved mahogany posts of the rice beds. It was not the Carrara marble mantles or the frieze-work molding that Jake wanted to learn about, but the history of the people who had lived here, especially Madeleine. Erica appeared absorbed by Sorio's every word, while Bobby followed behind, lightly fingering every fragile item whose sign warned: **Do Not Touch.**

"Oh my God, Jake," Kara breathed, pointing to the portrait of Albert Rosenburg hanging above the parlor's fireplace.

Jake studied the dark eyes staring down at him below thick brows, seeming to judge his every thought. The thick jawline, set firm in a stoic half-grin, warned he was not a man to accept 'no' for an answer. Rosenburg's black hair framed a perfect masculine face of the once admired prominent Planter in a world long abandoned.

"He looks just like you," she whispered, her awe all too relevant in her voice.

"By damn he does," Carlisle agreed, eavesdropping. He nudged Jake's shoulder. "You aged well, Mr. Rosenburg."

The resemblance was uncanny, even for Jake, but he waved his crew's words away with a sweep of his hand as if it were utter nonsense. Still, a seed of pride had been planted within his mind.

"This home was built in seventeen twenty-five," Sorio continued. "Marvin Rosenburg, who traveled here from England at the age of thirty, bought this property…"

"Let's skip ahead to Albert," Jake interrupted, unable to bite back his growing frustration. He wasn't here for useless knowledge.

Sorio arched a haughty brow at him. Turning his back to Jake, he stated, "Very well." His bald head flushed as he continued walking them through the rooms, his bootees sharply clicking against the polished oak floorboards. "Albert Lee Rosenburg and his wife, Camille, were the third generation of Rosenburg's to own the plantation. By this time in seventeen sixty-nine, they owned four-hundred acres on which tobacco was grown, and forty-two slaves to bare the back-breaking work to keep this plantation running smoothly. Tobacco was a vital source of income for the people of Virginia. It brought in a profit for…"

"No. We don't care about tobacco." Jake trotted to the front, stopping Sorio in his tracks.

"Jake!" Erica scolded. "Let him do his job."

Peering around Sorio's piercing stare, Jake locked eyes with her. "We're here to learn the history of Madeleine and what happened to her. That's it. Not specifics about the furniture they sat on or what products they farmed. Those details will not be included in our investigation when we represent it to the network."

"Mr. Hagstrom," Sorio said, clearing his throat. "I understand why you are here. We discussed it in our phone conversation when you set up this meeting. I just thought you would appreciate a full tour."

Jake shook his head. "Don't get me wrong, the plantation is beautiful. But I'm here for facts that coincide with my investigation."

"*Our* investigation," Erica corrected.

Jake waved a dismissive hand. "Of course," he muttered.

Sorio sighed. "Well, Mr. Hagstrom, I was giving you the facts. What I'm now understanding is that you are here for the legend of this place. Nothing provable. No concrete evidence as what I've been showing you. Allow me to fulfill your desire."

Jake was certain that Sorio had uttered those last words countless times within a private setting with beaded doorways.

"Let's go outside to the summer kitchen and I will tell you a tale."

This is not mere folklore if the story, although passed down through the generations, has the entity to back it up as proof. And that is why I am here… to show the concrete evidence, you prick, Jake mentally sneered.

The weathered oak logs of the two-story kitchen still proved solid despite the centuries passed. Outside, a cool breeze offered minute relief from the morning's humidity. Inside, the mud mortar between weathered logs blocked out any such relief, trapping them in the stale heat of this small container.

"By having an outside kitchen, the main house stayed cooler in the hot summer months. Upstairs is where the scullery maids slept. In the cellar," Sorio said, eyeing Jake with a smirk as he spouted details of the building, "is where food was stored since it stays nice and cool underground." He tapped his foot on a three by four-foot door centered on the dusty plank floor. A modern padlock had been attached to the door to keep guests from venturing downstairs. A table centered against the far wall was long scarred by years of preparing meals for the main house. On each side of the stone fireplace stood matching windows looking out over the garden where fresh vegetables still grew. Sorio stood proud. He studied the cabin's details as if he were the one who had built the place himself. Stomping his right foot, he marched to the rocking chair setting next to an empty barrel once used for washing. He settled in, the chair's strained creaks threatening to drop him on his skinny ass any second. Dramatically waving to the bench before the table, he invited his guests to sit and join him, offering Jake a sardonic wink.

Or is he flirting? Jake shivered at the thought.

As Bobby and Erica sat on each end of the bench, Jake stepped up, spinning around to plant his ass right on the tabletop, using the bench as a foot stool instead. He shot Sorio a return wink and the smirk quickly melted off the tour guide's face.

Sorio announced, "*Legend* has it that Rosenburg was a passionate man who chose to covet his vows in the cabins of his slaves. This was not uncommon in the day. However, he took a special liking to one slave in particular, Madeleine Copperstone. It is said that her parents were traded off to another master, leaving her here alone without any family. Rosenburg moved her from the field to a position in the home to keep her close by. Eighteen and naïve, she took her master and his lies wholeheartedly, carrying on an affair, all the while believing Camille to be unsuspecting.

"Madeleine became pregnant, causing Rosenberg much worry that his wife would learn of their affair. Unfortunately, Camille was barren, never having the opportunity to fill their large home with children of her own. He threatened to sale the girl to Chandler, a man who'd become popular through the colony's Grapevine for the brutal beatings he dealt his own slaves, if she should breathe a word of their involvement. Forcing a field-hand to marry her and claim the child as his own, Rosenburg became aloof to Madeleine. Her heart was broken." Sorio rubbed his chin between his thumb and forefinger as if pondering on what to say next. Finally, he snapped back to reality with a smile as grand as the one he'd greeted the crew with upon their arrival.

Strange little fuck, Jake thought, wanting nothing more than to impale Sorio with the iron stoker from the hearth.

Clearing his throat, the guide continued, "Madeleine worked the main house as a scullery maid alongside Harriet, the Rosenburg's cook. On July sixth, the women spent the afternoon scrubbing floors and windows, readying the house for Camille's weekly Assembly of Ladies.

"Nearing her due date, the strenuous work in the summer's afternoon heat took its toll on Madeleine, zapping her energy until she was practically useless."

"Girl, you need some fresh air," Harriet said, *snatching the mop out of the young girl's hands. "You're as pale as the master's ass."*

"How would you know how pale the master's ass is?" Madeleine asked, unable to contain her laughter.

"You kiddin'? He don't always shut that outhouse door." Patting the girl on the back, *Harriet said, "I can finish up this here moppin'. Take you a walk. It'll do you some good."*

The heat was suffocating. Madeleine sat down in the shade on the west side of the barn. Leaning her head against the oak planks, she closed her eyes and drifted to sleep.

A high-pitched whimpering woke her moments later. In a trance between reality and dream, she thought perhaps upon opening her eyes, she'd find her precious bundle of joy cradled in her arms. Just wishful thinking. Rubbing sleep from her eyes, she listened intently to the pitiful whines coming from behind the barn. Curious, she arose to her feet to investigate. A hound, tied to a fence post, stood erect upon seeing her. He panted in the sweltering sunshine, his ribs protruding through a sagging black and tan coat. Madeleine's heart ached for this pitiful, defenseless creature.

"You poor thing," she whispered, venturing closer.

"Don't go near that dog!"

Madeleine spun around, finding herself face-to-face with the mistress.

"He bites," Camille Rosenburg said, her thin lips bearing a cold grin.

"But he's starvin'. Jus' look at him."

"My dear," Camille said, edging closer. "I believe you are confused about where your priorities lie. Just look at you, on the verge of becoming a mother and you're out here worrying to death over a mere mongrel. Now how silly is that?" She crossed her arms and impatiently tapped the toe of her boot on the ground. "Get back to the house, girl. You've got work to finish."

Madeleine retreated from Camille, unaware that she'd backed into the dog's line of reach. With no forewarning growl, the hound lunged, knocking the slave girl face-down. The dog's weight pinned her to the grass. Vicious bites to her arms and back couldn't compare to the searing pain seizing her abdomen. Crying out for help, she reached towards Camille, eyes pleading for the mistress to be her savior. Camille surveyed the scene curiously, cocking her head to one side.

Harriet Terrell rounded the barn. "What's goin' on 'round here?" she called, holding her skirts in a wad so as not to trip. "Madeleine!" she cried, pushing past Camille to grab the girl's hand, pulling her out of reach of the dog. She used her apron to dab the blood running down Madeleine's arms. Staring up at the mistress, she said, "Snap outta whatever dream you're in and help me! We gotta get this girl to the house!"

The veil lifted from Camille's eyes. She shook her head as if disappointed. "Take her to her quarters," she mumbled.

"By myself?" Harriet asked, dumbfounded.

Camille stared down at Madeleine in disgust. "Yes, Harriet. I'll not stain my hands with her blood."

Madeleine's labor lasted into the early morning hours. Harriet sat with her, speaking soft encouraging words while keeping the girl as comfortable as possible. Camille paced the kitchen below demanding that Harriet make the girl stop screaming.

"She's having a baby, Ma'am," Harriet called out. "Not much I can do 'cept shove a rag in her mouth."

"Then do it!" Camille yelled, her boots clicking impatiently.

"Oh Lordy," Harriet exclaimed, "the devil's done gone an' got that woman by the reins."

"Don't clean the baby when it's out," Madeleine whispered between contractions. "Promise me."

Harriet frowned. "Why would you ask such a thing?"

Unable to meet Harriet's gaze, she said, "His... his skin. It'll be too light."

"Oh girl," Harriet choked, "what has you gone and done?" She kept shaking her head. "What in the Lord's name has you gone and done?"

By two a.m. Madeleine had given birth to a healthy baby boy.

Upon the baby's first scream, Camille entered the room. "Hand it here," she ordered.

Harriet hesitated. "The momma should be the first to hold her own baby, Ma'am."

"Do as I say, Harriet." Camille etched closer; her stern stare unwavering. "I'd hate to see you lose your position in the kitchen. Those tobacco fields get mighty hot this time of year."

"Yes, Ma'am," Harriet muttered, carefully handing the child to the mistress.

Camille guided Harriet to the corner of the room and whispered in her ear.

"Ma'am, please, I just can't." Harriet glanced at Madeleine, wide-eyed.

"If not, I'll make the Master sell you to Chandler. I'll convince him that you stole from us. What will happen to you then? Or your family? They will not be going with you."

Tears rolled down Harriet's eyes. She left immediately, choking on whispered prayers.

Camille licked her finger and stroked it down the infant's bloody cheek. She studied the child's face while humming softly to him.

"I want to hold him," Madeleine whispered, extending her arms.

"Aren't you beautiful?" Camille cooed, rocking the infant in her arms.

"Please, Ma'am," the girl pleaded, watching Camille with the trust of a mouse within a cat's reach. "I want to see him. Hold him."

Camille pinned her with an icy stare as her lips curled up maliciously. "He looks just like his father, girl." She rocked the baby faster. "What do you think?" she asked, her sweet tone belying her eyes. "Shall you name him Albert the Second?"

Madeleine's blood froze in her veins.

Turning on her heel, Camille hissed, "Remember that damn dog you were so concerned with? I believe it's time to feed him." She raced from the room.

"MY BABEEEE!!!" Exhausted and weak, Madeleine struggled to follow the master's wife down the narrow ladder into the kitchen and out the front door. "Gimme my baby!" she screamed, tripping over the threshold onto the scanty porch.

Camille stood at the base of the steps in the moonlight, glowing in selfish pride. Turning to face the wretched girl, arms now empty, she howled, "Cursed be all cheating hearts! May they pay with their life!"

Harriet knelt in the yard bawling, holding only a rope.

A black shadow sprinted across the ebony lawn, gripping its screaming prize between locked jaws. Shawled by only her blood and sweat, Madeleine pursued the dog into the shadows of the night. Camille's rancid cackles hauntingly tainted the air.

Albert Rosenburg dismounted his perch on the wagon, unable to comprehend what had ran out in front of him. He didn't need this after a long day of trading. Home lay a half mile ahead and all he craved now was sleep after the long trek into town. Kneeling, he nudged the naked woman laying behind the wooden wheel, turning her face-up. He sighed as the lantern's glow kissed her face. What a waste, he thought, remounting the wagon. I should have sold months ago. He shook the reins for the horse to continue on its way.

"It is said that the hound was found dead a mile down Hallow Road strangled on the femur of an infant child. Although many people have claimed to see Madeleine's spirit searching for her baby, it is Camille's curse that scares the superstitious hearts of local folks, especially those who have deceived their significant other. It is also said that only the unfaithful can see the hound on Harrow Road, and it isn't long before they meet their demise." Jake clicked stop on the digital recorder.

"Great story, Boss," Bobby Carlisle said, the PT100 temperature gauge aimed toward a nearby grave. "It was better than the first thousand times you rehearsed it."

Jake shook his head, saying, "Well, Bobby Boy, this is the last time you'll have to suffer." He held the recorder towards Bobby, adding, "Unless you want to play it back for yourself."

"Can I?" he asked, his eyes round with exaggerated excitement.

The night stood silent with not even a breeze to kiss the leaves of the surrounding forest. The crowding pines mingling with towering maples, redbuds, and cypresses cast eerie shadows along the border of the premises. Jake shivered, ashamed of himself for this sudden feeling of uneasiness. He was a professional. He spent countless nights in haunted areas. *Six-hundred and forty-seven to be exact, ole boy!* He collected data from his findings just as a doctor collects data from test results. Were doctors afraid of catching an incurable disease from the blood samples they collected? Of course not. *Then why should I suddenly be spooked by shadows?* It made no sense. Still, the chill of dread massaged his nerves.

"You feel something, don't you?" Erica asked.

Oh yes! By damn I feel it. It clenched his gut relentlessly in an iron-clad fist. It grabbed him by the shirt-collar, shaking him violently, spraying spittle into his gaping mouth as if threatening to pummel his ass right here.

"Something. I'm not sure what." He wasn't about to admit to her it was fear. Despite the cool air, beads of sweat traced his brow. "The air is becoming thick." *Thick with what though?* He wasn't sure, but the tension seemed to penetrate his pores, clawing its way deep into the marrow of his bones. "Start recording me," Jake managed to squeak.

Eventually fear would decide to let go of his collar *(hey, nothing lasts forever… not even an ass-beating)* and he would drop to the cold earth dead from a heart attack. He could see the newspaper headline now:

Paranormal Researcher Literally Frightened to Death in the Middle of a Cemetery.

"He never had a ghost of a chance," states Medical Examiner gravely.

Icy fingers caressed his spine, sparking a chill from his scalp to the arch of his back. The thickened air rotated around his body with the F-5 strength of a tornado, making it impossible to breathe. If he wanted to run, it would be no use. His steps would be reduced to the maple-syrup strides in the grip of a nightmare.

"Jake, what is it?" Erica persisted.

She's here with me. I'm feeling her presence.

He couldn't move. Couldn't breathe. The air grew frigid. Something... No! Someone was touching him. Stroking his neck. His ear. Oh God, his lips. It was penetrating into the depths of his soul with slithery tentacles.

"Carlisle," Erica shouted, "get over here! Something's wrong with Jake!"

The wails of a distant dog rode the night from every direction, pervading the air with its mournful song.

Carlisle ambled across the cemetery. "What the hell?!" he panted, bending over to ease the stitch in his side. "He's fucking floating!"

Erica's shaky hands held the recorder on him as she screamed, "Help him!"

Jake's body levitated horizontally above their heads with his face aimed toward the ground. There was no need for him to speak even if he could cough out the words. The terror on his face screamed everything he was thinking.

As Bobby reached for his boss' hand, Jake floated higher, just out of reach. "Holy shit, I did not sign up for *this*."

Erica dropped the recorder. "Lift me up," she demanded, stepping in front of Carlisle. He encircled his sausage fingers around her waist, grunting as he lifted her high. Jake floated higher. "Ohhh, it's no use," she groaned.

Master. Master...

The words floated within his skull as his body hovered in her embrace. *I'm not your master,* he tried to scream. How the hell does one convince a fucking spirit that it's mistaken? He'd come here expecting to find what he'd found at most of the other areas he'd investigated; nothing more than a residual playout of past events by lingering souls shadowing the night. He'd come here hoping to record Madeleine running through the twilight hours searching for her baby. Perhaps record a few EVPs to impress the producers. *I sure as hell didn't expect to be strung up like a pinata. This shit doesn't happen in real life!*

As if at last convinced by his protests, the binding power released him at once. He slammed down onto the ground as a puppet cut loose of his strings. His mouth was bearded in blood as he rolled onto his back.

"Oh yeah!" Carlisle announced. "That nose is shattered."

Before Jake could cradle his gushing nose, his arms jerked cruelly above his head. Erica barely jumped out of the way as invisible hands pulled him headfirst into the thicket of the forest's boundary.

Thorns, rocks, and sticks ripped his back as he slid across the forest floor. Jake kept his chin tucked to keep his head off the ground. *Last thing I need on the way to my death is a concussion.* "What do you want with me?" he cried out.

Master…

"I'm NOT Rosenburg! You have to let me go." Jake struggled to reclaim possession of his arms.

Maaaster…

"Let me go, Madeleine!"

Jake dug his heels into the mossy dirt. He turned his head and saw light ahead. *Is this the light at the end of the tunnel? Am I already dead?* Surely this couldn't be for he could still feel briars slicing through his jeans. *The dead cannot feel pain. Can they?*

Didn't Madeleine still feel the agony of losing her baby? Could she not still fathom the anger towards Camille? Didn't she still feel the heartbreak of being rebuked? *If not, then why the hell am I being dragged to my death by her?!* As he veered closer to the edge of the woods, Jake could see that the light was nothing more than the moon's beacon spotlighting a narrow rutty road.

"Oh *shit!*" Jake grabbled at the brush with his legs, refusing to be to dragged onto Harrow's Road peacefully. She… it… *whatever* the hell had ahold of him released as he hooked his right knee around the thin trunk of a young maple.

On hands and tattered knees, Jake watched a mist take human form in the middle of the road. It beckoned him forward with an ethereal force. "No!" he shouted, scrambling to clutch the sapling with both hands. "I didn't cheat on her."

Didn't you?

Was that his own thoughts interrogating him, or her. He didn't know.

"It wasn't like that," Jake insisted, shaking his head at the apparition. "I just wanted to be held."

Master…

He'd been drunk on misery. He had leaned his head into Suzanna What's-Her-Name's ample breasts, closed his eyes and pretended she was Kara. The resilient pull of the entity's summoning slid his legs forward. White-knuckled, Jake clutched the tree harder. "I know what it looked like, but *she* kissed me." Jake's legs lifted off the ground as the hurricane-force grew desperate. "*She* pulled me into the bedroom." Jake countered.

The spirit commanded his company on the road. As if a hurricane had blown inland, Jake's grip on the sapling was slipping as his entire body lifted from the dirt. He glanced around, expecting limbs to come crashing down on top of him from the nearby trees, but all was still. All except him. Only he could feel the fervent energy inviting him into the eye of storm.

"But I didn't," he screamed. "I didn't give in to temptation!"

"Boss? Boss!" Bobby emerged from the forest, Erica in tow.

Madeleine vanished, leaving Jake lying on the soft earth. Gulping waves of fresh air, he peered up at his crew and said, "By God, I think we've got something!"

Erica and Bobby arrived together. Neither bothered knocking before entering the front door.

Jake greeted them with bottles of chilled beer. "Did you get enough rest?" he asked them, immediately turning away to head into the living room.

Bobby nodded. "You finally look halfway handsome with that gauze covering half your face."

Jake ignored him. "Damn, last night was awesome!" His slur proved he was already a good three bottles ahead of them. He picked up his cell phone, checking the screen before tossing it back on the coffee table.

"Will Kara be joining us," Erica asked, claiming a spot on the tattered sofa.

"Fuck no!" Jake held his beer high in the air with a celebrating grin. "Kara and I are officially over as of today. It is final."

"Jake!" Erica started.

"Nope. It's time for me to move forward. *I shouldn't have to walk on eggshells in a relationship. Besides, as a bachelor, I can see whom I please. Fuck whoever I want guiltfree. I don't need a relationship tying me down when I'm trying to start a career.*"

"And her response," Erica prompted.

"Still waiting on it. She's letting all my calls go to voicemail."

Erica shook her head.

Jake plugged the digital recorder into the television and joined Erica and Bobby on the couch. He fought back the bitterness of regret. If only he'd paid more attention to Kara then she'd be here with them, holding his hand as they waited for the camcorder to reveal an image from centuries past.

"You were right, Boss," Carlisle said, sipping his brew with his feet propped on top of the coffee table, "the night scopes definitely weren't needed. Great view of you staring at the grave." He belched between chuckles. Erica questioned herself as to why she even hung out with these morons.

As the recorder played, a familiar mist began forming around the image of Jake. A thin haze weaved around his head like smoke from a fine cigar. It began to take form. Jake gasped as the smoke sprouted arms which clearly wrapped around his body. Yes, there was no doubt now that Madeleine had mistaken him as her Master... her lover. *This is it! This is my foot in the door,* Jake thought, already counting dollar signs in his mind.

He laughed loudly, giving Bobby a hard high-five. "We're moving on up!" he whooped.

"Hell yeah," Bobby said, toasting his boss.

"Oh God," Erica whispered. "It can't be." She knelt before the television with her ear planted against the speaker.

"What?" Bobby asked, frowning at her.

"Turn the volume up, Jake," she ordered as she rewound the scene of the spirit embracing Jake. "Loud as it can go."

They watched the apparition form, its head leaning close to Jake as a staticky whisper spoke through the speakers. *"I finally made it, babe. I took a shortcut on Hallow Road..."*

The Iron Jaw
Laszlo Tamasfi

Eric Peterson woke up, like he did so many other nights, drenched in sweat. It was almost midnight, and he was just lying there with his heart pounding in his chest, listening to the noise coming from the living room.

He could hear it, clear as day. It was the recliner, going up and down, opening and closing, over and over again. It sounded like breathing, as if a giant mechanical beast fell asleep in there.

He knew what would happen if he got up to check on it. It would stop the moment he'd open the door, like it did so many times before.

But he wasn't crazy. It was Grandma's recliner alright.

***

"I'm so incredibly frustrated, I can't even begin to tell you." said Sarah as she poured herself another glass of wine.

Eric nodded. They were standing in the kitchen, trying to get away from the craziness in the house.

"Did you know I bought her a Life Alert?" she asked.

"No." It took him a long moment to realize what that meant. "Jesus."

"And I think she just threw it away. I looked for it everywhere. Her medicine cabinet, the drawers, the nightstands. I even checked her car, although she wasn't supposed to be driving anymore." She sounded defeated "And she sure as fuck wasn't wearing it."

Uncle Jeff came in to grab a box of tissues from the pantry, but left quickly and without saying a word. He could probably tell that the grandkids were in the middle of a conversation.

"Okay, this is going to sound awful." said Sarah as she took a sip "I hope she had a moment, you know, when she realized that no one would just miraculously stop by to help her, and that she would, in fact, die on that floor…I hope she had a moment when she thought of me and that goddamn Life Alert."

Eric put the cork back in the bottle of pinot noir.

"That *is* awful!"

Sarah didn't seem concerned.

"Yeah. But you know what is even worse?" she asked.

"What?"

"The stain under that rug in the foyer. The fact we had to tear the carpet up. After she fell, she managed to drag herself there…"

"So I was told." He didn't want to hear it.

"Well, did they tell you that her body got so gelatinous that she fuckin' seeped through the carpet, into the hardwood floor, and all the way down to the concrete foundation?!"

She took another sip.

"All because she was too embarrassed to wear that goddamn Life Alert."

***

Eric got up from his bed and tiptoed to the door.

He pressed his ear against it.

It was still there. The mechanical breathing, coming from the recliner. Opening and closing, up and down. It sounded almost like Grandma's CPAP machine, the one she used for her sleep apnea.

"Grandma?" he asked, but he immediately regretted it. He didn't want anyone—or anything—to answer him.

He took a deep breath and cracked the door open. Just wide enough to peek through.

The breathing stopped.

He could see the recliner, and it wasn't moving.

***

It was ridiculous. Eric used to joke that it was the physical embodiment of *American exceptionalism*, because it was the very best version of what was, at the end of the day, an armchair. It was an armchair on steroids. It had a cooling cup holder, a hidden compartment for the TV remote, a USB port, an electric footrest, and even a heating element for those cold winter nights. It was covered in real leather and it smelled like a new car.

It was so high tech that the department store had to send a technician out to set it up. Eric was there, in case they needed to move some of the furniture out of the way, which they did end up doing. The recliner was much larger than it looked in the showroom.

"Ma'am, this is important." said the tech as he lifted the cover off the seat "Can you see these steel bars?"

"I sure can." said Grandma, as she leaned closer.

"Once it's all said and done, this recliner will be the most comfortable piece of furniture you ever owned. But you have to remember what's inside of it."

He tapped the metal rod to illustrate just how sturdy it was.

To Eric, this whole safety bit felt very rehearsed. The technician sounded like he already gave this speech verbatim a thousand times before. Like a bored actor in an instructional video.

"The frame underneath this cushion is *very* powerful. You've got to respect that. It's a hydraulic system strong enough to lift a five-hundred pound man…"

He looked at Grandma to make sure she was paying attention.

"Just keep it in the back of your mind when you use the controller. Don't go crazy with it. It has a very strong grip."

He pulled the cover back down.

"Think of it as a giant, iron jaw."

***

"Do you want the chair?" asked Sarah.

Eric wasn't sure. It was huge, and tacky, something he would never actually buy for himself.

On the other hand, it was very comfortable.

"I don't know. What about you?"

She frowned.

"Hell no. I don't even think I could get it through my front door. It's a beast!"

They were going through her belongings. It was a thankless job. Grandma was an avid collector of knickknacks, and they had a really hard time differentiating family heirloom from junk. They had to look at everything, one by one, and it was tedious.

"Didn't Aunt Mary put dibs on it?" asked Eric.

"No, that was for the rocking chair in the back. The only person who wants it is Grandma's church friend."

"Who?!"

Sarah was struggling to describe her.

"Fuck if I know her name...The lady with the purple hair from the service. I guess they went to the same church. Remember that small group of old people in the yard, doing that prayer circle?"

"Vaguely."

"Yeah. She's one of *them*. She was quite pushy about it, too...Rachel? Something with an R?"

Eric sat down in the recliner. He could feel his body relax as it seeped into the cushion.

"Takes some balls to ask for something this expensive!" he said. "Were they even close?"

"I highly doubt it. I didn't see Aunt Mary say hi to them, which—to me—means that she didn't know them. So how close could they have really been to Grandma?"

He reached for the control at the side of the recliner, and pushed a button. The footrest slowly rose up under his legs.

"Yeah, I don't want to give this to some random."

Sarah shrugged.

"Well, it's yours, as long as you get it out of here by next Tuesday." she said. "The realtor's sending someone to take pictures of the house, and it makes the living room look tiny."

***

Eric let the door go, and it swung open with a loud creek.

Then he waited. He kept his eyes on the recliner, to make sure that it didn't move.

A long moment passed.

Nothing happened.

The only light in the room was the green dot on his computer charger, and it covered everything in a sickly yellow glow. But even like this, he could tell that the recliner wasn't moving; it was facing the television in the same position he left it hours ago. And it wasn't making any sounds either. He could only hear the faint buzz of the refrigerator coming from the kitchen, and the occasional car driving by.

There was no mechanical breathing. No sign of the noise that woke him up.

He felt very silly. He walked into the living room and turned the lights on. He squinted, but a second later he was able to look around.

Everything was normal.

Maybe he wasn't quite awake yet when he got up, he thought. Maybe the sound was just a dream: a recurring nightmare that startles him, night after night. Nothing more.

He picked up the TV remote, and sat down on the recliner. He started clicking through the channels.

But despite telling himself that everything was fine, he couldn't relax. His heart was still racing, and his hands were shaking. His muscles were all tense.

He didn't even realize it, but he was bracing himself...for *something*.

***

It took Eric a couple of days to remember the lady with the purple hair. He *did* meet her at the service. When Sarah described her, he imagined a deep purple, a color you would dye your hair when you tried to look young and cool. Hers wasn't like that at all. It was that faint, pale purple that old women used to end up with all the time. It was *unintentional* purple.

He only remembered because he saw her again, on the day he picked up the recliner.

A friend of his came to help him carry it out to the truck. It was heavy: a real back killer, so they were struggling. They finally managed to squeeze it through the front door without banging up the door frame, and they sat it down on the lawn to regroup.

"Hey, what's up with the creepy neighbor?" asked the friend as he lit a cigarette.

Eric looked around, and spotted the woman. She was standing on the sidewalk across the street.

"I think she knew my Grandma."

The woman was staring at them. She didn't pretend to be walking by, or talking on the phone—she was just straight up staring at them, with the same disappointed look that teachers give when they hear that the dog ate your homework.

"Good morning!" shouted Eric, and waved to her.

She didn't wave back, but she did start talking under her breath. He assumed that she was cursing them out. Maybe she was still hoping to inherit the goddamn recliner.

"Well, fuck her." said Eric "I think they were trying to lure my Grandmother into a cult."

He and Sarah spent the last week going through her belongings, and they found a *lot* of religious material. Some were just the generic Christian literature one could expect: prayer books, Bible study schedules, and handouts about electing Republicans to end the murder of unborn babies.

But there were others.

It appeared that this congregation was obsessed with the Devil. They didn't think of it as a metaphor, but as a literal, flesh and blood creature who rages a war on all of God's creation. It struck Eric as rather naive.

"You know, we were all sweating like pigs when the lawyer opened her will...These churches are like vultures." Eric said.

His friend agreed.

"I heard that as you age, the part of your brain that tells the difference between fact and fiction deteriorates. That's why the elderly are so easy to scam. Why they eat up everything on Fox News, and why they end up leaving the family house to their church. Instead of, you know, their families." he said, and he flicked his half-smoked cigarette onto the driveway "It's a shame."

They got back to work. It took them almost twenty minutes, but they managed to get the recliner onto the truck in one piece. As they finally pulled away, Eric glanced at the sidewalk, and the old woman was still there, whispering something under her breath.

What a long-winded curse, he thought to himself.

***

"I can't take this anymore! Oh my god, I can't do this!"

She was hysterical. Her hands were tied behind her back, and she was kneeling in a pool of blood.

"For the love of god, let me out!" she screamed.

Eric was confused.

He must have dozed off, because the last thing he remembered was that gothy scientist from *NCIS*, and this was clearly something else.

There was blood on the walls, too, and when they cut to a close up, Eric learned that it was trickling out of a freshly decapitated corpse. It was dangling—somewhat comically—from a hook, like cheap Halloween decoration.

The pool around the girl was getting bigger.

"Pleeease!" she begged, but she fell silent as soon as the door behind her opened. The string music soared, and a shadowy figure raised his axe.

Eric turned the TV off. It was quite enough. He didn't mean to sleep out in the living room, and it was time to go back to bed. His head was all foggy, he could barely think.

He grabbed the armrest, and tried to stand up...

But he couldn't.

The recliner was simply too comfortable. He was too tired, too sleepy, and he just couldn't bring himself to do it.

He made one more halfhearted attempt to get up, but his legs wouldn't obey him. He finally leaned back into the cushion.

It was soft, and warm, like a mother's embrace.

He closed his eyes.

It was like heaven.

***

"Such a tragedy, what happened." said the woman with the purple hair. It was right after Aunt Mary read the poem, and everyone was still crying. "But the best we can all wish for is to die in our sleep, right?"

She petted him on the shoulder and gave him a comforting smile.

Eric was confused. Grandma didn't die peacefully in bed, but in agony, crawling around the floor with a broken hip. The doctors said that it took a couple of days.

"I'm sorry?!" he asked, but she has already moved on, to give somebody else her condolences.

He hated when old people just said whatever popped into their heads. As if age gave them a license to be crazy.

He probably would've remembered that strange exchange if there wasn't a shouting match on the front lawn mere minutes later. That's when they all learned that Uncle Fred wasn't sober after all.

***

It was dark.

As dark as a night can be—as if all the light in the world went out.

But he wasn't scared. At all. This darkness was like a womb: he was safe here, and there was nothing to be afraid of. He was floating in a sea of warmth, away from all the problems of the world. His life felt like a faint memory, something that happened a long-long time ago. Like a dream.

The only thing that existed here was the beating of a drum. Each beat echoed through the darkness like an otherworldly message.

BUMM.

Then came the all-consuming silence, and after what felt like an eternity, another set.

BUMM-BUMM.

Somewhere, far away, someone was beating a giant drum.

BUMM-BUMM.

He finally recognized that it was his own heart.

It was strangely comforting. If he listened carefully, he could even hear his blood rushing through his arteries after each beat, and it was like standing on the shores of the ocean at night.

He felt whole.

BUMM-BUMM.

But then came the pain.

It was a dull, gentle pain, in his lower back. It started out small, barely noticeable. But then it grew, and grew, until there was nothing else...

And that's when he snapped out of it.

He gasped, like he was taking a breath for the very first time.

He opened his eyes. He was still sitting in the recliner, and the afternoon sun was blazing through the windows. It was so bright he could hardly take it.

He reached behind his back and pulled out the thing that was stabbing him. It was a torn up piece of plastic. A small remote control, or maybe one of those garage door clickers.

He only recognized Grandma's Life Alert when he saw the tiny logo on it. The strap that was to keep it around her neck was all torn up, as if it was chewed on by giant teeth.

Then he noticed his hand. It was extremely skinny: he could see the cartilage between each digit of his fingers, and the veins running on top of his knuckles. He had to be sitting here for days, if not weeks, to lose this much weight.

He tried to scream, but his throat was so dry that no sound came out of his mouth.

He had to get up. He leaned on the armrest, but he immediately pulled his hand off of it. It felt different: it wasn't covered in leather anymore. It was skin.

The footrest opened up to grab his legs, and that's when the scream finally broke through his windpipes.

Hard iron rods crushed his shins.

Blood started to pool on the carpet.

He dug his fingers into the recliner, but it wouldn't ease up. It was shaking him, and its mechanical breathing sounded so much like growling that the neighbor's dogs started to growl back at it.

***

"Hello?" asked Sarah as she answered the phone. She could barely stop crying long enough to speak. "Who?!"

Uncle Jeff put his hand on her shoulder. He was the first one there: he came as soon as he heard what happened to Eric.

Sarah listened for a minute, then hang up without saying another word.

"What was that?" asked Uncle Jeff.

"That bitch." she whispered. She was shaking. "I can't even…"

"Who?"

"Grandma's church friend."

She took a deep breath and looked at him in disbelief.

"She's still asking for that fuckin' recliner."

Little Places
Dawson Goodell

I never much cared for little places, where you can't stretch out both your arms and legs till your muscles creak and your whole body shakes just a bit. I make do buying a house with an "open" layout. Closets are walk-ins and when even that seems too small, I ask my wife. When something breaks, I hire a professional to crawl under the house.

It isn't a big deal. I drive a hatchback with enough room to lay down in the back. The only thing claustrophobia really ruined for me was Harry Potter. I didn't make it past where the boy lives in a little room under the stairs.

I dream of little places sometimes. It's dark, but warm—too warm really—and when I kick, my leg hits something with a hollow woody sound. It's just inches above me. I try to push the object off of me, but whatever is holding my feet isn't laid across my chest. Instead my arms reach straight up into the darkness. So I wriggle, trying to pull my whole body into the gap, but I can't move my legs.

***

In the real world, my phone is ringing. It's late, and my wife doesn't respond to the angry chirp of my phone. The screen tells me it is 2 am, and answering the phone is just a foggy reflex without conscious thought behind it.

It's my mom.

"He's gotten worse," she says, but her voice isn't sad. It isn't anything except maybe tired.

"Do I need to come?"

"Yes," she says. "I'm not going to, but he's your father."

She washed her hands of him long ago, but next of kin is next of kin.

I wake my wife.

"My dad is dying," I say.

She nods silently and rolls over. I'll ask in the morning if she processed what I said.

I'm up for now, so I grab a beer and collapse in my chair out in the darkness of the living room. I email my boss from my phone and buy a couple of plane tickets.

***

It's a seven hour trip: four in the air, one in Minneapolis, another in the air, then it's an hour from the little airport down into the valley. My father dies when we're somewhere over Iowa. I'm relieved that I've been spared having to see him, but I still have to finish the trip. I have a funeral to plan, a grave site to buy, and my father's house. In the end, the funeral is small and we opt to cremate my father. The house is unfit for sale.

It's an ugly 70s sprawl with a large first floor and a second floor loft tacked on as an afterthought. The hallways are narrow and the living room sits a couple of steps lower than the dining area and kitchen it's tied to. The walls are wood paneling, but the thin kind that splinters. The floorplan leaves hallways dark and far from windows.

"It's charming," my wife says as I pull into the driveway.

I put the car in park and turn off the engine. "Not how I'd describe it," I say.

"It needs a new coat of paint and some things," she says.

"It needs bulldozed."

"Hush," she laughs.

I don't feel like laughing, but I do anyway.

The house is bigger than I remember, opening up from its double wide green door with a knob right in the center.

The door opens straight into a wall. To the right is a small sitting room and to the left is the kitchen and bedrooms.

My wife comments on the family crest displayed proudly on the wall.

"Yeah," I said. "My dad liked to go on and on about just how Irish we really are. As if the O' in the name didn't give it away."

"Should we take it with us?" she asked.

"What? No."

"Just a thought," she said. "This place is pretty nice."

"It's alright," I said.

"No, I just mean that I thought you were poor," she said running her fingers around a framed mountain painting on the wall.

"We were, sort of, I mean. My dad worked in the mines most of my life. Got a job with the union later on and eventually became union treasurer. We did alright."

"I see. Where is your room?" she asks with a smile.

"I'm sure it's just storage now."

But it wasn't. The room was just empty save for the bare mattress I slept on as a child.

"It's rather spartan," she says. She is still laughing easily; she knows that her laugh calms my nerves.

"Well all my stuff is gone, obviously," I said, but I was scared to tell her the truth. The room had always been bare. I had made an effort to plaster the walls with band posters and sports stars, but when I was grounded my dad ripped those things off the wall. I was grounded a lot, so I stopped trying.

"So this is where you first discovered masturbation," she said.

"I suppose so," but I didn't laugh. I really should have laughed. "But I remember it for other things."

"Like what? First joint?"

"Can you imagine?" I asked. "If I were that stupid? My dad would have killed me, and my mom, well she would have let it happen." I paused to look at the bare bed. "Let me show you the rest of the house."

She flopped down on my old bed. "Ew," she said jumping back up. "Smells like pee."

"Dad kept a lot of cats after I left."

"Sure, cats," she chided.

She was trying to lighten the mood, but the comment upset me.

"I didn't spend much time here," I said. "If you really want to know what it was like growing up we need to see the school and the library and the park and—importantly—the woods!"

"Lead on," she said.

I took her out the kitchen door into the patchy grass behind the house. From this side, the house appeared much older. The siding had never been replaced. The trim had never been repainted. The bare dirt between patches of thick crabgrass made this look like the yard of a trailer. All it needed to complete the picture was a line of old vehicles on blocks.

"My dad was never persnickety about the lawn, well except when I was between the ages of 8 and 18."

She laughed. "A good lawn is a character builder. That's what my dad said."

"You had brothers."

"Right, and they needed to build their character more than I did," she smirked at me and I couldn't help but grab her hand.

"Come on," I said and took off dragging her behind me into the stands of elm, birch, and maple behind the house. "I used to play way back here," I said almost at a jog through the thick bed of leaves. "It goes on for miles!"

"How far are we going?" she asked.

"Up for a walk to the creek?"

"I don't have any idea how far that is, so yes?"

We walked far back into the trees, past the point where the sky grows dark as the trees close over it. The wind was whistling a trill note through the bare branches, a note I felt more in the hairs on the back of my neck than heard with my ears. It wasn't accompanied by the chill of the autumn breeze, not down near the rot of fallen leaves.

"I don't remember it being this thick back here," I said stepping through the leaves and fallen twigs with heavy crunching footfalls.

"You were much smaller," she said. "Oh look, a rock-a-pile!"

"A rock-a-pile?" I said.

She was pointing ahead. Someone had piled a little stack of rocks on top of a little mound of leaves and dirt.

"That's called a cairn," I said.

"No normal person knows that. It's a pile of rocks, a rock-a-pile, and it means kids still play back here."

"I guess so," I said pressing on past the little marker, but I thought it a strange thing to find unless the precarious stones had somehow stood a long time. There weren't many houses in the area, and no proper neighborhood bordered the trees. When I was younger, there had been a few houses—maybe three in total besides my own, but they were long abandoned by the time I hit high school.

"Perhaps one of the hospice workers had a kid that played back here," I said.

"Maybe," she shrugged.

The walk to the creek was impossibly long as a child, but as an adult it could be done in about 15 minutes. The creek was small and narrow, flowing swiftly as it babbled over exposed roots and stones. A kid of around 12 or 13 could have jumped it in a pinch. An adult could step right over.

"It was bigger when I was little," I said.

"Are you sure? I think perhaps you were just littler when you were little."

"Nah," I said sitting down on a fallen tree. "It's still nice though, right?"

"It's a good picnic spot."

I put my arm around her and we sat in the woods just listening to the soft lapping of water. When we grew chilled and bored, we started our walk back to the house. The path we had tread in on was easy to see in the leaves, but thirty minutes passed without emerging into the backyard. I thought perhaps we had stayed too long at the little creek and that I had misread my watch when we left, but as day drew into twilight and our stomachs began to rumble, it was clear we had been walking too long.

"We must be going in circles," my wife said. She was exasperated though it wouldn't be the first time my directional skills had led me astray. Our light jackets were no longer enough to hold the cold at bay, and a chill had started to eat its way to my bones.

"I just followed the tracks," I said.

"Well it's not working. We must have looped back on ourselves."

"But we've never gone any way but uphill," I said putting my arm around her. She went to shrug me off, but she was nursing her own chill and pressed against me instead.

"We haven't even passed that stupid rock-a-pile," she said.

The wind was crying, but there was no breeze. The leaves didn't rustle in the trees above us. I had never felt something so terribly wrong, and with my eyes closed I listened to the sound and struck out of our old trail in the opposite direction.

"What?" My wife said, noticing the sharp climb in our speed.

"You're right. We've been walking in circles," I said.

"Did you find the way?" she asked.

"Yes," I lied. But in a few minutes we popped out of the woods just a quarter mile down the road from my old house.

We didn't speak of our time lost at dinner. We went to a little drive-thru place then back to the hotel to sit in silence. She was still mad that I had gotten us lost. I was still scared that maybe I hadn't.

***

My wife and I explored my other old haunts, the high school, the library, the local parks. We didn't hit any hiking trails and I didn't suggest it, but in the end she ran out of time off, and I still had not started the odious task of cleaning out my father's home. With no other options, my wife bought herself a plane ticket and returned home while I set out to get as much done as quickly as possible. I didn't want to be there much longer, especially without her. I checked out of our relatively nice hotel near downtown and into a motel on the edges. One of those motels with a number after the name that doubles as their rating out of 100. It was closer to my father's house, but more importantly it was $30 cheaper a night.

It was a cramped, dirty room. Just walking through the door set my nerves on edge, but it would do for a night's sleep.

I woke in the darkness of the motel room to the sound of the heater kicking on with a heavy clunk. I opened my eyes but there was no light creeping through the curtains. I felt like I was floating in a sea of black, drowning in it. I rolled to turn on the bedside lamp but found the blankets tied tightly around my feet.

The part of my brain, normally buried by higher order functions turned on, and I thrashed my legs trying to move up the bed and away from the hot, ghastly grip of my own covers.

The side of my face began to hurt like it had been slammed against something and without realizing it I had started to cry. I shouted my wife's name into the dark, but in that instant it was gone. My feet came loose of the sheet like nothing had happened. The dim lights of the digital clock illuminated where I was laying.

I flicked the light on and spent the early hours of the morning reading. I grabbed breakfast from the hotel lobby, store bought cookies and the cheap brand of yogurt, before heading back to my childhood home.

Daylight had chased away any real fear and now I just feel tired, numb.

It was still early morning when I arrived at my father's house with a couple of sandwiches from the local grocery store in a sack and a long to-do list. My father had died in the living room. He had spent the last few months of his life there on a rented hospital bed, next to a rented wheelchair, hooked up to a rented IV drip and a rented oxygen tank. The blankets would need laundered, the chair and bed disassembled and returned.

There was paperwork to be done, too. I'd need to find the deeds and titles to my father's house and car to take possession.

I had not expected it to be night when I finished, but as I closed the house door behind me, darkness had set in save for a single point of pale white light back in the trees. It was a small point and although I knew there was nothing but more trees back in that direction, I told myself it was merely a flood light on some distant house. I took a few steps off the porch towards the car and the light grew behind me.

I turned.

"Hello?" I said timidly, half expecting some hiker or local boy to come walking out of the woods. Another part of me, the same part I think that dreams of dark rooms, knew that the light was coming from some unnameable thing that stands entombed in those old woods.

A space as large as a truck was now filled with an iridescent glow, and I forced myself to step towards it. One small step then another, straining my eyes into the light. It was like moonlight, soft and cold. My legs tensed and my fists shut tightly.

I could make out a figure in the center. At first I thought it to be tall and lanky, but while she—and it certainly was a she though I cannot say how I came to determine that—had long arms hanging to her ankles she was not tall. She was floating three or four feet from the ground and while I looked I her I squeezed my keys so tight that the metal bit into the fatty underside of my fingers.

I took a single step backwards then stumbled as I turned and bolted towards my car.

But the figure in the light was faster. It shrieked like a cat in heat as it sailed by me. I didn't stay long enough to see where it stopped. Instead I turned and sprinted back into the house, slamming the door behind me.

I sunk against the locked door and covered my face with my hands. I was too afraid to move even as far as the light switch, so I sat and rocked myself peering through my fingers into the shadows on the wall. I didn't dare look through the window behind me at the unnatural light seeping through. I hugged my knees and waited.

When the family crest fell from the wall with a heavy bang I leapt from my resting place and bolted to my old bedroom. The door was shut and although I shook the knob I couldn't push it open.

I found myself sitting against another wall in the house between my door and the door to a second room whose purpose I couldn't recall. I must have fallen asleep in the hall because when I next opened my eyes the strange glow had been replaced with the first lights of dawn. I stood and opened the door to the room beside my bedroom. Beyond the door was a mirror image of my own room—a single bed, a single blanket in an otherwise spartan space. I felt strangely disoriented and rushed back to my room and threw open the door just to be sure that I was seeing things correctly. It opened easily now that day had come. The house had two bedrooms, mine and another.

***

It took me awhile to work up the courage to leave the house, but eventually I made my way to a coffee shop where I caught up on my work and current events. By mid-afternoon I had decided what to do with the house. It needed to be gutted and ripped apart and for all the memories living there, I needed to be the one to do it. Once the memories were gone I would hire a contractor to tear down the final beams. I'd sell the land and set aside the money.

I packed up my things and headed to the local hardware store, a little family place that had stood in the town for some 50 years. The front door opened directly into a mixed help / checkout table so that the employees could greet you as soon as you entered. I remember coming here on my own as a teenager and dreading it every time. I always felt bad telling the employees that I knew where I was going and how to find what I was looking for.

It was an old man behind the desk today.

"Kin I help ya?" he asked.

"Yeah, I'm looking for—" but he cut me off.

"You're the O'Connell boy, aren't ya?"

"Yeah," I said.

"I'm sorry for bringin' it up. Ya look just like 'im. Same brow. Same hair."

"Receding," I said.

The old man smiled. Same humor."

I wouldn't have known. I don't recall my father joking around much, not when I was around at least. But he was well-liked by coworkers and his fellow unionists. I didn't tell the old man this.

"I was sorry to 'ear he 'ad passed. Condolences," he said but the word *condolence* rolled out of his mouth like it was a proud trinket he was showing off. A five dollar word in a sea of pennies.

I thanked him, trying to hide my discomfort.

"If I'd've known you was coming I would have gotten ya a card with a bible verse."

"Thank you," I said. "I appreciate the sentiment."

The man smiled broadly. "How can I help ya today?"

"I need a sledgehammer," I said.

His demeanor changed and I wondered if I mispronounced the word somehow—as if perhaps I had so mangled the sentence as to have been offensive.

"You betta not be tearin' the old place down. Your dad, he loved that house. Put a lot work inna it."

"I'm not tearing it down," I lied.

"Then lez get you that hammer. I 'member your father coming her one night after I closed up. Must've been some twenty years ago to buy hammer, nails, an' paneling. 'Member it cause he woke me up. Looked like he'd seen a ghost. Think he jus' buildin' a shed."

The memory flooded back to me. Years ago my father had put up a little storage shed in the back yard to store his lawn supplies. It was a bit of a surreal memory. I left the house to go to school and instead of being at work he was in the yard hammering together a little wood frame. I was too afraid to say anything to him, but that wasn't unusual. I was often afraid of the man.

Somewhere in that recollection I also remembered him hauling wood into the house while I hid. I don't know if it was the same memory. It seems unlikely that wood for a shed would have ever been inside the house.

"That shed fell down if I recall correctly," I said.

The old man laughed.

"I think he was a better miner," I said with a smile, but there was something in the back of my mind clawing its way forward and without thinking I asked, "Did he buy anything else?"

"Oh I dunt 'member that. Lye, p'haps. He wud always buying cleaners. Why you asking?"

"I just feel like I remember that night for some reason."

"Wudn't surprise me. It was odd."

I paid for the sledgehammer and headed back to the house. I didn't expect it to be growing dark when I arrived, but I barely took note of the falling twilight. Time had not made any sense since I arrived here. It's noon then it's 3 and then it's nearly 7 and the sun is starting set without me seeing any of the time in between. I entered the house—sledgehammer in hand—in a sort of disoriented fugue.

I swung first at the family crest that had fallen the night before. It bounced up off the hard floor so I poured myself into the next blow, bending knees as the hammer fell. The crest burst apart. For good measure I put the sledgehammer through the wall where the crest had once hung.

It wasn't the first time that wall had a hole punched in it. Being the first place my father saw when he entered the house it was the frequent target of his indiscriminate rage. The paneling had been patched and replaced several times, but the sledgehammer didn't care that the wall was old and calloused.

I took the hammer into the kitchen and swung it from over my head into the corner of the kitchen sink where my father had held me upside down under the water. I was 6 and he was upset that I had cursed. It is one of my earliest memories that I remember with any clarity. It took several strokes before the cabinet shattered and the sink fell in, held up only by the heavy metal drain pipe.

I took the hammer into the hallway with my room and knocked the knob out of the door so that it would never be locked in on me again. Finding that insufficient I struck again and again until I had knocked the door from its hinges and the hinges from the frame. I flipped the bed in the room against the wall. It was not as cathartic as the damage I had done to the door and kitchen so I lifted the hammer back up and took it to the wall of the master bedroom.

I smashed a hole in the wall where I had cried listening to my mother and father fight on the other side. It was also where my father had knocked two of my teeth out. I was fourteen and I got between my fighting parents. I reduced the wall down to its studs and when only the skeleton of the room remained, skinned by my hand, darkness had fallen complete.

Panting in the chilly, drafty air, I noticed for the first time that my work was lit by the eerie glow from the trees—filtering through the master bedroom's windows. Like that glow, something was seething from deep inside my mind, hammering its way out.

Unready to face it again, I ran down the stairs, sledgehammer still in hand. When I reached the bottom of the stairs, I turned, gasping for breath, but the windows were dark again. I told myself the moonlight was just cutting through the clouds—that nothing unusual was happening. I was good at these kinds of lies. I'd been making them my whole life.

The front door creaked open and then crashed loudly against the wall, but I didn't dare turn around. The light was behind me now, illuminating the wall from just over my shoulder. I thought to run back upstairs, leap from a second floor window and dash to my rental car, but the light was there too now—slowly advancing towards the stairs.

The only way left to me was through the wall under the stairs. The wall that was always rotting—dry but moldy—and my father would paint over it again and again and the black mold would appear again. It was rotten now. Black with mold like dried blood drops.

I know I screamed as I swung my hammer into it.

The paneling splintered like matchsticks.

Behind the wall was an old door to a storage area, long ago nailed shut.

"No," I said. "Please."

But if the figure heard she didn't care. I could feel her now, directly behind me, her light illuminating the door in front of me and casting my long shadow on it. I dared not turn around.

The figure's hand crept over my shoulder and I screamed, swinging my hammer into the door. The sledge caught on the other side and I tugged with everything I had.

The nails pulled from the spongy wall and the hinges gave way revealing the inside of a tiny storage room and the little, decayed body of my older sister.

The figure passed through me like a wave crashing across a rocky beach and felt simultaneously cold as the grave and warm as sunlight. The force of it shoved me into the room so that I struck my head on the low bridge of the door and stumbled helplessly over the body in a pantomime of my sister's death. The figure and its light were gone now, but the moon shown through the windows and down the hallway into the room.

We were face-to-face, my sister and me, and for just a moment she looked as she once did. Her bright blue eyes stared up at me one last time then they were gone again.

I was eleven when she died. I had hit puberty earlier than my friends and my arms shot out, spindly, thin, and awkward. I spent my seventh grade year pretending I wasn't growing up, holding on to my childhood for the normalcy it gave me. Cassie was 13, and just the opposite. She was eager to grow up—precocious, fiery—a mountain of trouble.

Dad was always mad at her, and I never understood why. Perhaps because she grew up too fast or because she looked too much like her mother whom he also hated. I don't recall the specifics of the fight, there were so many to misremember. As I grew older the fights became intertwined, confused with one another. I do remember he ordered her into timeout and she didn't go.

My last memory of her is him grabbing her by the front of her shirt, seizing a handful of hair in the process and lifting her off the ground. He carried her roughly to the door under the staircase where we went for timeouts and threw her through the doorway. Her head cracked on the top of the door.

I don't know what I did the next day when she was gone and the room was walled off. I was afraid. So scared so I forgot she ever existed.

A week and a half after we buried my father, we buried my sister. The funeral was larger with most of the town coming to offer their condolences and to tell me that they thought she had gone to camp, or been taken by her biological mom or some other falsehood started by a small town rumor mill. My mother—her mother—didn't bother making the trip.

The local paper ran the headline "House on Knoll Hill St Holds Dark Secret." But it hadn't. Not really. Everyone knew who my father was. They knew he had a temper. They knew he drank. They knew he had a daughter. They just didn't care. It wasn't their business, and how could I blame them. I too had forced myself to forget.

I never told my wife about my sister's specter, though I did tell it to a counselor—framing it as a dream I once had. The house is still there, still empty, nearly reclaimed by the forest. The forest can have it.

The Red Spot Murders
Eric Nash

T he line of tower blocks resembled groyne posts stained and encrusted by the urban ebb and flow. A handful of Josh's students came from Sunnyside; he knew its reputation, but during the phone call yesterday the woman's voice transformed the problem housing estate into a tingling promise.

The battered playground ahead, intimidated into redundancy, had been commandeered as a gallery of tags and pictorial satire that could challenge even Hogarth. A barrage of outraged idiosyncrasies layered by decades of frustration spread to the surrounding high-rise concrete where historic vulgarity exploded in vivid colour against disturbing images daubed in varying shades of darkness, spotted with tampered signs. One not-so-talented, yet humorous, artist had tampered with the sign of the next tower block so it read, S***** H*i**t*. The filthy concrete rose out of the patchwork of violence, beauty and self-loathing, and, with a wave of excitement, Josh wondered what waited for him up there in Flat 314.

"Flowers! Fuck!" A hero would have brought his date flowers. And she wanted a hero according to the ad in the Daily Echo: *Female, 30, seeking a hero, must have GSOH and a big sword.* Those who didn't think teachers were courageous and noble weren't used to thinking much. And the students at Meadowdown Comprehensive were always telling him that he had an epic sense of humour. He just had to win Maeve over before unclipping his scabbard.

Mayyy … Mayyy … vvv … ah. He thought her name was the sound of longing.

Past a swing throttled by its own chain the ever inviting warmth of a fluorescent light emanated from a shop doorway. The yellow and black sign above it read, Brahma's News. It was not Interflora, nor Texaco, but probably his last hope.

Inside the musty interior, nine scrawny bunches of daffodils were dying against the side of a black bucket. He picked up four and waited for the pursed-lipped cashier, with an indicative complexion similar to a raw prawn, to finish serving the other customer.

"They should string the bastards up."

"Mmm."

"I mean, what her parents must be going through."

"It is awful."

Josh scrunched his mouth into a knot. He was going to be late: an instant death for a first date.

"That sort of thing was never heard of when I was growing up."

"Mmm. That's sixteen fifty then please."

"Oh, and a packet of Rothmans, love."

"Let's hope they find her soon, eh?"

"Oh, I do hope so. Poor little mite."

"Hello, dear. Sorry for the wait."

Josh beamed.

"Who's the lucky lady, then?"

"My mum. Any chance you could wrap them in some nice paper?"

"Go on then."

In the stairwell of S***** H*i**t*, his shoes struck the concrete steps and echoed loudly as he dodged spilled refuse and hurried to the first floor. The sound haunted his ascent nonetheless—as did the smell of chip fat and urine: the odour of surrender.

"Oi!"

His heart leapt into his throat, or felt like it had so much that he gasped. Josh glanced up, down, up again. He saw no-one. The voice had come from inside an apartment; the shout not directed at him. He continued up the next flight of steps as the shouts subsided replaced by a baby's sorrowful wail. A raw and weary cry; a shadow of the abundance of breath held in his infant niece's lungs, and it lingered upon the hairs of his arms and crept onto his skin until he reached the third floor and saw the sign, Flats 311 – 320 pointing toward the balcony.

The city lights on his left warmed him like Christmas decorations, though the festive season had been left drowned in dirty, curbside slush. The sound of a siren reached him – Flat 311 – the invasive noise gained urgency - Flat 312 - pealed in his ears, yet the street below was empty - Flat 313 - the siren faded away. Flat 314.

A wizened face grinned a mouthful of rot at him through the kitchen window, yet the number plaque and the damp piece of paper crumpled in his palm matched. Before Maeve's invite to dinner, they'd discussed his line of work and circumstances, but little about her; perhaps the old woman was her grandmother. He had expected to meet in a public place initially, joking to himself that they would be chaperoned. He never imagined it happening.

"It's open, Joshua." Her voice as gnarled as the features.

He smiled, hoped it displayed earnestness, and opened the door to a rich smell of caramelised meat that masked the reek of piss from the outside. He frowned, unable to distinguish what animal roasted in the oven. He concluded game. It tugged at his belly.

"Thanks. Um…is Maeve about?"

"Won't be long."

The woman wore a long nightdress, about as old as herself. The straight sleeves were rolled high and her skinny arms, which appeared covered in a coppery down so thick that it could have been called fur, were elbow-deep in a sink full of bloody water.

"Washing machine's buggered," she said, wringing out a shirt. "Saw you coming, sweetheart, so I made you coffee. Black, one sugar?"

"Good guess."

"I can tell what a man likes. Don't mind the decorating. Just moved in."

"How you liking the place?"

Used paint brushes and a hardened roller had been barged into the clutter of half-filled mugs and dirty cutlery, glasses, crusted plates and opened food tins serving as Petri dishes on the counter. Decay as well as paint were smothered by the oven's sweet aroma. The walls bare, ready for painting, other than five party Polaroids attached with blue push pins to a small corkboard above a collapsible table.

The vividness of the paint drew his attention. "I'm told red's quite popular at the moment."

"It's Raspberry Bellini."

The grandmother glanced at his feet and trailed her gaze upward. Her shoulders rose, then deflated. "Yep, you'll do. No more needed, now."

A dubious compliment. "How long is she going to be?"

"Like I said already, sweetheart, I won't be long." She dried her hands in a teacloth, a red stain leeched on the material, then she moved toward a mug on the windowsill. The movement caused an odd clacking noise, and her to trip over the skirts of her nightgown.

"Sorry, I meant Maeve."

"Get this coffee down ya and you'll see her soon enough," she said. As she exited the kitchen the clack accompanied her.

Josh's old man used to tell him if he wanted an insight into future romance check out the mother. Every rule had an exception, right? And the coffee was good. Very. It had a complex taste, neither fruit nor chocolate overtones that despite swishing the hot liquid around his mouth as he studied his surroundings remained a mystery. But he felt the buzz from it after two gulps.

He stepped further into the kitchen to the table on which was an old Instamatic. The shlick shlick sounds of his soles on the linoleum stopped when he placed the daffodils beside the camera. The Polaroids on the board weren't party photos as he thought. Four of the headshots featured a different man, the fifth a child. The men appeared to be asleep and very pale, the girl awake and terrified. All had a central red smear on their lips—similar to the lipstick of the Geisha—an obscene kiss. The images resembled crime scene photographs; a peculiar thing to showcase, but not as weird as keeping one's freezer well-stocked with rodents like Mary. Mary did have a boa constrictor, perhaps Maeve was an art student. He shuddered, backed away from the wall, his head so full of tinnitus that he clapped his hands over his ears. It eased as he retreated, until it disappeared.

Alongside the camera, two dinner plates, a wooden-handled carving knife, and a wet, stained teaspoon. Also, numerous dark, glistening splashes at the edge of the table, more by his feet. He dipped his finger, smeared his thumb. The substance was too gelatinous to be coffee, it also lacked paint's invasive VOC odour, plus coffee wasn't the colour of rubies. With a grimace, he wiped the stuff off his fingers onto the counter, feeling like he was walking alone at night through a deserted underground car park wishing he'd parked nearer to the stairs.

"Joshua?" At the hallway, the old woman's bony, elongated fingers twirled the lank hair framing her foul grin.

Blow this! Josh shlicked, shlicked toward the front door.

"There you are!" A new voice made him turn back. Maeve. She stood, draped in a burgundy dress that ran down her curves and splashed onto the floor, in the exact spot where her granny had been moments before.

"Maeve."

Her widening smile drew him closer. His hand slipped from the door handle. There was no way Maeve would ever end up like her mother. Not that it mattered.

"I see you've finished the brew, Joshua."

"She makes good coffee, your—?"

"It's effective. Are those lovely flowers for moi?"

"Yes. Yes they are."

He interrupted his view of her retrieving a vase to glance at the corkboard. "I haven't seen Polaroids for years. I used to have lots of party ones on my wall at Uni. What's the story behind yours?"

"It's an art project."

"Of course." He smiled a little too generously. "It reminds me of an exhibition at the Metropolitan Museum of Art I heard about a while ago."

"Really?" Maeve tucked a stray lock of hair behind her ear with elegant paint-stained fingers. That engaging smile continued to massage his heart until it beat in time with her breath. Christ, he'd flipped? His head struggled to gather anything other than lovesick thoughts. She'll be pushing him out the flat at this rate.

"Really. What was it now? Something and foul play, I think it was called. It attracted massive crowds. Suitably gruesome, I guess.

"Look, shall we go out? I know a great place near the Wharf."

"No. There's a joint in the oven. You're not vegetarian, are you?"

"Um, no," Josh replied, smelling the delicious aroma anew and hearing his stomach rumble, "but what about your grandmother?"

"That's a relief. I admit I haven't yet met a hero who was."

"What about your—"

"*There*'s just me and you, Joshua."

Josh had been in sight of the apartment's only exit since arrival, but did he really want to blow any chance of seeing Maeve again? "Do you only date heroes?"

"Wouldn't you? They keep my house safe," she said. "Now, you're in the way, so sit at the table and let me check on dinner."

Half expecting to be hit by a second barrage of tinnitus, his arm rested next to the flowers, their fading blooms drooped over the rim of a dirty pint glass. Maeve bent over to open the oven, her dress taut. The air seemed to thicken with the succulence of sizzling meat. His stomach groaned as she transferred the roast to a hot plate and placed it on the hob, then wiped her hands down the front of her dress. The act of spoiling her sumptuous outfit shocked him, it also left a greasy trail as evidence of where he imagined his hands.

"Well, I've never been treated like this on a date before."

"Are you a serial dater, Josh?" She wrapped her hair into a loose knot.

"No...well, I've been on a few, I guess. What about you?"

"Men are easy to find, heroes not so. I need new ones whenever I relocate."

"Do you relocate often?"

"When the magic wears off."

Pragmatic and honest, both qualities could become dull over time—she hitched the dress over her thighs and squatted in front of the open fridge—both qualities were also very desirable. A stray tangle of hair brushed the nape of her neck. He ignored the urge to stroke it away and tickle the bare, downy skin with a kiss, then the fridge shut with a flick of her hips, and Maeve stood holding a Perspex jug filled with red wine. She broke the surface of the liquid with her nail then sucked on it.

"Too cold. Bugger, I should have taken it out sooner."

"Do you normally put red wine in the fridge?" Room temperature had risen sharply since the industrial revolution, so it was not such a crazy idea.

"No. This is blood."

For the first time since she appeared at the doorway, a tremor of uncertainty unsteadied him. Artist or not, this woman probably had issues. And the mother was a hag. Thinking about it, he'd quite liked Kerry with the big boobs from a few weeks back.

"What did you do, drain a chicken?"

The question tickled her; the laugh charmed him, and thoughts of Kerry dissipated.

"It'll thicken the gravy. Take some thyme from the windowsill, sweetheart, and chop it into little pieces for me. Knife's next to you."

Drop by drop, she stirred in the blood and sang his name to the beat of his tapping knife. Their bodies touched, caressed, as he sprinkled the fragrant leaf into the bubbling stock.

"Dinner's ready. Sit down. I don't want the stock to catch."

She reached over the sink and pulled down the blind. Romantic, until she switched on the overhead bulb.

"Here you are, sweetheart."

Two blackened shanks were pushed onto the already-crammed table making the flowers rock.

"What a treat. Are we having vegetables?"

Maeve's eyebrows dived. "You aren't vegetarian. Eat." She poured thick, bloodied gravy over his shank.

She fingered her roasted joint, rotated it with her fingertips like a spit. He did the same. Their teeth sank deep and tore away the bloody, tender meat so ravenously that pieces fell onto the plates in clumps, splashing the table with gravy. These were retrieved and fed back into their mouths with such speed that they were lucky not to nip their own fingers. Both pressed the shanks against their lips, each turn exposed more creamy-white bone, eyelids lowered like some dog's licking out marrow.

Her bare bone clattered on the plate. With a chin bathed in pink, greasy juice and her dress spattered with blood, Maeve announced: "It's time."

She gripped his wrist and shoved his hand under her dress. His fingers enveloped by a viscous heat. Her fingers tightened, forcing his knuckles against her sex as Josh tried to pull away.

"Stop it!"

Still she controlled him, raised his cool, bloody hand from her and positioned it in front of his face.

"I put this in your coffee to enchant you." She jabbed his knuckles into his lips.

He tasted her blood. The Polaroid flared. In the resulting blindness, he felt his neck sliced open. Josh was dead in three minutes.

After a further twenty-nine seconds he blinked. He had no comprehension of his heart having stopped, he had no sense of his body at all, and only aware that he hung upside down and stared at a yellow-coated tongue poking between teeth the colour of bark. Maeve's grandmother, the hag.

His mind signalled his feet to kick but when Josh peered up to see if he was indeed kicking, he saw only the bare kitchen bulb swinging with the regularity of a pendulum. The hag shuddered, too. No, it was he who was being shaken. The constant jarring made his head feel like a Teflon ball bouncing against a spinning roulette wheel. He tried to fling his arm and grab some sort of anchor but it remained just a thought as two inflated cheeks and a set of puckered lips appeared inches from his. Spittle speckled his vision like drizzle on a windscreen. Through it the other men and that little girl pinned on the corkboard appeared a panoramic blur until he stared at another little, blue pin held between the hag's stained and stumpy thumb and index finger. The sharp point pushed nearer. He scrunched up his eyelids.

"Don't go anywhere, will you, sweetheart?" The sound of her clacking limp faded.

Below, the daffodil's bright heads bowed. Ahead, the wreckage of draining board life, the window, and beyond the blind the neon cityscape twinkled, comforting, out of reach. Josh refused, for as long as he was able, to look at what lay slumped on the lino, keeping it a shadow in his peripheral vision. When he gave in, he saw his own body laid face-down in a puddle of blood deep enough to splash in. He retched; the action, like those of his limbs, a memory.

"Nonononono. No! No! No!" That wasn't him: it couldn't be him spread out on the floor several feet away soaking in…in…his—

There was a sniff above his head. The hag had not reappeared, but who else could it be?

"Who's there?"

A voice, as brittle and tiny as a ladybug, replied, "Once upon…What did I taste like?"

"Oh, God, what's happening?" Josh cried out. "Wake up, wake up!"

Somebody else: "Hi, Josh, I'm Steve: the first one." Deep and resonating, yet the kind of voice that, in the real world, came with a smile and probably delivered bad news. "Sorry to be the one to tell you but that isn't going to work: you're dead. And so are we. At least you're not alone, eh?"

"Who the fuck are you? What the fuck is going on? Why can't I move?"

"Like I said, you're dead, Josh. I would have jumped in and saved you, being a paramedic and all, but you see my predicament. Don't worry, things will become easier to deal with when she gets your corpse out of the kitchen."

"No, I can't be dead. I'm having a conversation."

"And keep doing so, mate. Else you'll end up like the other three here who seemed to have lost their tongues, metaphorically speaking I hope, within hours of joining me. Where are you from, anyway?"

"Eh? Look, if you aren't going to help get out of here, then shut the fuck up."

"Once upon…What did I taste like?"

"Kaci? Kaci? It's okay, love."

Josh didn't want to know about Kaci; he wanted her to go away.

"Once upon…What did I ta—"

The hag tripped back into the room with an open tin of emulsion. "This wretched nightdress gets on my tits!" Placing the paint near the puddle, she levered her way out of the material. A patchwork of reddish fur and tanned skin stitched together with scars covered her wiry frame. Her muscles snaked and twisted on her skeleton as she bent over to undress him. The instrument that clacked when she moved: a cloven hoof in place of her right foot.

"What the fuck is that?" Josh demanded.

"Who cares? Isn't important now."

"I fucking care!"

"Watch your language in front of Kaci."

"Oh, like *that's* fucking important! Can that thing hear us?"

"Don't think so. I've been trying to talk to it for days and it's not given me the slightest indication that it can hear me." Steve sounded less upbeat now.

Josh's clothes were in a pile by his side. "Where's Maeve?"

"That is Maeve, you pleb."

"No. That's her grandmother—oh dear God."

"She used her menstrual blood to do the hoodoo on you, Josh. It's an ancient practice, I believe. Works a treat doesn't it? Made you think that she was your wettest dream, didn't she?"

Josh could tell Steve was smiling, again. "You're sick."

"Listen. She did it with all us blokes. I experienced it, saw it happen twice. How else was she going to do this, really?"

Maeve hadn't pretended that there had been another person in the apartment: it had been Josh's natural assumption. Maeve had said about looking at her through different eyes. He remembered the blood on the table below and the taste of it in his mouth.

"Now you get it?"

Josh didn't want to *get it*. Perhaps Maeve had drugged him and he was hallucinating that Maeve just hauled his corpse from the kitchen and was on her hands and knees wringing his clogged and dripping shirt into the tin of Raspberry Bellini. He didn't fucking think so.

"Tell me what she wants."

"Blood. Apart from Kaci, me and the rest were drugged while she siphoned it off."

"Once upon…What did I taste like?"

"Kaci? Kaci?"

"Shut up! Why does she keep saying that?"

"It's the story that Maeve told her when she was…before she was trapped in the photo."

"Once upon—"

"A time," Josh interrupted. He wasn't sure he should hear the story but certain he didn't want to hear that bloody question any more.

"A time," Kaci said, "in the Coit Mawr, there lived the woman of the wood and happy was she until Men came. They tore down her forest and hunted the beasts that shared her home. And when they had killed all the creatures, they hunted her, but they never caught her. As time passed, from amid the dwindling trees, she saw men build their own homes. Fortifications were built on the bodies of children, and mortar was mixed with human blood to hold it strong."

Maeve hauled herself off her blood-stained hands and knees. "Where's my paint brush? I do need to get on," she muttered, clacking out of the room, "They'll be here soon. Ah, here we are." She returned with her brush, and a pair of steps and a mixing stick.

"And she learnt, this woman—for she was as wise as her brother the owl—that the blood of heroes, men blessed by gods, is strongest."

Maeve was rotating the stick in the pot, blending Josh's blood with the congealing paint. She immersed the brush and scooped out the mixture, slapped it onto the walls in clots and spatters.

"Then one day the last Mother Tree of the Coit Mawr was felled."

So swollen was her brush that it dripped thick, meaty, pink splodges onto the floor and peppered the counters with each flick. Her hoof clattered against the metal step-ladder as she climbed to splash paint higher on the walls. When she raised the corkboard and painted underneath, the kitchen was complete. She leaned back to admire her freshly-daubed walls.

"And the wise woman was forced out into the men's world. Here she would be caught and slain for certain if she did not use her wits like her sister the fox, and so she conjured Man's magic herself. She sacrificed a child then found a hero, knowing that if they were her heroes and her innocents they would be the most potent of all, protecting her from those wishing her harm and keeping her safe in the heart of mankind."

"Oh God, no, no, no!" Josh screamed. "This isn't real. I need to get out of here. I need to get back to work. What have you done to me?"

Maeve chucked the brush and tin into the sink and pulled the blind a couple of inches away from the window to peer along the balcony. "Ah, here they are."

"She lived happily ever after because she listened to her cousin, the viper, who said that Man was fearful and superstitious. And she knew that fear is often best stirred with tongues."

Clacking to the front door, Maeve left it ajar then lifted Josh and the others from the wall. They slapped against their killer's spindly pink-spattered thigh until they were swung into the glare of a newly-decorated living room, and hung above a vacuum cleaner on the back of an open cupboard door. The heroes were left swaying against a cloth bag-tidy while Maeve took her place in the centre of the room.

"Shit!"

Five naked corpses had been lined up on the sofa behind Maeve like fanned tarot cards, with Josh's crusted and blood-stained body sprawled across their laps in a grotesque, erotic pose.

"Jesus," he whispered, suppressing another urge to vomit.

"Who are the other two?" Steve asked.

"Possibly, the previous occupa—"

A knock at the door.

"Help! Help!"

"Hello?" The visitor had the whining twang of a Birmingham accent. Beyond the sofa, the curtains shivered.

"Hello? Police."

"Yes! We're in here! Help!" Josh's shouts smashed the silence of the other souls. A torrent of voices begged release, pleas escalated to demands, demands twisted into threats as the noise swelled.

The new arrivals couldn't hear the shriek of the dead, like Josh. He wanted to clamp his fists over his ears but his hands were employed on the sofa, so he shouted louder than he'd ever shouted before, to drown them out, but nothing did. Until the little girl screamed.

"Did you hear that?" the Brummie asked.

"What?"

"We're conducting a door-to-door enquiry concerning a missing child. Anyone home?"

"Hell—"

"Jeeeeesus!"

"It's all right, Martin, it's paint. Look in the sink. And the walls are wet. What's the matter with you? You're acting all spooked."

"No, I'm not. I'm just saying that my kids do a better job at decorating than that, Tom. Look, it's all over the floor."

The schlick, schlick of footsteps got louder.

"Dinner's warm," Tom said. "Mmm, tastes like pork."

"Jesus, don't do that. 'Ere, that doesn't look like paint——Fuck, it's blood."

The two policemen appeared at the doorway.

The dead erupted in howls: a raucous audience for Maeve who, centre-stage, stood on hoof and foot with her hand between her legs. The vivid paint reflected on her nakedness and gave her skin a burnished glow.

"Fuck!"

"Call it in, Tom. Call it in!"

"Oh God, there's loads of 'em."

Fumbling with the radio attached to his lapel, Tom turned and stared straight at Josh.

Josh had a chance; his chance to…to what exactly? Be saved? He was dead already. "Help me!" The ferocity of his scream fuelled, not by desperation, but by anger: he was beyond saving.

Tom came closer, peered at the grim line-up attached to the corkboard while radioing-in the discovery. A crusty rock of rheum was still glued to the corner of the man's eye. It made Josh stop for just a moment to pointlessly debate whether the man was working the night shift.

"Help us. Help us get out of here!"

The copper couldn't hear him, and looked above Josh's head.

"What's that noise, Tom?"

Over by the sofa, the Brummie seemed to regard Maeve on her knees, her hand still busy.

"I can't hear anything."

"Sounds like…a dog?"

"Hey, Martin, I think this is Kaci Withers."

"Why can't you fucking hear us!"

Martin brought the photograph out from his uniform and stood next to his colleague. "Christ.

That *is* her. Get back on that radio, Tom, while I check upstairs. What the fuck is that noise?"

"There's something here: something bad. I can feel it."

Maeve convulsed. She threw her head back and unleashed a growl.

Tom was pulling on his partner's arm. "I need some air." Both officers were backing out of the room.

"No! Don't fuckin' go! Come back! Come back. Take us with you!"

Schlick, schlick, schlick, schlick, the front door clicked closed.

Clack, clack, clack, the closet door slammed shut.

Between sobs, Kaci Withers said the words, "The End."

The Toilet Zone

RESTROOM READING AT ITS MOST FRIGHTENING!

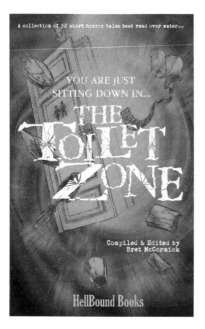

Compiled and edited by the grand master of 80's schlock horror, Bret McCormick, each one of this collection of 32 terrifying tales is just the perfect length for a visit to the smallest room....

At the very boundaries of human imagination dwells one single, solitary place of solitude, of peace and quiet, a place in which your regular human being spends, on average, 10 to 15 minutes - at least once every single day of their lives.

Now, consider a typical, everyday reading speed of 200 to 250 words per minute - that means your average visitor has the time to read between 2,500 to 4,000 words, which makes each and every one of these 32 tales of terror - from some of the best contemporary independent authors - within this anthology of horror the perfect, meticulously calculated length. Dare you take a walk to the small room from where inky shadows creep out to smother the light and solitude's siren call beckons you?

Dare you take a quiet, lonely walk into… The Toilet Zone

Tremble

Widow and single mother, Rebecca Noland, wants nothing more than to rekindle the passion with her overworked fiancé, Detective Dan Slaviche.

Expecting to surprise him by slipping into his apartment before he comes home from work, her curiosity gets the best of her when she discovers the key to unlock his desktop. What she finds there is a nightmare that sends her, along with her seven-year-old son, running for their lives.

Terrified and broke, her only option is to flee to her family's estate in Tremble, Tennessee where memories of her mother's violent death still haunt her childhood home.

But bad memories aren't the only thing that await her.

As Dan abandons all morals in his attempt to locate his bride-to-be, Rebecca struggles to make the house a home for her son while growing closer to her next door neighbors.

Her sanity comes into question when she realizes the entity responsible for her mother's murder is lying in wait, intent on destroying anyone who tries to come between it and the object of its deadly obsession… her.

The Children of Hydesville

When the terrifying entity that Maggie and Katie Fox unleashed in Hydesville in 1848 returns in 2018, a gallery owner, his wife, a journalist and her boyfriend join forces to battle it.

Manhattanites Derek David and his wife Edith receive an invitation to visit the Keilgarden Colony. Founded in 1948 with funds from Derek's great grandfather, the Colony is a secluded community dedicated to nurturing children with psychic abilities. Located five hours north of the city in the village of Hydesville, the compound was built on land that includes the cottage where Maggie and Katie Fox first heard the ghostly rappings in 1848 which started the Spiritualist movement.

But what begins as a late-summer respite swiftly turns into a confusing and terrifying ordeal for the couple and Derek's brother, Oswald. From the moment they are greeted by the Colony's beautiful yet mysterious host, Vanya Avery, they begin experiencing bizarre and disturbing events: Memory loss, unsettling visions and dreams, otherworldly manifestations, voices and apparitions that repeatedly beckon them back to the haunted Fox cottage.

An Unholy Trinity Volume 2

**FOUR HORRIFYING NOVELLAS,
FOUR EXCEPTIONAL AUTHORS,
ALL IN ONE PHENOMENAL BOOK!**

THE BLOODMOON EXPRESS - M.R. Wallace

Following a failed case in London three years before, Ian DeWitt finds himself on Le Train Bleu. The famous passenger train will ferry him to the warm shores of the Mediterranean for a much-needed rest. Ian soon finds that the horrors of the past have followed him, and the resplendent luxury train becomes the hunting ground for a monster all too familiar to the beleaguered Scotland Yard detective. Running out of time and woefully unequipped to combat such a beast, DeWitt must discover the identity of the creature and attempt to stop it before they are torn to shreds.

SAVAGES FOR REVENGE - Alex Marroquin

Failing as an artist, Derrick de Sousa travels to Argentina to recover his artistic inspiration after his college sweetheart invites him to reunite with her at Buenos Aires. Instead, he finds himself forced into a path of murder and cannibalism by a madman convinced that all humans must die in order to preserve the natural world for himself.

This mysterious killer, armed to the teeth for his 'war against humanity,' forces Derrick to follow in his bloody footsteps across Argentina. But with each life he takes, Derrick finds it harder to drop the weapon in his hand.

GARVEY'S EATS - Kenneth Seward

Deep in the backwoods of Texas sits a diner named Garvy's Eats, famous for its burger, the Garvy Special. Whitney and Tegan, best friends since Jr. High, are on a road trip to Mexico before college starts in the fall. After a thunderstorm forces the friends to take a detour, they end up at the diner where Roy Garvy wants the two girls for meat on the Garvy Special. Now with a monstrous, sick and twisted man known only as the Hellbilly hunting them down, the two girls must fight for their lives or risk ending up being served on a bun with a side of fries.

BONUS NOVELLA: MILK TEETH – Wren Pasdot

**A HellBound Books LLC
Publication**

http://www.hellboundbookspublishing.com

Printed in the United States of America

Printed in Great Britain
by Amazon

64834812R00253